Ullr's fangs

Katharine E. Wibell

Katharine E. Wibell

Phaesporia Press

Ullr's Fangs

Printed in the United States of America.

First Edition April 2018

Visit us on the Web! KatharineWibellBooks.com

Phaesporia Press

Copyright © 2017 Katharine E. Wibell

ISBN-13: 978-0-9983779-2-6

DEDICATION

To all my friends and family, who encouraged and motivated me
to recreate this manuscript after the original was destroyed

CONTENTS

SPECIAL THANKS

To April Wells-Hayes, my editor; to Karen Wibell, who served as reader and preserved my sanity; to Stephanie, Bob, David, Marilyn, and the Madison Writers Group, who reviewed content; to C. M. Soto for digital and artistic assistance, and to OliviaProDesign for the cover.

And I tip my hat to all those who told the stories that became the myths and legends that I read while growing up—and still do.

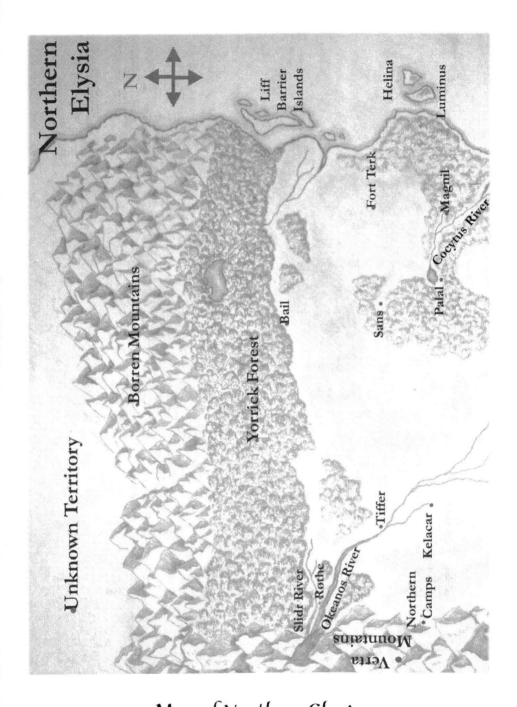

Map of Northern Elysia

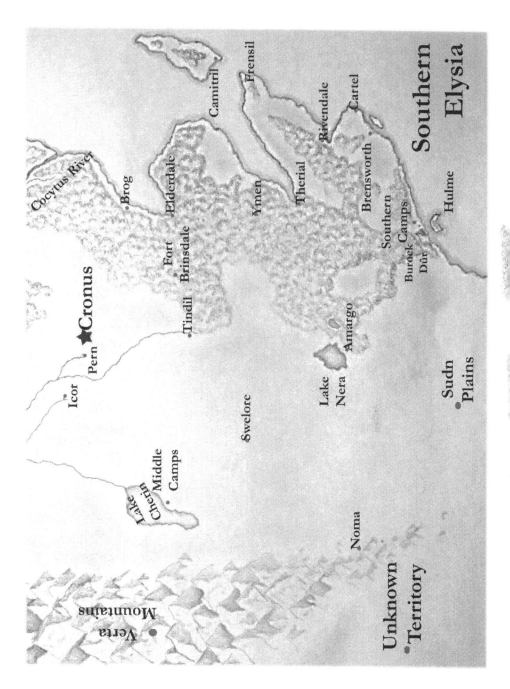

Map of Southern Elysia

ULLR'S FANGS

PART 1

Prologue

A dark shadow glides across the moon, briefly interrupting her continuous gaze on the drowsing city below. Masked faces turn up to the slit-like window high overhead, pausing to watch the unaware owl glide ever onward. Reassured of their safety in the doorless tower, they cautiously breathe a sigh of relief.

Turning back to their circle, obsidian masks eternally grimace from under heavy-hooded cloaks like dismal effigies of their creators centuries ago. Hearts pound quickly, though muffled by the thick weave of their encasing garments. Time is running out. Soon they will be forced to disperse back into the shadows of the kingdom.

Almost inaudibly the youngest of them, still past his prime, alters the course of the conversation with three words.

"What of her?"

Silence coils around them like a snake squeezing the life's essence out of its prey. Slowly, several of the Ancients turn to one another and nod before the eldest speaks. "Her destiny has been sealed since the time before her inception. She is on the correct course and should not be interfered with. Her fame is only pushing her forward on her predestined path, which will soon lead her to the others. When that happens, the day we have been waiting for since our initial formation will have finally arrived."

The fear in the mind of the youngest does not abate at these words. He asks anew. "And what of her prince? There are rumors..."

He is quieted by the appearance of the elder's knobby age-tarnished hand. The dusty voice speaks again, "She is destined for another. That we all know. Her fate is etched in the stars. Fear not her partner, their paths will diverge soon enough."

"And if they don't?"

Something moist glints behind the two slits of the Ancient's mask.

"Then we intervene."

Chapter 1

The Parting

Only a steady scratching sound was heard as quill pen scrawled over paper. The sheer impulse to write had awakened Lluava in the predawn darkness. After several minutes of contemplative scribbling, the teen paused to appraise her work. Satisfied, she bent over and blew on the still-moist lettering.

Carefully folding symmetrical creases one upon another, Lluava reached for her partner's seal and wax on the far edge of the small writing desk. The flickering candle gave off enough heat to melt the golden rod. As the liquefied droplets fell onto the parchment, Lluava quickly pressed the royal insignia into the puddle of wax. Even though its form was minuscule, she could discern a crowned raven perched above a prostrate lion. Gliding her finger over the cooling image, she could not help but think, Long live the king.

The grumbling of wooden floorboards in the neighboring room alerted Lluava that others had awakened. The day had begun, and the town, on the mend from the summer's war, was beginning to stir. Soon the steady thud of hammers and the snarl of saws would accompany multiple melodies of builders' songs.

Pocketing the letter, Lluava donned her simple uniform, a white short-sleeved shirt and black pants. Snatching up Issaura's Claws, her well-used weapons of war, she headed downstairs and exited the grand, three-story house. When the rebuilding had begun, the mayor and his wife offered to lodge some of the soldiers, including Lluava. Although suspicious that her own invitation into the prestigious household had something to do with her military partner's bloodline, she still appreciated the gesture.

Once outside, she slid the golden Claws over her hands. The three sickle-shaped, protruding daggers on each claw sliced through the chill of the morning air. To have weapons on her hands was now second nature to Lluava, though she had to keep reminding herself that the danger had passed. The presence of Issaura's Claws was comforting.

Knowing that her military partner would soon follow, Lluava headed down the main street of the town. Beams of fresh-cut wood served as pale scars on damaged shops. More than half the buildings were unsalvageable and would have to be totally reconstructed. At least all the charred timber had been removed and the ashes swept away. Although the memory of the newly expanded graveyard dwelt in the minds of its people, the town of Ymen seemed to stir with new hopes and new dreams.

A sharp whistle made Lluava turn. Yamir, standing near the skeleton of a home-to-be, waved to Lluava to join him. Once an arm's length from her, he handed Lluava the end of a rope and gave her a broken smile.

A voice shouted from above, "On the count of three, pull!"

Lluava recognized Talos's silhouette in the new morning's light as he perched precariously upon one of the roof beams.

"All right," she responded, and waited for her command.

Lluava studied her earthbound friend. Dark circles hugged Yamir's oval eyes, and crusted patches of mud almost blended into his ruddy skin. He was unusually thin, and his hair was long and unkempt. Its new length made it impossible for him to maintain his preferred spikes without the use of unreasonable amounts of wax. Yamir had intended to trim it but rebuilding a town had left little time for personal care.

"One!"

Lluava gripped the rope tightly. Her callused hands had become accustomed to the physical labor required in her current occupation.

"Two!"

Yamir stood in front of Lluava. The two were nearly the same height, and Lluava observed his back tense in preparation for their task. Behind her, someone picked up the end of the rope.

"Three!"

At once, the row of people pulled the rope with all their strength. At the far end of the structure, the frame of the fourth and last wall lurched upward. Its weight was considerable, even with the aid of the pulley system. Feet slipped over the slick ground that had been repeatedly aggravated by early autumn rains and the tread of countless workers. Halfway up, the wall swayed as the rope began to slip from their hands.

"Pull!" Talos shouted as he, too, struggled to tug at the mud-encased rope.

For a moment, Lluava thought they would lose their grip. Then, as if finally consenting to their wishes, the wall began its upward trek. As soon as it was upright, several workers with hammers at hand attacked the wall, pinioning it to the frame in a prison of nails.

Turning around to smile at the man behind her, Lluava formally greeted him. "Good morning, Your Majesty. I hope you had a pleasant sleep."

Her partner rolled his eyes at her playful sarcasm. Varren must have observed that Lluava's platinum-blonde hair had been tied back messily. Several strands floated freely in front of her emerald eyes. The contrast was always striking. "Your hair looks nice when it's pulled away from your face. It complements your cheekbones."

Lluava's laughter caught him off guard. She replied, "I never knew you were one to care about such things."

"I am an admirer of beauty."

Lluava could not help but blush at her partner's flattery. This unaccustomed feeling was still somehow unsettling. She wasn't sure she would ever get used to it. Yamir, oblivious to the situation, chimed in, "That seemed to go well."

With the mood broken, Lluava inquired, "How else can we help?"

Before Yamir could answer, their attention turned to Talos, who had climbed off his ledge and joined in the conversation. "Varren, we could use your help with this house. The more hands we have, the quicker the results. As for you, Lluava, Rosalyn requested your help with her rounds this morning. She is already waiting."

"I'll see you later, then." Lluava sneaked a peek at her partner. He, like Talos, always seemed to find time to keep up his appearance. Varren's thick, dark locks, which had disappeared temporarily as he pulled his shirt off in preparation for the day's work, now reappeared as loose curls bouncing back into place. Talos, too, had pulled his shirt over his golden head. Both men were prime examples of ideal masculine beauty, and the local women blatantly acknowledged this fact. Lluava, like many of the female Ymenites, loved to watch these aristocrats indulge in manual labor, although Lluava never made an obvious show of gawking. A smile twitched at her lips as she continued toward the sick ward.

After the slaughter, Ymen had designated a quadrant of the devastated town to serve as a medical ward for any townspeople or soldiers who required aid. Rosalyn used her skills where they were most needed. Having had some nursing training, Lluava helped when she could, always under Rosalyn's authority.

The putrid smell of infected flesh and crusting blood had dissipated over the past weeks as the number of tents for the wounded shrank. Now only a half-dozen tents still held their unwilling captives. Since the weather was rather pleasant, many of the injured lay on rows of stretchers that had been moved outside. Rosalyn believed the fresh breeze somehow encouraged quicker healing. Although the local doctor had originally balked at this treatment, even he had had to acknowledge the unusually high recovery rate.

Rosalyn looked like a spirit of grace, with porcelain skin enshrouded in a pristine white nursing uniform. Her raven-black hair, in stark contrast, heightened the image of an unearthly presence. She knew everyone under her care by name and always took a moment to talk to him or her individually. They all adored her. Excusing herself from conversation with a soldier recovering from a leg amputation, Rosalyn smiled at Lluava and asked her to tote fresh water from the town's well to the large cauldrons. The few spare strips of cloth needed to be boiled in order to clean them before bandaging wounds.

For the rest of the morning, Lluava busied herself with her new task, occasionally taking the longer route to the well to check on the men's progress. Each time she passed by, she and Varren would share a smile. By noon, she was helping to refresh bandages after Rosalyn cleaned wounds.

"Talos received a post from Byron yesterday." Rosalyn's melodious voice rang clearly, moving away from their light gossip. "He says he is doing well, although he is still looking for a new position."

"I wonder how hard it really is for him since he's only known an active soldier's life. How's his leg doing?" inquired Lluava. It had been several weeks since any of them had seen Byron. Breaking many a girl's heart, he had left in the hope of finding work at Fort Terk.

"He will never be able to do what he did before; however, he told me that he has made peace with his injury and his discharge from military service," noted Rosalyn as she inspected a particularly nasty burn on a little girl's hand.

"That's good. Will Talos follow his partner? Terk is way up north." Lluava was curious whether the rumors about Talos finding a position in the south were true. If so, what had Talos decided?

Rosalyn gently rubbed salve on the child's hand. "I know he wants to stay near his partner, but he must wait for word about the possible offer from Durog. He believes that a drill sergeant's life will be much safer for us once we are married." Rosalyn waited while Lluava wrapped the burn with ragged strips of cloth, then hesitantly began, "That brings me to something I want to talk to you about."

Lluava raised an eyebrow.

"Tomorrow, a large number of the injured will be released. As my services are no longer required, Talos is going to escort me home. We will visit Selphy on the way to Amargo. Did you know she is better now?" Without waiting for Lluava to respond, Rosalyn continued, "Anyway, as soon as I return, Talos's father and mine will begin the wedding plans."

"That's wonderful!" exclaimed Lluava. She knew that Rosalyn had waited a long time for this. Although Talos and Rosalyn's betrothal had occurred in infancy, they were fortunate to live in neighboring estates and had fallen in love with each other years ago. When the draft was instated,

Rosalyn volunteered to represent her family so she could be close to Talos. Lluava found their situation highly romantic, though a bit crazy. They were not even twenty. "When will the ceremony take place?"

"If all goes well, in the next few months. Selphy is going to be my maid of honor, but I would be truly blessed if you would be one of my bridesmaids. I cannot imagine myself getting married without you there."

A full-blown smile streaked across Lluava's face. She reached out and gave her dear friend an enormous hug, careful not to squeeze her too hard. Rosalyn always looked so delicate. "Of course I will! I'm honored that you asked me."

Upon release, Rosalyn gave a sigh of relief. She had known not to be worried, yet she could not help herself. "Last night, Talos invited Yamir to stand with him; he will ask Varren today."

"Isn't Yamir leaving tomorrow as well?" Lluava inquired as she realized that all of her friends were about to disperse across the kingdom.

"Yes. He is heading off to Cartel to care for Chat's parents. Adopted or not, Chat was their son, and, well…." Rosalyn stopped. They both knew that this had something to do with Chat's last request. Although Chat had been like a little brother to all of them, losing him had been hardest on Yamir. He was never the same afterward; a darkness seemed to have enveloped him. It was a good day if they could tease out a half-hearted smile. Lluava hoped Yamir would find some peace once he arrived in Chat's homeland.

"What will you do when you leave Ymen?" Rosalyn politely inquired. Neither wanted to dwell on the past.

"Well," Lluava began after a pause, "I guess I'll return home for a bit. I really miss my family." Lluava's thoughts drifted to her mother and her siblings before returning to the present and to helping Rosalyn turn an unusually frail old man onto his side. While Rosalyn tended to his wounds, Lluava admitted, "I have been craving my mother's cooking for a long time."

"Will you stay in Rivendale, then?"

"I guess. At least until Varren needs me at court."

"Oh, yes. You are a future Head Councilman. You will love the capital and the court. Its splendor is remarkable. I recommend that you visit the palace gardens. They are always in bloom."

"Good to know." Yet the words carried little importance, since Lluava's thoughts were on her own homestead. Her sister's school year must have begun. How well was her baby brother talking? It would be very different without Gramps.

Rosalyn left Lluava to her thoughts while they finished the rounds. After a late lunch, it was time to start all over again. By nightfall, Lluava was gladdened by the prospective discharge, tomorrow morning, of so many of those under their care. Several patients were released that evening, and they thanked their lovely caretakers profusely.

In the failing light, Lluava sat her weary body down on one of the cut logs that served as benches around the ever-blazing cooking fires. She ached from an exhaustion that was more than physical. In her hand, she held a steaming bowl of clumping porridge, or maybe repurposed hash. Although its taste was barely better than its looks, this mysterious gruel was the only thing the town could provide to feed the army for their extended stay. Lluava had grown accustomed to its bland taste and grainy texture. It might not be ideal, but it kept everyone's strength up when they needed it.

"May I sit next to you?" Varren's formal upbringing emerged even when there was no need.

Nodding, Lluava shoveled down the sludge. Eating quickly was her trick to keep the so-called food from sticking to the back of her throat. In contrast, Varren sat down, whispered a prayer of thanks, and began to eat. They remained silent until Varren had finished.

Wiping his mouth, he said, "I would like to head back to the capital tomorrow. Since you are my military partner—no, that is not the reason." Varren seemed flustered. He was not one to fumble with his choice of words. Eloquence had always come naturally to him, so why could he not state a clear thought now?

"Yes?" inquired Lluava, hoping to coax him to continue.

Varren stood up in his most formal manner and asked, "Lluava, would you come with me to the royal palace? I want to introduce you to Grandfather and the High Council and, well...I would like you to be with me when I return to court."

Lluava understood his fear of what he was about to do, for altering an age-old law was all but unheard of. Nevertheless, excitement fluttered inside her like a newly fledged bird. Varren wanted her near him. This was his way of admitting how much he needed her at his side. This day had truly brought wonderful news.

She was about to say yes when a new thought crossed her mind. "How long do you expect to be at court?"

"I do not know. Why do you ask?"

Lluava fingered the carefully folded letter in her pants pocket. "Well, I had hoped to visit home. I haven't seen my family since the draft."

Thoughtfully, Varren said, "I will not force you to come. You can leave at any time. However, I would like you to be with me when—"

Lluava interrupted. "Don't worry. I'll be standing by your side from now until eternity." She grinned at her pathetic attempt at poeticism.

"That is good. That is great!" Varren could not hide his relief. "Well, I will say good night to you now. Tomorrow will be a new and exciting day."

With that, Varren gently took Lluava's hand and kissed it, which sent a tingling sensation up her arm. As he left, Lluava thought, Oh, what am I getting myself into?

Next morning, Lluava ran to the shanty that served as Ymen's dispatch headquarters. Since a large portion of the Southern army was stationed here, the king's messengers came to the town every two weeks. Lluava had to hurry so as not to miss the chance to send off her own letter. She had forgotten to do this errand the day before, and with her departure imminent this was the only chance she would have before she left.

Attempting to catch her breath, Lluava retrieved the letter from her pocket. It was surprisingly unwrinkled. Perhaps the gods were watching over her. She handed the parchment to the small man loading full satchels onto his horse. Annoyed at the last-minute arrival, he began to lecture Lluava on the importance of punctuality. She in turn quietly reprimanded herself for her forgetfulness. Satisfied with his thorough scolding, the letter carrier asked Lluava in a disinterested manner, "Are you human or Theriomorph?"

This simplest of questions caught Lluava off guard. An inner heat coursed through her body as she growled out the formal reply.

"I am Lluava Kargen, daughter of Haliden Kargen, and I am Theriomorph."

Chapter 2

A Capital Concern

In a lackluster manner, the messenger shoved Lluava's letter into the recesses of his left saddlebag. Before he could leave, a woman hurried up behind Lluava and presented him with another envelope. To save time, he held back his lecture on punctuality and asked his question again.

"Human or Theriomorph?"

"Human, sir," the older woman tittered and scurried away.

If Lluava had left a moment earlier, she might not have seen the little man carefully place the parchment in the right satchel, the one clearly labeled Human. She might have maintained control and gone about the rest of her day as usual. This, however, did not happen.

The idea of dealing rationally with the situation flickered momentarily in Lluava's mind before her primordial thought process took control. Her inner heat was sweltering. Pressure built, forcing a release. Lluava's pupils elongated in their felid way as her senses went into a state of heightened alert.

Not again. That impression of a thought formed and dissolved as Lluava turned toward the unaware man. He was testing the stirrups before mounting his horse.

A rumble trembled up from her vocal cords, and Lluava's lip twitched involuntarily. As the sound grew louder, she strode over to the squat letter carrier and effortlessly shoved him out of the way.

"What in God's name are you doing?" he cried, stumbling to catch his balance.

Not again. The thought pounded in Lluava's brain, making it difficult for her to discern several onlookers' exclamations as she hoisted the saddlebags off the whickering mount. One bag at a time, she dumped their contents onto the chilled earth. Snarling, she knelt and began to mix the letters up until there was no hope of telling which letter came from which bag. Lluava stood and took several breaths while she regained her control.

The little man was beside himself. His face took on the shade of uncooked meat as he futilely attempted to sort out the pile of letters. Realizing it was impossible, he turned to his offender and half screamed, half spat, "By what paganistic belief did you do that?"

"I am Lluava Kargen, partner of Varren Mandrun, Crown Prince of Elysia. By his name, I decree that you will no longer sort letters by race."

Trying to cool his temper at the ridiculous order, the messenger inquired with distaste, "How would you have me sort the letters?"

The idea was so simple and so obvious that Lluava wondered why no one had thought of it before now. "By destination, of course."

Enraged at her insolence, the red-faced man waved parchment-filled fists in the air. "You will pay for this!" But he knew he had no chance of successfully fighting a soldier, especially one trained at Durog. He would have to find another means of seeking reparation.

Ignoring the human's empty threats, Lluava stormed away.

***

When it was time for Lluava's friends to say their goodbyes, they gathered near the stables. Varren held the reins of Ulder, his thoroughbred, as well as those of another well-built mare. The horses pawed at the ground, sensing the mounting agitation of the people.

Yamir finally spoke. "Well, I'll be off, then."

With the silence broken, the group was forced to begin their goodbyes. Lluava hugged Yamir and whispered in his ear, "Take care of yourself."

"I will. Don't worry about me. Shall I say hello to Chat's parents for you?"

"Please," said Lluava before turning to hug Talos goodbye. "Protect Rosalyn, okay?"

"With my life," vowed Talos stoically.

At last, Lluava approached her oldest friend. Rosalyn's broken smile mirrored Yamir's. Rosalyn collapsed into Lluava's arms, and almost instantaneously the raven-haired teen began to cry. Lluava's eyes began to respond instinctively.

"No, you don't," Lluava halfheartedly demanded, pushing her friend back. "You have no right to make me cry. I was doing so well not to."

At that, Rosalyn laughed through her tears. "We will see each other soon, will we not?"

"Yes, we will."

"Until then..." Rosalyn wiped her face with a handkerchief Talos handed her. The two young women hugged once more.

Turning away, not looking back, Lluava mounted her smoky steed. As she and Varren rode toward the capital, the tears welled up once more. Lluava spurred her horse on so she could blame them on the wind.

Eventually Lluava and Varren slowed to a steady trot. This rhythmic pace was so trancelike that they continued in silence, deep in their own thoughts. It was only as the sun was setting that Lluava realized they had ridden away the day. She shifted position, and her new saddle sores warned her to be gentle. It had been a while since she had ridden so long.

"How much farther do you wish to go?" Lluava inquired as she searched for the position that would give her the least discomfort.

Varren took notice of the late hour. "We can retire now if you wish."

"I do wish!" Lluava slowed her horse to a walk and began to look for a desirable area to make camp.

After supper, Lluava's sorrow dissipated, replaced by excitement for this new adventure. For as long as she could remember, she had yearned to visit the capital. She had always loved the wonderful stories and tales told by traveling peddlers passing through Rivendale, her home. All the local children were captivated by descriptions of castles whose spires reached into the clouds, festivals so amazing that they spanned three days, gilded carriages, galas, exotic gardens, and beautiful balls. Lluava was no exception. She was thrilled to finally have the chance to experience all this herself.

"Other than attending court and observing how policies and laws are made, what else am I expected to do?" Lluava asked, hoping that there would be ample time for her to explore.

"Court is held from midmorning until all daily issues are dealt with, which can take the entire day." Varren began to gather and wrap the leftover food.

"And for how many days is it held?"

Placing the scraps into a saddlebag, he replied, "Court is held every day."

"Oh." Lluava made no attempt to hide her dismay.

"I do not expect you to be there every day. You are not my High Councilman yet. Or should we change that to High Councilwoman? You would be the first of your gender." Lluava smiled at these words as Varren continued, "I will assign several loyal subjects to help educate you on proper courtly etiquette, among other things."

"Like what?" Lluava rolled out her blanket on a pile of leaf litter.

"For example, how to handle a situation involving prejudice toward your people without indulging in one of your fits." Varren eyed her carefully as he smoothed his makeshift bed. Though only twenty, he always had the air of someone far older.

Lluava wanted to shrink down into something very small, if only she could. She had never felt so young in all her seventeen years. "You heard about that."

"I am neither deaf nor dumb. Ymen is not as large as it appears."

"It's just so frustrating. After all the work to become respected by humans and treated as their equal, one person takes it all away."

"Lluava," Varren soothed, "try to understand. Yes, some progress has been made in the military, as well as in many of the towns that we have marched through. Yet this is only a small portion of the kingdom. Elysia is moving on the right path, but it will take time. Your point about the mail is perfectly valid, yet there are much more rational ways of dealing with prejudice, especially when you are working at court. With you at my side, think of the positive impact we will have on Elysia."

The excitement was back.

"First, you will have to learn to master your anger."

The truth of Varren's words was clear, but he couldn't understand how hard it would be. He was only human.

"I'll do my best," promised Lluava with a smile.

Varren's eyes sparkled as he returned her smile before turning away. "We should get our rest." With that, he retired and left Lluava alone by the fire.

The next day was much the same. Although the scenery slowly changed from dense forest to lightly wooded areas, then to tree-speckled grasslands, the hypnotic ride toward the capital encouraged little conversation. At night after their meal, Varren would hastily slip off to bed without even a goodnight. Lluava tried not to dwell on such things.

As they neared the center of the kingdom, the pair began to pass through towns and cities, each grander than the last. The road widened, leveled out, and transformed into newly laid cobblestone. The unification and structural improvement of all major roads had been planned for several years. Unfortunately, after the draft last spring, progress had been halted.

One day as evening approached, Lluava caught her first glimpse of the capital. Lanterns flickered like thousands of hovering fireflies the purple haze of night. A respectable wall embraced an overgrown metropolis, hugging tight all it could hold, yet hundreds of households seemed to have slipped outside of its grasp. The vastness of the city was far more expansive than Lluava had ever dreamed. She wondered how there could actually be enough citizens to fill all the buildings.

Lluava's heart leaped in her chest as she scanned it once again. There, snugly centered among it all, was the castle. An enormous masterpiece of masonry and art, it had been designed by the greats as an immortal dare to all who might try to surpass it. Level upon level rose up into the night, sending spires high into the atmosphere as if trying to break into the heavens. Huge buttresses like external ribs helped brace its body; towers like massive limbs secured it to the ground. A doorway of solid iron stood dark and impenetrable like a jaw sealed shut to all but the choicest offerings. Lluava could almost sense a heartbeat pulsing from within. This castle, this city, was certainly a thing of dreams.

The outer gates were beginning to close. With a click of his heels, Varren spurred his horse onward as Lluava hastily followed. With each clack of hoof upon stone, Lluava willed her mount to move faster. If they could not make it through, they would have to overnight in one of the outer inns until morning. The idea of being so close and yet so far was almost unbearable.

Hurry, thought Lluava, hurry!

The gates were closing too quickly.

"We can make it!" Varren shouted; Lluava hoped it was true.

The light of the lanterns disappeared behind the thick beams of oak until only the centermost lantern remained. Varren's horse leaped in front, leading the way; still the doors continued to close. Lluava dug her heels into the sides of her mount. The steed lurched forward at a frightening pace. There were only two options now: make it through or crash into the unforgiving doors.

At the last moment, she willed her eyes not to close. As she vaulted through the gate, Lluava could feel her thighs scrape past the ever-shrinking opening.

They had made it. She had reached Cronus, the capital.

Cursing and screaming, people leaped out of the way of the charging horses. Varren reined in his mount to prevent a minor calamity. Slowing her horse to a walk, Lluava followed Varren through the labyrinth of roads.

Inside Cronus's walls, overcrowded streets teemed with inhabitants, yet they did not seem to be settling down. Rather, they moved about like vast groups of watchmen changing their shifts. As some folded up shop overhangs and closed their shutters, others lit lanterns and swung open their doors to receive their nightly crowds.

The vibrant city life was unlike anything Lluava had ever experienced. Multiple melodies poured out of taverns only to collide in the crossroads of the streets. Unintelligible voices sang out beyond open doorways, and the thrum of the familiar notes thrilled Lluava. Men still hawked goods at crossroads even though the day had ended.

The people on the road were so intent on getting to their destinations that they barely lifted their heads to take notice of the newly arrived travelers. Only when one small boy loudly exclaimed, "Mummy, the prince looks like he needs a nap!" did others become aware of the pair and move out of the way. As news of the prince's return spread, those whom Lluava and Varren passed bowed low, a courtesy that Lluava discovered she liked.

The roads were an impenetrable tangle to the young woman. She lost track of their path to the castle, for the twists and turns were more than any non-Cronian could remember. Varren explained to her that this purposeful maze had been designed as a safeguard to prevent an invading army from charging straight up to the castle. The small roads made it impossible for large numbers to move quickly, and the seemingly haphazard design would confuse interlopers.

Although Lluava would not remember the specifics of their approach, she would always remember the warm glow that seemed to envelop her when the intricately carved inner gates opened as though deeming her worthy of seeing the hidden contents inside. Several groomsmen appeared and took their horses to the royal stables. The steward on duty tended to Lluava and Varren.

"Welcome home, Your Majesty," he said with a low bow, hat clutched in one hand, bare head displaying a large bald spot.

Without looking at her, Varren made the introduction. "This is Lluava Kargen, my military partner."

Partner—the word hung in Lluava's mind. It felt cold and distant. But that is what she was: his partner.

The steward turned to Lluava. "Welcome to the royal castle, m'lady." With a second glance at Lluava's appearance, the steward motioned to them. "Follow me, and I will show you to your quarters."

"I wish to speak to my grandfather," stated Varren.

The steward halted. "King Thor has retired for the evening and does not wish to be disturbed."

"He will wake to see me," Varren said wearily.

The steward wanted to protest but gave a quick nod. Another man appeared as if signaled, and the steward commanded, "Wake the king. Tell him his grandson has arrived. Alert the councilmen, too."

"No," Varren corrected the order. "I wish only to see my grandfather. The High Council will have their chance in the morning."

The steward looked displeased but said nothing. After the second man had disappeared without a word, the steward said again, this time hesitantly, "Please, Your Majesty, allow me to lead you to your quarters until the king is ready." Varren nodded and followed the small man.

It was hard for Lluava to take in the grandeur of the castle. Inside the expansive foyer, beautiful blue marble columns stretched up to the vaulted ceiling. The floor, a polished black marble with fine silver lines running through it, captured the sound of their tread and amplified its echo off the walls. They entered a wing through a large arched doorway. Brilliant woven tapestries of historical scenes decorated the hall, while portraits of former royals in heavy gilt frames seemed to stare at them as they ascended a delicately curved staircase.

"This is your chamber, Lady Lluava," said the steward, opening one of the doors of a well-lit hall. Lluava stepped through; then, realizing she was not being followed, turned back. The steward was about to shut the door, but Varren had his hand on it.

"I will wait with my partner until my grandfather is ready."

"As you wish." With that, the steward left.

Lluava took note of her new quarters. They were a great improvement upon her last, to say the least. The main room in which she stood was a sitting area. Cushioned chairs and a velvety couch and chaise were positioned slightly off center. To the right, an open archway allowed Lluava a glimpse of the heavily cushioned four-poster bed with emerald-green curtains tied behind it. Yet it was the far wall that drew her eye. A set of double doors was propped open, beyond which was a lovely private balcony illuminated by moonlight.

Without moving, Lluava stared out at the stars and felt the cool touch of the breeze on her skin.

"Lluava." The tenderness in Varren's voice was something that she had been longing to hear. A smile slipped past her lips as he gently placed his hand upon her shoulder.

Then her anger seared up. Jerking her body away, she snarled, "No. I'm only your partner." As soon as she said the words, Lluava regretted it. She never wanted to be the cause of the hurt that was written on Varren's face.

"I'm sorry. I didn't mean that."

Running his fingers through his thick waves, Varren sighed. "I know what you want. I feel the same way. But right now, I cannot give that to you."

Lluava made no move to respond. She watched as the loose curls fell back into place over his forehead.

"I am still betrothed to Illia. Until I have publicly nullified that arrangement, I cannot pursue any interest I have in you other than our military partnership."

"Will that happen tomorrow? At court?" Lluava questioned hopefully.

"I fear not. This is a delicate manner. No betrothal has ever been revoked. I will not allow Illia's reputation to be marred by this act. Though both she and I want to be allowed to follow our hearts as common people can, I must deal with the High Council as well as my grandfather. This decision will have repercussions. The whole culture of our matchmaking will change. I have to approach the situation with care." Varren implored her to understand.

Lluava had not considered the implications. The situation was completely unfair. He was the prince. Why couldn't he just say he was through and that be it? Why was it so complicated?

To hide her disappointment and her longing, she walked out onto the balcony. Pretending interest in the glowing city below, she concentrated on steadying her breath. When her eyes teared up, she clenched her jaw. Why was she being so foolish? She was seventeen, old enough to act with a level head. Besides, Varren had said he would be with her. She just had to wait. Yet patience was not an attribute for which she was known.

Soft footsteps approached behind her. Lluava's heart picked up its pace.

She felt herself tense and focused her attention on a distant lantern on one of the buildings. She felt Varren's presence before his touch. Strong arms wrapped themselves around her, pulling her body close. Lluava willed him to hold her tighter. She could feel his heartbeat against her back, the warmth from his skin, his soft breath on her neck.

They stood for a time, Lluava afraid to move and end the moment. Turning her head, she looked at Varren, to memorize every detail softly illuminated by the moon. Dark hair famed his strong yet gentle face; kind blue eyes sparkled like the stars above; her eyes traced his perfectly shaped nose and softly smiling lips. Lips that parted slightly and slowly moved toward her. Stopping so close that Lluava heard the catch in his breath.

Leaning upward, their lips met, fitting perfectly with one another. A warm, tingling sensation coursed through both with their touch. It was so simple, so wonderful. When they parted, Lluava felt as if she were in a dream. There was something surreal about standing so close to this man, her prince, her partner, her....

"Lluava." Varren breathed her name as if he, too, were testing the reality of having her before him.

She looked into eyes that were filled with unspoken emotion. Finding no words, she waited until Varren could continue.

"I want you to know how much you mean to me," Varren said, her hands in his. "We will be together."

Smiling at each other, they leaned in once more.

There was a sharp knock on the door. The mood was shattered. Varren quickly stepped back from Lluava, yet his hand lingered long enough in hers to convey his disappointment.

She watched the formal expression slip back over Varren's face. Until he nullified his betrothal, this was the last time she would experience his embrace. Lluava could not help but loathe the steward's interruption.

From the doorway came the hollow announcement, "The king will see you now."

Chapter 3

Lips of a Child

Without the guidance of the steward, Lluava would never have found their destination in the ever-expanding labyrinth that Varren called home. She overlooked the beautifully decorated halls, the lavish furnishings, and the intricate details of the stained-glass windows. Instead, she followed the quick-footed man but remained in a deepening sulk.

If Varren was as disappointed as she with this turn of events, he hid it well. It was clear his thoughts had shifted to matters unknown to Lluava. He toyed with his ring, rubbing the royal insignia repeatedly. His face grew more serious with each step.

Lluava discreetly reached out and touched the back of his shoulder just long enough for him to register contact before letting her hand drop down to her side. The brief gesture was enough. She knew from his expression that he wanted to share what was on his mind, yet the presence of their escort loomed, barricading Varren's tongue.

What did he want to tell her? Was there some warning about what she should expect? Perhaps some last-minute advice concerning political etiquette? Lluava pondered her questions until the trio stopped in front of a small arched doorway protected by a pair of surly-looking guards.

Lluava's heartbeat quickened. They had arrived. Panic welled up inside of her. What was she missing? She wished Varren would tell her, yet he remained silent.

The steward rapped twice. Lluava started to move forward as the door opened, but the steward entered first and shut the door almost in her face. Flustered, she looked at Varren. He motioned for her to wait, and after a moment the steward reappeared.

"You may enter."

The room was disproportionately large for such a small door. Two rows of high-backed chairs bordered the side aisles, which led to the pair of raised thrones upon which sat the very people of legend. For as long as she could remember, Lluava had heard about her king: Thor the mighty and just, Thor the beneficent, Thor the people's champion.

Lluava realized she was holding her breath and released it with a sigh of dismay. This must be some sort of cruel joke. The person before her could not be the king.

Seated on the larger of the two thrones was a man well into his sunset years. Whatever strength he once had, had crumbled like the walls of a forgotten city. A once-powerful chest had sunk to his gut, and his thinning frame struggled to remain upright. Propped up on his left arm, he looked like a tree twisted and broken by the wind. The crown weighed down his balding head like a symbol of the ruler's burden that he had carried for countless years. He blinked groggily, licking his lips with a dry tongue.

"Your Majesty," the steward began, "Prince Varren has returned from his triumph on the coastal line. His partner, the Lady Lluava, is with him." Bowing, the steward backed to the door, allowing them a symbolic privacy.

"Varren..." King Thor seemed to test the name in the air. "Varren?"

"I am home, Grandfather," Varren replied and waited as the old man caught sight of his grandson.

Turning to the person on the smaller throne, Thor said, "Look, Enya, Varren's home."

For the first time, Lluava took note of the queen. Here the rumors were true. The child looked Lluava over in a disconcerting manner, and Lluava shifted under the gaze. Enya herself was a pretty little thing—rosy cheeks on alabaster skin; big, beautiful eyes lined with lavish lashes; thick, dark tresses spilling down her gaudy nightwear. She looked like one of those dolls that sit in shop windows and are never sold for they are always overpriced. Just like the toy she so resembled, Enya's face seemed frozen in an eternal pout.

How old was she? Twelve, maybe thirteen? Lluava remembered the seemingly unending gossip of the women in her town when word came that King Thor's new bride was "just out of the cradle." Lluava had assumed that, like most rumors, this was an exaggeration, yet it was not so. Two years ago, Enya was crowned queen. Had she even reached bleeding age then? Lluava tried not to look disgusted. These were her rulers. She must be respectful.

Without looking at her husband, Enya replied in a voice that wavered on the edge of puberty, "I see him."

The creases in the king's face turned up, creating an exaggerated grin, while the little queen continued to pout, clearly not amused at this reunion. Or was it because of Varren's untimely arrival at the capital? The hour was late. One had to take that into consideration.

"Grandfather," Varren began, "if you would permit me to speak." The prince waited until he received the king's signal. "Many of the villages devastated by the battles are well into the process of mending. All subsequent signs of the Raiders indeed seem to verify their sudden retreat. Yet we cannot take lightly the threat by their so-called ambassador, Hadrian Alcove."

Thor looked momentarily puzzled, and then his furrowed brow softened.

Varren continued, "I implore you to command the northern and central training camps to begin moving toward the sea. Also, all the other forts should be notified to be ready to move at any moment. I want to meet the enemy head on if they try to breach our borders again. In addition, I also believe it is time to double the forces at Cronus's walls. We cannot risk enemy entry to the city."

The king seemed to gather his thoughts as he repeated choice words and phrases like *war, move armies, battle*. Finally, he replied, "Damian, if you want to play Kings and Crowns, set up the game."

Lluava was stunned. She looked from the old man to Varren and back. Varren seemed unusually calm. He stepped closer to Thor.

"I am Varren, Grandfather. Damian is not here."

"Varren," the old man muttered.

"Yes. Varren," said the prince.

Thor's cool eyes stared at his grandson for a while. "Varren, where is your father? He wanted to play a game of Kings and Crowns."

Annoyed, Enya blurted, "He's dead."

Thor's lower lip trembled as he questioned the queen. "Damian dead?"

"Yes, Damian is dead. You know that." The queen screwed her lips together even harder as she fussed with the wrinkles in her gown.

Varren intervened affectionately. "He has been deceased many years now. Remember the fire?"

"The fire…yes." Thor nodded. His clear eyes lost focus for a time, then rested on Lluava. "Hello, there," he said in a firmer manner. "Are you the female warrior I was told about?"

"Yes, Your Majesty." This whole conversation was making Lluava uncomfortable. She shifted position again.

The King pushed himself higher in the throne to get a better look at her. "You are very pretty."

"Thank you, Your Majesty," she replied as Thor smiled kindly down at her.

"She is dirty," the queen observed, and wrinkled her nose as if smelling something foul.

Lluava blushed. The grime of the past few weeks seemed suddenly to weigh her down. The desire to wash her hands was overwhelming. "We have only just arrived, Your Highness. I have not had a chance to bathe."

"Hmm…." Enya's mouth almost broke into a smile. "How dreadful."

With a wave, Thor commanded, "Step closer so I may look at you."

Lluava did as she was told. As the king inspected her, all she desired was to look away from his direct gaze. Yet she stared back into his eyes. They were his most startling feature. Stormy gray, yet clear, they took her in, holding her tight.

"Warrior with the moonbeam hair…" Thor began; then his thoughts drifted away. Enya continued to scrutinize Lluava while absentmindedly playing with the ends of her own locks.

"Grandfather," Varren began again in earnest. "Will you command the armies or permit me the right to move them? I fear that the Raiders will return."

Thor looked back at his grandson and cogitated. "You truly believe that is their intent, to return?"

"Yes."

"Even now, after they have retreated across the ocean?"

"Yes," Varren responded a bit forcefully. In a more restrained manner he explained, "Elysia and all her people cannot endure the horrors of another attack. We must be prepared."

"I will discuss this with the High Council in the morning."

Thor did not miss the displeasure on Varren's face. "It is their right to be heard on all major decisions regarding the kingdom."

Varren nodded slightly.

Once again, Thor's features softened. "I will, however, alert the Shadows to keep their eyes and ears open. Regin," he called. A figure dressed entirely in black seemed to manifest from the darkness behind the throne.

Lluava froze. She had not even sensed this other presence. Had he been there the entire time? This thought was disconcerting. She peered into the room's dark corners, looking for other forms, but there were none.

Thor commanded, "Tell the Guard to keep watch." The dark presence nodded and slipped back into the shadows.

This was almost too much to absorb. In one night, Lluava had met King Thor and the child queen and now had glimpsed the leader of the Obsidian Guard. She clawed at her memories pertaining to what little was known about the sovereign's personal soldiers. Founded two centuries earlier to protect the human rulers from Theriomorph attacks during the Landon Wars, these elite guards exclusively served the king. They still dressed in black, although today their obsidian-clad armor was used only for ceremonial purposes. Shadow walkers, silent warriors, rarely talked of and less often seen, their reality was a question often debated. Now Lluava, a Theriomorph from a humble fishing village, had been permitted a glimpse of their current commander.

"Are you all right?" inquired Varren.

Lluava tried to clear the dazed look from her face. She could barely force out a yes.

Turning back to his grandfather, Varren humbly thanked him.

"I am glad you have returned," Thor admitted with a yawn. "It is late. I think it is time to adjourn for the night."

Varren stepped up to the old man, then bent down and kissed his outstretched hand. "Goodnight, Grandfather."

"Goodnight," replied the king before adding, "Tomorrow maybe we could play Kings and Crowns."

"Yes, Grandfather," Varren said as he turned to leave.

"Goodnight, Your Majesty," Lluava said.

Thor looked at her and grinned. "Do you like Kings and Crowns? Damian loves Kings and Crowns. Maybe you both could play."

Without hesitation, Lluava responded, "If you wish, Your Majesty." Then she slipped quickly out of the room. Outside, she tried to shake the feeling that was knotting up her stomach.

Once Varren and the steward entered the hall, the three headed back to their quarters. As they walked, Varren asked the steward, "How long?"

"It changes," the man answered. "Today, like most days, he worsens the later it gets."

Varren nodded in understanding. "What have the doctors said?"

"Of what I know, which is not much, he is deteriorating—rapidly."

Talking primarily to himself, Varren acknowledged, "I should not have awakened him."

The steward kept quiet.

Varren breathed deeply. "I plan to breakfast with him in the morning."

"Will the Lady Lluava be joining you?"

In an untimely manner, Lluava yawned. The desire to rise early seemed to seep rapidly away. "No, thank you."

"You are more than welcome to join us," Varren earnestly invited.

"No," declined Lluava. "You should spend time with your family." Before Varren could counter her, she said, "I will be catching up on much-needed rest."

Wordlessly, Varren mouthed a thank you as they turned a corner.

The steward nodded, "I will make arrangements accordingly."

When they reached Lluava's room, Varren stopped at the door and said, "This is where we part."

"Goodnight, Varren," Lluava said. Her voice was husky with exhaustion.

"Sleep well," he replied, then gently picked up her hand and kissed the back of it. A tingling sensation ran up Lluava's spine. Again she wished the steward were not present.

Bowing politely, Varren took his leave.

"Is there anything you might need before I retire for the evening?" inquired the steward.

"No," Lluava began, then quickly changed her mind. "Wait—what was it that you and Varren were referring to back there?"

"That is something of a family matter."

Lluava's curiosity could not let this slide. "Varren was going to tell me."

The steward looked at her doubtfully.

"Truly," Lluava continued, "He was about to tell me in my quarters right before you summoned us." She hoped he wouldn't suspect her lie.

The steward contemplated her for a long moment. "Then Prince Varren will tell you in the morning."

Lluava refused to beg anymore. She would have to satiate her curiosity another way. "Thank you," she sighed. "I will know soon enough."

For the first time since they had met, the steward smiled. Was this funny to him? Lluava felt indignant.

"Since you will find out eventually," the steward began, "and since you are the military partner of Prince Varren, I will tell you in confidence." He stepped closer. "His Majesty, Thor, has fallen ill with the Wasting Disease."

Those two words explained it all, yet the steward continued, "As you are aware, it is incurable. Our best doctors are doing all they can, but…." He glanced around as if expecting the walls to sprout ears, then continued in a whisper, "We fear he does not have much longer." Returning to his normal tone, the steward stated, "Long live the king."

"Long live the king," echoed Lluava as she watched the steward move down the hall. Glancing around in the gloom, she shivered. Dying kings, child queens, shadow people—the capital was anything but what she had expected. She paused, trying to sort out her mixed emotions. Failing, she moved toward her room.

At last, sleep in a real bed was just moments away. Tomorrow Lluava would settle into her new lifestyle. Right now, with her senses dulled from exhaustion, rest was her first priority.

The door was heavy and groaned as she opened it. Candles flickering in the draft from the open balcony doors cast eerie forms on the walls and ceiling. It would take her a while to become acquainted with her new surroundings.

As Lluava moved to the alcove containing the large four-poster bed, she stopped. Nothing was out of place. Her room was just as she had left it only an hour before. Yet the fine hairs on the back of her neck stood up. The unmistakable scent of musk wafted through her chamber. Thick to her hyperactive senses, it was clear to her. Someone was in the room.

Chapter 4

Council on High

Shadows shivered in the shaky light. Peering from one to another, Lluava sought the source of the musk. Sofas, chairs, balcony, and bed all kept the secret. Lluava's mind raced with various reasons for the intrusion as well as possible courses of action.

Finally, she uttered, "I know you're here. Come out."

A moment passed with no response.

"I said, show yourself!" Again her demand went unanswered. Where was the odor coming from? The whole room was saturated with it. There was no way to pinpoint its source.

Lluava felt her canines sharpen as her lip twitched in agitation. So, they want to play a game of cat and mouse, do they? Let's play.

The thick curtain wavered. Was it only the breeze?

Spinning around, Lluava swiftly moved to the curtain and flung it back. Nothing.

The room shimmered with pulsing shadows. Where was the source? Her neck prickled even more. Glancing back, Lluava ran to the bed and lifted its skirt. Only darkness greeted her. Scanning the alcove where the bed stood, she finally set eyes on a different movement. Earlier, her travel pack had been carried up to her room and deposited on a dresser. Now the flap was undone, and its two most valuable contents were laid out next to it.

Lluava moved to the dresser and rested her hand on one Claw to steady its rocking. The cool metal against her skin did not help to slow the pounding of her heart. A sudden fear crept over her. Issaura's Claws, the weapons bestowed upon her during training in the southern camps, had almost been stolen. She carefully picked up each one and inspected the three curved blades before sliding the Claws over her knuckles.

Someone had some explaining to do. Closing her eyes, she tried to regain her calm. Fear was similar to anger; it would cloud the mind if given the chance.

A scuffing noise from leather shoes on stone in the main room was enough to make Lluava charge back to the seating area. The source was already gone. She hastily moved onto the balcony. Empty.

Where had the intruder gone?

She moved to the edge and peered down. No one could have jumped from that height and survived. She scanned the ledge. Finding nothing, Lluava began to step inside, then caught the fading trail of musk wafting from the ledge next to the wall. Leaning over, she took closer note of the narrow ribbon of stone wrapped around the tower. Its decorative intentions now served another purpose: an escape route. The minuscule ledge was barely wide enough for someone to stand on and only if that person pressed himself against the wall. Lluava's large dual form would be of no service. If she were a different Theriomorph and could transform into a bird or even a house cat, the ledge would be easy to traverse, but a full-grown tigress would find it impossible. Her human form would have to do.

Carefully climbing over the balcony, Lluava tentatively placed one foot on the stone, testing its strength. It held. She slid down and slowly began to inch sideways. She was only a body's length away from her balcony when an updraft of wind tugged at her, causing her to lose her balance. Time slowed as she wavered forward. The city seemed minute from this height. Forcing herself backward, she pressed her body against the cold stone. Her head throbbed. The musk had disappeared. The trail was lost.

Glancing sideways, Lluava wondered who was beyond the bend. Another bout of wind buffeted her, and her hair blew wildly into her eyes. Abandoning the endeavor, she moved carefully back to the balcony and stable footing. Once inside her room, she closed the balcony doors and latched them securely. After testing the lock several times, she crawled onto the bed, tucked the Claws under the spare pillow, and fell asleep.

***

"Lady Lluava?"

A voice like a dove cooed its way into Lluava's dreams. "Lady Lluava? It is time for you to get up. Lady Lluava?"

With a low moan, Lluava blinked awake. "Yes?" she croaked as the grogginess began to fade.

A small girl, perhaps nine years old, stood before her. "Good morning, Lady Lluava. My name is Juniper, like the tree. You may call me June if you wish." Lluava blinked at her. "I will be your personal chambermaid." The girl reached over to the bedside table and poured water from the pitcher into a washbowl. "Do you not like the sheets? I can change them to a different fabric if you wish. Or was it the goose down in the pillow? Tell me what you like, and I will get it for you."

Lluava's mind began to function again. Looking about her, she realized she had fallen asleep so quickly that she had not even slipped under the covers.

"No, no. They're both fine."

"Are you sure? It would not be any trouble."

"They are fine. Truly," Lluava insisted. Bending over the bowl, she splashed cold water on her face. Now she really was awake. Before she could even ask, June handed her a soft towel.

"Thanks," said Lluava into the plush fabric. "What time is it?"

"Seven o'clock, m'lady," chirped June as she removed the damp towel and handed Lluava an ivory mirror. "How do you like your hair styled?"

June had picked up a matching brush and comb and now gestured to a chair in front of the open window. Lluava realized that the girl intended to groom her. This was a strange notion, but as June looked so eager to please, Lluava did not argue.

Instead, Lluava sat down and took in the breathtaking view from the tower. The city was alive and thriving. Insect-sized figures crawled over the labyrinth of roads and walkways like an ant pile all astir with the discovery of nearby crumbs. The weather itself was noticeably warmer than on the coast. Watching the dance of the sparrows high above, Lluava quietly enjoyed the tingling feeling of the steady strokes of the bristles over her scalp.

"Lady Lluava, if you will permit me, I will review your daily schedule." It was clear from the tone of her voice that June was proud of her new job.

"Go ahead," responded Lluava. Her eyes were partially closed with pleasure. She could get used to this aided grooming.

"First, I must inform you that Theriomorphs are never, ever allowed to shift into their dual forms inside the castle. That is considered a hostile act." The girl eyed Lluava warily as if waiting to see if Lluava would be upset about this information.

Lluava nodded. She knew about humans' fear of this very basic Theriomorph capability.

June went on, "After your breakfast, I will lead you to the private baths. Once you are bathed and dressed, you will meet with the royal family at court for the Open Council."

"Open Council?" questioned Lluava.

"The time during which the High Council allows members of the public to present their grievances. After the midday meal, the Closed Council, which is restricted to council members and royalty, will convene to discuss the issues and to strategize."

"Okay," mused Lluava. "How should I prepare for that?"

"Um, I..." June fumbled. "I really don't know what happens behind those closed doors. But you do not have to worry about that, Lady Lluava. You will not be returning for the Closed Council. You will have etiquette sessions, followed by swordsmanship training in the evening."

"What?" Lluava's question was not intended to be answered but more to express the disapproval of what she had just been told. How dare Varren think she needed subsequent training? After all the battles and blood spilled, did he think so little of her skill? And what of this etiquette? Was she that rough, that unpolished, that she needed lectures on manners?

"That is your schedule as I was informed, m'lady," peeped June.

"All right," huffed Lluava.

Switching the subject, June asked, "How would you like your hair done today?"

"Just leave it down," instructed Lluava. There was no use in doing anything special today. Why waste the time?

"Down? Very well...."

When June stopped brushing, she disappeared into the main room, leaving Lluava to continue to enjoy the morning's warmth. A moment later, the girl returned and announced, "Your breakfast is ready. I will serve it in your sitting room."

Though the food was delicious and beautifully presented, Lluava took little satisfaction in it. She was still too insulted about her assigned daily tasks.

Her bath, however, was another story. Entering a large room illuminated by several skylights, Lluava could not help but be impressed at the half-dozen large pools sunk into the floor. Each contained some scene from history or myth portrayed in mosaics on its bottom. The first two pools had chunks of ice floating in them. Ice was a rarity out of season and even then rarely found in the south. The ice bobbed in the water like a child's forgotten toys. The next two pools were twice as large as the others, while the last pair steamed continuously.

Lluava instantly moved to the farthest pair and waved her hand over the water. Dipping her hand in to test its temperature, she quickly exclaimed, "Hot water!"

"Yes, m'lady," said June. "One of the reasons the royal family settled in this location was because of the natural hot springs."

Awkward as it was to strip down in front of the girl, Lluava could not have cared less once she had submerged herself into the steamy basin. The grime of travel slowly dissolved, and she let out a sigh of contentment. Unfortunately, the blissful feeling was short lived, for June insisted that they hurry lest Lluava be late.

Before she knew it, Lluava was dressed in a fine though somewhat overdone dress. Wrapped in its heavy layers, she felt like a caterpillar unwillingly cocooned.

"You must look your best for your presentation to the court and

Council," explained June as she finished lacing up Lluava's bodice.

Sourly, Lluava could not help but think, So they can see me as they would like? I'd rather them see me as I truly am.

The image of a roaring beast in the center of the great hall causing everyone to quake with fear made her smile as she followed the small girl through the castle.

They stopped before a large pair of iron doors. "This isn't the room I saw last night!" Lluava exclaimed.

Laughing, June assured her, "These doors lead into the Great Hall. You must have visited the king's private chambers last night."

"But the thrones and the seats—" The words had barely slipped past Lluava's lips before the trumpeted fanfare announced her arrival and the massive doors were heaved open.

Able to comfortably hold several thousand people, the Great Hall was marvelous to behold. The vaulted ceiling was higher than any Lluava had ever seen. Long, thin, arched windows allowed slivers of light to illuminate the people below. The windows were grouped in threes, and a large tapestry hung between them, helping to muffle the rising chatter. Around the room was wrapped a raised area containing high-backed chairs that looked almost as stiff as the figures seated in them. The High Councilmen wore dark robes, each adorned with different colored stripes. The number of the stripes also differed; the systematic variations made it clear that the stripes were more than decorative. The royal family was seated at the far end, above a two-tiered dais. Their thrones were set on the top tier, a level higher than the Council, whose private dais contained two grand thrones that split the four smaller, decorative chairs. An ever-shifting crowd filled the marble-floored room; people barely paused their conversations to spare a glance in Lluava's direction.

As the steward formally announced the new guest, and people realized who the stranger was, the room quieted. King Thor, much more alert than last night, gave Lluava a reassuring smile. To his left was the little queen, dressed in a flamboyant yellow gown; to his right was Varren. Seeing the prince, Lluava felt a bit more confident. Seated next to the queen was another figure, older and well-groomed, who wore a gown with a rainbow of stripes. He stared back at Lluava as if processing information before coming to a conclusion.

Receiving a nod from King Thor, the steward commanded Lluava, "Follow me, please," and proceeded to lead her to the royal family's seating area. As they approached the dais, Lluava could feel her temperature rise. The countless eyes of the kingdom's elite and privileged seemed to bore into her.

At the top of the stairs, Lluava made an attempt at a curtsy, then quickly sat down on Varren's right. The observers remained reasonably quiet until the steward had returned to his original position; then, like crickets in the evening, indistinguishable chatter erupted once again.

"Lluava," Varren began, "I would like to introduce you to Head Councilman Finch Themis." He motioned to the figure on the far side of the queen. The man continued to appraise Lluava expressionlessly.

"Hello," Lluava said pleasantly.

"Themis, I would like to introduce to you my partner, Lluava Kargen."

"Pleasure," he coolly replied. With that, he turned his attention back to the court and announced, "Send the first one in."

The wide doors cracked open, and a weathered figure stepped through. Wide-eyed, the man was led to the foot of the stairs, where he nervously flicked his eyes between the figures on the royal dais.

"What has brought you here today, my good man?" King Thor questioned.

The person took a moment to find his voice. "I…I have come to humbly ask for your help. My cattle are being stolen by my neighbor. I want to be paid in full for them."

"What proof do you have that your neighbor is indeed taking your livestock?" questioned Thor.

"The number of head of my choice herd has dropped by forty-five, and my neighbor's herd seems to have suddenly increased."

"Do your animals have a brand?"

There was a moment of silence while the man fumbled with the straw hat in his hands.

"No, Your Majesty."

"Then how can you tell that your neighbor's herd has increased because of your beasts and is not due to breeding or purchase?"

"I know every cow I have ever raised. I can identify them immediately. He has my cows."

Themis and Thor exchanged a few words. Themis nodded his head as Thor announced his verdict. "I do not doubt your knowledge of your animals."

The man began to smile.

"Unfortunately," Thor continued, "I cannot command recompense based on pure conjecture. This kingdom is run on fact and physical proof. Unless you can produce some substantial evidence that your neighbor is indeed stealing your cattle, I cannot force him to pay for your loss. Until you are able to gather proof, I suggest you find means to brand your herd."

The man seemed to sink into himself as he was led out of the Great Hall. Those remaining in the room resumed their loud banter. Lluava watched as those of class gabbed and gossiped among each other as if this were merely a social event.

Finally, Head Councilman Themis announced, "Send in the next one."

Once again, the heavy doors opened, and another timid person stumbled through to voice his grievances. The rest of the morning continued in this manner.

During another raucous pause between sessions, Varren inquired above the din, "Did you have a pleasant sleep?"

Remembering her night for the first time, Lluava admitted, "I had a visitor."

Varren's full attention was on her. "A visitor? What do you mean?"

"Someone came into my room last night. I think they were after Issaura's Claws."

"Did you see the intruder?" he hastily asked.

"No." Lluava lowered her voice almost to a purr. "I sensed him. A scent...one I am not familiar with..."

"A scent," Varren repeated.

Lluava knew he was impressed by the Theriomorph race and their capabilities, yet she felt sorry that he would never, could never, truly understand.

Before he could ask, Lluava answered, "Out the window."

"Flight?"

"No, I think earthbound. He used the decorative ledge to escape."

"I'll have you moved to another room."

"What are you two whispering about?"

The pair turned to look at the elderly councilman, who inquired, "Do the politics of the kingdom bore you, Lady Lluava?"

"No, Head Councilman," Lluava felt her cheeks grow hot. "I find it all highly fascinating. We were just—"

Varren finished for her. "We were discussing the Lady Lluava's room arrangements. Since we arrived quite late, I had not made sure they were satisfactory. I wanted to see if she preferred a different option."

Lluava knew where he was going and cut him off before it was too late. "I was just about to tell Varren how much I love the room. I am happy to reside in it for the duration of our stay."

Varren turned back to Lluava. "Are you sure that is what you wish?"

"Yes."

With that, the conversation ended and Themis summoned the next subject.

It was hard to concentrate on the lanky man standing below her. Over the hours, the hard, wooden seat had become increasingly uncomfortable. Positioned on the outer edge of the dais, her mini-throne was not adorned as the others, which became progressively more luxurious the closer to the center their position. Hers, unfortunately, did not even contain a padded pillow like Varren's did. She shifted around a bit before giving up. Her rump would have to deal with it for a bit longer.

Turning her attention back to the room, she noticed that the councilmen seemed more than partially alert. Casting her eyes downward, she observed that the person now before them must have some money—perhaps not enough to command any true respect based on his class, but from the numerous rings and floppy cloth hat, she judged he was not a common farmer.

"That's three wagons this season!" the man huffed, his face reddening with frustration.

"If I may, Your Majesty," Themis formally interjected. "We understand how distressing this is. With all the problems on the coast, we have let slide our interior protection. With His Majesty's consent, I will send several troops north to eradicate these villains."

Had her worst fear come true? The memory of fading screams came back to her with full force. Lluava stood erect and shouted, "Have the Raiders returned?"

Chapter 5

The Fundamentals of Formalities

Everyone within earshot froze; the sudden silence and stillness spread through the room like ripples from a pebble tossed in a pond. The unnatural quiet seemed to last forever when all at once laughter erupted from all sides. Puzzled, Lluava felt her cheeks flush. King Thor only raised an eyebrow, while the Queen giggled so hard she almost slid off her throne. Themis looked less than pleased.

Varren motioned to her. "Sit down."

Utterly humiliated, Lluava quickly took her seat. She yearned for the morning session to be over so she could escape from everyone's judgmental eyes.

After the crowd quieted, Themis continued, "As I was saying, it is far past time for all those bandits to come to terms with the authority of this great kingdom. The Clans' savagery will be stopped once and for all."

The Clans? Is that who he was referring to? Lluava wondered. Yes, it was true that the Clans' open refusal of Elysian law put them at odds with the kingdom. Their thievery from the wealthy was far too common, and on occasion a life was lost, but they had never purposefully hurt an Elysian. They also displayed many valiant attributes. Hadn't Yamir proved this when he, a Clansman himself, chose to enlist to defend Elysia?

"No." The word slipped out before Lluava had time to think.

"No?" reiterated the king. He seemed to find her brash interruptions interesting, a much more favorable alternative than the typical result of interrupted official proceedings. "Do you have an alternate plan, Lady Lluava?"

Lluava recognized the risk she was taking and did not tread lightly.

"The Clans are not evil," she declared. Varren gave her a cautionary glance. She continued carefully, "It is true that they follow their own code and partake in unsavory activities, but the Clans did help us defend our shores. They are good people."

"People who attack and steal from our wagon trains!" exclaimed a dark-skinned councilman.

"Yes..." Lluava could not refute that fact.

Themis noted, "The Clans' aid in our effort to defend our borders does not excuse their unruly and disobedient lifestyle."

"But," Lluava argued, "we should reach out to them. Why not send someone to negotiate a peaceful agreement?"

Themis looked annoyed. "Thank you for your input, Lady Lluava," he said without emotion. "We will take your comments under consideration."

"What is there to consider?" questioned Thor. "We shall send a diplomat to try to form a peaceful arrangement with the Clans. It is true this has been unsuccessful in the past, but saving lives in hopes of unifying the kingdom is our utmost priority."

"Your Majesty, we must consider—"

Thor cut him off. "This is my decree."

Themis gave a perfunctory nod, and the proceedings moved on to other topics.

By noon, Lluava was struggling to focus on the dull and petty complaints of the commoners. It seemed that everyone had some trivial grievance or trifling complaint. Her own thoughts had wandered toward friends and family by the time Themis banged his gavel and announced, "The Open Council is officially dismissed."

Lluava turned to Varren. "What do we do now?"

"Well, I do not know about you, but I am famished. We will retire to the banquet hall."

Lluava realized she was also hungry. "Why don't you lead the way?" Varren smiled and explained the proper order for procession into or out of the Council Room: king and queen, prince and military partner, head councilman, then other council members, two by two in order of status. The nobility followed and could come and go as they pleased.

Although not nearly as large as the Grand Hall, the royal banquet hall was still impressive. Long tables were positioned perpendicularly to the royal table, which was elevated on a dais at the back. Each table overflowed with sumptuous delights: stuffed goose, rack of lamb, enormous ribs, roasted turkey, and even an entire pig, apple in mouth. Silver plates on gilded chargers were decoratively adorned and carefully displayed against dark tablecloths. Platters of fruits and vegetables, boards of cheeses and honeycomb, and baskets of breads filled in the remaining spaces. So many delectable scents wafted around the room that Lluava's own sense of smell seemed to

34

convulse. Was this how they ate every day? she wondered. She salivated at the glorious sights and smells.

The seating arrangement at the royal table was identical to that in the Great Hall. Thankfully, her chair was cushioned. After she sat down, councilmen approached the front of the royal table for proper introductions. Before each greeted Lluava with a polite nod of the head, Themis announced the councilman's name and which region he represented. At first, Lluava attempted to remember all their names, but eventually they blurred together and faded from memory. It would take work to remember everyone she met.

As councilman after councilman introduced himself, Lluava took note of how few Theriomorphs were represented. Yet to be upset at this would be unfair, for it was only under Thor's rule that Theriomorphs had been allowed this elevated status. Someday, mused Lluava, she would be the first female on the High Council and all people of the kingdom would be represented. Would she be called councilman? Perhaps councilwoman or councilor?

After the council members had greeted Lluava, the rest of the court entered the hall and took their seats. Finally, with the king's first bite, the meal officially began.

Lluava did not know where to start; the options seemed endless. She ended up choosing her favorite, tenderloin on the rare side. She had just put the first forkful of oozing meat in her mouth when she noticed that another figure had approached the table accompanied by a herald.

The herald waited for Lluava to hurriedly swallow before announcing, "Lady Lluava, I would like to introduce to you Lord Edgar Sutton from Sutton Estates in the northern region."

"Hello," she said.

The man bowed and returned to his seat. Lluava returned her attention to her warm meal, but before she could take another bite, a new figure approached. This introduction continued like the previous one, and Lluava realized that she would have to postpone her meal until she had been formally introduced to the entire court. At least, couples and family members came up together. Though there were not many children present, the range of ages seemed appropriately distributed, with the exception of the rather large number of young adults. Maybe she would make a few friends at the castle.

At the end of the introductions, a young couple approached. Around Lluava's age, the woman was the embodiment of physical beauty. Although of average height, hers was a frame of sumptuous curves and a dainty waist. Soft sepia skin, several shades darker than Lluava's olive hue, accented her narrow arms and slender shoulders. Her black hair was carefully coiled in a complex and fashionable style favored by the privileged. Several ringlets dipped downward, leading the observer's eye to her two prominent and carefully displayed blessings, an artifice clearly not overlooked by the court.

Her facial features also beckoned the opposite sex. Crimson stained her lips, and thick black kohl set off the golden gems of her eyes. Her perfection seemed complete. Lluava could not help but compare her own toned but far less feminine form to this idealized vision of her own sex.

Lluava quickly glanced at her partner and found him coolly assessing her. Turning away, she looked at the woman's lanky male companion. He could not have been much older than eighteen. He was neither particularly tall nor particularly strong nor anything at all. Well, that was not entirely true. His angular features helped pull the eye away from his unusual hair coloration, black locks flecked with white patches. His pale skin almost matched his irises, which gave his facial features an unearthly look. He stared at Lluava with one eyebrow raised and a sly smirk on his face.

The herald announced, "Luka Fárbauti, son of Lord Axel Fárbauti of the Midlands, and his twin sister, Selene Fárbauti." The pair nodded, and as they turned to their seats Lluava saw Luka whisper in his sister's ear.

"How can they possibly be twins?" Lluava inquired.

"In truth, they are not twins nor related by any means other than legal documentation." While in the public eye, Varren had to speak even more formally than was his usual custom. "They were adopted by Lord Fárbauti at a young age and raised as siblings. Since there is only one month's age difference between them, they are often referred to as twins, especially here at court. They rather like the term, it seems."

"Is Lord Fárbauti Theriomorph?"

"No," stated Varren. "He is very much human. Why do you ask?"

"Because," Lluava explained as she watched the pair politely banter with those at their table, "they are."

Lluava realized that Varren wanted to ask how she knew, but he must have thought it more appropriate to hold his tongue. This was for the best, since she did not know how to explain it to him. A scent? A sixth sense? She had never actually thought about this ability, taking it at face value. It was part of her.

Once again, Lluava looked down at her plate—and gawked; her plate was gone. Looking around, she noted the flurry of servants clearing tables. The midday meal was over. Lluava growled softly, or maybe it was her stomach.

Sorry as she was to leave the hall hungry, her discomfort grew twofold once she entered the prim room of Madam Angela for her etiquette lessons. Surrounded by a pastel-hued décor of crisp linens, lacy pillows, polished silverware, and sparkling crystal, Lluava was instantly aware of her own lack of experience.

Madam Angela was a pleasant woman of moderate age and build, who welcomed Lluava in a most gracious manner.

"Pleasure to make your acquaintance, Lady Lluava," she cooed.

"Nice to meet you, too," Lluava replied, thinking, There were so many other things I could be doing right now. This is going to be such a waste....

"The pleasure is mine," stated Angela, catching Lluava off guard.

"What?"

"The most appropriate response would be to say, 'the pleasure is mine,'" corrected Angela as she motioned Lluava to accompany her to a seating area. "I would like to start by getting acquainted with you."

Lluava took a seat. Once she did, Lluava realized her chair was not nearly as soft and inviting as it looked. She thought sourly, I really hope this doesn't take long.

"First," Angela continued, "I want to further your knowledge about me. I have been privileged to teach the royal etiquette classes for more years than is proper to admit." She smiled at her own ostensible wit. "I provide private and group classes for the young ladies and gentlemen at court, as well as those who come from the outer regions to be educated. I have had many remarkable and noteworthy students, including the crown prince." It was obvious from her smile that Angela truly looked on that as a high achievement. "Now I would like to ask you a few questions so that I can better determine where you stand on your education in these matters. Let me begin by inquiring if you have ever had a formal etiquette class."

Lluava almost laughed. "No."

"Is that question amusing to you, Lady Lluava?"

"No, Madam Angela." She forced a much more serious demeanor for her inquisitor.

Angela considered Lluava a moment. "Where were you born?"

"I was raised in the southern fishing village of Rivendale."

"Lady Lluava, please answer the questions as I present them to you. Or was I not clear? Was that your place of birth?"

Lluava did not see the importance of these fine details; however, she replied, "No. When I was an infant, my parents moved into my grandfather's house to help him with our family farm. I can't remember where we lived before that. I was too young. Since my father was in the army—"

Angela lifted her gloved hand and cut Lluava off. "Thank you, Lady Lluava. That is all I needed to know. How did you and Prince Varren become military partners?"

Highly careful about the wording of her answers, Lluava began to explain. "We were assigned to be partners as part of the training process in the camps. We were matched based on several attributes, including skill level, intelligence, and the compatibility of my dual form."

Angela nodded. She seemed to be taking in all of the information without the aid of notes. "What is your dual form?"

"A white tigress."

For the first time, Angela looked as if she wanted to inquire more but, for the purpose of this session, held back. Regaining her proper demeanor, she asked her next question.

"How would you describe your partnership with Prince Varren thus far?"

A sense of warning formed in Lluava's mind. She had promised Varren to hold her tongue about their affection toward each other. Lluava carefully chose her words.

"Varren and I—"

The white glove was again raised in the air, cutting off Lluava. "One must never refer to the prince simply as Varren. Acceptable titles are Prince Varren or the crown prince. I know that in military proceedings you might reference him as your partner, and what you call him behind closed doors cannot be helped, but our society has standards, Lady Lluava. They must be followed.

"Since you are clearly unaware how to behave in a polished fashion," Angela said, regarding Lluava once more, "let us make it our first rule to never refer to Prince Varren in any way other than what I have just previously explained. Moreover—Lady Lluava?" Angela sat up even straighter. "Never leave your mouth hanging open. You are not a masticating cow."

The session continued in this manner for the next hour. Lluava left feeling ridiculed and judged as never before. She returned to her room and sulked during the interlude prior to her swordsmanship training. She snapped at poor June, who had tried to lighten the atmosphere. All Lluava wanted was to be left alone.

Grumbling all the way down to the training grounds, she entered the swept earth courtyard. Her mood immediately changed. The building that wrapped around the training yard reminded Lluava of the arena in the coliseums. Her heartbeat quickened, and her excitement was aroused. Finally, something she knew!

Her instructor, along with an assistant, awaited her in the middle of the courtyard. As she approached, he beckoned.

"Welcome, Lady Lluava! I was getting a bit worried that you had lost your way. I am glad you have found us." Although they both knew that Lluava could not have actually been lost since an escort led her, the pleasant humor was not unappreciated.

"My name is Domar, and I am the grand master chief who oversees the capital."

Domar was one of those people whose true age was difficult to guess; although his receding hairline made it clear, he was far older than he looked. His beard was groomed at a severe angle, in keeping with his facial features. Next to him was a younger twin who could only be his son.

"And this is Daniel. He will assist in your training." Daniel, whose beard was chopped down to a stubble, perhaps to allow observers to distinguish him from his father, nodded back at Lluava.

"Hello, Grand Master Chief Domar," greeted Lluava.

A grand master chief was the highest-ranking general in the army. It was very rare for a person to attain this rank, and there were very few in the entire kingdom. A sadness filled Lluava as she remembered the last time she had been with a grand master chief.

Turning to the other man, Lluava said, "Hello, Daniel."

"As hard as it may be for you, Lluava," Domar began, as Daniel moved over to the weapons rack, "refer to me as Domar while we train in private. The wordiness of my title can be rather wearisome. Here, I prefer informality."

"Sir! Yes, sir!"

"And we will have none of that."

Strange as it might be to push aside the formalities, at least for now Lluava rather liked the relaxed approach to conversing.

"Now," Domar began again, "I will have you face off against Daniel. I want to see where you are in your training. I know the sword is not your weapon of choice, but I believe it is crucial for every soldier to know how to use one efficiently. Many people use swords recovered from the battles on the coast; the enemy does, as well." Lluava followed the grand master chief to the weapons rack. The metal glinting in the late afternoon light sent a shiver up her spine.

"What if you were separated from Issaura's Claws? What then?"

Lluava looked up. "I would never let that happen."

"Nevertheless," noted Domar, "since the sword is the most common weapon, you need to know how to use it."

Moving her hand over the weapons before her, Lluava said, "With all due respect, I was trained to be able to use a variety of weapons, the sword included."

"I know how the camps train, Lady Lluava," stated Domar. "The question is, how good are you at using one?"

He observed Lluava pleasantly, challenging her. She was ready.

Domar ordered, "Select your weapon."

All the swords had the black, tarlike substance on their edges that dulled the blades. This allowed them to be used in training without fear of actual injury. However, they would still leave respectable bruises if given the chance. Lluava tested several, feeling their weight and balance before choosing a sword of moderate length.

Stepping to the perimeter of the courtyard, she looked across at Daniel. Her level of excitement rose yet again. For the first time since the war, Lluava would have the chance to fight. Her muscles tensed automatically. She took her stance. Locking eyes with her opponent, she waited.

"You may begin."

Chapter 6

Kings and Crowns

Daniel was upon her. Sword raised, slicing through the evening air, thirsting for its red nectar. Lluava skirted to the side and blocked the glistening weapon, glad that she had had the time to switch to more suitable attire. There would have been no way for her to move in that morning's suffocating garb.

Again Daniel attacked, and she dodged his swing. Lluava kept alert for the perfect time to retaliate, yet he did not allow her any. Sidestepping, ducking, blocking, and retreating—although she was supposedly the lesser warrior, she could not help but smile. The thrill of a fight resurfaced. Lluava had forgotten this feeling and all the heart-pounding sensations that accompanied it.

The song of swords reverberated all around them, and with each chorus Lluava became bolder. She began to assess her opponent's behavior. Was there a pattern? Perhaps a favored lunge or swing? Did he have a tell?

While weighing this information, Lluava could sense how much slower her own reactions had become. She had not used a sword in months; she had not had the need. Although Lluava was well aware of proper form, in her growing desperation to stay in the fight she became much less concerned.

At one point, almost cornered against the stone wall, Lluava caught a glimpse of Domar. She suddenly became aware of how unskilled she must appear. She was better than this. Why was she holding back? In an instant, Lluava went on the attack. Her movements, though far from practiced, began to turn the tide.

Did Daniel waver just then? Was he beginning to worry? Lluava could sense no fear in her opponent. His expression was calm as he concentrated on his goal. Lunge left, fake right, stab front—Daniel did indeed seem to falter. In her excitement, Lluava misjudged her opponent.

Without a moment to spare, she leaped out of the path of the angry blade. Losing her footing, she tumbled to the ground and felt *it*. Without a second thought, she raised her right arm, and sword bit sword. The impact, though expected, was shocking.

Lluava screamed. She dropped her weapon and automatically curled around the pain.

"Stop!" Domar shouted, but Daniel was already sheathing his sword.

Lluava's eyes watered, and pain blurred the figures beside her. She rocked in an instinctual attempt to sooth her shoulder.

"Let me see your arm," Domar commanded.

Trying not to think about her injury, Lluava unfurled and began to extend her throbbing limb. Hot daggers seared her muscles; she curled up once more.

"Lluava, I need to have a look." Domar's serious tone persuaded the teen to try again. Cautiously, she permitted Domar to inspect her injury.

After a moment, he stated bleakly, "The shoulder is dislocated."

Lluava blinked back her tears.

"We are going to help you up, Lady Lluava." Domar's voice was cool.

Carefully, Lluava was righted and led through the small wooden side door. Though the space was dimly lit, she could see that the recess contained numerous training weapons and devices. Lluava recognized many from the camps, yet some she did not. They stopped before one such machine.

Before she could attempt to guess its purpose, Domar motioned to the nearby stool. "I want you to take a seat and then slip your arm into this slot."

Lluava did as she was told. With each movement, the pain raced up and down her limb.

"Sit still," Domar said, as Daniel began to strap Lluava's arm down. "This will hurt. You may grab hold of me if you wish, but whatever you do, don't move your arm."

Before Lluava could protest, Daniel cranked the device. All noise produced by the machine was overpowered by Lluava's roar. Shoulder throbbing, she was unstrapped and asked to stand while Domar inspected her once more.

"Has this occurred before?" inquired the grand master chief.

Collecting herself, she answered meekly, "Yes."

"How?"

"In battle." Lluava held her right arm in her left hand. As the pain began to subside, her embarrassment grew. Would this day never end? Keeping her eyes down, she explained further, "It happened once before, when I was attacked by General Kentril."

"I see," said Domar.

Lluava did not want him to think she was unfit for war. She hurriedly replied, "It has not happened since!"

"Until today," he noted.

Lluava looked up into the general's eyes. "I can fight. Tomorrow it will be better, and I will fight."

"This sort of injury has a way of resurfacing, as you have just experienced."

Lluava's stomach dropped. By the gods of old, she swore silently to herself, don't keep me away from the front.

Domar continued, "Though you have courage and some knowledge of swordsmanship, my recommendation for military service is on hold until further notice."

Suppressing the desire to cry out again, Lluava silently pleaded with him to change his mind.

As if reading her thoughts, the grand master chief looked at her and relented. "We will continue your training, working around your injury and slowly building back your shoulder's strength. If your shoulder heals reasonably well, I will permit you to continue service. If not, you will be discharged."

Despite the severity of his tone, Lluava could not help but say, "Thank you!"

***

Tired and sore, Lluava was grateful for the long soak in the hot baths before she squeezed back into her dress and returned to her chambers. As she sat down on her chaise, there was a knock at the door.

June ran to open it, and the prince entered.

"Good evening, Lluava," he began as he glanced at little June. "I was hoping that you would be agreeable to accompanying me on a walk through the royal gardens before supper."

"I would love that!" exclaimed Lluava. Tired though she was, Lluava was eager to have some time alone with Varren.

As she followed the prince through the door, June called out, "Do you want your gloves, Lady Lluava?"

"I'm fine," Lluava called back as she slipped down the hall.

Somewhere in the heart of the castle, Varren led Lluava into what seemed like another land. Through doors on some middle story of the building, they entered what seemed to be a garden. Lush foliage draped the polished trail. Terraced downward, the intricate design was spectacularly arranged and held more exotic plant life than Lluava knew existed. Her jaw dropped with the beauty of vibrant flowers and greenery. Fully grown trees rose and unfurled like umbrellas over tucked-away benches and seemingly natural rock formations hidden away like a treasured secret in this interior courtyard of the castle.

Slowly strolling in silence down the path, Varren motioned her to be seated on a bench in a secluded area. Lluava took several moments, taking it all in, before acknowledging, "This is all so beautiful. It's amazing."

"The hot springs have enabled us to cultivate the land," explained Varren. "For me, it is like a sanctuary. An escape from…life's pressures. Expectations. See that flower?" He pointed to a display of irises. "The black and white one."

Among the plethora of colors was a single stem of a white iris striped in black.

"Yes."

"That variety," Varren said, "is called Theri. I can't help but think of you when I look at it."

The flower's name was fitting, thought Lluava. Its color pattern, resembling a white tiger, was suitable, since that was the dual form of the Theriomorph goddess of war. She smiled.

"It's beautiful." She could smell its pungent aroma—thick, heavy, almost fruity.

Varren turned toward Lluava. "I am glad you came with me. I know this is not easy."

Lluava's heartbeat quickened. "I'm glad I'm here too. Varren?" She took a breath. Why was she so nervous? "Have you told them yet?"

His sigh was answer enough. "No."

"Why not?"

"Breaking my betrothal could cause repercussions. I cannot risk Illia getting hurt."

"How could she be hurt?" questioned Lluava ruefully. "You told me she also wants this to happen. Isn't she in love with some other fellow?"

"I am not worried that she will be hurt emotionally, but I must consider her reputation."

Lluava raised an eyebrow, encouraging him to explain further.

"The High Council is the protector of human traditions. It has been thus since the end of the Landon Wars, when there was no further need for a council of war. With the integration of our races under one rule, the High Council has taken this responsibility quite seriously."

He lowered his voice, and Lluava moved closer to hear.

"Those who question the laws and structure of our society are considered dangerous and a threat. This is one reason why any significant change takes so long to occur."

The rustling of the leaves in the tree caused the pair to look up. Lluava glimpsed dark wings fluttering in the canopy. Still watching the mystery bird, she asked, "How do you make a plea for change?"

"One must present it in front of the Closed Council; it is during these sessions that all topics of note are discussed and laws are created or repealed. I will make the case."

Lluava turned to look at Varren, who continued, "But first I have to have everything ready: the facts, the rationale, the supporters. It will be difficult for the council to make such a significant change, but it is possible." Varren took her hand in his. "Please give me time."

"Okay," she said, as hope returned and a smile lit her face.

Returning her smile, Varren asked, "How was your afternoon?"

Should I tell him? she wondered. She had never kept anything from him before; yet looking into his eyes, she knew she could not tell the truth. Varren would try to protect her. If he knew her injury had recurred, he would prevent her from fighting.

She replied with a question. "Has Madam Angela always been that warm?"

This made Varren laugh, a sound Lluava wished she heard more often.

"Yes," he confirmed. "She has always been that way."

"That's what I was afraid of," Lluava said, chuckling.

Varren switched the conversation to a serious note. "In a couple of days, I will leave to visit Thad's widow."

Not knowing how to react, Lluava hesitated.

"I have not seen her since the attacks began. Thad was my closest childhood friend…" Varren's voice cracked. "I need to see her."

Lluava slipped her arm around his back, hoping to give him some sort of comfort. The action caused her to wince involuntarily.

Varren looked at her questioningly, and she shrugged it off with a smile. Then he said, "I want you to come with me."

Lluava was stunned. He was asking her to support him; how could she not? Yet to look into the face of the grieving widow—could she do that?

"Of course, I will come with you." She answered quickly, refusing to dwell on it further. She was his partner. She would be at his side.

***

Dinner was held in the king's private chambers. King Thor sat at one end of a large table, facing the queen. Varren was seated to Thor's right, while Themis mirrored him. To her dismay, Lluava was positioned next to the queen, too many seats away from the others to hear their quiet conversations.

Lluava gave a forced smile to Enya, who copied her action. Silently, they waited until the first course was served. Tendrils of flavored steam wafting above the crystal bowl of mint-green-colored soup toyed with Lluava's nostrils as Themis said grace. Absentmindedly licking her lips, Lluava dove in as soon as Thor took his first sip. She quickly swallowed, but it was too late. Tongue and throat scorched, Lluava forced herself to satisfy her hunger at a slower pace.

Enya clearly enjoyed Lluava's poor manners. Daintily the queen picked up her spoon, dipped it into the green soup; watching Lluava, she carefully blew on the liquid to cool it. Then she did the unthinkable and slid the spoon between her tight lips.

Lluava's tongue, still burning from the first course, prevented her from enjoying the full flavors of the main meal. She was thankful when dessert arrived. Scooped like balls of colored snow, the sweetened, frozen concoction was just what she needed.

As she savored each bite, Enya finally spoke in her sugary manner. "I want you to join me tomorrow. I like to take walks around the castle on occasion. I would forget everything I own if I did not."

Lluava knew this was not an invitation she could disregard, however unpleasant it would be.

"I would love to," she said, hoping her lie was believable.

The queen flashed another smile at her before returning to her chilled delight.

A feeling of loneliness started to awaken. Lluava looked at the far end of the table, where guests appeared to be engaged in jovial conversations. As if he sensed her thoughts, Varren looked up. Their eyes lingered several moments too long, but Lluava did not care. Varren was with her in his own way.

After dinner, the party moved into the living area, and Lluava realized that the royal chambers were actually like a house unto itself. She wondered how many rooms this wing actually encompassed. The living space was one of the homiest, most comfortable areas Lluava had seen in the castle. Mismatched chairs, side tables, couches, even a large harp in a corner—all seemed to work together. However, it was the smaller items that made the place feel like a home. Lluava took several minutes to become acquainted with her surroundings, pausing to look at miniature portraits, intricate boxes and bowls, and two beautiful lidded vases that adorned the ledge above the hearth.

In a way, this was her excuse to separate herself from Thor. His lapses of memory were worse tonight, and Lluava had an uncomfortable feeling in the pit of her stomach. She picked up one of the tiny frames and looked at the lifelike rendition of a crowned boy. Sensing a familiar presence near her, Lluava said, "You could have at least smiled."

Varren teased, "You cannot possibly imagine how long I had to pose for that painting. When a five-year-old child is told to sit still, time seems to last for an eternity."

"Lady Lluava." Themis's voice caused Lluava to turn. "Would you be interested in playing a round of Kings and Crowns with me?"

Taking a moment, she decided this would be more pleasant than trying to make conversation with the absentminded king. "Certainly, but you will have to refresh my memory on the rules. I haven't played in years."

After a quick review, Lluava was glad that she remembered some of the complexities of the game. The board consisted of two sides lined with various figures of war: princes, royal guard, foot and mounted soldiers and, of course, the most important piece, the king. The premise seemed simple: capture the enemy's king. Yet each figure moved differently, each had its own specialty and weakness. This game of strategy was a favorite with the upper class, for it was a battle of wits.

The first game, played in silence, allowed Lluava to refresh herself on rules and strategy. During the second match, seriousness replaced pleasure. This feeling intensified when Themis spoke.

"Varren is an amazing young man. That, I believe, we can both agree on."

Lluava looked up from the board, trying to determine the import of the head councilman's words.

Themis continued. "Strong, intelligent, courteous, and..." he locked eyes with Lluava, "pleasant to the eye."

Lluava felt her heart skip a beat.

Themis moved his guard diagonally across the board, taking out one of Lluava's foot soldiers. "Or am I mistaken? I thought that's what many a young lady believed."

How should she react? Lluava kept silent and moved her archer three spaces. "The ladies of Thowcelemine would agree with you."

Lluava hoped her reference to the female Theriomorph training camp that she had briefly attended would suffice. Maybe the councilman would not think too much of it, since she was known for her time at Durog, the men's camp.

Themis coolly commented, "At the very least, the prince is a heartbreaker. Those poor girls' daydreams will never come true. I cannot help but pity Lady Illia. Think of the many hateful glances and unkind words that are spoken about her. Such are the troubles of betrothal to the crown prince." He shifted his foot soldier to the side, countering Lluava's attempt at a strike.

Lluava silently studied her options on the board as Themis asked, "I wonder how many wish Illia were not betrothed to Prince Varren. How unfair it must seem."

He must have seen Varren return my look, Lluava thought reproachfully. She could feel the man's piercing eyes staring at her.

"Did you know that there have been several petitions in the past attempting to undo this noble tradition?"

"No," replied Lluava. She moved one of her mounts up and to the left. Themis was baiting her, and she did not want to bite.

"They never had a chance of being considered." Themis moved a soldier forward.

"Never?" Lluava saw an opening in the game. If she could distract him

46

long enough with feigned interest in his topic, she might win the match.

"Well," mused Themis. "That is not entirely true. There was one man who had gathered unusually large support for this plea."

While the head councilman talked, Lluava captured his last guard.

"Unfortunately, he died suddenly." With a swift movement, Themis's foot soldier captured Lluava's king, winning the game.

Lluava looked up in surprise as Themis remarked, "A shame that accidents can happen at such inopportune occasions. Better luck next time."

Lluava sat there stunned, heart racing, as Themis strode away. His threat was duly noted.

Chapter 7

A Threat Unchallenged

Part of Lluava wanted to leave the trials and tribulations of the previous day behind her; yet, as the sun's rays clawed their way into her bedroom, she knew she could not. Themis had threatened her, hadn't he? Who was he to do such a thing? She was the military partner of the prince. Lluava closed her eyes and tried to get comfortable once more under her sheets. Varren would find a way to change the law. Themis would not keep them apart.

The sunlight tugged at her eyelids. She growled and pulled the sheet over her head.

Themis was jealous! Lluava thought back on Varren's conversation. Had Varren discussed with Themis his plan to have Lluava instated as head councilman after him? If so, Themis might feel threatened. She could not assume that position until Varren was crowned; yet knowing you were going to be replaced and by whom would certainly be unnerving. For a human of a certain social standing, invested with the power to protect the kingdom's traditional customs and laws, any modification might be deemed unacceptable. Lluava was not only a female—and humans had never experienced a female in power—but also Theriomorph. Imagine a female Theriomorph as head councilman! Themis must be seething.

Lluava took a breath and sighed. No. Themis could not know that yet. He had been too calm, too centered. Lluava turned on her side. Well, that was for the best. Although she did not want to make political enemies, part of her wished that the head councilman knew.

The light was too bright. Lluava threw back her sheet with a huff. Themis had threatened her, that much was clear. Now Varren needed to know. And why was the room so warm?

Lluava moved to unlatch her bedroom window but stopped mid-step. Out on the windowsill, a large raven was preening itself.

A gurgled word slipped past her lips. "Chat…"

Lluava felt her jaw clench and her eyes began to blur. She froze and watched the bird finish its morning ritual before it cawed once and flew off. As the dark silhouette disappeared in the morning haze, Lluava thought of the bird she had released so recently at Chat's newly mounded grave.

"Lady Lluava?" June's voice called from the doorway.

Turning so the girl could not see her face, Lluava quickly wiped her eyes. Why was she acting so foolishly?

"Are you all right?"

"Yes," replied Lluava as she took her seat in the chair and waited for June to brush her hair. As the grooming progressed, she again refused June's offer for a special hairstyle. Her thoughts were focused on the need to talk privately to Varren.

Before Lluava entered the Grand Hall, June chirped behind her, "Remember to bring your weapons to swordsmanship class!"

Had June told her this already? If so, Lluava had clearly not paid attention. Had she missed anything else?

The massive doors groaned opened, and Lluava felt flustered as she took her seat next to the prince. The morning progressed much as it had the day before; the only difference was the faces of those who approached. Lluava kept glancing over at Varren. Yet each time she considered alerting him to Themis's threat, the sight of the head councilman dissuaded her. The midday meal was no different; Themis's hovering presence prevented Lluava from speaking to the prince.

As they parted ways for the afternoon, Lluava pulled Varren aside. "I need to talk to you before dinner."

Without hesitation, Varren replied, "In the garden." He gave Lluava's shoulder a quick squeeze before he headed to the Closed Council and Lluava to her etiquette class.

As if on cue, Madam Angela's syrupy voice welcomed Lluava before inviting her to take a seat. "A lady always crosses her ankles," Angela instructed.

Lluava made the correction.

"Now Lady Lluava, I would like you to put these on."

Madam Angela handed Lluava a pair of shoes unlike any she had seen before. These were made not of leather but of a coarse, stiff fabric that held its form. Unlike Lluava's regular shoes, the heel was lifted by a wooden block.

Lluava eyed the shoes warily before slipping them on. Before she knew it, she was wobbling across the room, trying not to fall on her face.

"Back straight, chin high!" chirped Angela between thin smiles.

This is barbaric! How could anyone ever think this was elegant? Lluava thought as she returned her instructor's smile with a false one of her own.

"Do not look at the ground, Lady Lluava," commanded Angela. "A woman always looks out in front of herself."

Lluava stifled a low growl. "Yes, Madame Angela."

There was a knock at the door. While Lluava tried to catch her balance, Angela went to see what the steward wanted.

"Tsk, tsk," Angela chastised upon returning. "Wherever has the time gone?" Turning to Lluava, she announced, "Our lesson is over for today. Tomorrow you will practice walking up and down stairs. A lady must be the epitome of grace at all times."

"Yes, Madame Angela," Lluava acknowledged with a sigh. She quickly changed shoes and left to follow her escort to the queen's chambers.

The child who was queen greeted Lluava petulantly. "You are late."

"I'm sorry, Your Highness," replied Lluava with an almost graceful curtsy.

Enya raised a tiny, gloved hand. "Take my arm. I want to show you my castle."

Linking arms with Lluava, Enya looked up at her, "You are quite tall. Your legs are too long. Do not walk fast."

With a dozen ladies-in-waiting in tow, Enya led Lluava down the hall. At first, they strolled in silence. Lluava wondered what to say.

Then, Enya's eyes narrowed as she gave Lluava another sidelong glance. "Do you dye your hair?"

Lluava was baffled by the question. "Um... no. I was born this way."

Enya gave a slight nod of her head toward the entourage. "Several of these girls try to lighten their hair with lemon juice and sunlight. I have never seen hair as pale as yours; it is almost as white as an old crone's."

Before Lluava could respond, Enya probed again, "What about your eyebrows? Do you darken them?"

"No. They're natural, too," replied Lluava.

The queen scrutinized her once again, clearly questioning her honesty. "How very odd," Enya remarked as she steered Lluava through a doorway.

"This is one of my guest chambers. We have...how many do I have, Else?"

One of the flock shadowing them chimed up, "One hundred and twenty-two, Madam."

"Ah, yes. I forget—there are so many." Enya searched Lluava's face to see if the girl was suitably impressed with her display of wealth. Not finding the reaction she hoped for, the child who was queen proceeded to show off chamber after chamber. Although each one was beautiful, polished, and perfectly decorated, all were cold, uninviting, and unwelcoming despite their physical splendor. Something was missing from this magnificent castle. Then again, since it was as large as a village, how could it possibly feel like a home?

Lluava thought of her family's aged and battered dwelling. The graying wood, the weed-choked garden, and the sparse furnishings did not diminish the feelings she associated with the poor abode, the love of her great-grandfather that breathed life into the rooms, the hearth, the land itself. Her great-grandfather had farmed the land, as had her father. And one day....

With sudden awareness, Lluava looked around her and realized *this* was now her home.

Observing the shocked expression on Lluava's face, Enya jumped to the wrong conclusion. "You do not like the colors..." The tone of the queen's voice betrayed her insecurity. "Just as I thought!" she shrieked. "This purple color is hideous. Else, I told you to have this room redecorated!"

"Again, Your Highness? It was just finished last week...?" Else was quaking.

"Yes, again! You are not here to question my decisions," snapped Enya as she eyed Lluava. "Lady Lluava," she commanded, "follow me. I want to show you the second floor."

Turning the corner of the hall, Enya strode past two large double doors, completely disregarding them.

"Where do these lead?" asked Lluava, seeking to engage in some form of conversation.

"What? Those?" Enya paused, looking at the dark wooden doors as if they had suddenly appeared out of thin air. "Why, Lady Lluava, those lead to the Burnt Wing. The wing was destroyed by fire a long time ago." She repeated herself as if the second time would make it clearer.

Lluava raised an eyebrow.

Enya continued, "That wing was Prince Damian's quarters."

So this was where Varren's father grew up. Lluava touched the heavy handle, her fingers brushing over the very knob that Damian had turned years before.

"That wing is off limits—for *everyone*."

"Why?" inquired Lluava.

"Thor believes it is a way to keep the memory of his son alive," Enya explained petulantly.

"It is sacred to him," Else added.

Lluava moved away from the door, but as she released the knob, she felt the door shift. "It's not locked!" she exclaimed.

The queen snickered at Lluava's ignorance. "There is no need. The Shadows keep everyone out. Come, Lluava, I have much to show you before your next class."

***

No matter how hard she tried, Lluava could not be anything but excited about her swordsmanship training. This time, she had Issaura's Claws with

51

her. It was clear even to Lluava that her confidence was inflated. Her weapons were extensions of herself, something she knew and trusted, not some foreign object she used to defend herself.

Domar explained his atypical request. "I asked you to bring Issaura's Claws today so that I might observe you in action as if you were on the field of battle. Since the sword is not your weapon of choice, I need to gauge your expertise with your own weapons."

Now it all makes sense, thought Lluava.

"May I inspect the Claws?" he asked. "I have only heard about them from reports during the war. They had been locked in the castle's treasury for many years prior to that."

Reaching into her satchel, Lluava pulled out the two gilded weapons and handed them to the general. As Domar lifted them up, they gleamed lethally in the sunlight. After a moment more, he respectfully returned them to the teen.

"They are magnificent," he acknowledged. "Your race had an unparalleled talent at metalwork. The fact that this skill and knowledge has vanished over the years is one of the greatest losses to both our races."

"It is," she agreed as she stepped to her starting position in the yard. Smiling, Lluava was glad that Domar had asked her to use the Claws today. This time, she was ready to put on a show.

"Issaura's Claws aren't coated." Lluava referred to the protective sheath used in training for swords and daggers. "I don't want to hurt Daniel."

Domar nodded. "Thank you for your concern, Lady Lluava. Do not worry yourself in regard to this matter. Daniel can hold his own. Just remember, this is a training exercise and not an actual skirmish."

"If you're sure...." Lluava looked at Daniel, who nodded back at her. Slipping the Claws over her hands, she automatically loosened her grip. This allowed the three arched blades to drop back before she balled her hands into fists, causing the blades to stand erect over her knuckles. Like a cat sharpening its claws, she continued to do this while she watched Daniel select the sword of the day.

"You may begin," announced Domar.

Lluava sprang into action. Though Daniel's blade gave him a longer reach, it was very heavy. This fact, combined with Lluava's agility and speed on foot, allowed her to easily hold her ground against his attacks. Yet without shifting into her dual form, she was often on the defensive.

Lluava needed to move in close. In order to do this, she had to predict Daniel's movements. His stoic demeanor made it impossible to read his face. Fortunately, like any creature his body language spoke for him. In just a few moments, she had maneuvered herself within arm's reach.

Like reflections in a mirror, the pair swung at each other. Their weapons collided at full force. Shock waves ran up Lluava's right arm, gnawing at her aggravated shoulder. She tensed; instinctively favoring the recent injury, she feared the worst. But nothing happened. A split second later, Lluava's left hand forced Daniel to retreat lest he be sliced into quarters. Lluava rolled her shoulders to loosen them. Her right side began to ache.

Lluava glanced at Domar. She refused to show weakness in front of this man, who had the authority to prevent her from returning to the front lines. I must not give him any reason to doubt my ability to fight, she thought.

In seconds, Lluava was again defending herself from Daniel's retaliation. Forced to use her right arm, Lluava gritted her teeth to keep from vocalizing the pain. Soon she was blinking back tears. Mercifully, they both were moving too fast for anyone else to register her reactions.

None too soon, Domar called out, "That is enough for today."

Turning her head down to prevent the others from seeing her face, Lluava tenderly slipped off her weapons and replaced them in her satchel.

"Lady Lluava…"

Lluava turned back to Domar. The general walked up to her. "You are very impressive with Issaura's Claws. I see now why they were given to you."

Lluava could not help but smile at the complement.

"Your race has many remarkable abilities. A human would not be able to wield these weapons as you do, at least not without some type of brace. Structurally, their impact on the forearms would be too much. How are you doing with your injury?"

Should she tell him the truth?

Domar continued, "There is no shame in injury, only folly in ignorance."

"It hurts more," replied Lluava softly.

"Tomorrow, we will begin working to build back your shoulder's strength," Domar told her. "No more work with the Claws, though."

Lluava nodded silently as she was released.

***

Taking several wrong turns, she finally found the royal gardens. Lluava followed the trail to the bench where Varren already waited. The sight of him made Lluava smile, and she soon forgot her throbbing arm.

He stood up as she approached and inquired, "Is everything all right?"

"No." Her response was a bit too blunt, so she explained, "Themis threatened me last night."

"He did *what?*" Varren's voice rose an octave.

"He knows we are more than mere partners. Or at least he knows that's what I want…."

Varren's jaw tightened. "What did he say to you?"

"It wasn't the words, exactly," Lluava tried to explain. "He just…I don't know how to describe it. He just threatened me."

"All right," Varren said as he clearly contemplated his options. "Lluava, you have to be extremely careful."

"Me?" Lluava was taken aback.

"Themis has a powerful sway over the council. While my grandfather is…" Varren's voice trailed off for a brief moment. "Themis's authority has grown. I knew this was happening, but I had not realized how far it had gone. While I have been away, Themis has become too comfortable with wielding power. If he suspects what I intend to do, he could thwart my ability to effect change in the traditions and laws by which I am bound."

Exasperated, Lluava exclaimed, "But you are the crown prince!"

"Yes," acknowledged Varren as he twisted the signet ring on his finger. "But until I am king, he has authority over me."

Lluava was fuming. "That's—"

Varren cut her off. "The way it is."

"How can you make any changes if he is always around?" Lluava could feel her anger rising. Varren motioned her to be quiet.

She took a breath and asked, "What about your family dinners? Can't you at least prevent him from attending those?"

"I cannot," Varren replied, his frustration evident. "He has the authority to attend any family function."

"Why?"

Varren sat down on the bench. His face seemed broken by the burden of the truth.

"Themis is my godfather."

Chapter 8

Hyrax

Themis is your godfather?" Lluava wasn't sure she'd heard him correctly.

"Yes. That is why he can attend all family functions," reiterated Varren.

Scowling, Lluava said, "He planned that, didn't he?"

Varren rubbed the back of his neck with his hand. "Who knows? What is certain is that after my grandfather, he holds the most power in the kingdom. Come, Lluava, it is time for supper."

When Lluava arose the next morning, the first thing she saw was the large raven ruffling its feathers outside her window. A light rain formed liquid jewels on its feathers. Fluffing up into a black ball, the bird shook the gems off once more as it huddled close to the windowpane.

Knowing that little June would soon arrive to begin their morning ritual, Lluava moved to her chair. As she sat down, the raven turned toward her as if it had just realized that there was another world on the other side of the glass wall.

"It can't be!" Lluava exclaimed.

"Can't be what?"

June, as punctual as ever, had appeared in the doorway.

"That raven has a scar on its face," Lluava pointed out. June moved closer to take a look. The bird had a healed gash that angled from the top of its head, over a dead eye, and down to the corner of its beak.

"It's an ugly bird, isn't it?" June noted as she started brushing Lluava's fine hair.

Lluava said, "It's Chat's bird."

"Who?"

"A boy a little older than you who died in the war."

June paused for a moment. "That's so sad."

Lluava kept her eye on the sopping creature vainly trying to take refuge on the ledge.

"I'm sure that's his bird. It has to be."

She stood and reached over to unlatch the window. As she did, the raven took wing, cawing angrily at the disturbance.

Throughout the morning, Lluava kept thinking of the raven. Could it actually be the same bird? She had released him by the sea. How could he have found its way here—and to her very window?

This particular train of thought made Lluava anxious. Since she had a little spare time, she decided it would be better to resume her exploration of the castle than to sit in her room and dwell on her questions.

Roaming through the corridors proved much more agreeable without the artificial giggling of her first guide. As she wandered around the fifth-floor halls, two figures approached.

"Might this be the Lady Lluava?" the young man asked.

His companion, a woman, responded, "Why, I believe you are correct."

A moment later, Lluava recognized the pair's distinctive characteristics. The twins greeted Lluava respectfully, Luka bowing and Selene curtsying gracefully.

"What are you up to this fine afternoon?" asked Luka coolly.

"Trying to acquaint myself with all this," said Lluava, motioning about her.

In a voice as smooth and polished as her brother's, Selene responded, "This must be a tremendous change for you. How do you like it here?"

Lluava phrased her feelings carefully. "It's been rather eye opening."

The twins shared a smile before Selene replied, "I am sure it has been."

"Would you care for some company?" asked Luka.

Wondering if these were the first two people she might enjoy getting to know, Lluava quickly replied, "Actually, yes, I would."

Before long, the three were talking easily, sharing stories, and teasing each other. Lluava felt as if she had always known them; their idiosyncrasies, mannerisms, and wit seemed so familiar. Laughing so hard tears were in their eyes, they turned a corner as Luka finished a tale of one of his many mischievous antics.

"...and that was when Enya ran out of her room screaming, 'My dolls are alive! My dolls are alive!' She has had them locked up ever since."

Between the image of the frightened queen and Luka's terrible attempt at a girl's voice, Lluava had to lean against the stone wall to catch her breath between uncontrollable bouts of laughter. Finally she gasped, "I can't. No more..."

Chuckling, Luka said, "I thought you would like that one."

"Isn't he horrible?" said Selene as she smiled kindly at her brother.

"All in good fun," Luka replied with a grin. Then he cocked his head for a second and stated, "We're going to have a visitor."

Lluava suddenly smelled a heavy perfume, and within moments a councilman turned the corner, almost running into the group.

"My apologies," he said as he bent down to pick up several scrolls he had dropped.

"It was our fault, I am sure," replied Selene. Turning to Lluava, she said, "Councilman Hyrax is one of the finest representatives of our race."

"I only hope to live up to your compliment, Lady Selene," said the councilman. Even though Hyrax was one of the younger councilmen, his dark beard was marked by two extraordinary white stripes on either side of his chin. Lluava noted a large medallion hanging from a wide maroon ribbon around his neck. On it, the engraved crest of a radiating eye was encircled by ancient symbols.

"Those markings," Lluava said, indicating the pendant. "They're ancient runes, aren't they?"

"Yes, they are," Hyrax replied, looking down at the emblem. "Can you read them?"

"Only a little," acknowledged Lluava, "but I don't recognize these."

"Ah, what a shame," said Hyrax. "Our people's great literary achievements are all but lost; only a few are able to decipher our written language." He shifted the scrolls under his arm. "It would have been exciting to meet another erudite Theriomorph."

Lluava's interest spiked. "I started to learn several years ago."

"That's admirable. Why did you stop?"

"My father began to teach me before he…" Lluava took a breath, "was killed."

"I am sorry for your loss," condoled Hyrax formally.

Lluava nodded and went on, "He believed strongly in the old ways. He wanted his children to grow up with the knowledge of our history, beliefs, traditions, and culture. After he died, my mother thought it would be easier to raise us in the human fashion. I was not allowed to continue my studies of the ancient runes."

Hyrax ran his hand over his beard, fingers pausing over the two white stripes. "Would you like to learn more?"

Still remembering her father, who had always understood her, Lluava replied, "Yes."

"Follow me, then." Without another word, Hyrax strode off down the hall.

Lluava turned to her two companions, who had been silent during their exchange. Luka waved her off. "Go."

"We will see you again, I am certain," affirmed Selene.

Catching up to the councilman, Lluava followed Hyrax up another flight of stairs. An oval doorway led to the castle library. Lluava sighed in awe at the countless books and scrolls stacked neatly on the shelves and cubicles built into the room's soaring walls. Her nose twitched from the strong odor of dusty leather bindings.

Moving to a table, Lluava sat down and watched Hyrax climb a narrow ladder to select a particular book and a pair of scrolls. Returning to Lluava's table, he opened them for her examination.

"These will help you learn how to read the Ancients' writings. Although crude in their simplicity, they are essential to begin." Handing Lluava the heavy tome, Hyrax explained, "This contains both religious books of the Old Ways: the *Karmasana,* which encompasses the creation stories and what has occurred, and the *Virisinu,* which contains all that is predicted."

"I have my father's *Karmasana* in my room," Lluava put in. "I brought it with me when I left home." She gently explored the pages of the heavy volume, gazing at the various symbols. "I was never able to actually read it. I just know the stories."

She paused to look at an inked image of Theri, the goddess she so resembled. The virginal goddess was depicted with her arms outstretched to the viewer. The light radiating from her symbolized her compassion for the Theriomorph race. A sleeping white tiger lay at her feet; Issaura's dual animal form was identical to Lluava's.

"Ah, Theri," acknowledged Hyrax, "more commonly known as Issaura, the goddess of war, wisdom, and womanhood. Not a bad goddess with which to be associated." He glanced at Lluava then, back at the table.

"Start with this scroll," he said, pointing to the nearest one. "It is devastating that our people have lost this once-common knowledge. Perhaps you can salvage some of it."

With parchment, quill, and ink, Lluava began to learn the basic symbols of the ancient language. The hieroglyphic nature of the written form was complex and confusing. As she practiced, Hyrax busied himself with replacing the scrolls he had borrowed from the library. Occasionally he paused to give her aid.

"I must leave now," Hyrax said as he moved toward the door. Uncertain of the time, Lluava thought it best to leave, too. Neatly grouping her materials at the end of the table, she hurried out the door, then doubled back to reclaim her notes. Her self-proclaimed studies would have to wait until after dinner.

Once in the hall, Lluava did not recognize her surroundings, nor did she know where to go. Trying to retrace her steps, she cursed herself for not leaving with Hyrax. As she jogged down a hall, she abruptly stopped in front of the first feature she recognized.

The doors to the Burnt Wing were slightly ajar.

I could just take a quick peek, she thought.

Moving closer, Lluava peered inside. The light was so dim that even with her hypersensitive ability to see in the dark, she could make out only obscure blobs in shadow.

This is crazy. Yet, will I have another chance? Opening the door just enough, Lluava slipped through.

Taking a moment to allow her eyes to adjust, the young woman crept to the center of the room. Thick curtains blocked any natural light, and heavy sheeting covered what she assumed to be furniture. Yet nothing appeared scorched. The walls still held their color; the carpets, though rolled, were unblemished. Realizing she was in a large foyer, Lluava moved into the next room.

"Ah," she sighed aloud. "Now I see."

This larger entryway clearly smelled of aged embers and torched tapestries. Smoke stains discolored the back recess of a former doorway. As in the foyer, furniture had been covered, but draped frames were also scattered about; some were still hanging, others were propped against walls or stacked at odd angles on the floor. Lluava moved to the largest one. As she tried to peek at the painting hidden under the material, the fabric began to slide off the frame.

No! No! No! she thought, vainly attempting to push the sheeting back in place. Too late! Slipping off, it enveloped Lluava like a funeral shroud. The covering swirled and twisted around her. For a brief second, the thought of being tied down awoke terrifying memories.

Trapped! Trapped! The words reverberated in her mind. Her mouth began to dry out. Was it her imagination, or did her skin suddenly feel stretched thin? The memory of her starvation and abandonment in the cells at Fort Brinsdale seemed very fresh.

Lluava's breath quickened. She flailed about, but that only knotted the sheet tighter.

I have to get out! she thought as she felt the heat rise from her core.

Lluava did not realize what had occurred until she crawled, gasping, through the shredded sheets. Picking up the tattered remnants, she knew there was no way to hide the claw marks that had dissected them.

Should she hide it? No. Nobody comes in here.

Lluava dropped the ripped drapes, and a dust cloud puffed up around her.

Trying to regain her composure, Lluava closed her eyes and took a long breath. When her breathing had steadied, she looked up—and stared into the eyes of Varren's young parents. There was no mistaking who they were. Damian had been painted standing next to his seated wife. Varren would look like this man if he were a few years older; hair, dress, and even stance were all mirrored in his living son. Varren had his mother's smile and her eyes. The crowned couple gazed serenely into the distance, past Lluava, past the scorched walls left by the fire that had consumed them.

"You never got to know your son," Lluava said aloud. "He has grown up to be a good man."

She wondered what might have happened had the couple not perished in the sabotage of the royal chambers. Would Themis have gained such power? Where would she and Varren be? Would they even have sent Varren to war? Would there have been a war at all?

There was no point in pondering such questions, Lluava reminded herself. People die. People die for horrible reasons. Varren's parents, Chat, General Argon, my father—for what? Because some empire from across the waters tries to lay claim to our country? They do not own this land. They do not own us. Even if their claim were valid, and Varren's ancestors had broken treaties, putting themselves in power, who were these foreigners to cause this devastation?

"Who?"

Lluava's question echoed aloud through the room like the ghostly voice of the dead.

Respectfully, she moved away from the painting; its lifelike nature was unsettling. She headed to the fire-marred entryway, amazed that the smell of soot was still so strong after all these years. Pausing, she turned back to the room. She stood for a moment in the dead silence, then moved toward the main tower room.

Suddenly she sensed them. Like shooting stars, two bladed projectiles embedded themselves in the stone an eyelash length from her face.

Heart pounding and heat rising, Lluava scanned the vacant room. The hairs on the back of her neck stood on end. No one was there. No scent of any kind, other than that of stale ashes, found her nose. Not a footstep or a shallow breath to tease her ears. Just silence, stillness, and solitude.

Her senses heightened, Lluava inspected the weapons. The toothed blades looked like lethal, radiating suns. Sinister to the touch, they had bitten deeply into the solid granite. As she stared at the gleaming surface, Lluava caught a movement of shadows in the blade's reflection. Something was in the room with her.

An unidentifiable form morphed into blackness; then three more sparkling projectiles burst from the darkness. Throwing herself to the floor, Lluava dodged the onslaught.

A warm sensation slid down her face. Touching her forehead, Lluava was thankful it was only a scratch, yet like most head wounds it was bleeding heavily. As the red oozed between fingers and down into her eyes, a crimson veil coated everything. As it trickled down her nose and over her lips, Lluava could taste her life. The embers inside her, lit by a match of blood, ignited.

Lluava lost control, released, and transformed.

Chapter 9

Red Holly

Silent flames crackled through her veins as Lluava's internal heat exploded like a volcano. Torching pain seared every sinew of her body as muscle tissue tore and mended itself. Bones elongated and shifted under boiling skin. She identified the sharp pain as her tail erupted from its base. She felt her fur spring forth, black on white. With teeth and nails growing sharp, pupils narrowing, ears folding back, she bolted around to face her offender. Guttural vibrations shook free, and the roar reverberated from every surface in the room.

In mere seconds, Lluava had shifted into her dual form. Her whiskers twitched as they responded to the vibrations around them. With her heightened vision, the chamber seemed much brighter now. Although shadows still flickered on the periphery, there were far too few to keep their secrets any longer.

Flicking her tail in agitation, Lluava sought out her attacker. She spotted the form rising out of the dark nothingness. Cloaked all in black, the figure appeared to float toward her. The shadowy material formed a mask of sorts, hiding the identity behind it; only the eyes were exposed. Green like her own. The form approached.

Lluava's claws slid from their sheaths, grazing the stone floor, waiting for their moment. She snarled, keeping her body aligned with the shadowy form.

The figure paused for the span of two tail flicks. Then, swiftly, the entity charged. Lluava lunged, but as she leaped, the phantom evaporated in the darkness. Stumbling to a stop, Lluava turned around, searching for her enemy.

The form rose out of the shadows to her left. Before Lluava could attack, two more glinting blades shot her way. In her larger tiger form, she struggled to avoid those serrated teeth. Evading one attack, she was bombarded with another. This time, it was a set of small, three-pronged daggers. Their skilled master deftly whipped them through the air. Lluava's fore claws desperately kept them at bay.

In and out of the darkness, the pair danced. Blackness momentarily consumed Lluava's prey only to regurgitate it from a different angle. Occasionally the enemy blades hit their mark, leaving ribbons of red in their wake. Yet none dug into muscle, which allowed Lluava to continue to maneuver. The entity glided to the side and quickly disappeared in the dark.

Lashing out, the tiger's claws slit the black material near the head, and the form vanished. For a moment, Lluava's attention followed the languid fall of a long auburn strand of hair until it landed in a spiral on the floor. Then the chase began anew.

Following the vibrations her whiskers detected, Lluava raced toward the door and the spiral staircase, the spine of the tower. As she lunged up the steps, a new series of projectiles hurtled down at her like silver rain. Whistling by her ears, they dug into the stone as she clumsily skirted them. As she glared up into the darkness, a new wave followed.

Lluava leaped across the open central chasm to the high level of stairs, across from the falling blades. As she gained her footing, the shadowed blur of a boot collided with her lower jaw. Several more jabs and side kicks followed. As the huge feline desperately grasped the ledge of the stairwell, the figure before her paused, as if considering various scenarios. With a sudden thrust, the all-too-familiar boot landed on Lluava's snarling face and shoved.

The sensation of falling, never pleasant, gripped her now as her stomach upended itself and her limbs flailed helplessly. Lluava torqued her body and landed on her paws. The force of the impact wrenched muscles, and her injured shoulder gave way. She screamed.

As the echoes of her cry died away, new sounds reverberated through the chamber, hushed and distorted in their overlap: "Leave now...."

Lluava thought, they sound as if—no, that couldn't be.

Lifting her wounded forearm, Lluava loped out of the tower and back into the main room. She glanced behind her and realized she was now alone.

As she stumbled over a piece of disheveled cloth, her stomach dropped again. In her haste, she had forgotten that she wore clothing woven by humans. These were the tattered remnants of her dress, which had been unable to change with her shape.

She was suddenly aware of her very precarious situation. She certainly could not move through the halls as a tiger: Theriomorphs in their dual forms were forbidden in the castle.

Every profanity she had ever heard flashed through her mind. Searching for a solution, Lluava finally accepted the only possible one. She shifted into human form—an experience to which she was now numb, having done it so often. Then she grabbed the cloth that had once protected the portrait and wrapped it around herself. With her spare hand, she collected the scraps of her clothes and then cautiously peered out the door. The hall was empty.

Lluava quickly slipped down the corridor. Taking only a moment to reassure herself that she was alone, she navigated the castle, leaving only a trail of curses in her wake.

***

"Lluava?"

She froze in mid-run.

"What are you doing?"

Turning slowly, Lluava flushed. The twins were looking out of a side room. Their expressions were a hybrid of curiosity and hilarity. As they approached, Lluava tightened her grip on the cloak. Her shoulder throbbed.

"I…uh…"

What could she say? What excuse could she offer? Breaking into the forbidden wing? Foolishly fighting an Obsidian Guard? Shifting in the castle, and in human clothing? The more Lluava realized how idiotic she had been, the more she fumbled.

Luka was clearly offended. "Well, if you don't trust us..."

"I do," Lluava hastily answered. "I'm expected for dinner now." She moved under the fabric. "And I seem to have gotten myself into a little situation."

"That might be the biggest understatement I have heard all day," Selene said smiling.

"Go!" Luka waved Lluava off.

"Come over to my apartment later," Lluava said as she moved away down the hall. "I'll fill you in, I promise."

Without further interruption, Lluava returned to her quarters and changed into her own clothes faster than she ever had. Arriving just in time for dinner, she wiped the perspiration and crusting blood off her brow. Varren's questioning look made her aware that she needed to come up with an excuse, and fast. She could hardly tell him the truth.

The evening began pleasantly. Thor was more lucid than normal, which lifted the spirits of those around the table. As the second course was presented, he spoke out.

"Lluava, I am glad that you are making yourself at home here. I do want you to be aware that there are certain areas of the castle that are off limits— to everyone. I will make sure that you are informed of the areas of which I speak."

The succulent piece of goose Lluava was chewing momentarily stuck in her throat. She tried not to gag as the king continued, "My eyes and ears inform me of *everything* that goes on within these walls."

The king shook his wrist; two Shadows entered from behind Lluava and moved to either side of the king. Thor introduced them.

"This is Regin, head of the Obsidian Guard."

Regin pulled off his mask, and Lluava recognized his name from her first night at the capital.

"And this is Holly, his second-in-command."

The other figure pulled back her hooded mask, allowing a waterfall of red curls to pour over her shoulders and back.

Lluava's jaw dropped as her mind raced. Her thoughts came in spurts. It can't be...she's a she...she's...human...women don't hold such positions...she can't...a female Shadow!

Unenthusiastically Holly looked at Lluava with her green eyes.

More profanities flickered through Lluava's mind. Holly had obviously informed Thor, but how much had she told him?

Thor finished, "They are my senses when I am not around."

As Holly was dismissed, she gave Lluava a look that was so clear Lluava could almost hear the echoing voice: *I'll be watching you.*

***

That night, Lluava left the enclosure of the castle walls for the first time since her arrival. The air was thick with the scents of day's end. She rode with Varren in one of the royal carriages along the winding roads and side streets, past closing shops and candle-lit houses. The sun was low on the horizon; with its dying light, Varren grew anxious to reach his destination.

Entering an area composed of notably large households, the driver stopped before one house with a pair of ornately carved doors. Varren strode up to the house and paused for a moment, hand outstretched as if mustering his courage, and then rapped twice. Lluava heard the shakiness of his breath and sensed his quickening heartbeat.

"It'll be okay," she whispered just as the door opened. The butler instantly recognized Varren and led them into a sitting room. Lluava took a seat in a wing-backed chair, while Varren moved around like a dog unsatisfied with its environment.

"Hello, Varren." The sweet voice drifted lightly from the doorway.

"Hello, Emily," Varren replied in turn. "This is my partner, the Lady Lluava Kargen. Lluava, this is the Lady Emily Sihia."

"Nice to meet you," Lluava replied automatically, and then felt foolish at the obvious falsehood This meeting was far from nice.

As Emily took a seat across from her, Lluava noticed how old the woman looked. Though she was not much older than Lluava, the effects of widowhood had carved themselves into the Lady Emily's features.

"Please join me for tea," their hostess said. Moments later, another butler arrived carrying a silver platter and the evening's beverage. As Emily began to pour the first cup, her hands started to shake, and the steaming liquid splashed onto the lacquered table.

"Oh! I am so sorry!" she exclaimed. "I do not know what has come over me."

Varren quickly pulled out his handkerchief and wiped up the spill. Lluava sat back stiffly, uneasiness brewing inside her. Should she have aided with the cleanup? Should she say something?

There was a long silence as the trio began to sip their tea. Finally, Varren began, "I wanted to visit you and tell you how sorry I am." His voice broke.

Emily attempted a smile but, with tears still fresh on her face, fell short. "Thad loved you like a brother."

"He *was* a brother to me."

As the pair began to reminisce, Lluava wished she could slip away. She had really liked Thad, but she had not known him well. He had been the comical friend of the prince, the one who could always make you laugh. However, she had only known him briefly. He had left early in the war on his last and fatal mission. Much as she enjoyed hearing about the joyous times of his short life, Lluava felt awkward and out of place.

Near the end of the visit, Lluava turned her attention outside the window. In the darkening sky, several vultures glided northward. For a moment, she wished she could float away from this room of tragedy and pain.

I want to go home, she thought longingly.

***

The following days trudged onward relentlessly. Madam Angela found new ways to take the simplest things and make them complicated. A lady must sit with ankles crossed, right over left. A lady must curtsy with grace, not grit. A lady must this, a lady must that—Lluava soon realized that she never wanted to be a lady. Taking a seat at a mock dinner party, she could not help but yawn as she was drilled on the plethora of silverware. Did anyone really care what a small, two-pronged fork was used for?

Lluava's swordsmanship lessons were progressing as well as could be expected with her injured shoulder. Some lessons were spent sparring with Daniel. These were the sessions she loved the most. Others were occupied by seemingly arbitrary tasks. She spent one whole afternoon picking up wooden crates, lining them up on a shelf, then taking them back down. This meaningless task was repeated far too many times. How was that supposed to help her in battle?

Every morning, the raven would sit outside her windowsill and preen itself. Soon Lluava fell into the habit of collecting table scraps and leaving them out on her balcony for the scrawny bird. The ratty thing would hop over to the bread crusts and caw excitedly.

One evening, as Lluava looked out over the city from her balcony, the bird fluttered down onto her shoulder. She froze, not wanting to scare it off. Carefully she turned her head. The raven with its one good eye was watching a flock of its own kind fly north. It cawed once, and its airborne fellows called out a reply.

"Don't you want to go with your friends?" Lluava asked aloud.

The bird silently watched the flock leave, then turned to look at Lluava.

"You really are Chat's old bird, aren't you?"

The raven cocked its scarred head, then hopped down to the banister. The ugly thing teetered in the wind.

Often on days when Lluava explored the castle, the twins would join her and fill her in on the newest, juiciest political and social gossip. "Did you hear that Lady Gelmend is pregnant? Her husband has been away for a year and won't return for the birth."

On other occasions, Lluava was summoned to accompany the queen. Lluava loathed the requests until she discovered that Enya loved to listen to Theriomorph tales. The little queen would sit captivated as Lluava told her about the gods or heroes of old. During those moments, Lluava saw some aspect of her little sister in the young queen's face.

Often Lluava took refuge in the library and worked on her self-assigned studies. She was thrilled when she finally deciphered a sentence of the *Virisinu*. She had not heard many of those stories until now.

Despite her busy life, Lluava missed the times she had spent in the camps, surrounded by friends. She often wondered how her friends were and what they were doing. Lluava had not heard from anyone since her arrival at the capital. She longed to repeat the hours spent sparring and training with Varren. Even though she knew the prince was needed here, Lluava loathed the council's demands on his time.

One afternoon, Lluava had explored all of the castle she cared to. Looking for another way to appease her curiosity, she decided to see the capital. The castle guards were a little confused—Why would she want to wander the city?—but they allowed her to leave.

Outside the walls, the air was a bit chilly. It seemed that fall had finally reached Elysia's heartland. Not knowing where to start, Lluava began a leisurely stroll down the roads. She peered into various shop windows, admiring the decorative displays of goods and wares. There was much to see and much variety. Some stores specialized in a certain product, like cheese or meat. One store's sole focus was on high-quality ladies' hats; another sold parasols.

As Lluava slowly moved away from the castle, the dynamic of the establishments changed, as did the merchandise. Exploring a small side lane, Lluava cut through a back alley and entered a busy street. The hawkers shouted loudly over each other, talking up their living goods. The men in the market pushed and shoved, trying to outbid each other for the object of their desire. Once bought, the porcelain-painted lady stepped down from her pedestal and led her temporary master away for an hour or, if he had paid enough, for the night.

"'Ow much?" a behemoth asked Lluava, cutting off her path.

"Not for sale," Lluava sneered back.

The man grabbed her wrist. Without a second thought, Lluava twisted around, torquing the offender's arm behind his back at an unnatural angle. He screamed and Lluava let him go. As those around him laughed, the man slunk off down the street.

The vile exchange was too much for her, and Lluava made her way to another market whose goods were more palatable. Somewhere between the tang of dried citrus rinds and the potent fragrance of herb bundles, Lluava scented a familiar odor. Tracking the heavy musk down streets and alleyways, she finally caught a glimpse of its origin, a hooded figure fingering some handcrafted medallions that hung from a moving cart.

The desire to confront the would-be thief overtook her, and Lluava shouted, "Hey! You there!"

The person turned and saw Lluava. A cluster of women chattered past, barring Lluava's lane. The cloaked figure started to move away.

"No!" Lluava began to panic. "Stop!"

The figure ran.

Chapter 10

Third Time's the Charm

The thief must not get away!

Pushing through the clusters of shoppers, Lluava desperately pursued the unknown person who had attempted to steal Issaura's Claws from her room. She had to know why. The musk trailing behind her prey helped Lluava track him around corners and down alleyways. The scent, thick and heavy, had alerted her that it was definitely a male.

A rolling cart took her by surprise. A cascade of watermelon splattered pink residue over enraged passersby. Slipping in the dripping mess, Lluava shouted an apology to the driver as she continued her chase. The scent was dissipating on the wind.

Lluava stopped at a fork in the road to home in on the scent trail, but she was unable to pinpoint the musk. Her hopes of catching a glimpse of the hooded figure faded, and she finally gave up her search. Once again, she had lost the supposed thief.

Taking note of her surroundings, Lluava stopped and stared at the gigantic building before her. She did not have to guess its purpose. The columned edifice had been built ages ago, for only one reason. The capital's Theriomorph temple stood proudly, defying the human sprawl, an ancient symbol of a dying religion.

A shiver trickled down her spine as Lluava slowly climbed the enormous steps. Pausing before the ornate doors, which stood open to all worshipers, she considered entering. Lluava had not been in any religious building, human or Theriomorph, since her father's death. He, like his ancestors, had adamantly kept the old ways, worshiping the gods. Lluava remembered riding with her father to the closest temple in a neighboring village. Her mother was unable to travel while nursing Lluava's younger siblings, so these occasions of age-old reverence served dually as a time to bond with her father.

When the soldiers delivered her father's uniform after he died, Lluava could not understand how the gods could have abandoned him as they did. She began to question the All-Powerfuls. Did she even want to worship these beings who could save a loyal follower's life yet chose not to do so?

Lluava ran her fingers over the wood frame of the doorway. Which god was this temple devoted to? For whom was it built? Temples today were either used as worship centers for the entire pantheon of gods or, worse, converted into human churches. By the number of humans milling about, this was one of the latter. The time had long passed since each city tribe prayed to its protector, the god whom the tribe credited with the founding of their city. Lluava turned away from the ancient structure and returned to the castle.

That evening, as June finished her habitual cleaning of Lluava's rooms, Lluava realized she did not know much about her little chambermaid.

"June, how long have you worked at the castle?"

"Me, Lady Lluava? I have been here for two years." She finished fluffing the bed pillows. "At first, I scrubbed halls and such. You are the first person they have commanded me to serve."

"Well, you are doing a great job," complimented Lluava. June grinned sheepishly.

Lluava did not know how to ask what she really wanted to know. She skirted the direct route. "How did you come to work here?"

"A man came and offered to pay my mother if I would work at the castle. Mother needed the money." June realigned the pillows. "I have twelve sisters and brothers, many of whom live at home if still unmarried. Mother said she needed the money for food."

Lluava was shocked. A mother selling her own children for money! How could anyone do such a thing?

"What about you, Lady Lluava? Do you have siblings?"

"I have one sister and one brother," said Lluava, returning her attention to June. "Maruny is five, and Tomius is almost two." Lluava had to catch herself from calling them by her pet names, Lamb and Mouse. Old habits died hard.

Lluava motioned for June to take a seat next to her. Plopping down on the plush material, the two began to tell each other stories about their families, times with their sisters, being raised by working mothers.

When she awoke in the morning, June was curled like a kitten under Lluava's left arm. They had both fallen asleep in the sitting area. After gently waking the girl, Lluava began her day.

When she returned during her afternoon gap to change quickly out of the heeled shoes, Lluava instantly noticed the new piece of furniture standing by her balcony. A large perch, once prized by the royal falconer, now served a new owner, the scrappy raven.

"Where did—" Lluava began.

"Do you like it?"

June popped out of the alcove, smiling. "It was going to be discarded. I saved it for your bird."

"He's not—" Lluava stopped. The raven ruffled its feathers, appearing almost twice its size. "Thank you. I think he likes it."

Leaving June beaming, Lluava hurried to the queen's wing of the castle. Enya wanted Lluava to pick up where she had left off in her latest Theriomorph story. Though she wasn't following the chronological order of the old religion, Lluava was sharing some of her favorite tales of the gods and goddesses.

"Issaura should have mated with Ullr. As the god of war, he would have been her only match. When Issaura realized that Ullr would not be faithful to her, she forswore him and chose to remain the goddess of virginity forever. In turn, Ullr's anger and rage grew and spread throughout existence."

Enya laughed. When she regained her composure, she sneered. "Since some call you Issaura, will you also remain a virgin?"

Lluava was silent, thinking, how dare Enya ask such a question? Yet the pain of the truth was there. Lluava glared back at her queen, a child still, yet far more experienced than she.

Enya proudly exclaimed, "I will bear the king many sons! They will be strong, powerful, and handsome. You will be married off to some second-rate nobleman. Being born of less-than-favorable class, it is the best you can do. Do not worry. The uglier he is," she smirked, "the less often he will ask you to look at him."

The inner rumblings moved up Lluava's throat, and she hurriedly forced them back down with a few coughs. She should not let this self-righteous girl get under her skin. Excusing herself, Lluava determined to leave those feelings behind. Later, however, after a lackluster swordsmanship class and an uncomfortable dinner, she realized that her loathing of the queen was here to stay.

As gently as she could, Lluava sent June away, and none too soon. Once the door shut, Lluava could feel the warm tears bubble up. Silently, she lay down on her couch and let her emotions saturate her thoughts and her pillows. After her father's passing, she had known she needed to be strong for her family, especially her mother, so she had learned to cry quietly.

There was a knock.

Before Lluava could compose herself, Selene, followed by Luka, stepped through the door.

"Lluava, what's wrong?" Selene hurriedly asked as she rushed over to sit by Lluava's side.

For a moment, Lluava considered lying, but the truth came out anyway. "Enya. She is a horrid, horrid brat," Lluava sniffed out.

"What did she do?" Selene asked. Luka took a seat on the arm of the couch nearest Lluava.

"She is heartless," replied Lluava. "She wants to marry me off to some ugly nobleman, saying that's all I deserve. And then she boasts about how she will mother future princes."

Luka consoled, "Enya is a half-witted little nincompoop. Anyone and almost everyone is better than her, especially you."

Selene laughed. "And any woman could be a better queen than she! I could be ten times the queen she is. Think of it—a Theriomorph queen! I would shake her out of her world of make-believe."

Lluava smiled as Luka brushed a tear off her cheek. He then inquired of Selene, "What would be your first command?"

An expression of pure satisfaction slid onto Selene's face. "I would begin by turning the High Council on its head. I have a list of names of those who should be dismissed." Turning to an imaginary figure, she announced, "Your services are no longer needed."

Standing up, Luka shooed, "Be off with you! Away!"

Continuing, Selene said, "I would make you head councilman, dear brother. And you," she said, turning back to Lluava, "with your knowledge of war, you would become the new grand master chief of the royal army."

"It would be an honor," Lluava said playfully as she wiped the rest of her tears off her face.

"Anyway, little Enya will not be able to back up her boasts," Selene asserted.

Lluava questioned, "What do you mean?"

Luka said to his sister, "I don't think she is aware of the situation."

"Let me explain," began Selene, "from the beginning. The High Council serves two purposes: one, to keep the human tradition alive; and two, to protect the royal bloodline." Lluava nodded as she listened. "The council was put in an uncomfortable situation when Thor's reign began after his father died. As all his older brothers were killed in the Landon Wars, young Thor was hastily married off to his betrothed. In truth, I think he did love her. Queen Rowana bore Prince Damian several years later. Although the prince was healthy, she was never the same and died when Damian was three."

"I remember learning this," noted Lluava. "Thor took care of his son by himself for a few years."

"Yes," confirmed Selene. "He would have been happy continuing in that manner, but the High Council got involved."

Luka interjected, "The fear of only one heir was too much. They pressured the king to marry again."

"Queen Sif," said Lluava.

Selene nodded. "The council finally wore Thor down. Unfortunately, at that time very few marriageable women were human, of class, and not already wed. They ended up selecting the Lady Sif."

"Hadn't she been married before?" questioned Lluava.

"She had, but her husband left for the wars and never returned," acknowledged Luka. "She was a bit older than Thor and rather plain to look at."

"May I finish?" asked Selene a bit impatiently.

"Sorry. Go on."

"After their wedding, the High Council slowly acknowledged the truth. Sif was barren."

"She had lost her first husband before anyone realized she was," added Luka.

Selene gave her brother a dark glance, which shut him up. "Anyway, Sif helped Thor raise Damian. The council stepped in once again when the prince was of age, and Damian was married to Lilyanna. Luckily, Varren was born before his parents perished in the fire."

Luka, playing with a pillow's tassels, mused, "Think of the poor council—in one night, their sense of security went up in those flames, leaving the future of the bloodline to a baby's fate."

Selene threw a pillow at him, which bounced off his face and landed on the floor.

"Too harsh?" he asked.

"What does this have to do with Enya?" inquired Lluava.

"I am trying to get to that," Selene answered as she glared at Luka. "If he would just shut up!"

Luka mimed locking his mouth and tossing away the key.

"Sif eventually died several years ago, allegedly of old age."

Luka wiggled in his seat.

Selene sighed and explained, "Luka thinks she was murdered."

"By the council?" Lluava asked.

Luka nodded exaggeratedly, "Or specific individuals on the council." He winked.

"Regardless," Selene continued. "The council yet again had a chance to pair the king off in hope of producing a secondary heir."

Luka blurted, "They went from hopefully experienced to hopefully fertile."

Selene smiled quietly at her brother, who slipped down into his seat. After a moment of silence, she began one last time.

"Enya is fertile. There you are right. But tragically, the king has reached the age of the cursed male affliction, impotency. She will never bear a son, for her husband will never again be able to erect his scepter."

Luka grinned. "I guess the council got what they deserved."

"Themis must be furious," acknowledged Lluava.

"They will try to save face," noted Selene.

Lluava asked, "How? Why?"

"There are several ways and several reasons," Luka answered thoughtfully. "They wouldn't want a bastard prince toddling about. The risk of a false bloodline would be disastrous for the council. They might consider ending Enya's reign, but she is so young and healthy; it would be too suspicious. The easiest would be simply to kill the king. He is far too old anyway."

"They wouldn't do that," Lluava asserted.

Selene chimed in, "No. Not until Varren is married."

***

That night, dark forms snarled and clawed their way through Lluava's dreams, tearing right through her soul. When she awoke, the feeling, raw and wild, stuck with her. That morning, during the Open Council, Lluava's attention focused more and more on Themis himself. It was all so clear now. She watched as Themis's words and pronouncements slipped from the lips of his old puppet.

Varren must be aware of this, she thought. Unfortunately, this morning Varren was not present. He was performing his civic duty, delivering a speech at a groundbreaking. Lluava would have accompanied him had it not been for her lessons. So, while her partner was fulfilling his princely obligations, she studied the puppeteer at work. Someone had to stop Themis.

The last supplicant of the morning, a Theriomorph, approached the dais. Assertively, the man began, "Your Majesty, my name is Olingo Kumar, son of Olio Kumar. I have come to humbly petition that Theriomorph mail carriers be allowed the opportunity to transport letters in their dual forms. In a dual form, the carrier can often fly over land or run faster than most of the pack horses we use. This would provide more efficient service to all areas of our kingdom. I have a list of names of those who approve this change." Olingo raised a tied scroll.

The steward retrieved the parchment and handed it up to the king. Thor's eyes drifted down the page in such a manner that it was obvious he was not reading it or was unable to do so.

"May I see that, Your Majesty?" Themis inquired. Examining the scroll, he said, "I see you have quite a few advocates for this request. How many of these are humans?"

"Councilman?" the man questioned.

Themis asked again, "How many are humans?"

Olingo began to worry. "There were a dozen or so that signed it, Head Councilman."

Themis inquired a third time, "Out of these thousands of signatures, only a dozen were humans?"

"Yes, Head Councilman, but if I may—"

Themis raised his hand, silencing the poor man. "Those numbers seem rather biased, do you not agree? I think that until you are able to produce a more representative mixture of names, this petition will have to be postponed."

Lluava looked at Thor, who said nothing. His tiny frame was slumped like a stringless marionette. Someone *had* to stop Themis.

Just as the man was about to be dismissed, Lluava implored, "May I speak, Your Majesty?"

Thor looked over at her and smiled. "Of course you may, my dear."

"During the war, we used Theriomorphs for this purpose. Commanding officers sent messages via dual forms from their tents to other soldiers who were out on the front. Not only was this a quick method, but it also prevented messages from being intercepted by the opposition. Since the military has used this system successfully, Elysia might also benefit."

"Lady Lluava," began Themis. "One must consider the grand scheme. An occasional document sent on the war front is far different than transporting many letters and documents over the entire kingdom. When you consider the term *efficient,* this is far from it. Then what benefit would there be in this new structure?"

Lluava's thoughts switched over to Thad's last and fatal mission. "If Theriomorphs had been allowed to send messages in their dual forms over long distances by themselves, you would have been informed about the battles by the sea before they were over. Yet since the current rule stood, the military partners who sacrificed their lives to attempt this were grounded and lost valuable time as well as their lives!"

Themis looked a bit tired as he countered, "I know the pair of whom you speak. Thadius Sihia grew up here at court; we were saddened by his loss and that of his partner, Horus Ethril. Yet if my memory is correct, they arrived at their destination, one that had already been taken over by the enemy. It would have not mattered if Ethril had flown by himself. The end result would have been the same: his death and no message."

Lluava clenched her jaw as she struggled with an appropriate response.

"If I may, High Councilman."

Who had spoken? Looking about her, Lluava recognized Councilman Hyrax.

"Lady Lluava might have a point. It is true that it would be impossible for every letter and parcel to be transported using Theriomorph means," Hyrax continued. He looked at Lluava. "Yet, there is some benefit for allowing dual forms to be used for this purpose. Consider this: if we allowed certain documents to be delivered in this manner, we could enhance our communication throughout Elysia. Moreover, we would create new jobs, which would strengthen the economy."

"Where would we get the money to pay for these specialty mail carriers?" inquired a councilman to Hyrax's left.

A second councilman stood up and asked, "And who would decide which letters would justify using this service? It would be impossible to open it to all."

Hyrax took a moment to consider, then spoke. "It is very simple. Those who require this faster service would pay more to have their letters delivered quickly. The extra funds would pay for the specialty workers. With proper management, this mail service could not only pay for itself but also add to the treasury."

With the heads of the council nodding in agreement, Thor pronounced, "We will implement this new system at once."

Themis was clearly displeased as Thor continued, "Councilman Hyrax, since you so eloquently backed the idea, you will lead the formation of this branch of letter carriers. Start small. Once it is tested, I will consider expanding it throughout Elysia."

"As you will, Your Majesty," assented Hyrax before taking his seat.

Themis closed the council, and they progressed to the dining hall. As they took their seats, a pair of councilmen could be heard talking to each other.

"Prince Varren chose his partner wisely," said one.

The other nodded and replied, "Lady Lluava will keep Themis on his toes. She is brave to oppose him in public."

Lluava wished they would be quiet. Suddenly she sensed eyes on her. With one glance at Themis, she knew she had made a mistake—one that he would not soon let her forget.

Chapter 11

Fructomancy

A n enemy is an enemy. Yet Themis wouldn't dare touch her, would he? Lluava lost her appetite. Stabbing at the fish head on her plate, she decided it was time to play by their rules—for now.

Instead of allowing her curiosity to get the better of her again, Lluava rekindled her studious side and worked extra hard at becoming the polished and erudite woman the court expected. This wasn't just a smart strategy, for she loved to learn, and a challenge—be it physical or mental—only pushed her to be better. She practiced etiquette and memorized terms of address and the nobles' hierarchy: duke over marquess, viscount over baron. Madame Angela was pleased with her progress.

Swordsmanship also went well, until one evening Daniel did not show up for class.

Domar explained, "It is important in the training process to allow students to practice with a variety of opponents."

Lluava raised an eyebrow.

"Students often become too comfortable sparring with a single partner. They learn to read their opponent's signals, begin to anticipate certain moves, and start to relax. When that happens, it is time to switch things up. In battle, your opposition will be new, their actions novel. Different opponents also bring aspects of their various backgrounds into the picture. A good soldier will always be on the alert, ready for anything."

Lluava wondered if Domar would be sparring with her.

"It is essential to be ready to defend against various styles of fighting, weapons, and enemies..."

Behind Domar, a figure stepped into the illuminated courtyard, one

Lluava recognized instantly. Her stomach dropped.

Holly took a position opposite Lluava. Her thick red locks were tightly bound in a large bun. Her pronged daggers were at the ready.

"Lluava?"

Lluava turned to look with distaste at Domar.

"You will use the short sword today to combat her sai."

Lluava picked up the weapon. It felt terribly foreign. Her shoulder, as if reading her cues, began to throb. Testing the sword's balance, she nodded at Domar. She hoped to get through this as quickly as possible.

Holly was dressed in the same tight, black material that she had worn during their first encounter. Choosing to remain maskless, she signaled that she was ready.

Lluava made an aggressive first move, hoping to force Holly on the defensive. She needed every advantage she could muster. Unlike their earlier encounter, Holly would not be able to retreat into the shadows; however, Lluava could not shift into her dual form, and the sword was exceedingly heavy.

Whistling through the air, the sai's silver spines, like a serpent's fangs, struck out at her. Lluava blocked one and narrowly dodged the other. Although petite, Holly moved with exceptional speed and agility.

Sucking in her stomach, Lluava felt the fabric of her shirt tear as the pronged weapons barely missed their marks. Retaliating, Lluava swung left, faked right, and swung left again. Holly stepped back once, then twice. Lluava tried to keep up the offense, but the little inferno's swiftness was causing havoc. Several strands of her attacker's slicked-back hair escaped their confines, creating the illusion of Holly's face ablaze before her.

Just as Lluava was about to strike her opponent, Holly eluded her with a series of back flips. Lluava blinked. Did she see that correctly? Charging again, Lluava jabbed at her challenger. Holly escaped by running up the wall, kicking off, and leaping behind Lluava.

Forcing herself to move faster, Lluava combated the red rampage. Her shoulder was seared with pain. What if it dislocates again? she thought with gritted teeth. Should she take that chance? Nothing may happen, but there was always a risk...

Cautiously, Lluava began to hold back. Soon she felt the tiny pricks from the small daggers and was forced to accept defeat.

Lluava returned her weapon to the rack.

"Your performance today was respectable," Domar acknowledged. "Holly is highly skilled. Keeping her at bay for as long as you did was no small feat. Be assured of that."

Turning to thank him, Lluava realized Holly was nowhere to be seen.

***

It rained that evening, discouraging many of the more entertaining activities. Selene and Luka congregated in Lluava's apartments. Selene stretched out on the couch and feigned cooling herself off with her lace fan.

"Luka, will you be a sweetheart and shut the doors?"

Luka, leaning against the open doorway to the balcony, declined the request. "I like listening to a good summer rain."

Selene looked rather displeased. "Summer has ended."

"Only just," noted Luka as he turned back to the ladies. "Lluava enjoys warm rains." He stuck a hand outside, allowing the water to trickle down his arm. "Don't you?"

Remembering her childhood playing in the puddles with her baby sister, Lluava smiled. "They do bring back good memories."

Selene wrinkled her nose. "The only things those rains bring are the cold and despair that arise from winter's ferocity." She picked up an apple from the bowl on the table.

Luka just shook his head as he admired the raindrops that clung to his arm.

"I have an idea," Selene said, perking up. "There is a superstition from our home region that if you peel an apple in one long stroke and toss the skin over your right shoulder, it will land in the silhouette of your future spouse. Want to try?"

Lluava, amused by this children's game, agreed.

"I will pass," Luka replied sarcastically. "My obligation to my own gender dissuades me from joining in this endeavor."

"You're no fun," pouted Selene, not exactly surprised at his response. "Will you at least lend us your knife?"

Luka handed her his small blade. Each girl made several attempts before successfully peeling an apple.

"On the count of three," announced Lluava. As the word *three* passed her lips, they tossed the spiraling prizes behind them. The friends looked at Lluava's first.

"Um...well." Luka struggled to find the right words.

"He's monstrous," laughed Selene.

Lluava laughed as well. Her blob had no distinguishable shape.

"Maybe he has a great personality," noted Selene between giggles. Luka moved to the far side.

"From this angle, it looks like some sort of animal," he noted. "Maybe a dog?"

Lluava stepped to his side. Perhaps it was a beast, but calling it a dog was clearly a stretch. Selene's peel was next.

"You know," began Luka. "This one has a strange likeness to the prince."

"Why, that's just silly," Selene said, giggling even more.

"After all, he is engaged to Illia," Lluava said with a smile. Yet there did seem to be a strange similarity in the red profile lying on the ground.

***

The following day, Lluava was invited to attend the Closed Council for the first time. This was unexpected. As she was not officially a member of the council, she had to sit on the perimeter of the room. Council members sat along the semicircular table, with the thrones positioned on the uncurved side.

The man seated on the large throne was not Thor, who was nowhere to be seen, but Themis himself. Varren sat to his right.

Where is Thor? wondered Lluava. Shouldn't the king attend his own private council?

The gavel struck twice, quieting everyone. Themis announced, "I welcome all of you to the Closed Council. We will begin by attending to old business. First, the state of the southwestern crops."

Umber, a dark-skinned councilman, gave his report. "As noted yesterday, this will be the third sun cycle in which the drought has reaped the majority of the crops, especially our wheat production. Today we will decide on the creation of canals in the farming district."

"What are the advantages?" questioned Varren.

"The ability to mitigate the drought, thus saving not only essential food stores but also the jobs and income generated though the farming, harvesting, and sale of the crops."

"And the drawbacks?"

"The amount of royal funds required to pay for this feat is substantial. Then there is the secondary concern of spending monies that might be better utilized by the military in the event of war."

"Any discussion?" Varren asked.

Council members took turns arguing the points. Some clearly supported the idea, while others complained of the financial burden. During the debate, both Varren and Themis remained impassive, considering the various viewpoints while interjecting new ideas to consider.

What would she do? Lluava thought. She hated that people were starving, yet spending Elysia's resources to build canals could hurt their defensive measures. Governing the kingdom was complex and clearly not to be taken lightly. In the end, a compromise was reached, though it was obvious that there was no perfect solution for everyone. As the afternoon progressed, Lluava's thoughts went back to her preliminary question. Where was King Thor?

When the council broke for dinner, Lluava asked her partner, "Where's your grandfather?"

"His…" Varren searched for the right word, something he was beginning to do all too often. "His episodes have been getting worse during the afternoons, preventing him from making sound judgments, which is critical during these sessions."

"How long has this been going on?"

"It has been on and off for a while, but over the past several days he cannot seem to concentrate at all." Varren, a person raised to be self-assured, was clearly worried. "Lluava, he is not well. I do not know how much longer he has."

Lluava reached over and hugged him. Lingering in his embrace, she breathed in his scent and felt the gentle touch of his loose curls as they brushed the side of her face.

"It will be okay," she said hollowly.

A fear began to hatch inside her mind. If certain people discovered the king's weakness, would the kingdom hold together if war broke out? By Varren's look, he was also considering these possibilities as well.

"Thank you for being here with me through all of this," Varren admitted earnestly. It was only to her that he dared show his weakness, his fear.

"I will always be here for you."

"I know, but thank you all the same. This cannot be easy for you."

Lluava shrugged. "What is?"

When she returned to her room that night, she noticed a bouquet on the table. The vibrant colors captured the heart of the royal gardens. Tucked into the center was a single stem of her new favorite flower, the Theri iris.

The raven cawed from its perch.

"Do you like them, O carrion eater?" Lluava asked. The bird fidgeted on its stand.

Lluava was elated. The ribbon on the vase was bound in the center by a wax seal that bore the royal insignia. Smiling, Lluava bent down to breathe in the thick, fruity perfume. Something else tugged at her nose.

The bird cawed again.

"Jealous, are you?"

Suddenly the world seemed to bend. Lluava reached out to steady herself as color grayed into nothingness. Objects lost their definition, and a smoky haze seemed to swallow her whole.

The feeling of elation consumed her as she felt herself begin to fall. Down, down, down, she tumbled into darkness. Would the bottom of this empty chasm ever come? Lluava's stomach danced inside her, causing her to laugh, though no sound emerged.

The air had a texture, thick, like honey oozing from its waxy chambers. She could not see her arm, but she could feel the atmosphere ripple when she moved. Lluava did not know whether she moved willingly or by another's command.

Music or some musical sound kept her company as she fell into the deep. The undulating melody was pleasant. She could feel the vibrations from each chord shake her as she sank weightlessly.

The haze seemed to lighten, forming clouds that swirled about her. Light, like rays of the sun, peeped out and then hid their golden beams. Smoky tendrils curled up like ferns at night, then reached out to grab Lluava, pulling her inside. The clouds parted, and through the dimness she perceived cloaked forms. She must have been lying on her side, for she could only see thick hems swish against a stone floor.

Lluava wondered who wore these strange garments. They were not the decorated robes used by the council. The fog drifted in once more, and the figures melded with the haze.

Could she be levitating? The ground seemed to have vanished; she was clearly floating. A tingling sensation began at the tips of her fingers and toes. Again, Lluava wanted to laugh, though silence swaddled her tightly.

Light was returning. A scene materialized before her, broken up by the graying clouds that tumbled about her. She was looking at a well-constructed ceiling that peaked directly above her. Beams of light moved diagonally downward from her left side. What window they bled from, she could not tell. She was still unable to move.

Screeching syllables could be painstakingly deciphered into words that, in turn, became a conversation. One voice harshly questioned its unseen comrades.

"I do not care. Is there any possibility of error?"

Lluava wished the voice were kinder. Its anger seemed to sear right through her sinews.

A cloud languidly drifted above her, then mingled with a smaller one. She watched until it slid out of sight. She wished she could continue to float, but her body was beginning to feel heavy.

Audible voices muttered around her, a respectable number, based upon their various tones. How strange. They seemed so…so… Lluava could not pinpoint it. Whatever it was left a bitter taste in her mouth.

The cloud thickened and then dissipated again.

Voices returned, although these were different.

"The northern members have been silent too long. We cannot wait for their vote."

The tingling in Lluava's hands became a prickling. She wanted to move them but could not. Maybe one of the people would scratch her feet. They were beginning to itch like crazy.

Another voice spoke out above an irritating rumbling noise. "She is their puppet, a marionette for public show."

Lluava was growing increasingly uncomfortable. She wanted to move. Why wouldn't they move her?

A new, raspy voice silenced everything. "…the time is close at hand."

Lluava wanted to listen longer, but her arms and legs erupted with fiery pricks. One, much sharper than the others, made her leg kick out.

A shifting cloud vanished as a slick, shiny black mask drifted down from above. Carved in an eternal shout, only the whites of its eyes flicked through slits in its fearsome surface. An almost recognizable voice gurgled, "She's coming to…"

What came next was only blackness.

Chapter 12

The Unborn Truth

Through the blackness, she could hear its breathing. Animalistic—steady, repetitive, subtle, yet clearly making itself known. The beast of the deep was watching her, yet she did not know from where. Although unable to pinpoint its origin, Lluava sensed its intent. She must get away. Now.

Standing. She was standing. That much Lluava knew. Reaching out, she stumbled in the darkness. Her arms extended before her, she tried not to run into anything. Yet as she moved, the breathing followed her, closing in.

Soon the muted sounds of war became audible, an evil white noise that confounded her judgment. Was the thing still in pursuit? The clatter of weapons and the screams of the dying cloaked everything else. Lluava's heart thrummed faster and faster. Voices cried out like a chorus of the damned, some in unimaginable pain, others begging for mercy that would not arrive. A sudden fear overwhelmed her. She didn't know where to turn.

Lluava smelled smoke. Rising before her, an amber glow bedeviled shadowy wood. She turned and ran, the heat and the blaze in full pursuit. Scrambling through underbrush, Lluava struggled to keep her momentum. Glancing behind her, she saw the fire consuming everything in its path.

Get away! Get away!

The faster she tried to run, the slower she became. Soon the heat clawed at her back. Lluava struggled to move, but her body grew numb. She struggled to breathe and then coughed, choking on the smell of scorched fur.

A tree next to her shattered and fell. With the last ounce of her strength, the young woman rolled out of the way. The trunk thundered to the earth, and the vibrations shook her body. In the midst of her fiery pyre, Lluava was once again aware of the sound of breathing. A primordial growl arose behind her, circling her. Unable to move, all she could do was watch as the veil of smoke split and a creature leaped through, landing on the fallen tree.

The orange haze illuminated a monstrous silhouette. As the brute's hackles rose, Lluava sensed its next action. She would not let it take her. Not without a fight. As the beast leaped at her throat, she found the strength to vault up, shift, and combat the monster.

She landed with a thud, claws screeching on the stone. Even in the dark, Lluava recognized her nightmare-tossed sheets. She was in her room. It had all been a dream.

The raven's screams broke the quiet. Whether due to the rude awakening or to the fact that a white tigress now stood in front of it, the bird would not calm down. Lluava shifted back.

Still trembling, the teen looked mournfully at her ruined nightgown. Helpless against the emotions flooding her body, she wept hunched over on her hands and knees, the tears pooling onto the stone floor. Something unwholesome stirred inside, feeding on her fears.

***

Throughout the day, Lluava felt drained. In Open Council, she sat quietly, half listening to the discussion of mundane topics. Only one proclamation snared her interest, when the council ruled that the elopement of a highborn girl with one of her family's field hands would be dissolved and the girl returned to her father's household. The field hand did not fare as well as his lover.

Driven by poor sleep or perhaps restlessness, Lluava decided that she had had enough of the government's backward policies. It was time to force Varren's hand. He must either stand up and make a change, or—

Varren would just have to make his stand. There was no other way.

Before excusing the assembly for the noonday meal, Themis announced proudly, "We are all quite aware of the important celebration that will occur over the following days."

Are we? Had she forgotten some special holiday, festival, or religious ceremony?

Themis continued, "It gives me great pleasure to announce the grand ball and tournament in honor of the eightieth birthday of His Majesty, King Thor Mandrun, direct descendent of the great King Landon."

Applause erupted from all sides, along with smiles and lighthearted chatter. The kingdom was in need of an exorbitant celebration and public demonstration. Thor was smiling, too, although it was unclear whether he had really understood the announcement.

Lluava also clapped, although she had to force herself to politely stay seated. She liked the old king when he was *there*. He had been a great man, a wise and strong leader. Who wouldn't want to celebrate the remarkable achievements of her sovereign's youth?

"The invitations have been sent out to all highborns and nobles throughout Elysia," Themis continued, "including the beneficent Lady Illia Alcazar, Prince Varren's betrothed."

Lluava stopped clapping.

No! She wanted to scream out. She did not want Illia to arrive at the capital. She did not want her near Varren at all. No! She did not want to see this woman who had rights that Lluava did not yet have.

Varren looked as shocked as she did.

So, he had not been aware of this plan! Scowling, Lluava glared at Themis, who appeared extremely pleased with the response to his announcement. Lluava icily hoped his time would soon be over.

***

As Varren escorted Lluava to her room that evening, she could wait no longer.

"You must abolish the tradition of arranged marriages and contractual engagements," she told him.

"Lluava, I have explained—"

Lluava cut him off. "I know what you've said, but Themis is up to something. He always is."

Although clearly displeased with Lluava's outburst, Varren tried to be reasonable. "I do not have enough support even to consider moving forward with that endeavor."

But his calm analysis only spurred Lluava on. "So when are you going to do something? When you are riding off to your matrimonial chapel?"

Varren raised an eyebrow. "Are you jealous of Illia?"

"No! I want you to stand up for yourself for once in your life!" exploded Lluava.

Her words drew blood. Varren scowled. "What do you think I have been doing? Themis has kept me close, always watching during council. I can only attempt to rally supporters at night. Where do you think I have been?"

Lluava had wondered but never asked.

"I have spent countless hours riding into the city to meet secretly with highborns and others who have vast sway. I have campaigned relentlessly, sacrificing sleep and sanity for this effort."

Eyeing Varren in this new light, Lluava realized how tired he looked. How could she have missed the darkened skin under his eyes?

"I am doing everything I can, everything I know to do. I have had no time to socialize or relax."

Lluava growled, "Is that what you think *I've* been up to? Playing games while you are at work? You are the one who organized my schedule. You made me go to those classes when I would have rather been by your side. You did not invite me to your nightly meetings. All I want is to be with you."

Lluava jabbed her finger into Varren's chest. "You left me alone in a city I did not know, with people I did not know, to deal with ridicule and judgment that I did not deserve. I am going home." The words had escaped on their own, but Lluava realized they were absolutely true; she had just suppressed the desire.

Shocked, Varren was speechless. Lluava spun on her heel and headed to her chambers. She knew this was the right thing to do. She had not seen her family since the draft. It was time to return to Rivendale.

When she was halfway down the corridor, Varren shouted, "Stop!"

Lluava's anger flared again. "Are you telling me or commanding me?" she said, scowling over her shoulder.

A desperate "Please…" was uttered by the prince.

Taking one more step, Lluava paused. She listened to the thud of footsteps as Varren ran up behind her. She turned to face him.

"What are you so scared of?" she demanded.

Through his distress, he managed to say, "I do not want to lose you."

Taking a shaky breath, Lluava consoled him. "You're not going to lose me."

Varren shook his head. "I am so afraid that if I make the wrong decision, the wrong choice…You know how hard it has been for me to make any decision of weight. The choices I make can hurt others."

This concept was all too familiar to Lluava. Hoping to comfort her partner, she chimed "But you always make the right choices."

"Not always."

The sternness of his voice startled Lluava.

Hollowly, he told her, "There is something you need to know."

"About?" she prodded.

"Me. Themis. Why I am the way I am."

Lluava's heart began to race. She knew that whatever he was about to tell her would not be good.

"But first," Varren said, holding up a hand, "we need to be in the privacy of your room."

Once seated on her couch, Lluava noticed a new vase of flowers on the low table. Although the vase held several varieties, one was clearly familiar— the Theri iris.

As she fondly eyed the flowers, Varren took her hand in his and began again.

"When I was a boy, fourteen sun cycles old, I was very stupid. I guess it was a rebellious stage. My friends and I would wreak havoc in the castle, constantly causing trouble and getting into mischief. We were a proud lot, pretending we were tough yet knowing we were not."

It was hard for Lluava to picture Varren acting this way, but she did not interrupt.

"I remember how we listened to the young lords of that time boasting about their crude exploits. We began to dare each other to do the things that we believed would make men of us. The dares became increasingly challenging and serious."

Varren looked almost apologetically at Lluava before continuing, "I was a stupid, stupid boy. I should have said no. I should have lied. At fourteen, I became a man. Other than feeling quite satisfied, I thought that was the end of it."

What did he mean? Lluava thought worriedly. But Varren's next statement made it irrefutably clear.

"She was a scullery maid, a girl I had never seen before and would never see again. Shortly after, she came to me and told me she was with child."

Had she heard him right? Lluava was not sure. Yet she could not verbalize her question. She sat there, still and silent, and waited.

"I was afraid, Lluava." Varren seemed to be willing her to understand. "I did not know what to do. I could not confess to my grandfather. I was so scared. Instead, I turned to the one person I thought I could trust, whose judgment I need not fear."

"Themis," Lluava said.

Varren looked away briefly.

"He was my godfather, a trusted adult, and one I considered a friend. He told me not to worry, that he would take care of everything." Varren shifted uncomfortably. "He told me he would send the maid west to work at his home estate. As the years passed, I thought nothing more of her or the child."

Lluava's jaw tensed involuntarily.

Varren continued, "When I was about your age, I wanted to know what had become of the child. I knew, by then, that I had to face the responsibility that I had evaded for so long. As hard as I tried, I could not find any scrap of information about the girl who had been sent away years before. I approached Themis and confronted him. He told me... he told me that there had been a carriage accident resulting from an attack by bandits and that both mother and child were lost."

Varren reached out to touch Lluava's hand. She sat frozen like a statue as thoughts raced through the forest of her mind. Varren had fathered a child. She had never asked about his childhood and adolescence. She had just assumed...

"Because of my youthful indiscretion, I ruined the life of that young girl and am responsible for her death and her unborn baby's. I did that. My stupid, moronic, rash choice killed two innocent people. I vowed never to make a decision again without thinking it through completely. I cannot bear to cause innocent people harm. I cannot..."

Varren seemed to be searching her face—for what, Lluava wondered?

Compassion, understanding, absolution?

"I know this is a lot to absorb…"

"You're not a virgin." Lluava needed to say this, to hear this out loud.

Varren, appalled, stared at her. "Have you not heard a word I said?"

Sliding her hand out from under his, Lluava suddenly realized that she did not want to touch him. Someone else had touched him, kissed him, and…. She struggled to remain calm. Anger, sadness, and disgust collided like storm waves against stony cliffs.

"I'm tired. Goodnight, Varren." Her voice was icy, although her insides felt scorched.

Her partner clenched his jaw. Before submitting to her cold command, Varren declared, "I am not done."

Lluava snarled back, "I said, I am tired."

Varren stood up, blocking her escape. The violation of her personal space enraged her. She wanted to lash out. She wanted to chase him away. More than anything else, she wanted to be left alone.

"You need to hear this," Varren insisted. "I looked into the accident. There were no reports of a wagon attack or damage to any carriage. The only truth was an unmarked grave that I visited with an understanding far greater than before. Themis promised he would take care of the situation, and he did. Themis is a person you do not want to cross."

Although Lluava now felt revulsion for this man who was her partner, she understood that he had revealed this to protect her. Knowing he cared for her, she had her own confession to make.

"It's too late."

Varren had clearly not expected this. "What?"

Lluava reminded him of the threat Themis had directed toward her as a result of her interest in Varren. "He is also angry that King Thor backed my idea regarding the postal service. It has nothing to do with the letter carriers, only with the fact that I willingly opposed him in public and won. That infuriated him. He does not like me. Not at all. Maybe he will change his mind about me. I mean, I have worked hard at trying to be proper and everything…"

Varren's eyebrows drew together unpleasantly. Lluava wondered what was going on inside his head.

After a moment, he said, "You are right. You must go home."

"What!" Lluava exclaimed. She rose to face him.

Looking down at her, Varren explained, "It is too dangerous for you to be here now. If there is any risk that you have pushed him too far—I will not let him harm you."

Lluava said coldly, "He could not hurt me if he tried."

"Please do not take offense, but you are hot tempered and—" Varren purposely did not allow her to get a word in, "—have a talent for getting yourself into unpleasant situations. As long as you are inside the capital's walls, you are in danger."

Taking hold of Lluava's shoulders, Varren gently ordered, "Go home. Protect your family. Themis's reach has always been longer than anyone suspects. Lluava, I fear for your family's safety—and yours."

Chapter 13

All Eyes on Him

As hard as it was for Lluava to admit her troubles, it was harder still to back away and run. Once she had promised to head home, Varren left her quarters. They had agreed she would depart after the Grand Ball. To leave any sooner would draw suspicion.

Lluava grabbed the vase of flowers and hurled it at the hearth. It shattered among the neatly aligned logs. She stood for a moment, wondering why she had done that. The flowers had been beautiful; now they lay besmirched with soot. Pulling out the iconic iris, Lluava twirled the sorry-looking specimen in her fingers. Then, stepping back to calm the ruffled raven, she thought about her next steps. It would not take long to pack for her journey homeward—only the few items she had brought with her and some food. Of course, she would take Issaura's Claws.

The preparation for King Thor's birthday celebration was another story entirely. Three new dresses had to be made to order: one for the outdoor tournament, one for the grand feast, and the third for the ball itself. Lluava had not only to maintain her daily schedule but also to find time to meet with three different tailors, each one's sole job to construct one of those outlandish gowns. Lluava felt like a doll or, better yet, a pincushion, as the tailors buzzed around her brandishing needles and trimming threads. She desperately tried to hold still. Madame Angela's lessons focused on the specific etiquette for these events. A refresher of common dances was incorporated into instruction in appropriate small talk and polite applause.

Outside the classroom, Lluava was especially cautious. She was the epitome of social grace, never talking out of turn or causing trouble of any kind. This façade, although it seemed to suit her, was a front. She had vowed to General Domar to keep quiet until the appropriate time. One last secret would not be terrible. Anyway, with so much to do, no one had time to care about such business.

As the days passed and Lluava thought about her treatment of Varren, her embarrassment grew. She had acted childishly. Yes, Varren had been unfaithful to his betrothed, Illia. This was hard to accept. Yet he was only twenty. Had she really thought he was chaste? Then there was the more important issue. He had fathered a child and, as a result, two people had died. Her focus on Varren's lack of virginity was petty. Was she that immature?

On the few occasions when she crossed paths with her partner, she knew that Varren was disappointed in her. He had said nothing, but Lluava could almost taste it in the air around him. She must apologize to Varren, must show him that she was not really so childish. But how? Lluava's emotions were in as much turmoil as the rest of the castle during these preparatory days.

Still, each evening brought a freshly cut Theri iris left on the table in her quarters. Without the flourish of vase or other flowers, it seemed almost humble and a bit lonely by itself on the silver tray. Lluava was somewhat puzzled by the gesture. Was Varren reaching out to her even through his disappointment? She really should say something to him.

***

Two evenings before the celebration, Lluava was in the library decoding runes when Hyrax burst in, clearly displeased.

"Is something the matter?" she asked.

"You are a Northern-born, correct?"

Lluava shook her head. "I grew up in Rivendale. Southern."

Hyrax blinked. "Oh. Right."

"What's the matter?" Lluava was now quite curious.

"The capital's mail carriers are a good-for-nothing lot. I sent important documents out weeks ago! My letters do not seem to be getting through. Drat this postal service! I wonder what the excuse is this time: the Clans, early snowfall, a case of laziness?" He sighed briefly. "I do apologize. It is unseemly to act this way in front of Prince Varren's military partner and future royal advisor."

"Future advisor?" questioned Lluava. "Where did you hear that?"

Hyrax, looking a bit amused, admitted, "Why, from Head Councilman Themis, of course. He has informed the entire council of the prince's intentions."

So Themis did know, thought Lluava. Now, more than ever, she wanted to head home. Trouble was brewing, and she had to escape it.

"Are you all right, Lady Lluava?" Hyrax asked.

"Yes, yes, I'm fine." Lluava hoped her lie was believable. "I just didn't realize they were ready to make the announcement."

"I see," said Hyrax. Quickly selecting a scroll, he left; but as he did, Lluava overheard him mutter, "Well, I am certainly tired of this 'North is quiet' nonsense."

Something about that phrase reminded her of the strange dream she had had. Hoping it was nothing, Lluava went in search of her partner. If something was happening, he should know.

She was familiar with Varren's habits, so her partner was easy to track. She found him studying dense tomes on government policy in an alcove of a small library off the second-floor balcony. As Lluava spied him hard at work, she experienced a sudden twinge of guilt over their earlier argument. However, the feeling dissipated when the she remembered his past indiscretions.

Varren looked up from his reading and motioned to a chair opposite. "Please, take a seat."

"Varren, I was wondering," began Lluava as she sank down on the cushioned chair, "if you've heard from Illia."

By the look on his face, Lluava realized he assumed this conversation was headed in a different direction. "I meant, do you know if she has accepted the invitation to the celebration?"

She could sense both bemusement and displeasure radiating from her partner. He responded, "Themis sent the invitations. I do not know when or how. I assume any confirmations would be returned to him. Why?"

"I've just heard some talk that 'the North is silent'. It seems there may be problems contacting people there. I wanted to know if you'd heard anything."

Varren considered this. "I have not, but neither have I tried to send word to our northern sectors. I will send a message to our northern forts and strongholds and make sure it is received."

"Yes. That would be wise." Lluava nodded. She knew Varren still respected her counsel even if he was disappointed in her. "It may be nothing. But I'd like to be sure."

***

The morning of Thor's birthday celebration was like no other. New banners hung from the castle's balustrades; decorations adorned all available space; the royal emblem appeared everywhere; and the entire city seemed to dress in the royal colors, moss green and gold.

Lluava awoke to the lively thrum of music rising from the street, mixed with the sounds of laughter and singing. Stepping onto her balcony, she could see that the festivities were well under way.

Excited, she quickly donned her first dress of the day. The gray-green material—the exact color, she had been told, was diaphoranthema green, not to be confused with the brighter dicranum green of her second gown—was soft to the touch, although not that pleasing to her eye.

As June finished lacing her up, Lluava said, "I have something for you."

"For me?" repeated the girl.

"Yes, it's under the bed."

Lluava smiled as she watched June scurry over and lift the skirt of the bed. Pulling out a wrapped present, June began to beam.

"You really shouldn't have!" June grinned as she tore open the parchment and twine. Her eyes glowed when she saw the little dress. Though not nearly as frilly as the one Lluava wore, the petite, muted-green gown looked quite pretty against June's auburn hair as she lifted it up to check its size.

"Oh! Thank you! Thank you! Thank you, Lady Lluava!" exclaimed June as she twirled, holding her new dress.

"You deserve something special for helping me this past month," stated Lluava, almost purring with pleasure.

Lluava headed to the tournament grounds outside the main walls of the capital. Green and gold awnings stretched over seating areas for the most prominent guests. There were five fields, one for each of the different events: archery, wrestling, swordsmanship, jousting, and the main event, melee.

Representatives from many noble households as well as the forts had come to compete. Theriomorphs were not allowed to use dual forms in any event except the melee group battles. In accordance with human tradition, women were barred from the events. Regardless, Lluava was thrilled to watch the competitions.

Archery began the day while the morning air was still cool. As the temperature began to rise, several attendants waved their ostrich-plumed fans over the royal representatives. Enya had had a fan created from peacock feathers just for the event.

After the noonday meal was served, Lluava excused herself. With a smile at Varren, she slipped out the back of the tent. Varren made an excuse when Themis asked, "Where is she going?"

Before long, Lluava listened as the herald called out the names of the next pair of competitors.

"In this swordsmanship round, Lord Jamison Cromwell of the West will combat the Theriomorph lieutenant, Haliden Kargen of the South."

Stepping out of the private changing tent and into the sun, Lluava instantly felt the heat rise inside her borrowed suit of armor. As a Theriomorph, she never used armor, as the need to shift was more important than metal bindings. Armor was primarily used by castle guards or on special occasions like this one. The excess weight was a greater burden than she had anticipated. Yet here she was, sword at the ready, preparing to put on a show.

Hearing the cheers of the crowd, Lluava made a note to thank General Domar for registering her in the tournament under her father's name and lending her a temporary wardrobe. With her natural build and the metal helmet hiding her tied-up hair, she could pass for a small male.

The cheers turned into applause, and Lluava spun around to see why. On the podium, Varren had stood up. Would he call her out and prevent her from competing? She still did not know whether his personal feelings toward her had changed since the other evening. Something glinted in his hand.

The herald announced, "The prince has chosen his champion."

Varren tossed the object to her, and Lluava caught it. In her palm lay a large golden token stamped with the royal insignia. Tucking it inside her breastplate, she knelt down to acknowledge her royal backer.

There was no time for Lluava to consider this honor, for the trumpet sounded and the game was on.

Though Lord Cromwell was a large man, any skill from his youth had been dulled by lack of active duty and a life of ease as an adult. This boded well for Lluava, who could not muster the same force behind her thrusts as her challenger. Their swords clattered and clanked as they vied with each other. The weight of the armor began to take its toll on the teen. She struggled to swing her weapon and dodge Cromwell's attacks.

With a rather loud *thunk*, Lluava was shoved to the ground. As she regained her footing, she realized the gold token had slipped out and fallen onto the dirt. Cromwell grunted and lunged to grab the piece.

To have the token stolen by an opponent was a horrible dishonor! Lluava could sense the eyes of the entire royal family upon her. She would not be shamed in this way.

Heaving forward, Lluava struck at her opponent's hamstring. Cromwell had to sidestep to avoid the impact. His pause gave her time to grab the token. Backing away, she heard him struggle to catch his breath.

So, he, too, was struggling, Lluava realized. It was all the motivation she needed. Getting her second wind, she moved in for the kill. Several strokes later, Cromwell yielded, and Lluava stood triumphant.

As applause erupted around her, Lluava knew she would never be recognized for her feat. She could not reveal who she really was. This was a celebration, and spirits were high, but there were rules and traditions that could not be broken—not here and not now. At least her father was here, if only in name.

Lluava withstood four more rounds before being eliminated in the quarterfinals. Although she had not achieved the dramatic win she would have loved, she was pleased with her success. General Domar would not be shamed. Varren's name was honored, and she had found a new comfort with the sword.

In the private changing tent, June helped braid her hair to hide the streaks of sweat, and Lluava returned to her seat under the canopy to finish watching the competition. Varren shook his head, grinning at her, and Lluava shrugged a reply.

Moving to the melee field for the last major event of the day, Lluava observed the various teams engaging in group combat. Unlike the earlier competitions, this one sent a feeling of discomfort coursing through her. Swords were swung, daggers flew, and mounts flailed, entangling themselves in horrid cacophony. Soon it became too much to bear.

Excusing herself, Lluava returned to her quarters. It must be the heat. Why else would she feel this way? After taking extra time to wash and dress for the banquet, she stepped out onto her balcony to watch the royal procession heading back to the castle. Banner carriers led the hundred-strong Obsidian Guard, dressed in their ceremonial costume. The burnished black obsidian armor with faceguard helmets was an awe-inspiring sight. Though merely decorative, the costume gave the guard its official name. Behind them, ivory chargers drew gilded carriages, one for each of the royal family members, followed by another hundred guards.

The streets teemed with people, who waved and cheered as the entourage passed. Musicians, singers, fire-eaters, jugglers, and stilt walkers took part in the festivities outside the castle walls, while the nobles joined the court inside for the feast.

Lluava took her seat at her partner's side in the Dining Hall. Wearing his silver circlet, Varren looked like a prince out of legend. His smile could melt the coldest heart. More than ever, Lluava wanted to tell him how sorry she was, how petty she knew she had been. But not here, not now.

Servants began to bring out platter upon platter of decadent dishes with such rare ingredients as purple pheasant and white truffles. These preparations had taken the better part of the week. Artfully presented, the chefs and cooks had certainly done their part for this lavish affair. As musicians played, jugglers challenged the guests nearby to toss something for them to spin in the air. It was impossible not to feel lighthearted and carefree in the festive atmosphere. To her surprise, Lluava found herself laughing with the others, including Enya.

Varren caught her eye. As she returned his gaze, Lluava sensed that she was at least partially forgiven. Under the table, she moved her hand to touch his. He took it and gave hers a light squeeze. Perhaps it was the splendor surrounding them, or maybe the result of the honeyed mead, but Lluava realized that she would miss the capital.

By the time Lluava changed into her final gown for the evening, she was feeling rather pleasant. This dress had been created by a Theriomorph tailor, who was not as constricted in his vision of what royal garb should entail. He had chosen a golden material that silhouetted Lluava's form rather than drenching her in layers of cloth. The gown was sleeveless, but matching above-the-elbow gloves conveyed a strong-willed modesty.

June was allowed to style Lluava's hair and decorate her face with various powders and paints. The young girl had been yearning to do this since

Lluava's arrival. Now, she could barely restrain her excitement.

"Ready?" asked June when she had finished.

"Ready."

Turning to look in the vanity's long mirror, Lluava paused, almost afraid to believe what she saw. The woman in the reflection looked absolutely beautiful! She took several moments to admire the vision before her. Yet one thing was missing.

She quickly moved to the table. Pulling out the contents of her satchel, Lluava sifted through her father's old letters, removed the *Karmasana*, and found the diamond-shaped emerald necklace her mother had given her.

Slipping the gem around her neck, Lluava thought, *Now* I'm ready.

A pair of trumpets heralded her entry into the music-infused hall. The lords and ladies had begun to segregate themselves on opposite sides of the room in anticipation of the first dance. Through the thinning crowd, Varren emerged wearing a suit of silver cloth. A matching circlet haloed his loose curls.

He looked about the room momentarily before his gaze found her. Was it her, or did his eyes widen? Did he just blink? His features glowed as he smiled at her, and for a moment she pushed aside her uncertainties. Presenting his arm, Varren escorted Lluava to her seat. At a nod from King Thor, the gala officially began.

As Lluava watched the dancers, her nervousness grew. She knew that Varren had chosen her to be his partner during the ceremonial Dance of Suns. The entire court would watch and judge. Would she trip in these heels or tread on his feet? Forget the steps or lose the beat?

She was still mulling over everything that could go wrong when there was a lull in the music. Thor slowly stood up. "Thank you for this wonderful celebration. It has pleased me to see so many of you enjoying yourselves. My only regret is that my son is not here to see this day."

Lluava was not the only one on the dais who was worried by that statement. Was King Thor entirely *here*? Would this be the moment in which all of Elysia would discover the king's condition?

Thor took a moment to lick his parched lips. "The Dance of Suns will instead be performed by my grandson, Prince Varren, and his fair partner, the Lady Lluava Kargen."

Lluava could almost hear her heartbeats. They had narrowly escaped that catastrophe for now.

Suddenly, Themis took the floor.

"If your Majesty pleases, this would be the perfect moment to announce the exciting news."

What news? Lluava wondered.

The old king took a moment to consider and then pronounced, "Although it is unfortunate that the Lady Illia Alcazar cannot be here for this great celebration—"

No! Lluava thought worriedly. Nausea slithered inside her.

"—it pleases me to announce that the royal wedding of the lady and Prince Varren will occur before the harvest celebration during the next moon."

Both Varren and Lluava rose to their feet. Lluava could barely contain her rapid breathing, while an expression of shock masked Varren's usually calm features. Lluava's focus shifted to one person. Themis's smirk was enough to coax a low rumble from her throat. She could hear the confident beat of his heart. He was sure he had won.

In a firm voice, Varren spoke up. "Grandfather, we must discuss—"

The rest of his words were drowned out by the blaring of trumpets. Moments later, the large doors groaned open. A colonel dressed for combat strode through the room, followed by a dozen foot soldiers. Stillness paved his way to the dais. The man moved so quickly that the herald stumbled to keep up. At the base of the step, they stopped.

Without fully catching his breath, the herald announced, "Colonel Wayland Bern, representative of Fort Terk of the Northeastern region."

Colonel Bern pulled off his helmet and tucked it under his arm. Locking eyes with the befuddled king, he stated bleakly, "The enemy has breached the North."

Chapter 14

A Will to Fight

Iluava's worst fear had come true: the Raiders had indeed returned. She would be going back to war. She tried to catch Varren's eye, but he was focused on Colonel Bern.

The commander spoke. "We need more assistance at the front, or I fear we will lose everything north of the Cocytus River."

"War?" questioned King Thor. "There is no war. The war is over."

"If it pleases you, Your Majesty," Themis was quick to reply, "allow the council to reconvene in the Lesser Hall to discuss this issue. I would not want you to miss the rest of your festivities."

Thor nodded blankly. "This is a nice dance, do you not agree? Such a nice dance."

Enya, annoyed at talk of war, interjected, "I agree with Themis. Why ruin such a pleasant party?" Turning to Colonel Bern, she inquired, "Is the enemy at our gates?"

"No, Your Highness," stated the colonel, a little taken aback.

"Will they be here before sunrise?"

"No, Your Highness." Bern was clearly confused now.

"Then let the dance resume," ordered the little queen.

Throughout the Grand Hall, members of the council left the room as discreetly as possible. The worried nobility and other guests of honor whispered hastily among themselves. Themis's displeasure grew in proportion to the fears of those around him. He nodded to the musicians, and they began to play. Two by two, couples took the floor.

"We are speaking about war," Varren said harshly, causing his godfather to pause. "The time to sing and dance is over."

Themis leaned in and hissed, "The war is here, which is exactly why we have to keep our heads, Your Majesty. If we cancel the festivities now, the guests will realize how dire the situation truly is. There would be a widespread panic. I cannot allow that."

Lluava's thoughts were racing. A panic could cause serious problems. She envisioned streets flooded with worried city dwellers running around haphazardly, unintentionally disrupting the army's ability to mobilize.

Varren's jawline twitched. Lluava sensed that he, too, was having second thoughts. "What would you have us do?" he asked.

"Finish the Dance of Suns, just as Thor promised."

Varren clearly disliked that idea, but Themis continued, "Then, if you wish, you may excuse yourselves and join the council."

Varren took a moment to consider his options, then looked at Lluava. As much as she hated to admit it, Themis's suggestion made sense. Lluava nodded, and Varren agreed to the head councilman's terms.

As the traditional Song of Suns began, Varren escorted Lluava to the vacant dance floor. Beginning with hands palm to palm, he led her around the circle of attendees. Lluava caught a curious look from Luka. Selene was too enthralled with the trio of men around her to notice the dancers.

"Shouldn't King Thor attend the council?" Lluava questioned as Themis left the hall.

Varren looked at his grandfather. "It would not matter if he were there."

As she spun around, Lluava caught sight of the king. His eyes were those of a man lost. Thor was not anywhere, not really.

"What happens now?" Lluava asked when her lips were near the prince's ear.

Varren turned around twice as Lluava mirrored his action. "We will head back to the war front."

Lluava's first reaction was happiness. "Fortunately, the war will prevent the wedding," she said without thinking.

Just as quickly, she realized how tactless she had been. Yet Varren's look of sudden displeasure somehow prevented her from apologizing. Why should she? It was true, wasn't it? Then her cheeks flushed. Once again, she had behaved immaturely. What was wrong with her?

When the dance ended, Lluava and Varren made their way to the Lesser Hall. Lluava took her seat along the perimeter, as she had the first time. Themis was in mid-sentence, debating with the other councilmen about the number of soldiers they should send from the capital.

"...too many," he said dismissively.

A sallow-looking councilman countered, "We need to assure our borders' safety."

He was cut off by a heavyset councilman to Themis's right. "But not at the risk of the capital. We need to keep sufficient troops here in case the

Raiders decide to cut the head off our country."

The sallow man jabbed a bony finger on the tabletop. "If we do not send enough soldiers to the front lines, the Raiders will make their way to the capital. We were lucky last time. Do you think we will be so fortunate again? By God, we did not even hear about the war until after it ended! Not one word!"

"General Argon failed us on that point," a third councilman hissed. "That's what we get for placing a Theriomorph in charge."

Hyrax chastised him. "Was it his fault that we all disapprove when the military sends word by Theriomorphs alone? Argon could have sent aerial Theriomorphs with the message, which would have gotten to us quickly, but it was this council that ordered him and all other Theriomorphs never to send one of theirs without a human counterpart if they dealt with *any* news of importance. Can you understand what sort of hindrance that was? We were grounded from the beginning."

"Enough!" roared Themis, at last losing his temper. "We will send one cohort of our best soldiers. The rest will stay here and protect King Thor. Long live the King."

The others responded, "Long live the King."

"Is that all, Your Honor?" inquired Colonel Bern, clearly disappointed.

Themis looked displeased by the question. "That will be all. We will send word to the western forts to move troops northward. That is all we can do at the moment."

Varren interjected, "Lluava Kargen and I will travel with you and help give you what aid we can. Our swords are yours."

"That is out of the question," disagreed Themis. "You are to stay behind these walls, where it is safe."

Varren's voice rose. "It is my duty to protect my kingdom."

"It is your duty to stay alive," countered the head councilman. "You are the sole heir to the throne. The risk is too great."

"You may control all proceedings and government policy, but I am the crown prince," asserted Varren. "You are only an advisor. You have no authority over me, and thus none for this decision."

Themis's eyes widened in surprise and then narrowed into slits. He made as if to stand, then held back. "As your advisor, at least take this advice: allow me to send a special unit of soldiers to protect you, since you are so adamant about risking everything."

Was Lluava the only person in the room to sense the prince's strange emotional state?

"As you wish," agreed the prince.

After hours of mulling over the particulars, the council adjourned for what was left of the night. As Lluava headed to her quarters, she could still hear the lilting melodies rising from the Grand Hall. How, Lluava mused darkly, can they be so secure in their frivolous lifestyles as to have not even a second thought about the rekindled war?

In her room, she struggled to fall asleep. As the sun's rays kicked at the sky, she drifted at last into fitful dreams. When June awakened her, Lluava found the stillness of the castle eerie. The chaos and disorder that she had expected to see were nowhere to be found. All too methodically, the pair prepared for the day. Brush, breakfast, bathe, dress, and then head to the council.

As if nothing were awry, Thor sat on his throne and dealt with the trivialities presented to him. Not a word was breathed about the Raiders. Not a whisper of fear about the war. It was as if the whole thing had been a bad dream, forgotten upon awakening. As the day progressed, even Lluava began to have doubts. She started to feel a bit crazy, surrounded by people who acted as if this day were no different from those that had preceded it.

Her sanity was finally restored as she headed to the training yards. Out in the courtyards, rows of soldiers were practicing critical maneuvers. General Domar was overseeing their progress. The ranks of men executing series after series of movements in perfect unison were awesome to watch.

After a few moments, Domar seemed to sense Lluava's presence and approached her.

"No training for you today," he said. "I need to work with these men and select those who will join the cohort."

"What am I to do, then?" she inquired.

"Rest."

Lluava's first inclination had been to argue, but as she headed back to her quarters, her previous night's lack of sleep began to catch up with her. Maybe a nap wouldn't hurt.

Several hours later, Lluava woke up, still feeling groggy. What time is it? she wondered. Before she had a chance to crawl out of bed, June slipped into the room carrying a tray of food.

"Your dinner, Lady Lluava," she peeped as she placed the tray on Lluava's lap. "I tried to keep it warm for you."

"Wait?" she questioned. "What time is it?"

"A quarter till ten, m'lady."

"Ten!" Lluava growled. "Why didn't you wake me?"

June looked aghast. "I'm sorry, m'lady. I thought you would prefer to sleep."

Seeing how upset her handmaiden was, Lluava suddenly felt bad at her uproar. Silently she ate her tepid supper.

Eventually June spoke up again, more quietly this time. "Your friends came by to see you while you were asleep. The brother and sister pair."

"What did they want?"

June shuffled her feet uncomfortably. "To say goodbye. So...does this mean you will be leaving me soon?"

For the first time, Lluava realized that June would be left behind. "Yes," she replied.

"Will you come back?"

"I hope so," Lluava responded with uncertainty. She could not lie to the girl.

"Is Onyx going with you?

"Onyx?"

"The bird, Lady Lluava. I thought he should have a name."

"Oh," Lluava glanced at the raven, who seemed to be listening in on their conversation. Did she want to bring an animal into that bloody chaos?

"I guess not." Turning to June, she smiled. "I think Onyx will be much happier here with you."

June returned her smile. Removing the tray, she left Lluava alone for the night. After only a brief series of stretches Lluava wriggled back down under her sheets. She would have more time to worry about the uncertainty of the future tomorrow.

***

Lluava awoke with a start. Someone was shouting her name. No, more like an assertive whisper. Before even pausing to blink, she leaped out of bed, ready to confront the man in her room.

Varren stood there, partially surprised, partially prepared for her quick reaction.

"Varren, what's wrong?" she asked hastily.

"We need to leave right now."

The hour was early. Lluava demanded, "Leave? Where? Why?"

Motioning her to be quiet, Varren explained, "Themis is holding an emergency council about Mandate Eleven, which gives the High Council the power to act to preserve the purity of the royal bloodlines."

"What does that mean?" Lluava was still unsure what all this was about.

"Essentially it means he will be able to prevent our departure."

"How is that possible?"

Varren repositioned his travel cloak. "It is the High Council's responsibility to make sure that Thor's heir will produce heirs of his own."

"But you are the only heir—" Lluava cut in.

"Yes, and legally the council can prevent me from doing anything that places my life at risk."

Finally Lluava understood. "So you would not be allowed to fight in the war."

Varren nodded, "I would have to stay here."

Lluava solemnly added, "As would I…"

"We have one chance to leave."

"If the council agrees, can they force you to abandon the battle?"

"This is not a sound plan, I know," acknowledged Varren, "but a nation's fighting spark is best ignited behind a single tangible cause. If their ruler is not willing to risk his own life to protect his country, why should the common people? I need to be there to inspire and motivate them or, at the very least, to serve as a sort of encouragement. Lluava, will you come with me?"

There was no need to ask. Lluava's very essence called her to the front lines. She answered with a simple question.

"What are we waiting for?"

In moments, Lluava had dressed in her old training uniform and slipped on her Endun boots. She grabbed her satchel. It was light. Too light.

"Wait," she called out to Varren, who was already in the main room. Upending her bag, she saw everything she needed—everything but her two most precious possessions. Issaura's Claws were gone.

"Where are they?" she exclaimed aloud as she ransacked drawers and armoires.

Varren returned to the bedchamber. "Lluava, what is wrong?"

"The Claws—they're gone."

"Gone?"

"Varren, I can't find them."

Without being asked, Varren helped her search. Lluava tried to remember when she had last seen her weapons. She had not needed them since her duel in the practice fields. Had they been in her satchel during the dance? She could not remember seeing the Claws when she had looked for her necklace.

Her breathing suddenly became labored. Could the intruder have returned and stolen her weapons?

After futilely sweeping through her chamber three times, it was all too clear that Issaura's Claws were indeed missing.

"What do I do?" Lluava cried out, at a loss.

Varren, holding her satchel, stood by the door. "Lluava, this is our only chance to leave. We have to go now."

Could she leave the Claws? If she did, she might never see them again. If she stayed, then what? She still might not find her weapons. What was certain was that in staying, she would be giving up her only chance to return to the battlefield. There was no question that she must support her partner. Even more, the idea of war thrilled her. What a loss if they were not able to defend their country, to combat their enemy! Lluava had to choose: her weapons or her call to fight.

She wanted to challenge someone, to cry out, to claw the face off any unfortunate soul who thwarted her. Scanning the room one more time, she spotted Onyx glaring at her coldly. He must not have enjoyed his rude awakening.

Fighting back her angry tears, Lluava left with Varren. As quietly as possible, the pair slipped down the halls, evaded patrolling guards, and made their way to a small side door that opened to the main yard. A pair of horses waited, pawing the cobblestones. She recognized Domar as they approached.

Lluava was suddenly happy that she would be able to say goodbye. She was leaving many who would not understand her decision.

Handing over the reins, Domar silently nodded to Lluava as she mounted her steed.

"Domar," Lluava began as her horse shifted restlessly under her. "Issaura's Claws are gone."

Even in the dark, Lluava discerned the scowl on her teacher's face. Without hesitation, he unstrapped his scabbard. Handing his own sword to Lluava, he said, "Take this. May it protect you and bring you home."

"I can't," Lluava protested.

"Take it," he ordered as he backed away. "Her name is Vjeran. May she be the most faithful amongst the faithless."

"Thank you," Lluava whispered, then with a quick click of her heels against her mount, she and Varren were off, heading north, toward their dark destiny.

Chapter 15

Bracing for Impact

Varren and Lluava spent the first day putting distance between themselves and the High Council's sway. By the second day, the pair suspected they were being followed. They spotted a trail of smoke from a distant campfire, and Varren caught sight of a cloaked figure in his spyglass. Lluava had a tingling feeling in her gut. They began to avoid the hamlets and villages, stayed off the main road, and camped in forest and field. No matter what evasive moves they attempted, their pursuer kept coming. Worse, he was closing in.

Lluava realized their only option was to confront their pursuer. At last check, the hooded figure was now only an hour behind them. Surely he was not alone.

Lying low, not far from where they had made camp, Lluava shifted into her dual form and waited. One could never be too cautious. Varren, reluctantly acting as bait, busied himself by harassing the small cooking fire with a stick.

Soon they heard steady hoofbeats rustling amid the underbrush. Lluava crouched low. When the dark head of the steed broke into the firelight, the tigress crept forward. The horse, smelling the predator, sidestepped. The cloaked rider reached down and patted the side of its neck, attempting to sooth it.

Varren, looking back, called out, "Who goes there?"

The rider slid off the horse and approached the young prince. The stranger pulled off the hood, revealing a mane of red curls.

"Holly?" questioned Varren, a bit shocked.

Lluava, recognizing her red-headed rival, shifted back, thankful that her

Theriomorph uniform shifted with her. Endun was a marvelous material.

"What are you doing here?" asked the prince.

Holly loosened her riding gloves before answering. "I have been trying to catch up to the pair of you." She glanced in Lluava's direction, even though Lluava knew she was out of sight. "I have brought something for Lady Lluava."

Lluava cautiously stepped into the circle of light.

Holly reached inside a hidden pouch in her cloak and removed what could only have been Issaura's Claws. Yet, they had been altered. Straps and bindings hung from the grips like a tangle of spiderwebs.

Lluava rushed forward. "You stole them? What did you do to them?"

Holding the gilded weapons tightly, Holly indignantly responded, "I did not steal them. I had them removed from your quarters to have them fixed."

"There was nothing wrong with them," countered Lluava. She reached out her hands, waiting for her weapons' return, but Holly was not ready to relinquish the Claws. Infuriated, Lluava growled, "Give them to me. They're mine."

"Not until you let me explain," said Holly. Small as she was, Holly was not about to back down.

Varren, too, wanted to know the reason behind this strange action. "We are waiting."

"I had your chambermaid relinquish them to me so that these braces could be constructed." She pointed to the hanging materials. "They will help distribute any impact during a fight. They are perfect for your—"

Lluava quickly cut in. "My request. Thank you. I had forgotten about that." She did not want Varren to know about her arm.

Holly looked from Lluava to Varren and back before responding, "Yes. Your request."

"But you should have told me first," reprimanded Lluava. "May I please have the Claws now?"

"Of course. But let me show you how the braces work."

Holly helped Lluava slip her arms through the interlocking bars and tightened the straps. "This joint," Holly pointed to the corner of her grip, "swivels just enough so that the Claws are not too rigid."

Lluava tested them on imaginary opponents. They were snug yet not overly tight. The Claws could rotate backward against her hand; yet when erect they aligned perfectly with the brace, allowing them to lock into place.

"You made this?" Lluava asked in awe, momentarily pushing her anger aside.

"I designed them for you. Two other Obsidian Guards actually constructed them."

As Lluava admired the new modifications, Holly added, "I planned to give them to you upon your departure from the castle. I was unaware of your sudden change of schedule. One thing you must know, however, is that the braces will not shift with you. They will break if you do so."

Lluava considered this information. "What do I do if I need to shift?"

"Take the braces off. They come apart, but that will take practice."

When Varren stepped away to tend the campfire, Holly whispered to Lluava, "Unfortunately, this was the best option for your arm. Why have you not told Prince Varren about your injury?"

"I've worked too hard to get General Domar's approval to let me fight. I don't need to prove it all over again to Varren," Lluava explained as she unstrapped the braces.

Holly snorted. "Grand Master Chief Domar did not believe you were battle ready."

Lluava stared at her. "What do you mean?"

"Never mind," Holly said quickly. "Now that you have Issaura's Claws, I must return to the castle."

"If General Domar did not believe I was ready, why did he let me go?" questioned Lluava. "Unless...you vouched for me, didn't you?"

Holly blinked back at her. "I have no idea what you are referring to."

Softly, Lluava said, "Thank you."

Holly looked at Lluava for a long moment. Then, pulling up her riding hood once more, she mounted her steed and sped off toward the capital.

"Where is she going?" Varren had come up with a plate of food for their unexpected guest.

"Back to the castle," answered Lluava as the rider disappeared into the darkness.

***

The morning air had a definite bite to it. Lluava clutched her saddle blanket around her tightly, shivering nonetheless under its coarse fabric. "I hate cold," she muttered as she gathered food parcels.

Varren grunted from under his cover. He, too, was reluctant to move.

Near the embers of last night's fire, the bowl containing their dinner leftovers had been upturned. Sulkily, Lluava looked at the spoiled food scattered about. Then the bowl jumped sideways. Lluava cocked her head, and the bowl jerked again.

"What the—" she began as she bent to pick up the cracked ceramic ware. An explosion of dark feathers flew up at her. The raven fluttered in midair for a moment before landing atop Varren's saddlebag.

"Onyx?" she asked it. The bird tilted its head to look at her with his good eye. "What? How?"

Varren walked over and pointed to the raven. "Is that your bird?"

Onyx cawed indignantly, as if insulted by the question.

Lluava shrugged wordlessly in amazement.

"Well, we need to get moving." Varren eyed the raven. "If he wants to follow, he will."

Once packed, Onyx decided to settle on Lluava's shoulder rather than fly. She was initially worried he would fall off but, as they galloped, the bird held on tightly.

They were nearing the outpost on the northern side of Sans. Based on Colonel Bern's report, that was where the Elysian army was making a stand. As they closed in on their goal, Onyx began to mutter. Lluava glanced at the bird and saw that he seemed to be watching the sky.

Reining in her horse, Lluava called out, "Varren, look up."

Flocks of birds were traveling in their V-shaped formations.

"Don't birds migrate south during this time of year?" asked the young woman. "These are flying north."

It became clear that these groupings were not actual flocks but mixed clusters of different avians. They did have one thing in common: they were all carrion feeders.

Varren's voice was filled with apprehension. "Let us go."

After a hasty trek that fed upon the greater part of the day, they finally arrived at their destination. The once-nameless outpost had swollen to the point of bursting. Tents and makeshift shelters oozed from the wooden walls like pus from a gangrenous wound. Muddied from the smoke of campfires, the yellow-green uniforms painted the whole panorama a putrid color.

Nearby, trees that should have been changing color had forgone their vibrant hues to don brittle browns. Many of the branches were stained with the dark-feathered hijackers that roosted upon them.

Spying their arrival, several soldiers gave a shout. Soon a welcoming committee arrived that was anything but expected. Lluava gasped as she looked around at old friends. They were all there: Talos, Rosalyn, Yamir, and Byron.

Leaping from her horse, Lluava cried out, "You're here? All of you! Talos…Rosalyn… I thought you both were headed south. And you two!" She looked over at Yamir, then at Byron. "Weren't you heading to Cartel and you to Fort Terk?"

As she and Varren began to embrace their comrades-in-arms, Rosalyn turned toward her fiancé. "Talos, they do not know."

Talos, shaking his dusty blond head in bewilderment, asked Varren, "Did you not receive any of our letters?"

"No letters were delivered to us," declared Varren, who now looked worried.

Themis. The name sprang into Lluava's mind as Varren asked, "What happened? How did you come to get here?"

Talos looked around then said, "Follow me to my tent, and I will explain. After you and Lluava left for the capital, a messenger rode into town alerting us of an attack to the north. He requested the aid of all available soldiers. As it was our responsibility, we came here."

As they walked, Lluava could not help but notice the many injured soldiers. They passed by rows of cots on which the most severely afflicted were stretched out. Late-summer flies swarmed in levitating orbs through the camp, their monotonous hum only temporarily muted by the caws and cackles of the perching birds.

"Varren," Talos continued, "the war never stopped. We have been fighting the entire time."

Lluava cut in, "That's impossible. We would have heard something before now."

Yamir sneered. New piercings above his eyes made his expression even more sinister. "You did know. The High Council sent us one excuse after another for not sending reinforcements. When even those communications stopped several weeks ago, one of our commanders, Colonel Bern, left to request help and press the urgency of the matter."

Varren voiced what Lluava was thinking. "That cannot be…"

They began to weave through a series of tents that housed the active fighters.

Byron interrupted, "This is what we have been doing in the six weeks since you left."

Had it only been that long? thought Lluava. It had seemed like an eternity, but she realized he was right.

Pulling back the flap of a tent, Talos ushered them into the small space. "Regardless of how we arrived in this position, here are the facts: we have been fighting in four shifts a day. Every second shift, those on the field are relieved by those at camp, to prevent exhaustion. Regardless, we have been losing the towns and strongholds east of here. The Raiders push us back daily. Our injured outnumber those still able to fight. The worst is that the Raiders have been methodically taking out our commanding line. So far, we have not been able to stop them."

Lluava glanced worriedly at Varren. He seemed to sense her anxiety and returned her gaze.

"One officer," interjected Rosalyn, "was pulled from the front lines after he had some sort of nervous breakdown. He has been raving for weeks that this enemy is different, that they have inhuman abilities."

Varren asked for clarification. "What does he mean by that?"

"I do not know," replied Rosalyn. "His ravings are hard to follow."

"Is he insane?" asked the prince.

"I am not skilled enough to make that decision," Rosalyn replied wearily.

Talos picked up his sword. "As far as I know, they are the same burly marauders that we fought off before." Strapping on his scabbard, he added, "Varren, I would advise you against fighting on the front. Human or not, these men are dangerous. As you are the one true heir, it would be too great a risk."

Varren considered what he had been told. Themis had used the same reasoning to try to keep him in the castle. However, here he could at least be of some service to motivate and encourage the army. "I have always valued your council, Talos, even when I did not like the truth. I will stay at camp."

Lluava's mood darkened suddenly. Outside the tent, the sounds of battle rent the air. Nearby, men were laying down life and limb for their country while she—

"Lluava."

She refocused on her band of friends. Varren looked directly at her, his expression one of pain. "I want you to go and fight. I need you to be my eyes and ears on the lines. Yamir," he said, turning to his spiky-haired friend, "will you serve as temporary partner for Lluava?"

Yamir, who had lost his partner in a battle by the sea early in the war, had been fighting solo ever since. While Talos and Byron protected each other's backs, Yamir had often stuck near young Chat before the boy's death.

In a tone on the cusp of optimism, Yamir replied, "It would be an honor."

Soon Lluava strapped on the Claws. Then she, Yamir, Talos, and Byron marched with the evening shift to the front lines. The air was cool, and a shiver slithered down Lluava's spine. Heading into the frantic melee before her, Lluava thought, here we go…

It was as if she had been born for these moments: evading arrows, dodging swords, deflecting battle-axes. Lluava had forgotten how many layers of thick animal pelts the Raiders wore. Making adjustments to her points of attack, the sea brutes fell before her, their horned helmets crashing against the churned-up ground beneath her feet.

A bird cawed above, and Lluava glanced up to see the raven. She had forgotten about Onyx. The raven gave another shrill cry, drawing Lluava's attention to a raider charging from behind.

Growling, Lluava crouched low and prepared to attack. Her inner heat seared up, then, with her quick realization, was smothered unforgivingly. Lluava could not shift without risk of destroying her braces. Hand-to-hand combat was her only choice.

The Raider held one of their thinner swords from across the sea. The pinprick blade appeared fragile against the man's girth, yet Lluava knew how lethal it was.

Snarling, Lluava lashed out. Claws missed their target. Before she could strike again, she was deterred by the sword's hot temper. As Lluava countered, she spied a second attacker approaching. This one carried a thick mace. Bits of flesh and hair were entangled in its spikes.

Switching to defensive maneuvers, Lluava stood ready to receive a blow from either direction. When the first man grunted, they both went into action simultaneously. There was no way she would be able to protect herself.

At least I will take one out, Lluava thought stoically. Choosing the sword-bearer, she ducked under his swinging blade and tore into his torso, her Claws freeing the man's imprisoned intestines.

Spinning round, she saw two arrow-like projections protruding from the second Raider's throat. The red of his grisly beard mixed with the blood he spat out. Leaving her would-be offender in his death rattle, Lluava turned to nod thanks to Yamir. His throwing quills had done their job.

As the fight wore on, Lluava realized that although the braces were indeed preventing her injury from flaring up, the need to shift was much more important. Moving to the edge of the main clearing, Lluava took advantage of an atypical rock formation. Squatting low, she unstrapped the bindings around her arms. Lacking the time to figure out how to detach the braces from Issaura's Claws, Lluava hid both the weapons and the braces deep in a crevice in the rocks.

In the blink of an eye she had shifted, bolting from her hiding place. Like a striped fiend from hell, Lluava tore through opponent after opponent. The stink of blood and death intermingled with a smoky odor that she could not identify.

A war horn blew twice.

She sensed a shift in the enemy's mood. The men began backing away from her, the ring of Raiders reminding her of the judgmental high councilmen she had so happily left behind. The circle of men separated her from Yamir. Then the crowd split.

A man like none other strode forth. A head taller than the rest, his helmet sported an uncut set of adult steer horns. Stopping in front of her, he let the head of his maul slam into the ground. The face of the weapon was as big as her own. The strong smoky odor wafting about made her eyes water. As she blinked back tears, the man's bloodshot gaze caught hold of hers. Then the hulk cried out—a sound far from human.

The man-thing before her charged, swinging his weapon wildly. Lluava turned tail and ran, clawing her way through the onlookers. Breaking through the circle, she charged across the battlefield. There was no way she could defend herself against a creature like that. Behind her, the massive shape swept past the warriors, laying low everyone in his path, Elysians and Raiders alike.

In her mind's eye, Lluava carried the image of the Raider's bloodied mouth, the slivers of flesh stuck in his teeth.

Skirting a trio of marauders, Lluava listened to their cries as they were tossed out of the way by the behemoth. The heavy tread of his feet did not diminish. He would not be shaken off her trail.

Lluava was nearing the Elysian side of the field. The soldiers moved forward to give her aid. Nothing could prepare them for the unstoppable force that would send them to the afterworld.

I can't lead him to our camp, though Lluava in a panic. Veering to the left, she began to lead her pursuer away from her comrades. A sharp catch in her side caused her to stumble. She tried to run through it, but to no avail. She could not continue this pace much longer.

A thick spear hurtled over her shoulder. Lluava recognized it as Yamir's. With a thunk, the weapon sank into its mark. Lluava looked over her shoulder and saw the giant Raider still moving toward her, despite the shaft of the spear that skewered his left shoulder. Oblivious to his injury, the man raised his maul above his head.

A second serrated spear severed the man's wrist.

"Watch out!" Yamir cried. Lluava quickly skidded to a halt to prevent herself from colliding with a small marauder. Slicing through the man with tooth and claw, Lluava glanced back once again. As impossible as it seemed, the massive Raider had vanished.

Yamir ran up to her. "What was that?"

"I don't know." Looking at the pools of blood soaking into the earth, Lluava said, "He won't last much longer."

Yamir cautiously circled the massive maul, to which the hand was still attached. Its shaft was as long as he was tall. Turning to the carnage in their wake, Lluava was stunned. "If there are more like him, we are in trouble."

Chapter 16

Past Ghosts

After her shift ended, Lluava returned from the field. The image of the gargantuan Raider was still vivid in her mind. Without bothering to wash up, she rejoined her comrades outside of Talos's tent, where Varren was also conversing with several officers. It seemed that the army's commanding officers were being apprised of the current situation at the capital.

"Lluava," Varren called out, "I would like to introduce you to the officers present at the front. This is Captain Jamison Cault." Varren indicated a man elderly in years but not in physical presence. Jamison's whiskered face broke into a smile as he nodded to her.

"And this is Lieutenant Vidrick Bern. His father, Colonel Bern, brought us the news of the enemy attacks."

Although Vidrick looked to be only about twenty-eight, his uniform displayed the evidence of numerous honors already earned.

"This is my military partner, Lluava Kargen."

Lluava nodded to the officers. "Hello, Captain. Lieutenant."

Captain Cault turned back to Varren. "As I was saying, don't worry about the morale of the soldiers. They know their duty and will fight regardless. There is no need for you to take any risks."

Varren was displeased with the conversation.

"We wouldn't want to jeopardize your safety," added Lieutenant Bern. The crisp breeze freshened and tugged at Vidrick's hair, the vibrant red of late autumn. As the young officer stared back at Varren, Lluava sensed an undercurrent. What was it, exactly? Lluava could not put her finger on it.

"Well..." Varren huffed, and then abandoned the subject. He glanced at his partner. "What is it, Lluava?"

Lluava focused her attention on the two commanding officers. "I have a report to give you from the front lines."

"You may speak freely," Jamison acknowledged formally.

"There was a strange Raider on the field of battle today. He was larger and more volatile and seemed impervious to pain. Your fellow officer might not be delirious or crazed; this might have been the same monster."

"You are referring to Corporal Merl. I fear his sanity is highly questionable," noted the captain. "Was this Raider the only one?"

"Yes. He has been mortally wounded and will not be harming anyone in the future."

"You are positive?"

"Nobody could survive the wounds he received."

The officers nodded.

"Very good, then," noted Cault.

Varren motioned toward his friends, who were ladling stew from a pot. "Will you both join us for dinner?"

"I would enjoy that," answered the captain as the scent of the simmering meat toyed with Lluava's nose.

Vidrick, on the other hand, quickly shook his red hair and left without another word.

As Varren entertained Cault, Lluava sat down next to Rosalyn. "How have you been?"

"I am well," she answered with a gentle smile.

Lluava was not content with that statement. "You know what I mean. How are you handling this? After all, you were supposed to head home to be married."

Rosalyn blew on her steaming spoon. "Honestly, I wish we had left when you had. I cannot stand waking up every morning wondering if this is the day Talos will not return." She tucked several loose strands of long black hair behind her ear. "I keep myself busy tending to the wounded and cooking and whatever else I can do to help. Yet, every time I see a man carried back on stretchers, my heart skips a beat. I think, what if it is he? What if...? How about you?"

"Don't take this the wrong way, but I'm actually quite happy to be here with everyone. The capital and I don't seem to agree."

Rosalyn looked across the fire at Talos, who was seated next to his partner, Byron. "Well, right now, I would trade with you."

Lluava grunted as she spooned down some of the hot liquid. Hearing laughter from Captain Cault, she asked Rosalyn, "So, who is in charge here?"

"Colonel Bern, before he headed south for help. That left us with Jamison and Vidrick—if I disregard poor Merl."

"Only two?" Lluava was astounded. The seriousness of the matter began to seep in. Another bout of Cault's laughter rose through the air. "I like Cault, but what's Vidrick's story? He seemed a little standoffish."

Rosalyn lowered her empty bowl onto her lap. "His behavior could be due to his atypical past."

"Battle scars?"

"No. His are more personal. Vidrick was one of those sought-after bachelors. Though not of high class, his military successes and pleasant personality made him quite attractive."

Lluava realized where this was going. "Yet he never married."

Rosalyn nodded her confirmation. "No. He neither married nor even attempted to court a lady, as far as I know. Some people say he never developed an affinity for the fairer sex. I prefer not to believe gossip."

"I noticed he looked at Varren strangely."

Bemused, Rosalyn remarked, "You had better watch out, Lluava. You might have some competition."

Lluava quickly retorted, "I don't know what you are talking about."

***

The sound of wolves' howling woke Lluava like an unwelcome alarm in the early morning hours. In the tent next to hers, Lluava heard Varren rising quickly to receive the news. In the center of a ring of tents, a dozen timber wolves trotted in, led by their larger black leader. As if on cue, the entire pack transformed, causing Lluava to smile.

"Derrick!" she exclaimed, running up to hug the dark-skinned leader of the pack. His bristly chin prickled her cheek. Lluava ignored it, relishing the fact that yet another of her friends was here with her.

"Lluava, Prince Varren, when did you two arrive?" Derrick asked as the rest of his group loped off to their respective tents.

"Late yesterday," Lluava responded.

Varren inquired, "Where have you been?"

"My pack and I have been scouting the northern edge of the kingdom in case of enemy attack."

"They are among the few troops who dare to breach the borders of Yorrick Forest," noted Byron with a yawn. Stretching, he added, "Since it's haunted and all…"

Lluava laughed. "Well, I'm glad you're here."

Derrick nodded. "If you will excuse me, I am going to rest before my next shift. I am glad you, too, are well."

"And I, you."

As Derrick disappeared behind a yellow-green tent, Varren spoke up. "Lluava, I need to talk to some of the soldiers this morning. Care to come?"

"Sure."

Grabbing several chunks of salted pork from their supplies, Lluava accompanied Varren on his rounds. It was soon apparent that the morale of the men was very low. Between the losses of both lives and ground, the soldiers seemed to be on the verge of deserting, although the presence of the prince gave them some hope. This issue needed to be dealt with, and quickly.

Varren and Lluava entered the officers' tent along with a few prominent soldiers like Talos. Since Vidrick had retired after leading the evening shift, Cault was currently in charge of determining the morning's movements.

"I want to fight on the front today," said Varren authoritatively.

The Captain countered, "As I told you yesterday, that is not an option."

Varren was ready for Cault's response. "The doubts of this army are like an infection of the soul. As it stands, their faith in this effort is weakening as the wounds of their hope fester. They yearn to believe in something tangible. I can be that beacon, that light for which they search."

"You speak eloquently," noted Cault, "but pretty words do not affect the grim reality. Elysia almost lost you, her one true heir, during the battles near the sea this past summer. The enemy knows who you are. I will not allow such a rash decision. The cost would be too great."

Lluava's imagination took hold. She had felt the rush—the incredible rush that is only born in battle—dissipate as she stood restlessly by Varren's side in the safety of the camp. She had to speak up.

"Captain, why would common men fight in a war when their greatest leader will not? How can they place their trust in a man who will not stand up for them?"

Talos, always rationalizing, responded, "It is the duty of the soldiers to follow their orders. They are well aware of the great costs that could occur in defending the kingdom."

"You speak as if they have no feelings," argued Lluava. "What if you were told to wait at camp while Rosalyn fought on the front lines? Would you be so content?" Lluava could see she had touched a nerve. "The love and protectiveness you feel for Rosalyn are exactly what Varren feels for his people. Don't you see? There is no difference."

Varren looked at Lluava. She sensed his respect.

Cault interjected, "Emotions cloud the mind, Private. They need to be eradicated before true rationalization can occur. This is why major decision-making is not left to your sex."

Lluava almost took a step back. The physical presence of his words smote her.

The captain continued, "The individual feelings of the soldiers do not change the hard facts. It is too risky to send the prince out to fight."

Varren briefly caught Talos's eye, and Talos raised a questioning eyebrow.

The prince spoke assertively. "Not long ago, I was given some advice that I have held dear ever since. I was told that as Elysia's prince, I had the power to order a change if I believed in something and took a stand." Varren regarded the disapproving expressions around him. "It is time to take a stand. As the prince, the one true heir of this kingdom, I have made the decision to fight on the front lines."

Cault began to protest, but Varren silenced him.

"I have found my motivation," he went on, with a glance at Lluava. "No more hiding behind others. I will ride out to battle with the morning's troops."

"Go, then, and prepare," responded the defeated Cault. "Meet Lieutenant Bern at the eastern side of camp in thirty minutes."

Excited, Lluava arose to retrieve the Claws but stopped in mid step.

Varren inquired, "Is something wrong?"

"Issaura's Claws. I left them on the field."

"What do you mean, 'left them'?"

"I couldn't shift with them on, so I hid them in a rock formation. I forgot them during my encounter with that giant, and—"

Cault's furious voice came from behind them. "You left Issaura's Claws in enemy territory? Maybe someone as foolish as you should not have been given such a great gift. Private Rein, lead Private Lluava to the armory so she can select a new weapon. We seem to have more than we require."

Private Rein stepped out from the officers' tent and motioned for her to follow.

***

"Where did the weapons come from?" Lluava wondered aloud as she looked through the tent flap into an overburdened armory.

Rein explained, "They are what we have salvaged from our fallen comrades."

Dead men's weapons. She would have to fight with someone else's possession. The thought of it soured like milk.

"I have another weapon. A sword, actually," Lluava said, referring to Vjeran, which Domar had given her. The least she could do was use it, yet she felt wretched. As she and Varren headed to her tent, Lluava voiced her thoughts.

"Maybe Cault is right. This is the second time I have lost Issaura's Claws."

Varren shook his head. "Do not let the captain's words upset you. He is angry at my decision and is taking it out on you."

"But I left the Claws—"

Varren placed his hand on her arm and turned her to face him. His voice was low and gentle. "Issaura's Claws have been in the Vaults, my family's treasury, since they were initially acquired several generations ago. You are the first person to be considered worthy of them. Do not believe that this decision was made lightly. You were meant to possess the Claws."

"Even if I lose them for good?"

"You will get them back. Even I can sense that."

Regardless of his kind words, Lluava's guilt remained. She had left her weapons and not given them a second thought until now. Lluava glumly made her way back to her own quarters as Varren veered off to his.

As she approached, she heard her friends' voices. Talos was speaking.

"Everyone understands what to do now? Good. We need to protect Varren at all costs. Remember, neither he nor Lluava must know."

"What's going on?" Lluava questioned as she stepped into view. Byron and Yamir were with Talos. Their expressions were like rats caught gnawing on one's cheese.

Byron attempted to explain. "We just want to keep him safe."

Insulted, Lluava snapped back, "I can keep him safe."

"He is our prince, Lluava," Talos responded. "We want some extra insurance for his well-being."

"He is my partner. *My* partner!" exclaimed Lluava, jabbing her finger into her own chest. "I'm the person to watch his back!"

Annoyed, Talos said, "Then act like his partner and protect him. Convince him to stay off the front lines."

"No. Varren can make his own decisions."

"Then we will be there to give him aid if the need arises."

Lluava snarled, "I wonder what Varren will say about all of this?"

Talos took a couple of steps toward her, then stopped. "He must not know. Lluava, if Varren worries about anything but fighting, his concentration and awareness will be split. That could cause him more harm than good. He cannot know."

Why were they doing this? Lluava thought. She was a more capable fighter than any one of them. It was the duty of partners to protect one another. *She* was Varren's partner. His partner! Not one of them.

Spinning on her heel, Lluava stormed off.

Talos called out, "We have to protect him!"

Lluava shouted back, "He is *my* partner!"

Fuming, Lluava spent the few extra minutes she had left prowling around the camp before she joined the troops who were preparing to leave. Soon enough, a tired-looking Lieutenant Vidrick gave the signal and led the men to the front lines.

Lluava was quite comfortable being the only female marching toward battle. The source of her current discontent was the constant awareness of the nearby presence of her friends. She wished they would fend for themselves and not stick their faces into her business.

On the field, the troops charged over the clear-cut area, climbing over fallen trees and men. Varren fought at her side as they slowly hacked their way through the enemy lines toward the rock formation and Issaura's Claws.

Her own senses were stretched thin. Too many things demanded her attention: Varren at her back, facing a marauder he could clearly overcome; friends fading in and out of her peripheral vision; Raiders blocking the way to her destination. Sensing a second familiar presence shadowing them, Lluava hurried Varren forward. Yamir needed to take the hint and get lost.

Suddenly she heard an awkward cry from her ruddy-hued companion. However, with a Raider breathing down her neck, Lluava could not afford a backward glance at Yamir. Her heart thrummed.

The Raider before her sneered, his curled lip exposing a small tattoo. He gripped his mace and attempted to thrust it into Lluava's chest. But his attack was thwarted as the mace met the steel of Lluava's sword; before he could react, the young woman had thrust Vjeran into the brute's torso.

Turning around, Lluava spotted Yamir, who had slain his opponent with a lance through an eye. But rather than moving on, Yamir continued to plunge his weapon into the fallen Raider's face. Up and down, up and down he jabbed, as if trying to liquefy the crushed contents that had once been a head.

Lluava wasn't the only one who took note of Yamir's vicious actions. Several marauders closed in on her friend.

"Yamir!" she called, but to no avail.

Varren shouted, "I am going back for him."

Before Lluava could follow, another Raider blocked her path. Beyond him, she could see Talos attempting to pull Yamir away from the disfigured corpse.

Taking more time than she liked, Lluava fended off her opponent just as the trumpeting sounds of retreat rang out.

No! she thought. I can't leave now; Issaura's Claws are so close!

She scanned the wooded edge of the clearing. Her friends were already moving into safer territory. They must be expecting her to follow. But the Claws... Lluava mournfully assessed her situation. She should turn back.

Before she realized what she was doing, Lluava had charged toward her hidden weapons. A Raider rose up in front of her. She shoved her sword into the thick hide covering his back, and heard his ribs splinter. With her boot, she shoved the corpse off the blade.

Almost there, she thought.

Through the chaos around her, a smoky scent caught hold of her nostrils. Turning around, Lluava stared up at the monstrous Raider she thought she had killed the day before.

It couldn't be...!

Lluava blinked. The figure was real. His nub of an arm. Dried blood staining his fur coat where Yamir's spear had pierced it. The sweat of his brow running down into bloodshot eyes.

Staring at her, he raised a thick sword with his good hand and grunted. "Theri."

Chapter 17

Victim Unfortunate

heri."

Hearing the goddess's name once more, Lluava did not doubt whom she was being called. How did this brute know of the goddess? How did he recognize Lluava's physical similarity to Theri? Did he really believe Lluava was that ancient figure, or was that just the name he had chosen to give her? After all, she was the only female warrior on the field.

The image of a man flickered in her memory, but she couldn't place him. Could it be the Raiders' leader, Ambassador Alcove? After watching him sail away, she had not given him much thought. Was he the source of this superstitious nonsense?

She had no time to ponder further, for the giant Raider lifted his sword into the air. Lluava clutched Uppsala tightly. The hilt of the sword was still unfamiliar to her and therefore far from comforting. Compared to the massive size of the enemy's sword, her own weapon was meager.

Any twitch of muscle that might have alerted Lluava to the Raider's next move was hidden under the layers of fur the behemoth wore. His sword crashed down; vaulting aside, she felt the vibrations from his weapon's impact on the burned earth. The sword left a deep cleft in the surface.

That could have been her. Adrenaline coursed through her body. As the brute swung again, Lluava narrowly dodged the vengeful device. A low growl rumbled from her throat. With his next attempt, she stumbled back, her inner heat growing at an unprecedented rate. Something deep inside her stirred. Something dark waited to be born.

Her mind reeled with inner dialogue. What *was* this man? His wound, recently cauterized, did not seem to affect him. The stain on his shoulder oozed anew, yet he persisted in his attempt to fell her. How could a man like this exist?

Other thoughts fought for her attention. What about Yamir? What had happened to him? Was he also losing his mind? No. She wouldn't lose another friend. Yet how else to explain his unhealthy fixation? And what of Varren? Had he escaped? Was he safe behind the lines, or was he returning to find her? Talos would not let Varren risk his life, but the prince's determination and confidence had grown over the summer. Could Varren be stopped? Lluava found it hard to concentrate. Her mind was pulled in countless directions simultaneously.

She had to stay alert, to think, and there was only one choice. Lluava discarded the sword, whose weight and balance she had not yet fully tested.

Each time the behemoth attacked, Lluava desperately tried to stay focused. As she struggled to avoid the Raider's blade, she realized she was losing any chance of gaining the upper hand.

Panic. Panic rising. How long could she keep up the defense? Just one strike from his blade, and she would be no more; Varren and her friends would be left to struggle on. What if they lost? What then? What would happen to her family? What about the kingdom? Her heart thrummed rapidly, and her temples rang with every beat. Sweat chilled the back of her neck.

Lluava looked about desperately. Was she about to slip up? No one else was nearby. I can't, I can't, came the frantic thought.

Stepping back, she tripped over the cold body of the smaller Raider. And as she fell, in that moment of utter failure, her instincts took command. She shifted.

As Lluava turned to combat her opponent, her senses heightened and her strength renewed, a new sensation claimed her. She felt as if something else were in control, in her skin. It was as if she were pushed aside; at the same time, she had never felt more in tune with her actions. And as she struck out at her opponent, the colors around her slowly began to drain away and fade out. Soon everything had a blue-green tint. All other colors, with the exception of red, had vanished.

The behemoth seemed to sense the change in her, though it had nothing to do with her felid form. No fear emanated from him. He clearly did not view her as a threat.

As the Raider brought down his blade, the tigress sprang aside to evade it. When he lifted his weapon again, the enraged animal vaulted up and sank its fangs into the flesh of his forearm. Warm liquid oozed down Lluava's throat, triggering blackness.

***

She was standing in human form, that much was certain. Her feet, partially engulfed in thick muck, made stomach-knotting sucking sounds as she lifted each foot. Looking down, she saw that the mud had taken on a much darker tint due to the liquid that had fed it.

Next to her lay the corpse of the giant Raider. At least, she hoped it was a corpse. The body was prostrate and facing away from her. She detected no trace of movement, no murmur of breath. Lluava inched closer. No reaction. She slowly moved around to the other side of the man and gasped.

The Raider's face—or where his face should have been—had been entirely stripped away, hollowed out like a dish holding entrails. The sight was foul and deeply affecting. Lluava's legs felt as if they had lost all muscle and were melting into the ground.

What on earth had happened? she thought as her body began to tremble. Her strength vanished, leaving her weak as a newborn cub.

What *had* happened?

The question was overwhelming, but Lluava was in the open, and there was no time; she needed to get out of sight. Looking around, she saw that the field was quiet. No one was near—at least, no one alive. Had the number of corpses grown? Sounds of blood and heartbreak could still be heard in the distance. Was anyone approaching? Lluava glanced at the trees behind her, then back at the behemoth's body.

What had happened?

On shaky limbs, she snatched up her discarded sword, crawled to the sanctuary of the woods, and did not stop until she reached the rock formation. Dropping down behind it, she began to sob, head tucked between crossed arms, tears rolling like waves down her face. Whatever had happened, it had left its impression on her soul.

Some time passed until, drained, she finally looked up. The sun had begun to put itself to rest. How long had she been there? Sounds of battle still resounded not far off, and Lluava knew she had to make her way back to the encampment and Varren.

Taking a breath, Lluava reached into the hollow in the rocks, hoping beyond all hope that those precious items still remained. Her fingers brushed against something smooth and cool. Pulling them out one by one, Lluava strapped on Issaura's Claws once again. They gave her the solace she had craved.

After carefully looking over the field of battle, she stood up and took off toward the promise of safety. The phantom of the dead, faceless figure clung to the back of her mind, giving weight to her limbs. She pushed on, knowing that if she stopped she might not be able to force her body to move again. Fortunately, the only creature to spot her dashing form was Onyx, who cawed angrily above her.

Lluava ran past several lines of comrades, only stopping once the moss-green tents surrounded her. She bent over her knees and concentrated on her breathing.

"Lluava!" Varren's angry voice cried out. "Why did you not follow—

Lluava? Lluava, are you all right?"

As soon as his hands touched her, she sank down onto the ground. Her whole body shook uncontrollably. Varren quickly bent low and turned her face toward his.

"Are you hurt?"

It took Lluava a moment to shake her head no. Varren scowled, not angrily but because her lie was so obvious. Without turning toward the growing number of onlookers, he commanded, "Bring Rosalyn! Someone call the nurse!"

After inspecting her for obvious injury, Varren gently helped the trembling girl to her feet. Sending the crowd away, he led her deeper into the encampment.

As the first clear knowledge of safety washed over Lluava, she felt smaller hands fussing about her. Rosalyn expertly began her examination even as the three of them moved toward the makeshift medical ward. When the dark-haired woman asked questions, Lluava did her best to answer. Yet her mind still roamed over the battlefield, desperately trying to recapture the memory she had lost.

Rosalyn gently ordered, "I want you to sit down and rest."

As Lluava was helped to a chair, Rosalyn asked, "What happened out there?"

Lluava looked at Rosalyn. It was the first conscious direct eye contact she had initiated since the horrific ordeal. "I need to speak with Captain Cault."

Rosalyn shook her head. "No. You are to stay here until—"

"I *will* speak with the captain."

Varren interceded before Rosalyn could attempted to quiet Lluava again. "The Captain is now leading the troops. He will not be back until later. You can rest until then."

"If Cault is fighting, then Vidrick should be here. I will speak with him."

Rosalyn scowled. "I will not advise—"

"Where is the lieutenant?" Lluava could not allow her friends to hold her back. They did not know. Everyone needed to know. She stood up quickly and, before Rosalyn could stop her, pushed past the woman as if she were no more than a breeze. She heard Varren apologize, saying he would watch over her. Lluava kept on walking toward the officers' tent.

When Varren reached her side, he said distastefully, "You did not have to be so rude."

"She would have kept me there. This is important."

"That may be," noted Varren, "but Rosalyn is also your friend. She is concerned for you. As am I."

Varren's hand briefly touched her arm, and a subtle sense of remorse made itself felt. Without slowing her stride, Lluava looked at him. "I will let her finish her exam, but I must do this first."

Outside the officers' tent, there was quite a commotion. Several men held down a writhing figure. A Raider! They had captured one alive! Vidrick was giving commands to his men, and they began to drag the still-fierce prisoner away.

Vidrick said to the man watching beside him, "He may not want to talk now, but he will later."

"Of course," noted the second as he headed toward their captive.

Lluava called out, "Lieutenant Bern, I must speak with you."

Vidrick looked at the approaching pair. All expression left his face. After a moment, he nodded to them. "You may speak freely."

"Have you been informed about the giant Raider?" she asked.

"The one you killed. Yes."

"Well, I didn't exactly kill him. At least not then. He found me on the field earlier. He fought as if he had not sustained those normally crippling injuries."

Varren stared at both of them. The young officer shared his look of unease.

Vidrick asked, "What happened to him?"

"Oh, I killed him," Lluava quickly acknowledged. "His body is lying near the edge of that island of trees." She pointed to the area.

"How?" Vidrick asked again. "How did you kill him?"

Lluava felt her heartbeat quicken. What should she tell him? The truth? And what was that? Did she even know?

"I did it by accident. I doubt I will be that fortunate again." Changing the subject, Lluava stated, "If there are others like him, we need to find that out."

"You saw our new guest, I assume?" inquired Vidrick. "He will be the perfect informant on that and other matters of importance."

Lluava nodded.

Vidrick glanced over at Varren, then back at Lluava. "I will let you know what we find out, if that will calm your mind."

"Thank you."

With that, the pair was dismissed. They headed back to their own section of camp to wait. As the hours slipped into night, no word came. The prisoner kept as silent as the death he wished upon them.

Seated by the campfire, Lluava felt restless and constantly compelled to shift her position. Varren reached over and placed his hand on her leg, which settled her momentarily.

"You should get some rest," he told her.

Beyond that expression of concern, Varren kept his questions to himself. Lluava knew he wanted to ask about the incident on the field but was holding back. But he needed to know.

So, in a hushed voice Lluava began, "When I was out there, something happened." Although it was clear that none of her other friends were listening, she would not risk capturing their interest. "That giant attacked me in a moment when I felt torn."

Varren raised a questioning eyebrow.

Lluava swallowed. Her throat was terribly dry. "I could not concentrate on him. I was thinking about a thousand things at once. Yamir, that man, you…"

She felt Varren's hand tense as she continued. "I…I let go. I felt as if something else, some other force, took me over. I lost control and I…blacked out."

Pausing, Lluava observed Varren's reaction. She needed to see how her news had affected him. "When I came to, the Raider was dead. But it is *how* he died that worries me. His face—skin, tissue, bone—all had been removed."

Lluava realized she was trembling again. What was wrong with her? This couldn't be fear. Why was she acting so weak? The whole conversation was terribly discomfiting.

Before Varren could attempt to console her, she spoke up again, more firmly this time. "The captive must speak. We need to know what he knows. We have to find out about the giant Raider."

"The lieutenant's men are working on it as we speak," answered Varren. He had read her previous reaction and taken his hand away. "All we can do is wait."

"I can get him to speak," said a third voice.

They turned with a start. Derrick stood behind them, stretching after his much-deserved rest. The wolf pack's leader spoke confidently.

"You are talking about a prisoner, yes? I will get him to talk."

Varren gave the dark-skinned man a quick nod, and Derrick left, presumably to carry out his new order.

Time dragged on, and Lluava finally turned in.

***

She awakened from a dream filled with swords and blood.

"I told you she would be startled," Varren said to Talos, who still had his hand on Lluava's shoulder.

Outside her tent, another figure wiped his hands on what had once been a handkerchief. "He will talk now."

Derrick led the way to the prisoner's location, then left to rejoin his men on another scouting mission. One of the few buildings of the original trading post had been stripped of its contents for its new purpose as a cell for the enemy. Although the wooden structure was sturdy enough to hold a Raider, several men flanked its entrance. Vidrick slipped through the doorway, and the rest followed.

The sight inside caused Lluava to catch her breath. Completely bare, the modest room now sported a thick wooden post at its center, where metal shackles bound the hands of the Raider above his head. Yet it was the fresh red color splattered over walls and ground that caught her attention. Gruesome redecoration, courtesy of Derrick and their guest.

The marauder did not raise his head to look at his hosts; his body slumped limply as far as his restraints allowed. Scarlet designs around his forearms drew Lluava's attention to the thick shackles that dug into his wrists. But it was his hands that held Lluava's gaze. Every fingernail had been peeled back like the skin of a ripe fruit. Pulpy stubs protruded where the last two fingers of his left hand should have been. They had been gnawed off.

Varren was the first to return to his senses. "You said you would talk now."

The Raider winced at those words. He nodded slightly, still gazing down at the darkly stained floor.

"Whom do you follow? Who commands you?"

The Raider's voice sounded drained and hollow. His accent was heavy and thick. "One who can't be stopped."

"Does he have a name?"

"He does."

After a pause, Lluava took a breath and asked, "There was a Raider on the field of battle. He was larger, stronger than the rest of you. Who was that man? Are there others like him?"

No response.

Was that a smile on the brute's lips? From where she stood, Lluava could not tell. Haughtily she asked, "Is something funny? Well, that man is dead. You have lost your giant."

The prisoner tilted his head in her direction yet continued to keep it lowered. "When one is killed, 'nother'll rise in 'is stead."

"What?" This was not the answer Lluava wanted to hear. "There are others? Where?"

The marauder gave no reply.

Vidrick broke in. "You said you were willing to speak. Do not make this more difficult. You know we are in no such mood. What are your plans, your strategy?"

The Raider raised his head and looked directly at the red-headed lieutenant.

"They will rain from above."

He turned to Varren. "Take the head; kill the body."

Shuddering, the prisoner sank down with a low moan and did not stir again.

Chapter 18

Mandate Eleven

I s he…" Lluava hesitated as Varren shouted to the men outside, "Fetch the nurse! Fetch Rosalyn!" Vidrick was silent as Talos whispered into Varren's ear.

Lluava knew only rudimentary first aid, not having completed her medical studies before she was transferred to Durog to train as a soldier. But should she even try to help this man? He was the enemy. He would have fought to kill her if they had met on the battlefield. Still, she pitied him and could not imagine what he must be suffering.

Rosalyn entered the room, followed by Yamir, who carried her large medical bag. The two stopped short as if they had hit some invisible wall. Lluava wondered if she had done the same. Rosalyn's face grew dark.

"What did you do to him?" she hissed as she hurried over to the man.

"Derrick," Talos stated flatly.

"Yamir," Rosalyn barked, "come here."

Yamir did not move. He was frozen to the spot, eyes locked on the sight before him. Lluava approached him and removed the bag from her friend's grip. As she did so, he blinked and looked about. Then, with an abrupt turn, he left the premises.

"I will see to him," said Talos as he hastened after his friend.

Rosalyn was holding one of the Raider's wrists. After a moment, she touched a spot on the side of the man's neck. Lluava opened the bag and looked at its various contents. "What do you need? Cloth? Something to stop the blood?"

"He is dead."

Lluava stared. Rosalyn was completely serious. Their prisoner, their only source of information, was gone and his secrets with him. One by one, the small group vacated the building until only the men unchaining the body remained.

Another group approached the area. Five men with fiery intentions strode forth, Captain Cault among them. "You have a prisoner? I want a word with him."

A living prisoner was rare. Raiders had a tendency to fight to the death and refused to allow themselves to be captured alive. Nor had this opportunity yielded the fruits that were so hungrily desired.

Vidrick explained what had happened. Understandably, the captive's death was not to the captain's liking. After reprimanding the young lieutenant for his poor decision-making, Captain Cault shared new information.

"A second giant Raider is doing battle. He is taking down more men than I could have thought possible. Private Lluava, did you see any weakness in the other one? Anything that might help us?"

Lluava shook her head.

The Captain seemed to expect as much. "In the morning, I want you out on the field with me. You've killed one. Maybe you can do it again. Prince Varren," he said, turning to Lluava's partner, "I must insist that you stay here—at least for now."

"I will consider your advice," Varren responded as he looked at Lluava, "but I will make no promises." The pair returned to their tents to salvage what sleep they could.

Early the next morning, Lluava awoke to the howling of wolves. The scouts had returned. There must be more news. Lluava hurried to dress.

Varren was waiting for her; the results of a sleepless night apparent in his drawn face. Derrick had already dismissed his men and made his way to the officers' tent. Whatever the scouting party had discovered must be extremely important.

When Varren and Lluava stepped through the flap, sullen faces greeted them. Besides Derrick, only Captain Cault and Lieutenant Bern were present. Lluava quickly realized that she had been admitted only because of her partner's status. Even Talos and the other favored soldiers were not in attendance.

"Give us your report," Captain Cault ordered.

Derrick cleared his throat. "On patrol last night, our wolf pack spotted movement in the forest, deep enough in that it would not have been detected outside the woods. A score or more Raiders are heading northwest. They are all the larger sort."

Derrick stopped. Lluava felt that he was leaving something unsaid; however, she kept her questions to herself lest she lose her special privilege. She looked at Varren. He knew exactly what to ask.

"What is your plan of action?"

Cault, although he had anticipated the question, was clearly frustrated. Vidrick cast his eyes down. Derrick remained silent. As senior officer, Captain Cault began, "We—"

Suddenly, trumpets blared.

Startled, everyone looked about, then rushed outside. Another round of blasting horns. Lluava's heart raced, each beat seeming stronger with every blare. Did this alert indicate the battle was raging again?

Lluava turned toward the sounds. No. These were coming from the main road on the southwestern edge. The soldiers who had already left the field emerged from their tents to see the reason for the commotion.

Pennants came into view, snapping in the crisp fall air, gold and moss green. Embroidered on them was the royal emblem, a prostrate lion beneath the feet of a crowned raven. The bird's olive branch meant little now. The banner men flanked the few others riding in on mounts, while a line of battle-ready soldiers marched behind them.

Their leader was quite recognizable in his ceremonial uniform. Colonel Bern dismounted and made his way to the other officers. His cohort of men expertly set up camp as soon as they were given the command.

The officers greeted one another formally, as rank dictated. Lluava studied the features of the colonel and the lieutenant; both father and son shared the same strong jaw and rather small ears. Vidrick stepped aside to allow the colonel to approach Varren.

"Your Majesty."

"Colonel."

There was a tense pause before the silence was broken.

"There have been important events of late, of which you must be informed as chief officer," Captain Cault began. He proceeded to give the colonel the briefest, most succinct recap of the past few days. When he had finished, the question remained: How should they deal with this problem?

Varren addressed Colonel Bern. "What would you have us do?"

The pessimistic colonel responded, "Nothing. There is nothing we can do about that band of Raiders."

Varren was shocked. Without waiting for proper acknowledgment, he interjected, "What do you mean? Are you just going to let the enemy move their forces as they wish? We need to send soldiers to stop them or, at the very least, to discover their intentions."

Colonel Bern looked grave. Varren regarded the other officers. Not one made an effort to counter the colonel's assessment.

Lluava felt as horrified as Varren. She persisted in her partner's stead. "Can't we send a party after them? You've brought us fresh troops."

All at once, a new thought struck her. Lluava's eyes narrowed in concentration. "This is what the captive meant."

"What?" The question was asked by several at the same time.

Looking directly at Colonel Bern, Lluava explained, "Before he died, the prisoner said that they would 'rain down from above.' He must have been referring to those giant Raiders. They will attack Elysia from the north."

"And what of the rest of his statement?" questioned the lieutenant. His voice resonated with the same strong tones as his father standing next to him. " 'Take the head; kill the body?' "

Lluava paused for a moment. What did that mean? Surely more than just crazed words.

Derrick spoke up, "They might be targeting Prince Varren again. He will be the next head of the kingdom."

"The kingdom's head," mused Varren, more forcefully than even he seemed to expect. When the others turned their attention to him, he continued, "The capital. They want to take Cronus. If both the capital and our government fall, so will the rest of Elysia."

"They will have difficulty making it to Cronus," countered Cault. "There are hundreds of miles between the Yorrick Forest and the capital's walls."

Lluava chimed in, backing her partner. "If these other marauders are similar to the one I dealt with on the field, reaching the castle will not be as difficult as you might think."

Captain Cault looked sourly at Lluava. Yet he, too, had observed a giant Raider in battle just yesterday, with disastrous results. Turning to Colonel Bern, Cault reluctantly agreed. "She might have a point."

"Word will be sent to the capital to be on guard. That is all we can do," the colonel replied.

"All?" Lluava was angry. "Send soldiers after those Raiders!"

"Despite the reinforcements, Private, we are dangerously low on troops as well as officers." The colonel's raised voice could not hide his irritation with Lluava's insubordination. "All of which are needed here where the enemy is at its worst. We have no one to lead this mission."

"I will." Varren's voice was strong and sure. He was ready.

Lluava viewed her partner with admiration. Not long ago, he had shied away from assuming a leadership role. Now he was declaring his willingness to take command of an extremely dangerous mission.

A sigh escaped Colonel Bern's lips. "The High Council, by the authority of Mandate Eleven, has ordered you to return to the capital in the morning."

Varren grew still. Lluava felt his tension thicken like day-old pea soup. Then it hit her: she would be forced to leave as well. But they had just arrived! She couldn't go back, not now. Not while her friends stayed behind, not while the raiders ran rampant.

Infuriated, Lluava growled, "Well, somebody needs to send a troop after those giant brutes."

The officers exchanged looks with each other; it was clear they were privy to information that was not being shared. Even Derrick seemed informed.

Shaking his head, Captain Cault explained, "The Yorrick Forest is believed to be haunted."

"What? With witches and warlocks? Those don't exist," hissed Lluava. "The Yorrick wolverine? The Great Mountain bear? They've been extinct for years."

"That may be," admitted the colonel. By his tone it was clear that he, too, thought this superstition to be rubbish. "Whatever ghosts the forest contains are no concern of mine. However, the men believe it, especially those born around here. Faith is a powerful thing, and so is fear. The men will not enter the woods."

"What about Derrick?" Lluava gestured at her brooding companion. "His men are not afraid to enter the forest."

The colonel, looking rather exhausted, countered, "That may be true, but only the Theriomorph partners enter the woods. By themselves, they are only half a unit, and they only patrol the perimeter."

"So, send half."

"Theriomorphs will not be sent out without their military partners. This is the law, one you have no authority to question."

"But they—"

Lluava had pushed him too far. The colonel raised his voice and spat out his orders. "I will not allow partners to split up. They fight together or not at all. The men will not enter the forest. This includes most Theriomorphs. Remember your place, Private. It is at your partner's side."

Blatant fear from humans! Once again, that fear was overtaking reason, hindering progress. Lluava began to sneer before she remembered her place. If Varren would not stand up for himself, she would have no chance to continue to fight. She could not override the colonel's authority.

Her partner nodded slightly at the officers. Did he really agree with them? She scowled at the prince, but as she did, she noticed a slight gleam in his eyes. Something was on his mind that he did not wish to discuss with those around him. Maybe he did have a plan. She kept her emotions and her tongue in check.

Dismissed, Lluava, Varren, and Derrick left the officers to continue their strategizing. As they headed to their tents to prepare for battle, Talos and Rosalyn approached. When Talos stopped to have a word with Varren, Rosalyn strode forward and jabbed a finger into Derrick's chest. Her action caught everyone off guard.

"You killed that man," Rosalyn hissed.

"I've killed many." Derrick's matter-of-fact acknowledgment angered Rosalyn even more.

"You tortured him." The young woman's breath was ragged and exaggerated.

"He was the enemy," Derrick stated, slightly annoyed.

"He bled to death from the wounds you inflicted."

Derrick stated sharply, "We needed him to talk."

"*You. Are. An. Animal!*"

Derrick stepped closer to Rosalyn, pushing back her finger, which still jabbed his chest. Rosalyn's delicate coloring had always made her resemble a porcelain doll; now, Lluava wondered if Rosalyn were about to crack.

Derrick snarled, "I did what needed to be done, which is more than I can say for any of you!"

Talos rushed to Rosalyn's side as Derrick shoved past them. Placing a hand on her arm, Talos attempted to calm her. "Let Derrick be."

Rosalyn abruptly turned to her fiancé, her eyes scorching, "How dare you? You are supposed to be on my side!"

Talos countered, "We are all on the same side."

As the couple's argument escalated, Varren quickly steered Lluava away. "Some things are meant to be dealt with privately," he admitted before changing the subject. "Today, I feel, might be the longest one yet."

The day was indeed long. On the field, men fought, bled, and died. Lluava was hypersensitive. Anything that might signal the second giant Raider captured her attention immediately. Yet, throughout the long day, she did not get a single glimpse of the brute.

Returning to camp, Lluava trudged to her tent and stood inside for several minutes, attempting to clear her mind. She reeked of sweat and entrails. A bath would be nice. Maybe a dip in the stream. There was one not far from the main road, and this might be the last chance to clean herself until she returned to the capital.

The capital. The very thought sank in her stomach like a boulder in a lake. The phantom faces of Head Councilman Themis, Madame Angela, and even Queen Enya rose up before her. She shivered. Mandate Eleven was unfair. If Varren wanted to fight for his people, why shouldn't he?

Lluava's griping became audible. Kicking her blanket, she sent it flying into the back of her tent.

"I did not know the Raiders were sending bedding materials to fight for them."

Varren stood in the tent's opening. Although Lluava knew he was trying to lighten her mood, she was not amused. This was not what she wanted to hear.

When she did not attempt a witty comeback, her partner spoke more seriously. "Come to my tent." He turned and left.

Lluava blinked in the growing dark. What did he want now? She was tired, and she smelled like the rear end of a horse.

"Ah…" she grumbled as she headed over to Varren's tent.

She nearly tripped over Yamir as she entered. Byron caught her and set her upright. Talos shushed them as Varren motioned for her to take the remaining spot by the door. Crowded together almost shoulder to shoulder, the heat of their bodies intensified their unbathed aroma.

Varren must have something important on his mind to have gathered all of them together. Did it have anything to do with the earlier meeting? Lluava waited for him to speak.

"I called you here tonight because you are my most trusted comrades." Varren looked around him. "What I am about to say is highly secret and might even be viewed as treasonous." He paused. No one stirred. "If you do not want to be involved, please excuse yourself now. I will not hold it against you."

No movement.

A slight smile stole onto the young prince's face.

"Very well. I have been ordered by the High Council to return to the capital in the morning. That is something I cannot and will not do."

Lluava almost shouted in excitement. Themis would not win!

As Varren continued, his voice rose in confidence. "There is a band of Raiders making their way northwest. They are the larger sort and so are very dangerous. They are using the Yorrick Forest as cover. Many of the soldiers, especially those raised in this region, believe that this forest is haunted. As a result, they will not enter the woods. The officers refuse to discourage these long-established superstitions, thus enabling the enemy to move about freely."

These words were quite unsettling, especially to Byron, who was from the north.

Varren came to the heart of the matter. "I want to follow them. With your help, I think we can track these giant marauders in order to discover their intentions. We need to know what they are planning. This mission is not to fight," he clarified, "only to gather information. If they are moving into a position to attack, we might be able to warn the people or towns in danger. We could set up a defense. Prevent the Raiders from moving on the capital." He paused and gave each of them a few moments to consider fully the importance of his words.

"Will you come with me?" he asked them.

"Yes."

"Of course."

"Certainly."

Lluava smiled. "I would follow you anywhere."

"That is settled, then." Varren smiled too. "The next order of business is to figure out how to track the Raiders. Byron, you used to hunt. Could you pick up their trail?"

"That was a long while ago," acknowledged Byron, "and my skills were never that good."

"We could try to hire a tracker," Talos suggested hopefully.

Yamir shook his head. "The men around here hold true to their beliefs. I am from farther south, and even I remember hearing tales of all the dangers that lurk in these woods. I doubt you would find anyone willing to set foot into that forest."

"I know of one," stated Byron. Everyone turned to look at the man, who was rubbing his bad leg.

"They call him Apex."

ULLR'S FANGS

PART II

Chapter 19

The Crooked Pine

Apex?" Yamir asked aloud. "That's a funny name."

"It may be uncommon, but it is his," Byron explained. "And is Yamir that different?"

"Yamir is a clansmen's name," he snorted back.

"I'm just teasing." Byron smiled.

Yamir was less than amused.

"Who is this Apex?" questioned Varren. Time was of the essence; they had to act quickly.

"He is a huntsman, probably the best in all Elysia," stated Byron matter-of-factly. "It is said that he can track any animal, and he is known to frequent the Yorrick Forest. Some say that he was born in those woods and raised by animals." Byron hesitated as if aware that what he was sharing had never actually been proved.

"Anyway, he is the one you want."

"Good," Varren said. "Where can we find him?"

"That is the tricky part," acknowledged Byron. "He holds no affiliation to landholdings nor claims any town as home. Yet, based on his past endeavors, Apex typically frequents my hometown. Brings in the finest furs you have ever seen."

"What town is that?"

"Bail. Five days' ride west. Three if we push ourselves."

Varren considered this information while the group began to discuss their departure plans. Byron, however, was compelled to speak once more.

"I must warn you that Apex is…how can I put it nicely? Rough around the edges."

"If he is as good as you say he is, that does not matter to me. Not now," said the prince.

"And what of Rosalyn?" asked Talos.

For the first time, Lluava realized her female friend was not among them.

Varren looked at Talos and answered flatly, "I asked you to come alone to this meeting because I felt that this was for your ears, not hers. She is your betrothed; moreover, Rosalyn is one of the few healers we have. The reasons for my decision are two. First, I believe her skills would be better served here, where the injured can receive her treatment. Second, she has never been trained in combat. As she was raised as a privileged lady of the higher class, the physical effort required to complete this journey might be too much for her. However, I will leave it to your judgment if you wish to invite her along. You know her best."

Talos nodded seriously. It was clear that he was deep in thought.

"Varren makes a good point," admitted Byron. Rosalyn was the closest thing to a sister that many of them had. They all wanted her safe.

Talos uttered whispered words as he left the tent. "For the best…"

***

Before the sun had risen, Varren and Lluava were packed and had made their official farewells to the officers on the front. On well-rested mounts, they took the road that headed to Cronus, to ensure that their deception was believed. Not more than an hour later, several figures on horseback caught up with them. Lluava counted four.

She looked over at Varren, who was also surprised. Rosalyn, looking rather sour, nodded to Lluava as they came into sight. Lluava wondered what had changed Talos's mind. She hoped beyond all hope that they had all underestimated their female friend's capabilities.

Without a word, the friends followed Byron onto a side road that branched westward. Riding at a rapid pace, they made good time while distancing themselves from those they had tricked. Who knew when their lie would be discovered or whether a recovery party would follow?

As they journeyed on, Lluava noticed changes in the landscape. The trees seemed to don far brighter hues. No more brittle browns. Vivid reds, oranges and yellows painted a striking panorama. The cause for this was unknown to the girl. Did it have anything to do with the crisp chill in the air that had been building steadily? Maybe it was the unadulterated ecosystem away from the battlefield. Regardless, Lluava could not help but stare at the brilliant colors, far more vibrant than those found on the same trees farther south.

Onyx seemed to enjoy the cooler temperatures. He chose to take wing more often than not, cawing profusely all the time. But although both she and her bird reveled in the autumn alterations, Lluava could not help but notice a growing tension between Talos and Rosalyn. Apparently, they still had issues to resolve. Could Rosalyn really be angry with them? Talos had invited her. She could have stayed. Anyway, thought Lluava, it really isn't my business. Everyone argues at times.

As the third evening approached, the small band pushed on, for their destination was imminent. In the dying light, Byron was the first to make out the glimmers of lanterns from his home village.

"Bail," he announced, as everyone smiled excitedly at one another. The promise of sleeping in a real house was thrilling. Byron had told them they could stay at his mother's home. But first, they had to find Apex.

"Lluava, I want you to keep your hood up." Varren explained, "We may have been followed. We cannot be forced back, not now. All of us must be careful." His warning drew several nods. Turning back to his partner, Varren looked at her, "Especially you."

"Why me?" It hurt Lluava that Varren did not trust her. Did this have anything to do with what had happened to the giant Raider?

"You, out of all of us, have the most easily distinguished physical characteristics." He reached over and touched the ends of her platinum blond hair. "You are not only the single female warrior in the military, but you are also associated with your goddess. Both facts make it likely that someone will recognize you."

"And what of you?" Lluava retorted rather hastily. "You, the crown prince?"

"That is true; I must be cautious. Nobody should discuss who I am," he warned. "But Lluava, you must remember that not everyone knows what I look like. You did not recognize me when we first met."

Lluava felt her cheeks grow hot. "That was a foolish mistake. Anyone might have done that."

"Exactly," affirmed Varren. "For now, keep your hood up."

Lluava did as he asked. She was not about to complain again. Besides, her hood kept her ears warm.

As they neared the village, Lluava felt oddly at home. It was as if she had been here before, yet that was impossible. She was Southern-raised. She gazed at the wooden structures with admiration. At home, wood was a luxury, and most houses used mud as a base; yet here, where forests were plentiful, things were different.

Varren's furrowed brow alerted Lluava that the prince was focused on their mission. Their journey had cost them the better part of four days. Even she felt a concern about tracking those giant brutes.

Varren scanned the village. "We should find the stables and then search on foot."

"They are over to your left," Lluava responded without thinking.

Both Byron and Varren paused to stare at her. She felt her face flush.

"She's right," admitted Byron. "How did you know that?"

"I...I don't know." Lluava could not fathom where that knowledge had come from. "This place—it just feels familiar."

Byron thought for a moment. "Our fathers were military partners. Since mine was from here, maybe yours visited when you were younger. Just a thought."

Lluava nodded, still disturbed.

Byron added, "You can ask my mother later."

Once the horses were bedded down, Talos suggested the small party split up to cover more ground. Byron said he would go with his partner and suggested that Rosalyn accompany them. That left Yamir with Lluava and Varren.

"The best places to search for Apex," Byron explained, "are the taverns."

"How many taverns are in Bail?" questioned Varren.

"Three. Two down this road," Byron said, gesturing to his right, "and one at that end of town, near the forest's edge."

"We will take the latter," said Varren.

"Right. It's called The Crooked Pine. You can't miss it."

Each trio made its way to the appropriate destination. Just as Byron had directed, the tavern was at the very end of the road, slightly removed from the rest of the town. The gloomy-looking building might have been described as rather ordinary had it not been for its entryway. A large pine, listing greatly to one side, served as two-thirds of an arched door. There was no sign announcing the name, yet it was clear enough. The Crooked Pine was the obvious choice.

Without a word, Varren led them through the door. The humid air circulating in the tavern was so thick with smoke that it tickled Lluava's throat, and she muffled a cough. She blinked her eyes to clear her vision, while her comrades loosened their coats and stamped leaf litter from their boots in the doorway. Stepping farther into the room, Lluava's senses recoiled; she could almost taste the sour smell of spilled mead, the tang of sweat and men, and the vulgar odor of vomit that refused to meld with the bitter smokeweed undertones.

Lluava hoped they would find Apex quickly so she could escape to the crisp, frigid air outside. Pulling her hood forward to cover as much of her face as possible, she glanced about and noted the sparse crowd. None seemed promising.

Behind the bar, the gruff owner silently stared at the new arrivals. The meaning of his look was unmistakable. They were unwelcome. At the far end of the bar, two figures were so preoccupied with each other as to seem oblivious to the world. The man sat atop one of the bar stools, his back shoved against the wall, while a well-endowed wench balanced upon his lap and groped at his face. Her thickly curled locks entangled his fingers, which busily tested the strings of her overly tight bodice. Near the crackling fire, an elderly man sat slumped over in drugged sleep, his legs outstretched upon a former tree trunk that served as his temporary footrest. A half-empty glass was precariously balanced on his open palm. In a corner, three men sat around a table and talked quietly among themselves. With their faces half-draped in shadow, their features were indistinguishable. The rest of the tables were empty, and many had not even been set up properly, their chairs still perched upside down upon them.

Varren moved toward the tavern's owner. Tugging off one of his gloves, he pleasantly ordered, "Three, please."

Since money is money, the owner pretended hospitality and ceremoniously wiped down the countertop with a dingy rag so saturated that it dripped more dirty liquid than it absorbed. Looking them over once more, the tavern keeper filled three mismatched mugs until the fizzing slush poured over the rims, then deposited them in front of Varren. After receiving payment, the man poured himself a mug and took a swig as he continued to eye Lluava's cloak. The desire to pull her hood even farther around her face had never been so strong.

Lluava waited as Varren pretended to sip the thick liquid; she followed suit and did not drink hers, either. Yamir, on the other hand, seemed quite happy quenching his thirst with the potent home brew.

Why was Varren waiting so long? Just ask the question. Lluava eyed the prince and wished she could speak without drawing attention to herself. Time dragged.

Finally, Varren put down his mug and faced the still-observant bartender. "We are looking for a man."

The owner picked up an empty mug and turned his grim gaze to Varren.

"He goes by Apex," Varren said.

The man's expression remained unchanged, although he began to wipe down the mug with his sopping rag.

"Do you know where we can find him?"

The only reply was the squeak, squeak of the mug in his hand.

"I will pay you for your assistance." Varren pulled several coins from his purse. The owner threw down the rag and quickly grabbed his reward. His eyes glinted like the gold in his hand. He nodded toward the back corner and turned to deposit his newfound wealth in a safe place.

Allowing Varren to take the lead, Lluava followed as they wove around tables to the one in the back. The seated men continued to mutter to one another, watching them approach.

"Excuse me," Varren began. "Which one of you is Apex?"

The men looked at each other. The one nearest Varren whispered into the ear of his comrade, who was no doubt his brother, since both men shared the same features. The brothers turned toward the third, much smaller man, who was also older. They waited for him to speak. The snickering fire and the low grunts of pleasure from behind them filled the otherwise heavy silence.

Taking careful note of the leader of the group, Lluava could not see what the fuss over this Apex was all about. He was far too young for the soft white hair that encircled his rather large ears. His dark eyes glanced from Lluava to her companions and back again. She could almost hear him thinking.

"Who wants to know?" His voice was as small as his stature, yet there was confidence in it.

Varren, like Lluava, was not in the mood to play games, "I, Varren Mandrun, Crown Prince of Elysia, require your services."

The smiles slipped from the brothers' faces, yet their leader remained stoical. Lluava could feel the thump of her heart as she anticipated his next move. But even she was unprepared for what happened next.

"And if I decline?"

The question was simple, yet the harsh voice from behind made them all turn.

Standing not a rabbit's length away was a man whose characteristics could only be described as untamed. Powerful and strong in both presence and physique, he clearly was not one to be commanded on any account. With the back of his hand, he wiped lip stain off his bristly jawline. Behind him, the wench retied her bodice, clearly disheartened by her lover's abrupt departure.

"Well?"

The man's impatience was palpable as he moved in closer. Before Varren could reply, Apex tugged at Lluava's hood and pulled it off. There was a tense moment as he and Lluava locked eyes. His eyes—so fierce, so wild, so bold. Eyes that expressed the desire for a challenge. Eyes that seemed to see right through protective boundaries and dig down into one's soul. Golden spheres radiating crimson. They were unlike anything Lluava had ever seen before. But somehow, in some way, she recognized them.

Chapter 20

Of Fathers, Of Mothers

Every last hair on the back of Lluava's neck stood on end. She knew she had never met Apex before. How could she have? Yet that gut feeling of inexplicable familiarity was unmistakable. His eyes held hers, and she could not turn away. An electric tension kept her frozen in place.

The sound of Varren's voice broke the spell. "I want to hire you for a job."

Apex continued to study Lluava. His unfaltering scrutiny fed the uneasiness inside her. Apex replied with disinterest, "I'm not for hire."

Lluava glanced at her partner in a silent plea for his help to shatter her discomfort. For some reason, her voice failed her. Varren moved closer. His shoulder brushed against hers. None of this affected Apex's remorseless gaze.

"I may not have made myself clear," Varren began, his voice steely. "By my authority as Crown Prince of Elysia, I must insist."

Apex's eyes finally swept to the side to glare at Varren.

"By your leave," he answered, in a voice equally cold with a touch of sarcasm, "I will make *myself* clear." He stood erect. Although a bit shorter than Varren, Apex's presence was one of immense power. "I work for no one."

"As a citizen of Elysia, you must—"

Varren was cut off as Apex growled out, "I serve no king, no country, and *no* prince."

Lluava could feel Varren's frustration growing, and for good reason. If Apex did not align himself with them, their plan to stop the giant Raiders would fail.

"You will be well paid." Lluava's statement was simple, reasonable, yet Apex raised a questioning eyebrow. Lluava wondered if it was due to the offer or to her sudden interjection into the conversation. Regardless, she felt compelled to explain further.

"We," she began, gesturing to her companions and herself, "understand that if you help us, you would be losing valuable time—time you would have used for hunting and selling your goods. We are prepared to compensate you both for your time and for all money lost."

Lluava hoped she had not overstepped her authority. The money would have to come from the royal treasury. She did not dare risk a glance at her partner. Yet, if this was what it took to get Apex to agree to go with them, wouldn't it be worth it?

Apex cocked his head to one side in thought. He stared hard at the three men still seated at the table, then back to Lluava and Varren. Yamir was ignored.

"My comrades," Apex responded, with a nod toward the corner table, "will need to be compensated as well."

Lluava let out her breath. She had not even realized she was holding it until now. Fortunately, the unexpected addition of a few more men should not be a problem. Not entirely.

Varren, too, seemed more settled even though the details were not yet finalized. "Everyone will get his fair share in payment as long as he does his part."

There was a long pause in which no one spoke. The only sounds were the slight snoring of the man asleep by the fireplace and the irritating squeak of the bartender's cloth as he wiped down glasses.

"What is it I would be doing?"

Lluava relaxed; Apex was hooked. They pulled up chairs around the small table, and Varren quickly explained the situation and their flimsy but crucial plan.

When he had finished, the younger of the two brothers noted smugly, "Tracking men. Easy enough." Looking back at Apex, he shut his mouth as if realizing he had spoken out of turn.

"Since our lives would be at risk, the price per huntsman will rise," stated Apex.

"You are not hired for combat," responded Varren. "You are a tracker. As I explained, this is only to gather information. In the event of a skirmish, your men are not expected to participate. We have been trained for war." He nodded at Yamir, who seemed glad to finally be acknowledged. "You have not.

"As long as you understand that my comrades and I won't fight," Apex said. "If any confrontation occurs, we will disappear until it is over and reappear only if you win. Regardless, the price rises. Call it security."

Varren did not like being bested in a bargain, and at the rate they had already agreed upon this was nothing short of a swindle. Lluava nudged his foot under the table. Varren begrudgingly agreed, and they settled on a revised fee.

"Then we have an accord," stated Apex. "Now for introductions. This is Austro."

The diminutive man nodded in a way that drew attention to his large ears.

"Those two," Apex said, gesturing to the brothers, "are Wod and Monk."

Lluava was not positive which was which, but she thought Monk was the elder and Wod was the one closer to her own age. How odd, she thought; I wonder what use Apex has for those two humans. They don't appear extraordinary. The young men simply smiled; the younger one even winked at Lluava. She turned back to the huntsman.

Apex finished by saying, "We will meet here in three days—"

"No," Varren interrupted with an edge to his voice. Apex glared, but the prince continued, "We need to leave tomorrow. We only need to gather a few supplies. You can purchase yours tonight, or in the morning if necessary, but we leave tomorrow. Too much time has been wasted already."

Composing himself, Varren turned toward Wod and Monk and returned Apex's feigned hospitality. "It is a pleasure to meet you." Then, gesturing toward his spiky-haired friend, he made their introductions. "This is Yamir. And this is—"

Apex interrupted yet again. "I know who she is. Everyone knows."

Lluava expected to hear the name Theri or Issaura slip past his chapped lips.

"She is Lluava Kargen. The prince's military partner."

Choosing not to respond, Lluava waited as Varren reclaimed the conversation.

"We have three others traveling with us: the Lady Rosalyn; her betrothed, Talos; and his military partner, Byron. I do not expect that to affect your decision."

Without conferring with his companions, Apex said, "We will meet at the forest's edge, just beyond the town's northern gate, when the sun is higher than the trees. Agreed?"

Varren stretched out his hand. "Agreed."

Once the two men had shaken hands, Varren led the way out of The Crooked Pine, leaving their new partners to discuss this unusual turn of events. Outside, Lluava made sure to pull up her hood. The sudden change of temperature was jarring, and she hated the cold. Hopefully, Onyx had found a warm place to roost.

Not far from the main square, they were hailed by Byron, who was accompanied by Talos and Rosalyn. His look of discouragement was quickly replaced with pleasant surprise once Varren told him the news.

"We found Apex, and he, along with three companions, has agreed to work with us for a price."

"So Apex and his friends will be joining us in the morning," reiterated Byron, as if saying the words aloud would make it seem more believable. By the tone of his voice, Lluava realized he had not expected his plan to actually work. She was thankful it had.

Byron mumbled almost inaudibly, "Apex doesn't have companions."

Yamir, always the skeptic, had obviously missed Byron's statement. "I thought you said Apex worked alone."

"As far as I know, he does," acknowledged Byron. "The truth of the matter is that there is not much known about him, except he is the best at what he does."

"Tomorrow...." Varren's voice seemed distant, as did his train of thought. He was gazing away from them toward Yorrick Forest. Even in the dark, Lluava could imagine the gnarled trees twisting around one another.

"Tomorrow we head into the Outlands. We need to rest, save our strength for what is to come. Byron," he turned back to the blond-haired soldier, "where does your mother live?"

"She owns a little farm west of Bail. A twenty-minute walk. Tops."

Varren nodded. "Lead the way."

As they followed Byron out of the town, Lluava's thoughts shifted from the unshakable familiarity of the place to the unknown that lurked beyond Elysia's boarders. The Outlands. She knew stories, had heard whispers, about what lay outside Elysia's protected boundaries: ferocious beasts, wild men who periodically attacked the perimeters, uninhabitable terrain. As unfavorable as Apex and his fellows appeared, she decided that she was glad to have them come along.

A soft glow of candlelight signaled to the group that they were approaching the small homestead. *Humble* might be the first word to come to mind to describe the house. Yet even in the gloom, a warmth enveloped it. Above the stoop, a lantern illuminated the unpainted door. Before Byron reached it, the door was flung wide open. Two cats darted out from behind the dark silhouette that blocked their entry. One of the streaking felines almost tripped Yamir as it flew past.

"Byron! Oh, my boy," a woman's voice trembled into the dark. "You're home!"

"Mom!" Byron sprang forward and threw his arms around the woman. The others waited in the gloom as Byron and his mother embraced for the first time in months.

As soon as Byron released her, she ushered them all inside. "Come in.

Come in, all of you. Come in by the fire. Let's get all of you out of the cold."

As they stepped into the small abode, Byron collected their cloaks and introduced his friends to his mother. She gave each of them a warm hug.

"And this is Lluava Kargen," Byron said as Lluava pulled down her hood. "Daughter of Haliden Kargen."

Enfolded in the arms of Byron's mother, Lluava suddenly missed her own family intensely.

The woman, who shared her son's blond hair and kind features, paused for a moment. "Hello, Lluava." Turning to the group, she said with a smile, "Please call me Eleanor, and make yourselves at home. Any friends of my son are welcome here."

Byron motioned for them to warm themselves near the fireplace. His mother busied herself in the kitchen. Soon the entire group was seated around the small table, happily eating a tasty stew.

Lluava thought it was interesting that Byron's mother had not asked them about the war or why they were there, apparently just overjoyed to have her son with her, if only for a night. Lluava felt that she at least should have inquired. Wasn't the woman curious? Or did she fear the answers? Her husband had been killed during his military duty. Her husband. Byron's father. The man who had been the military partner of Lluava's own father.

Returning her spoon to her bowl, Lluava probed gently, "Did my father ever bring me here while he was on tour?"

Eleanor lowered her own spoon. "Children are not allowed along on such journeys."

"Did he—" Lluava began again and then stopped. Her question was foolish. What was wrong with her?

"Did he what, dear?"

Lluava asked, "Did he ever live here?"

Their hostess blinked, and then laughed. Her eyes sparkled just like her son's. "My dear, I was very close to your parents, especially your mother. We grew up together, you know. Where did you think Haliden and Maessa met?"

Lluava's eyes widened, and her mouth opened in surprise.

Eleanor studied the teen's face for a moment and then continued, "Your parents were dear friends of mine. I was actually Maessa's bridesmaid. Ah, when we were young... I wish they hadn't had to move so soon afterward. There was no time even to celebrate their union, but your grandfather needed help with the farm. How is Giam doing?"

The heat of tears welled up. Lluava forced herself to regain control. "He died this summer."

"I'm very sorry to hear that."

Lluava returned to her earlier question. "So I never visited? But did I live here when I was little?"

All of this would have made sense if only Eleanor had not shaken her head no. Byron's mother looked consolingly at the daughter of her friends. "I'm sorry if that's not what you wanted to hear."

That night Lluava struggled to sleep, but she could not still her thoughts. How could she be familiar with this town? Knowing that she was about to embark on another adventure only increased her restlessness.

As morning's light encroached on the horizon, the group hurried to purchase the wares they would need on their trip. Before leaving, Lluava said farewell to Byron's mother; she hoped to see her again. Then she followed her friends up the road.

For the most part, they found what they required. Talos retrieved their horses from the stables, and they made their way to the north gate. By the crooked wooden fence, four figures waited with horses picketed.

Good, Lluava thought. Let this begin. Then she slowed; a quick whiff of the crisp air caused the fine hairs on the back of her neck to stand erect. One of the four was not supposed to be there. She placed a hand against Varren's shoulder. They brought their own horses to a halt and stopped at a distance.

"What's wrong?" called out Austro.

Lluava was certain. One figure was different. One was a woman. Glancing at Varren, she saw he also looked leery. Was this a setup?

Varren's voice called out, "Where is Apex?" Pointing to the woman, he then demanded, "Who is she?"

Perched atop the fencing was a woman, slim and strong. Her facial features seemed timeless, making it impossible to guess her age. On the other hand, her long hair, tightly braided all the way down her back in a no-nonsense manner, was silvery gray flecked with strands of black. Lluava wondered whether she was older or just prematurely gray, as Austro appeared to be. The woman waited, quietly observing those approaching her.

In his small yet authoritative voice, Austro replied, "This is Mila. She is with us."

Looking displeased, Varren stated flatly, "You did not say anything about another person. Who else should I know about?"

"No others," Austro replied hastily. Lluava could not tell if his quick reply was a result of nervousness or part of his personality.

"And Apex?" Lluava asked again after reassessing the current head count. The tracker was the only one missing.

Austro's eyes shifted between Lluava and Varren. Saving Austro from responding, Mila volunteered, "I'll get him. You know as well as I that he should have been here already."

"I'll go with you," Lluava said. As she passed her partner, she gave him a look that expressed her distrust of the situation. He nodded, and Lluava followed Mila back into Bail.

After several fruitless inquiries, they were finally directed to a small barn owned by one of the more agreeable shopkeepers. A grumbling snore could be heard from the back stall. Mila strode toward the sound, Lluava at her heels. Though Mila was shorter than Lluava, the taller teen had to walk quickly to keep up.

In the dirty stall was Apex, nestled between two large swine. Lluava did not have to guess what had happened; the smell the man gave off was enough. The pungent tang of stale mead was so strong that Lluava's eyes began to water. The odor almost covered up the stench emitted by the hogs. A partially empty bottle, the remnants of the culprit, was clutched in one hand. With every rise and fall of Apex's chest, sour droplets sloshed out, only to be licked up noisily by one of the hogs.

Lluava was disgusted.

Mila was indifferent. Shrugging, she turned and walked away, while Lluava began to fume quietly about the mess they were in. How could he do this? Didn't he understand the importance of this mission? Didn't he have any respect? Was this the man they were supposed to rely on? The man responsible for the fate of Elysia? On the contrary: this filthy, swill-muddled drunk might well be responsible for the downfall of the kingdom itself. There had to be someone else. Anyone else.

Over her shoulder, a bucket of cold water was hurtled onto the slumbering man. A moment later, a string of profanities slipped past Apex's lips. As he leaped to his feet, his stall-mates ran squealing out the door. Focusing on the pair of women, Apex's face blazed red with fury.

"To the seven hells with you!" he bellowed.

Mila tossed the empty water pail at Apex's feet. "You're late," she stated, then turned and left again. All the chastising Lluava had intended to do disappeared. She decided the safest route was to follow Mila. Well beyond the gate to the barn, the pair could still hear Apex shouting insults.

Before anyone could ask, Mila announced to the waiting group, "Apex will be here momentarily."

Lluava wished she could leave it like that, but she needed to warn Varren about what she had seen. Once she had, his mood darkened. "I will deal with him."

When Apex arrived, he seemed to have come to his senses. Although he still reeked of the night before, he was much more alert, and his mood had mellowed. However, there was no word of apology on his lips. He pushed past the others and stopped at the edge of the forest.

Varren approached him. "There is one rule I must insist upon: no alcohol is permitted on this journey. We must all have our wits about us. Is this clear?"

Apex seemed to expect as much. He replied offhandedly, "You're the prince. You make the rules."

Varren studied the lead huntsman for a long while before stepping back, satisfied. As Talos mounted his steed, he asked, "Apex, where is your horse?"

Lluava had not noticed they were one horse short, not counting the two pack animals.

Apex replied coolly, "I don't need one." He turned to face the woods, then looked back over his shoulder at the others. "Ready to enter the Yorrick Forest?"

Lluava realized she was nodding, although Apex could not actually see her.

The huntsman led them onto a path barely worthy of a deer. She and Varren had chosen to ride side by side a few paces behind Apex.

The village was not yet out of sight when Lluava's horse flicked its ears warily, spiking Lluava's senses. The animal tried to sidestep, and she had to force it to move forward. As she did, a low growl rumbled from the scrubby brush in front of them.

Apex lifted his right arm, signaling everyone to halt. A creature crept into sight. A wolf-dog, teeth gleaming in a snarl, blocked their path. Its ears were flattened against its head, while its raised hackles exaggerated its size.

They had barely crossed into the Yorrick Forest, and the woods had let loose a beast upon them! The wolf mix took another step closer, snapping and snarling. It locked eyes with Apex, who was closest.

Lluava began to reach into her travel pack for the Claws. She moved extremely slowly so as not to draw attention and aggravate the animal. Yet none of that mattered. The beast's only focus was Apex. Before she could react, the creature leaped at Apex's throat.

Chapter 21

A "Hare-y" Situation

Although only seconds passed, for Lluava events unfolded in slow motion. There was a scream; someone scrambled for cover behind her. High in the forest canopy, Onyx screeched. Varren's mount shied, and the prince sprang to the ground.

The wolf mix leaped at Apex's throat, aimed at the jugular. The huntsman deflected the attack and retaliated, grappling with the animal in a fierce embrace. Then he stumbled back, but too late. The wolf-dog was at his face.

Apex's bristly features were being covered with a film of saliva. The animal was licking him.

Lluava's jaw dropped. What was going on?

Shoving the dog away, Apex smirked at his thunderstruck observers. He patted the wolf-mutt on its head and said, "This is Sköll."

With that, the huntsman turned to face the forest once again. "Move out," he barked and began walking forward, the canine by his side.

Over the next few days, the unspoken distrust between the two groups became more apparent. The huntsmen kept to themselves, refusing to join in any conversation struck up by Lluava or her friends. Sometimes one of the hunters would disappear for a time, to return with some small game hanging from his mount. At night, the two groups camped separately, though still within earshot. This was unintentional at first but quickly became routine.

To add to her discomfort, Lluava's keen ears had picked up the whispered words, "being followed." For no clear reason, Varren and the others were unable to shake off their unease. The huntsmen did not seem worried, although Apex pushed them deeper into the forest as quickly as possible. He was not one to take risks.

On the evening of the third day, Lluava was collecting firewood for their camp. Varren had assigned each person a task. This not only allowed everyone to pitch in but also offered much-needed distraction. Spending so much time worrying about their plans and their current situation had drained Lluava's energy. She was relieved that Varren had established order and provided some direction.

Lluava was gathering a small bundle of kindling when a rustle of leaves alerted her. She tensed. Cocking her head to one side, she strained to hear the sounds again. After a moment, there was another rustle.

Slowly placing the kindling on the ground, Lluava took a step closer to the area from which the sounds had come. The noise stopped.

Was someone—or something—following them? Had she scared them away?

Several minutes passed before the leaves rustled again. The teen held her breath. She knew she should return and alert the others, but her instincts said otherwise. Her curiosity was aroused.

Taking another step forward, she gripped Issaura's Claws tightly. If something was going to attack her, she would be ready. Slowly, pausing every few steps, she began to creep up on the unseen entity.

Crouching low behind an old pine, Lluava at last glimpsed the noisemaker. Twenty feet away was a large Arctic hare. She remained still and marveled at the animal. The hare rested with its back to her as it scratched a brown patch behind its left ear, flicking off small clumps of fur that drifted in the still air.

It would be a magnificent specimen once it fully shed its summer coat. Glancing behind her, Lluava realized it would be best to bring back dinner. The travelers had few resources, and those they had needed to be conserved.

Rolling her shoulders to loosen them up, she watched as the hare changed position and hopped closer. Lluava felt her pupils narrow into daggers.

Just a little closer, she thought. Come on, you're almost here. As she imagined the taste of rabbit, her mouth began to fill with saliva.

The animal inched forward again.

Lluava shifted form, then froze. Unfortunately, the hare picked up the snap of a twig as the tigress's front paws met the earth. Lluava wished her dual form's large size had not disturbed the leaf litter.

The feline dropped to the ground. She watched the hare's ears move in all directions as it sat on its haunches. It hopped forward one final time.

It was within reach.

Lluava leaped.

The hare began to *shift*.

In midair, all Lluava could do was retract her claws before she landed on top of her screaming victim. Reverting to her human form, she untangled herself from writhing limbs.

A man abruptly sprang to his feet, his face an angry red. The putrid smell of fear-induced musk tainted the air around him.

"You tried to eat me!" blustered Austro.

"I…uh…" Lluava fumbled.

"You tried to eat me!"

"I didn't…I didn't know." Lluava was mortified.

The little man glared at her. She could sense his contempt. Her face grew hot despite the chill air. Her mind still struggled to connect all the dots. "But you're a rabbit!"

"Am I supposed to be something else?"

"But you're a *prey animal*," Lluava tried to explain her shock, "and a *huntsman*."

"So?" Austro huffed as he brushed the dirt from his clothes.

"You hunt animals, even though—"

Lluava stopped. She felt ridiculous. This whole experience was extremely embarrassing.

Austro scowled up at her for another moment before his face softened a bit. "Being a prey animal allows me to think the way other prey animals do. Helps me catch 'em."

She nodded but still found the whole situation bizarre.

Austro turned to leave, then stopped. "Next time, try to make sure your meal isn't another Theriomorph."

Lluava felt her face grow redder.

When Austro had gone, she continued to chastise herself for not trying to sense the presence of others of her kind. Feeling sick to her stomach, Lluava sat down and leaned her back against the flaking bark of a pine. She closed her eyes and took slow, steady breaths to calm herself.

"Is it nap time already?"

Although Varren's remark was meant humorously, Lluava's grimace caused the prince to lose his pleasant smile. "Is something wrong?" he inquired.

"I almost killed Austro." Just saying those words made Lluava want to vomit.

"What are you talking about?"

"Austro's a rabbit. I didn't know that until I almost killed him for dinner."

Varren's sudden burst of laughter caused her to blink. Varren dropped his own bundle of wood to hold his sides.

"It's not funny," she hissed.

Varren wiped his tearing eyes. "Theriomorphs hunting each other! I did not know you could do that."

"Typically, we don't." Lluava still could not find the humor in this.

Varren plopped down next to her. "I apologize. That was insensitive. It is just that this situation is almost too ridiculous to be true."

Lluava tried to visualize the scene as if she were an outside observer. She was reluctant to admit that she, too, found it ironic, if only in a sick way.

Varren continued, "I have never thought about it before, but can you recognize each other for what you truly are in your dual forms?"

"Yes," acknowledged Lluava. Tapping her chest, she said, "There is a feeling, an inner sense, if you will, that allows us to register another Theriomorph close by."

"A feeling?"

"Yes. It's hard to explain. I can do it. My entire race can. It does take a bit of concentration, but one can tell the difference between animal and Theriomorph. It's not very specific, though. We can't tell what form they are taking, just their proximity." Lluava could tell from Varren's eyes that he was still a little baffled. There were some things that simply could not be explained to humans.

She ended by saying, "I just wasn't paying attention. I won't let that happen again."

Varren leaned back against the trunk and stretched out his legs. "You might have something here. This feels oddly pleasant."

"I wasn't sitting down to relax," huffed Lluava. "I needed to think."

"Well, it feels nice just to sit." Varren pointed in front of them. "Look at the colors raining down from the sky."

Brilliant leaves were falling, each at its own leisurely rate. The small, varicolored mounds that had piled up nearby reminded Lluava of her father's old paint palettes. She missed him.

"You are so serious. What are you thinking about?" inquired Varren.

"My father," she said. "He used to paint beautiful landscapes like these."

"I thought your father built furniture when he was not on active duty."

"He did. Painting was for pleasure."

Varren turned to her. His eyes were soft, comforting. "What did *you* do for fun, before all of this?"

"I don't remember," admitted Lluava sorrowfully. Not more than half a year had passed, yet her life in Rivendale seemed ages ago. All that remained were memories that either made her sad or made her miss everything she had given up.

"Hmmm." Varren pretended detachment. "Lluava the Sullen. Lluava the Brooding. They just do not seem to fit. Or," he said, cocking his head to one side, "maybe they do."

Lluava cracked a wry smile. "Oh?"

Her partner spoke in a more meaningful tone. "When people forget to appreciate the little things in life, everything becomes quite dull."

A yellow leaf landed on Lluava's face, and Varren chuckled once more. In response, the young woman grabbed a handful of leaves and tossed them at him. He blinked and brushed away the litter. All of a sudden, Lluava found herself laughing.

"Oh, well, two can play at that game." The prince grinned as he scooped up more ammunition. Leaping to their feet, the pair hurled leaves at one another until the whole atmosphere seemed to pour down warm hues.

Varren's smile became mischievous.

"What are you up to?" Lluava demanded, but her partner remained silent. Suddenly he lunged forward. She squealed and darted into the forest, Varren right on her tail. Dodging saplings and circumnavigating trees, their dance through the woods left a trail of laughter in their wake.

Suddenly Lluava stumbled. As she tried to right herself, Varren caught her arm. However, before he could shout, "I got you," he slipped, and the pair tumbled into a pile of leaves.

When was the last time either of them had laughed with such abandon? After a few moments, Lluava noticed that Varren had gone silent. She turned to face him. He lay beside her, so close that their noses almost touched. His breath smelled of rosemary and fennel; his tender blue eyes studied her as if he were trying to memorize every detail of her face.

Lluava's heartbeat quickened. She sensed that his had, too. Varren carefully removed a leaf entangled in her long hair. She relished his warm touch as his hand brushed her face, and she reached over to stroke the side of his jaw. The day-old stubble made her fingertips tingle.

Did he just lean in? Lluava wondered. She knew the prince could not show outward affection for her in public, but here, alone, maybe... Lluava's breath caught in her chest. She slowly leaned closer.

Suddenly an odd prickling arose at the back of her neck. Something was not right. A shadow fell over both of them. Varren turned, and Lluava followed his gaze.

At their feet towered Apex. His features were blank; even his eyes did not reveal what he was thinking. How long had he been watching them? For a moment, no one moved.

Then Apex spoke. "The fires need more wood." He turned and left as silently as he had arrived.

Varren sighed and helped Lluava to her feet. They retraced their steps to collect the wood they had dropped.

***

Back at camp, Mila had returned from the forest, the carcass of a large deer draped over her horse. Stopping her steed directly in front of Talos, she threw the dead animal down at his feet.

"For you," she said with a grin. She nudged her mount and continued to her own camp. Talos's body stiffened. He was obviously upset.

154

Wondering what Talos would do, Lluava hurried to stand next to him. "She may not know you're a stag."

Talos's grim expression did not change as he began to butcher their dinner.

After an unusually quiet meal, Lluava turned to Varren. "Should we thank them for our food?" What she really wanted to ask was if he thought Mila had been passing on a warning. Varren wiped off his plate with a rag. "Yes, we should."

The huntsmen's camp was almost a reflection of their own. Cooking meat crackled on spits; mounts were picketed nearby; saddle packs and blankets indicated beds. But unlike their camp, this area was all but abandoned. Only the low growl from Sköll alerted Lluava and Varren that somebody was keeping watch.

Apex was sprawled on the ground. An untreated deer hide was rolled up as a pillow under his head. His half-open eyes observed the amber flames that licked at the back of his upcoming dinner. His breath made Lluava wrinkle her nose.

Lluava narrowed her eyes in disapproval as Varren spoke. "Where is Mila? We want to thank her for her generosity."

The huntsman lifted the bottle he had been holding and took an overloud gulp, confirming Lluava's suspicions. He answered in a slurred voice, "If you don't see her, she ain't here."

"What is that?" Varren's voice was flat as he indicated the bottle. She could see the prince wanted to give their tracker the benefit of the doubt.

"Somethin' that'll put the coarsest hair even on your baby-smooth chest."

Varren's anger sizzled in the air. "I told you that there would be no alcohol on this mission."

Apex swirled the contents of the bottle before taking another swig. "You have no authority here."

"I am the Crown Prince of Elysia!"

The huntsman's eyes seemed to glow like the fire before him. "Look around you, Prince. You are not in Elysia anymore. You hold no power here."

Varren's eyes widened. It seemed he was about to speak his mind, but he spun on his heel and headed back to their own camp.

Apex watched him go and raised his bottle. "Now, I can drink to that."

"You disgust me," hissed Lluava.

"At least I'm not some human's pet."

Lluava felt her face flush, and she growled. How dare he say such things? And then she, too, stormed off before she could chase away their only chance at finding the band of large Raiders.

That night, Lluava shivered beneath her saddle blanket. The coarse material could not ward off the increasing chill in the air. Unable to sleep, she allowed her mind to wander. She thought of the giant Raiders they pursued. What would happen when they found them? If they really were anything like the monstrosity she had faced, any mistake could be their last.

And what about that first massive marauder? Why had he called her Theri? The name reminded her of her grandfather's words to her as she had prepared to head off to war. She knew that she physically resembled the goddess. Nevertheless, any notion that she was Theri, Issaura, the Lady of the Night and Moon, was entirely ridiculous. Surely if that were true, she would know. Surely she would have exceptional abilities, wouldn't she?

Nothing supernatural or extraordinary had ever happened to her. She was a simple farm girl from a small seaside village. Yes, she was partner to the prince and traveling through a supposedly haunted wood, but this honor was not an accident. She had earned it through hard work and her own merit. Nothing more.

So why did she remember Bail if she had never been there? Maybe Byron's mother was wrong. Maybe Lluava had visited the town when she was young. Yet that would not explain how she knew Apex and recognized his eyes. No, she really didn't know him, but that sense of familiarity was unshakable.

Before the sun rose, Lluava found Apex waking his comrades. "May I have a word with you?" she asked.

Apex did not turn his head in her direction. "You are paying for my time."

Without offering, Lluava began to fold his blanket. She asked, "When we first met in The Crooked Pine, did you feel anything strange when you saw me?"

Apex to turned to her as he contemplated her question, and Lluava wondered if she had explained herself clearly. "I mean, did you recognize me? Did you think that we had met each other before?"

"Have you been into the drink?" he responded as he inspected the contents of his half-empty bottle.

"I just thought—"

"Is this some kind of game?" asked Apex sourly. "I take my work seriously, as should you."

Before Lluava had time to protest, Mila strode up and announced, "We are ready to head out." She gave Lluava a sidelong glance before steering Apex away.

In the late afternoon, Mila rode up beside Lluava's mount and said, "Hunt with me."

Lluava was so surprised that the female huntsman had spoken freely to her that she almost failed to reply, "No thanks." Whatever Mila's intentions were, Lluava preferred to stay among her friends, where it was safe. The huntress did not seem offended. Instead, she handed Lluava her reins.

"Hold my horse."

After Lluava had tentatively secured the other animal to her own, Mila slipped off her mount and shifted into a spectacular snow leopard. The silvery feline slipped into the deepening shadows of the forest and disappeared from sight.

Barely an hour later, the sleek snow leopard bounded up to the caravan, ears flat against her head. She glided up to Apex who was, as usual, leading the way. Lluava and Varren were not far behind him.

"Our pursuers are close by. They have not been shaken," she announced.

Varren did not comment upon the lack of open information; rather, he inquired, "How many?"

Apex nodded to Mila to continue.

"Several. They are coming in at different angles."

As she shifted into her human form, Apex shouted to those in the caravan. "Halt! All ears toward me!"

The huntsmen and Varren's comrades crowded around as close as they could considering the numerous horses.

"This is where we split up," Apex announced. He turned to Varren. "As was our agreement, my comrades and I are not here to fight. There is a ridge just ahead where you can make your stand. He then indicated the other huntsmen. "We are leaving and will return only if you…survive." His last word hung in the air.

Talos did not like the idea. "If you stand with us, we will all have a better chance to defend ourselves."

"No, Talos. Apex is right," Varren acknowledged unhappily. "Our agreement excluded the trackers from engaging in battle." Varren looked Apex in the eye. "I am a man of my word."

"I had no doubt," replied Apex. He paused briefly and then led his comrades into the forest.

Varren quickly moved those who remained to the top of the small hill and positioned each person carefully so that all angles were covered. Within their tight circle, they waited with weapons ready. Rosalyn stood to Talos's side and slightly behind him. Lluava knew the young man would protect Rosalyn if he could.

Who were their pursuers? Lluava knew the question was on everyone's mind. Had the Raiders realized they were being followed and decided to attack first? Had Colonel Bern sent troops to force Varren to return to the capital?

They did not have long to wonder. The sounds of incoming movement erupted from three different directions, just as Mila had warned. Three figures charged up the slope—not figures so much as creatures. Wolves!

Chapter 22

The Swan's Song

The animals were upon them, a hungry pack hunting for their supper. Their leader quickly closed the gap. Large and dark, this beast was different. Before Lluava could say a word, Derrick transformed before them.

As she let out a sigh of relief, a new fear took hold. Had Derrick come to send them back? From the numerous howls in the distance, his men outnumbered Varren's three to one. Varren looked hard at Derrick. "We will not be returning."

Derrick's grin was wolfish. "I hoped you would say that."

"Then why have you come?"

Two other wolves loped up to the group. Standing behind Derrick, they shifted and awaited his orders as more wolves arrived.

Still grinning, the dark-skinned man announced, "We are here to help. Whatever you're up to, we want in." Derrick's eyes glistened with excitement. "You're after that band of Raiders. You have to be."

Varren was quiet for a moment. Talos and Byron exchanged looks. Onyx gave a deep rasping call and alighted on Lluava's shoulder.

Lluava felt the impulse to speak. "So, you really are not here to send us back?"

"I have come to offer Prince Varren my assistance. You see, we have a plan." Derrick stopped abruptly to read the prince's expression. He was baiting them, that much Lluava knew; but she had to admit the idea was enticing.

Varren gave in. "What is this plan of yours?" he asked tentatively.

"Well, first, I have to admit that deceiving the officers with that little trick of yours was highly surprising. I didn't think you had it in you."

Derrick relaxed his pose, and Lluava followed suit. Varren continued to stand tensely.

"After they realized you were missing, it was quickly determined that you were tracking those marauders." Looking over the group, Derrick continued, "Selecting so few to travel with you could only mean that you intend not to attack but only to follow. Am I right so far?"

Yamir, still clutching his throwing quills, countered, "So what if you are?"

"Well, I was hoping you would clarify your intentions for me."

"The purpose," Varren explained, "is to gather as much information as we can about the motives of that band of Raiders. If they are planning to attack, where and when?"

One of the two men behind Derrick whispered to the other. Derrick seemed pleased. "That is exactly what I needed to hear." He nodded to his comrades, who shifted into their canine forms and sprinted down the slope.

Varren quickly raised his sword and positioned it level with Derrick's throat. "We will *not* be heading back."

"May I finish?" asked Derrick as he eyed the sleek blade. When Varren did not lower the sword, Derrick took a step back. "As I was saying, I had hoped that this was your plan, for it dovetails perfectly with my strategy." With a respectful nod to the prince, he went on, "You see, Your Majesty, once you have gathered your information, you will need a quick and efficient means of sending the news to Elysia. If there were an attack, how long do you think it would actually take the soldiers to gather and position themselves where they were needed?"

The expression on Varren's face indicated to Lluava that he had been pondering that very question.

Derrick continued, "My men and I have developed a perfect solution."

Before anyone could get a word out, Derrick let loose a long, piercing howl. A moment later, a response trailed from the south.

"We can hear each other's calls several miles away. We will position ourselves so that we form a line of communication between you and Elysia and thus eliminate that wasted travel time."

Varren lowered his weapon. "Thank you. I must apologize for not trusting you."

"Wait," went on Derrick, "there's more. Lieutenant Vidrick Bern is leading a troop of his own men, accompanied by our human counterparts, along Elysia's northern border. They will alter their position based upon my nightly reports. As I said, you will need soldiers ready to fight whenever and wherever those brutes decide to attack."

"The lieutenant is willing to help us?" Lluava was as baffled as her friends.

Derrick smiled, exposing all his sharp, white teeth. "He said he believes in his future king."

"Thank you, Derrick," Varren said earnestly. He placed his hand on the dark-skinned man's shoulder. "Now let us go and find these Raiders."

***

Apex and his comrades had shown no emotion at the news of Derrick's participation. Sköll was a different story. That evening, the wolf-mutt continuously whimpered at Apex's feet, his tail beating against the huntsman's leg. The dog would eye Derrick and sniff the air before turning his scrappy head up to catch Apex's attention. The huntsman gave Sköll reassuring pats, but the dog would not leave his side.

Derrick did not question the subtle distance between the two parties. Begging exhaustion, he settled into Varren's camp and retired early.

Next morning, Lluava watched Derrick shift and energetically race ahead of the group. Without a mount, he had to travel in his dual form. No wonder he had been tired! Sköll continued to eye the strange black wolf, though he had ceased his whimpering. The morning crept on sluggishly. Even at midday, the sun had still not checked the cold. Lluava clutched her cloak tightly about her. By sitting at an angle that made her look like a hunchbacked crone, she found a small measure of warmth.

Mila's voice rang out behind her. "You should travel in your dual form." The huntress tethered her mount to one of the pack horses trudging near the rear, and shifted.

"Why?"

"The cold will help build up your winter coat. Out here, you will need it."

Lluava considered Mila's words. In the south, it was never cold enough to warrant consideration. As a tiger, with thick fur to insulate her she would be quite warm.

"Thanks for the advice," Lluava replied earnestly. Maybe Mila was not as frigid as she had first appeared.

"Hunt with me." Mila's statement was more a command than a request.

Lluava wanted to trust this woman, to learn more about her. She explained briefly to Varren what she was going to do, dismounted, and handed him her reins. Then she loped after Mila, and the two felines disappeared into the woods.

As they prowled through the underbrush, Lluava reciprocated Mila's overture.

"What made you associate yourself with those huntsmen? You seem capable enough on your own, and they're not the warmest bunch."

Mila cast her a sidelong glance. The end of her tail twitched in agitation. "I would not if I had a choice."

That statement struck Lluava as odd. "You don't like them?"

"I prefer to be alone."

"Well, why don't you?" Lluava paused and slowed down as she caught the scent of partridge upwind. "Hunt alone, that is."

Crouching low, Mila explained, "I can hunt as well as any man, but men don't want to purchase goods from a female, Theriomorph or not."

Lluava's initial inclination was to denounce the stupidity of that situation, yet she was well aware of the inequality of genders. "So, you work for Apex because he can sell your goods for you?"

"Nobody works for Apex. However, I do prefer to have a male market my wares for me."

They were approaching several birds hiding in a thicket of briars. Unexpectedly, the wind changed. Suddenly, feathers exploded into the sky. Their prey had escaped.

But not quite. A silvery form vaulted into the air and in a single bite seized hold of the male bird, bringing him to the ground. As Mila spat out her prize, Lluava silently chastised herself for not capturing its mate. Though Mila said nothing, Lluava wondered if the woman was disappointed in her.

As they made their way back to their comrades, Lluava resumed her previous inquiry. "Okay. Austro understands prey animals, and you hunt and kill as well as anyone, so why do you travel with those humans? Humans have such dull senses."

"True. Humans are an amazing species to have survived this long with such poor abilities," acknowledged Mila as she spat out downy feathers. "Wod and Monk are different."

"How so?" Now Lluava was thoroughly curious.

"Monk is remarkably skilled with the bow. He can shoot an animal over a hundred yards away with perfect accuracy." Watching a single plume float to earth, Mila continued, "Wod, on the other hand, is an expert trapper. His contraptions always snare a remarkable bounty."

"Wow." Lluava discovered a newfound appreciation of the brothers.

"Growing up in the Beltline forces one to develop such skills."

"The Beltline?" The question was rhetorical. Lluava knew the Beltline was the band of the Yorrick Forest that stretched from Elysia's borders up to the Borren mountain range. To live in the Beltline meant that...

"They are Outlanders!" Lluava could not help but exclaim. Another flutter of wings could be heard in the distance.

Mila seemed to nod her head without actually doing so. She then agreed, "Yes. Have you never met one before?"

"No." Lluava answered abruptly. "I'm an Elysian. Why would I deal with—"

Mila finished her sentence. "Someone from outside the kingdom? Isn't that a bit prejudiced?"

Lluava closed her mouth. Was she really that narrow-minded? Hadn't she just judged the brothers based on their place of birth?

"But Outlanders raid Elysian villages," she protested.

"Not all Outlanders are the same. Some are born here; others choose to live out here."

Lluava thought of Apex. Was he one of the latter?

"Wait until we reach Tinder's Keep. You will meet plenty more Outlanders."

"What? No. We are following the Raider's trail."

Mila's eyes sparkled. "If that were the case, why would we have veered off their track a day ago?"

Lluava's eyes widened as Mila stretched in a leisurely way. The snow leopard continued, "If you want to find the prince, he and the others are in that direction." She nodded. "I am going to continue hunting. I will return with no fewer than three birds."

Lluava quickly excused herself and bounded off in search of Varren. When she found him, she quickly shifted and then explained what Mila had told her. He was far from thrilled as he passed her horse back to her.

Cantering up to Apex, Varren positioned his mount to block the huntsman's path.

"Why are we not trailing the Raiders?" shouted Varren.

"Tinder is the last stop for supplies."

"We have already stocked up on all we need for this mission. We need to continue on."

Apex grinned. "Some goods cannot be packed."

"Wha—" Lluava was about to ask what he meant when she remembered the painted women in the capital. She shivered. "Uck," she gagged out.

Unperturbed, Apex continued, "Would you deny the men one last night in a *warm* bed?"

"There is a time and place for everything," acknowledged Varren. "But for now, we return to tracking the enemy. That is our first priority."

"If that's the way you want it," sighed Apex unconvincingly. "Had I known, I wouldn't have led you this far. Tinder's Keep is just over the next hill." He pointed ahead of them. "It would make the perfect resting place tonight."

"Humph." Varren, outmaneuvered, voiced his reluctant consent. "Very well. One night."

"One night," reiterated Apex, his eyes sparkling.

Just as Apex had said, Tinder's Keep was nestled behind the next hill. Late evening lanterns, already hung outside many of the buildings, rocked gently in the breeze. The village was small even to Lluava's eye. There was a handful of houses. Several were attached to a few structures built of sturdy wood. A stable contained an assortment of barnyard beasts. Nearby was the trading post, which doubled as the tavern if the name on the hanging sign were to be trusted: The Tankard. Directly across stood the largest building in the village, The Lion's Pride.

Studying the iconic feline silhouette carved into the tavern's sign, Lluava again recalled the painted women. She swallowed bile as she forced herself to follow the huntsmen, who were entering The Tankard.

Wod, seeing her reluctance, encouraged her, "Come on, Lluava. I want you to meet my family."

Wod's family. Lluava could not help but feel unsettled, first about working with Outlanders and now staying with them. They didn't abide by the kingdom's laws. That's why they lived in this wilderness. And hadn't Outlanders been involved in occasional skirmishes on the borderlands?

Lluava left Onyx to preen himself in a nearby tree and sulkily entered the tavern. The smell of heated mead sweetened the warm air. The room seemed rather commonplace, although she had never seen a bar in the center of the room before. However, she did not make a habit of frequenting these establishments.

Suddenly, she was pulled into an enormous hug. Her body automatically tensed when her feet left the ground. As quickly as she had been grabbed up, Lluava was plopped down in front of a large, smiling man.

"Lluava," Wod began the introductions. "This is my father." The balding man smiled pleasantly, as did the homely woman hovering next to him. "And this is my mother."

"Come here, my girl," the woman said, tugging Lluava to her side. "You must be thirsty. Elsa, Lanie, a round for everyone."

A half-dozen young women ranging in age from twelve to their middle twenties were scattered around the room. They shared the same features as Monk and Wod. The two girls managing the bar were already pulling down mugs of various sizes.

The family's business was obviously booming; the tavern was crowded. As the drinks were dispensed, Monk jumped up onto a table and pulled Wod up beside him.

"Time for a song!" the older brother roared. The crowd cheered. Soon Monk and Wod were belting out lyrics from a well-known song and stomping out its foot-tapping rhythm. The brothers, though not musically gifted themselves, ignited the room in joyful frivolity. Women clapped, men stamped, and soon everyone was dancing.

After a time, Monk glanced at his family's new guests and asked, "Will one of you sing us a song?"

Wod added, "Why not Lluava?"

"I don't sing." Lluava felt her cheeks flush. Why did he have to put her on the spot?

Monk pointed over Wod's shoulder. "What about you? Rosalyn?"

Rosalyn looked around. "I have not sung in quite a while. Forgive me if I am a tad off key, but one Theriomorph song comes to mind. I remember it being sung to me when I was little."

"Here, here," Wod encouraged as he and Monk helped her up onto the table with them, then stepped down themselves.

Taking a moment to clear her throat, Rosalyn began to sing, softly at first:

> *Red sky at morning,*
> *The gods say 'Warning.'*
> *Red sky at night,*
> *Delight.*

Her voice flowed smooth as silk. Lluava was not the only person in the room who was captivated.

> *The fire is burning,*
> *A heart still yearning,*
> *Hopes of the people take*
> *Flight.*

> *Morning sky red*
> *Tis' time to dread*
> *Red sky at night,*
> *Delight.*

> *Children are crying,*
> *A people dying,*
> *The fears of the family*
> *Affright.*

Rosalyn's voice gained strength as she sang even more passionately:

> *Red sky at morning*
> *A warning! A warning!*
> *Red sky at night,*
> *Delight...*

Suddenly her tone grew soft and sorrowful as she finished:

> *Red sky at night,*
> *Delight.*

The hush of her spellbound audience lasted several minutes. Rosalyn's face flushed. "I am sorry. I warned you that I was rusty."

At the back, a single pair of hands began to clap, and suddenly the entire room rang with applause. Talos helped his fiancé to the floor, and the brothers reclaimed their former positions. A lively ballad rang out, and the crowd was on its feet, singing and dancing.

Lluava overheard Byron asking her raven-haired friend, "Where did you learn to sing like that?" He, too, was awestruck, and his partner could not have looked prouder.

"May I have this dance?"

Varren stood next to Lluava with hand outstretched. She smiled, and her heart beat faster as she followed her partner into the throng of people. They began a quick-paced dance filled with twists and spins. Nearby, Talos led Rosalyn in the same manner, both their faces aglow. Glancing around her, Lluava thought she spied Byron dancing with one of Monk's sisters; she couldn't tell which one.

A little later, the uncomfortable feeling of being watched crept up the back of her neck. As she twirled about, she realized that Apex was observing her over the rim of his mug.

When the dance slowed, Varren pulled Lluava close. She could feel the beat of his heart as their bodies pressed against each other. Even after days of traveling, Varren still gave off the subtle aroma of fennel and rosemary, just like the first time Lluava stood near him. These fragrances, so reminiscent of home, were soothing; Lluava closed her eyes and breathed deeply.

As the evening wore on, Lluava's friends relaxed. With all the dancing, talking, and laughing, Lluava could not deny the comfort she felt in this Outlander village. Byron was entertained by a swarm of young ladies who stuck to him as if glued there. He clearly had no complaints. Rosalyn and Talos seemed to have resolved their earlier argument, or at least to have pushed it aside. Varren appeared to enjoy the intriguing conversations with their host and hostess about life in the outlands. Austro sat by himself, flushed but smiling. Only Mila had turned in early; the business of the tavern was not for her.

Lluava realized she had not seen Yamir in a while. She wandered among the revelers until she spotted him seated on a bench by the far wall, speaking with Apex. As she turned away, she overheard Yamir's question.

"So that's all it takes?"

Her sharp sense of hearing picked up Apex's response. "Just pay the money, and they will make you a man and so much more."

Lluava spun around to confront the pair. Yamir cast his eyes down quickly, while Apex gave her a slight nod.

Feeling her lip start to curl, Lluava grabbed Yamir by the shoulder and pulled him up and away. "We need to talk."

Yamir shrugged her off. "Quit trying to control everyone."

Lluava was flabbergasted. "Wha...I...no. I can't make your decisions for you," she agreed, then moved closer until they were face to face. "But trust me: some things are worth waiting for."

Yamir stepped back, almost tripping over a couple dancing behind him. He left the building briskly.

Lluava turned toward Apex, who was still seated. His gaze was remorseless as he continued to swig his drink. Snarling, Lluava stalked away. She really hated that man.

***

Next morning, Lluava awoke early. Nearby, Rosalyn breathed heavily, still tucked under the sheets. Lluava had an unsettled feeling. Something was definitely not right. Quietly slipping out of bed, she changed into her traveling clothes and headed down the hall.

The tavern turned out to be an extension of Tinder's inn as well. Wod and Monk's parents had allowed their sons' guests the use of a couple of spare rooms without charge. Although the rooms were well insulated, there was still a chill in the air, and Lluava shivered.

The door to Yamir's room was open, and she peered inside. The bed was still made up, the room untouched. A low growl slipped past her lips. What had Apex said to make Yamir do this? Ignoring the pleasant greetings that came from the kitchen, Lluava strode out the front door and almost tripped over the figure seated on the stoop. Yamir looked up at Lluava with sorrowful eyes.

"I couldn't do it," said her spiky-haired friend as she seated herself next to him.

Struggling to find the right words, Lluava tried to hide her relief. After a moment, she asked, "What made you change your mind?"

"A feeling..."

She wanted to ask more questions, but this was not the time. Instead, she placed her hand on Yamir's shoulder. Together they sat watching Tinder's Keep begin to stir in the morning light. As they watched people moving about, someone emerged from the Lion's Pride. Lluava's heart sank.

Spotting her, Byron paused for a moment as if debating what to do next before approaching his friends. But he neither spoke nor slowed his stride. Instead, he walked right past them and disappeared inside the inn.

"Apex!" Lluava hissed as she balled her hands into fists. He had gone too far. He was infecting her friends with his base ways. She would not allow that to continue.

Before she knew it, she had marched across the street and swung open the door of the dim entry of the one place she had never expected to set foot in. A thin, spidery man behind a small desk stood up. After looking her up and down, he asked, "Come to satiate an appetite? We have the most succulent variet—"

Lluava cut him off before he could add to her building rage. "Where is Apex?"

The thin man's demeanor became haughty. "I don't know what kind of operation you think we run, but this facility believes in client confidentiality."

Grabbing the man by the collar of his pressed shirt, Lluava roared, "Apex. Where is he?"

She could feel her pupils narrow as her inner rumble began to grow. The man's face blanched. "Third door to the left," he squeaked.

Releasing him, she strode off to beat on Apex's door. There was a shuffling of blankets and stumbling of heavy feet before the door swung open. Apex, eyes still blurry from intoxication, stood in front of her. He was stark naked. Lluava flushed but forced herself to focus her gaze on the huntsman's bristly face.

"Come to pay me a visit?" he asked coyly, leaning against the doorway as if it were sustaining his balance. "There is plenty of room."

Lluava's lip curled back. She pushed the door open even farther and stomped inside. Seeing his discarded pants on the floor, she thrust them in his face. "Put them on!" she demanded.

"Only if you take something off first," he teased, slurring his words.

Ignoring the movement behind her, Lluava snarled, "I said, put them on." She watched him stumble into his pants, all the while grinning at her. Was this a game to him? He was disgusting.

"Your turn," he said as he almost fell on his face.

She spun around in search of his shirt. The bed was a tangle of sheets and bodies. Half-drunk bottles, empty glasses, and pillows were scattered about the room.

"Out!" Lluava's yell morphed into a roar. "Get out, all of you!"

In a flurry of movement, several women scrambled out and ran past the seething teen without pausing to grab sheets to cover themselves—one, two, and three. As the trio disappeared down the hall, Lluava turned her anger toward Apex, who now faced her.

"You're a disgrace! Do you know that? What kind of a man does this?" Lluava's chest rose and fell with each statement. Trying to regain her calm, she waited for a response.

Apex let his hand drop from the doorframe. His body swayed ever so slightly as he cast his angry eyes toward her. "That just cost me a lot of money."

"I don't give a god's crap about any of that," sneered Lluava. The room reeked of sex and sweat.

"I paid for those women," Apex stated, more calmly now. He closed the door behind him and stepped close to Lluava.

"And I always get my money's worth."

Chapter 23

Ensnared

Lluava's heart beat wildly, and her inner warning reverberated. She had to get away—back to the others, back to Varren. She felt cornered, trapped. She would not let this happen.

Without glancing at the door, Lluava calculated her distance from the knob. Could she reach it with this brute in her way? Apex leaned an arm against the door for support and studied her with hazy eyes. Then, like a viper striking, he was upon her.

Before she could cry out, Apex had one hand around her throat, squeezing tightly, and his other hand grasped her waist. Her heart fluttered in her chest as a sickening feeling took over. Her growl was stifled by the iron grip of the huntsman's hand. She lashed out, kicking and swinging, desperately hoping one of her limbs would hit its mark.

Curling his lip, Apex slammed her back against the wall, forcing out whatever air she had left in her lungs. As she struggled to catch her breath, he slid her upward, lifting her legs off the ground. Lluava had not realized how strong he was. Unable to touch the floor and becoming lightheaded, she grew rigid. She could not believe this was happening.

Lluava reached up with both hands and struggled to peel back Apex's fingers, but her weakening grip failed her. Tightening his grip on her throat, Apex released her waist and began to untie his corded belt. Lluava clutched the arm at her throat. As the room seemed to waver and dim, she allowed herself to go limp.

Apex let his belt fall to the floor. His eyes danced. Lowering his prey, he loosened his grip just enough for his victim to gulp the humid air.

Lluava was too weak, now, to struggle or fight. But with every

168

inhalation, her mind became a little clearer. Then, when Apex moved in, she struck. The huntsman released her and swiped at the four claw marks erupting in red across his cheek. Without a pause, Lluava kicked him in the groin, causing him to buckle and collapse on the floor. She leaped for the door, swung it open, and raced down the hall. Apex did not follow.

She sprinted toward The Tankard's stoop. Yamir's shouts alerted those inside, and numerous faces appeared at the doorway. Her friends surrounded her, peppering her with questions. Lluava was shaking terribly and could not seem to stop. She could not focus. Had she tried to answer them? Was she crying, too?

As the adrenaline wore off, Lluava sank to the stoop and lay motionless. Rosalyn wrapped her arm around her friend in a protective embrace. Varren and Talos strode across the street just as Apex appeared in the doorway of the Lion's Pride. Without trying to run or fight, Apex stood there as Varren furiously shouted at him. Talos was unable to prevent Varren's punch from slamming into Apex's face. More shouting. Lluava's eyes lost focus. Blinking to clear her vision, she saw Apex turn in her direction. She quickly dropped her eyes and started to shudder again.

Much later, when her mind was functioning, Lluava struggled to process the conversations she had overheard. Apparently, Varren had fired Apex. To Lluava, there should have been no argument with his action; yet Derrick was quite perplexed.

"You are right that Apex must be punished," stated the dark-skinned man. "Yet who will track the Raiders if you let him go? The other huntsmen will not continue without him. We have nobody."

"We have Byron," Varren snapped back. Turning to the other northerner, he asked, "You did say you used to track, or am I wrong?"

Looking uncomfortable, Byron answered, "I did. But that was years ago. I was never very good."

"It will suffice," Varren replied sternly.

Byron looked as if he wanted to say something, but whatever it was, he kept it to himself.

Soon afterward, the now much smaller group headed out. It seemed Lluava was not the only one ready to leave Tinder and its debauchery behind. There were no farewells between the friends and the huntsmen. As they headed into the woods, Lluava thought she caught a glimpse of gray-dappled fur in the shadows.

On the second evening, Talos made a suggestion. "We should save our food and hunt when we can. Who knows how long it will take us to locate the Raiders?"

"We passed a deer trail not far from here," Byron pointed out with a gesture behind them. "The tracks seemed fresh."

"I know. I could smell them." Derrick grinned wolfishly.

Lluava's lips curled up as well. The thought of fresh venison was pleasing to her stomach. A hunt would help pull her thoughts away from Apex's assault.

"Very well," agreed Varren as he halted his horse. "Who wants to go? Talos?"

Talos shook his head. "Hunting deer was never one of my interests."

Lluava thought she heard Yamir snicker. She rolled her eyes.

"I'm not up to it this time," Byron admitted, rubbing his leg.

Lluava reached up and stretched. "I'll go."

"So will I," Derrick replied.

"I'll come, too," added Yamir.

Lluava wondered how Yamir was doing. Was it wise to let him tag along? Was he ready for that? She hated to admit it even to herself, but she was unsure of her old friend's stability.

Varren seemed to read her thoughts yet again. "Not this time, Yamir. Three is enough, and I go where my partner goes."

Yamir's expression grew dark, but he did not argue. Lluava felt sorry for him. Unlike the others, he no longer had a partner. He had lost so much over the summer.

"It's not personal," Lluava began.

Yamir shrugged her off. "Never is." He left to picket his horse and assist Rosalyn with setting up camp. Lluava was grateful for Rosalyn's presence.

Onyx hopped up to Yamir, tugging with his beak at the ragged trim of the boy's pants. Yamir gently picked up the bird and placed it on his shoulder. Though Onyx seemed to prefer Lluava, the ratty bird occasionally associated himself with the ruddy-hued boy and his endless supply of breadcrumbs.

The trio headed out on foot, leaving their horses in camp. The large animals would only alert their prey to their location. Lluava, like Derrick, chose to hunt in her dual form. She liked the feel of loose soil under her claws. It would not be much longer before the winter's cold would harden the ground. Why did it have to be so cold?

As they neared the herd, Lluava and Derrick moved in a wide arc around the deer, hoping to drive them toward Varren, who, as a human, possessed limited hunting skills. He would not be able to give chase, yet he could attack if given the chance.

It soon became clear to Lluava that Derrick had an ulterior motive for coming along on the hunt. "You need to tell Varren to reconsider his decision to fire the huntsmen," he confided. "We need them."

Lluava wrinkled her nose, causing her whiskers to flare sideways. "He only fired one; the others followed suit."

"Regardless, we are lost without them. Talk to Varren."

"I will not. He made the right choice to get rid of Apex." Lluava almost choked on that name. How could Derrick favor such a horrid man? And why does he think we would be lost without them? "Byron is capable," she argued.

"You don't really believe that, and Byron doesn't either." Derrick's amber eyes studied her sharply. "Have you not been watching him? Have you not seen the stress that clings to his features, or smelled his worry, his fear? He knows he can't do this. He knows that what he has been asked to do is far beyond his ability."

"Then why hasn't he said something?" questioned Lluava unhappily.

"Guilt? Pressure? Who knows?"

Lluava remained silent. Had she been in human form, she would have pursed her lips. A bird sang harshly above them, its high-pitched trill like nails on slate. Lluava wanted to wring its neck.

Derrick spoke up once more. "You could have stopped him, you know."

Lluava froze in her tracks.

"I *did*." Her voice came out in a whisper.

"You got yourself into that mess," affirmed the wolf. "You were fully capable of getting yourself out. You are a tigress—or did you forget?"

His stare cut deep. Lluava wanted to recoil into herself. The urge to curse at him dissipated as the canine continued.

"Lluava Kargen, embodiment of the goddess Theri, partner to the crown prince of Elysia, warrior from the south, was almost overpowered by some backwoods tracker. No. I won't accept it. You are trained in the arts of war; he is not. Your dual form is more powerful than most. You could have stopped him at any point. Whatever hesitation you had and for whatever reason, only you know. Never doubt your strength."

Derrick continued to study her. Lluava wanted this conversation to end. Perhaps, if Derrick thought she was considering his suggestion, he would be quiet. "Okay. Say you're right. What now?"

"You could have stopped him then, and you can stop him if it ever happens again. Lluava, we need someone who knows these woods, how to navigate the terrain, and—most important—how to track the enemy. Talk to Varren."

"Why don't you?" Lluava was growing irritated once more. She wished she had stayed with her partner.

"I tried, remember? Anyway, it is obvious he values your opinion above anyone else's."

The thought of being near Apex again was utterly repulsive. Lluava said, "I am Varren's partner. I will support any decision he makes."

Derrick let his own irritation show. His lip curled back to show the whites of his canines. "Do not let Elysia fall because of one individual's fractured emotions. You are better than that." The black wolf turned and loped ahead, leaving her to ponder in silence.

A familiar scent wafted on the air, and Lluava turned her attention to the prey. The deer were close and sheltering in the thicket. It was a large herd, and several females were in heat.

Stealthily moving forward, she crept through the underbrush. She hoped to spy a glimpse of tawny fur and not the white flag of warning. Already the scent was dwindling. Had she lost them? A small pile of round dung steaming in the chill air allayed her fears. They could not be far away.

Testing the air, Lluava remained downwind from the suspected area. In a few moments, she caught a glimpse of movement ahead of her. Five does came into sight. Although they were not particularly plump, Lluava could still imagine their succulent taste. The deer grazed at leisure on low-lying brush and fallen acorns; the one farthest from her was grooming its haunch.

Lluava needed to position herself farther to the right if she was going to herd the animals toward Varren. She knew she had to be careful. She did not want to lose this wonderful opportunity, especially with so many choices meandering before her.

Step by step, she made her way to the most advantageous point of attack. After each step, she paused to ensure that the animals were not alerted to her presence. Step. Pause. Breathe. Step. Pause. Breathe. She was there.

As she readied herself, a shadowy movement caught her eye. Derrick had also moved into position. Was he waiting for her? A sharp bark sent the animals careening toward her, and Lluava charged. The buzzing of contact calls between animals intensified with their fear.

Clawing at the closest doe, Lluava suddenly heard snuffing and wheezing noises, and a dagger-like object sliced at her rib cage. She let loose several short growls as she fought off her opponent—a huge stag, its impressive rack still aimed at her.

Nearby, Derrick was working the does as if they were a herd of sheep. She could hear every shift they made as their hooves churned up divots from the ground. They had almost reached the place where Varren lay in wait.

Lluava knew she should let this buck go. Varren and Derrick would certainly kill one of the does, and they only needed one. But what if they failed? Without fresh meat, they would have to use valuable supplies. The animal before her was a fine specimen. Healthy and vibrant, he could feed them all for a while.

The buck waved his pointed weapons in the air. The rage of rutting season made him a violent target. Should she risk it? Her side stung where the antler's tip had left a long scratch down her side. Not deep, but painful. She should let him go.

Without warning, the animal charged her. Snarling, Lluava leaped aside and spun around to face the beast once more. She clawed at its antlers. Their numerous points jabbed at the air in over a dozen places. Lluava gave him one good swing that knocked back his rack, and the buck halted. Did it sense how dangerous a creature the tigress was, or the imminent danger to its own life? The white of its tail flashed into the air as it leaped away.

Lluava concentrated on the bounding body, and not the white of illusion. She knew that once the animal gained distance, it would flip down its tail. The white signal would disappear, leaving most predators with one less meal. She would not be tricked so easily.

Charging after the stag, she forced her large form through the dense thickets, still keeping the buck in sight. The animal was fast, due to its strength and streamlined form. Lluava wished she could say the same. Tigers were quick to tire. Not designed for distance runs, they preferred close-up, sneak attacks. There was no need to surprise this animal, so she forced herself forward.

The distance between the pair increased.

No! she snarled, and lunged. Still too far ahead, the buck was well into a safe zone as Lluava landed. Her prey had escaped.

All at once, the buck flew up into the air as if it had wings. Impossible, thought Lluava. It was as if an invisible predator had pulled it into the sky like an osprey snatching a fish from the ocean. As Lluava spotted the rope snare, she attempted to skid to a stop.

Too late. In mere seconds, a tight pressure around her rear leg jerked her upward. The loss of contact with solid earth was not as gut-wrenching as the realization that her weight would soon hurl her back to the ground. She had no chance. The earth seemed to leap up toward her. She slammed into the ground and into blackness.

Chapter 24

Whistles and Wonderings

Lluava's hands barely brushed the ground below her. She felt a hot pressure building in her face and heard the steady drip of her blood onto the dry soil. A cardinal chirped above, and the teen's eyes fluttered open. Unable to maintain dual form once consciousness was lost, she was in human form.

Carefully turning her head upward, Lluava stared at the snare that bound her leg and held her, dangling, in midair. The cord was not particularly thick, yet it bore her weight securely. The carcass of the deer hung limply alongside her. Its neck had been broken when it smashed into the ground. Lluava was thankful that she had not ended up like her intended prey.

She fought through the intense pounding in her head and the throbbing in her leg. As she took a breath, she tried to swing herself up to grab the snare. The sharp pain from the long cut down her side caused her to cry out.

Should she call for Varren? Perhaps Derrick would hear her, but what about those giant Raiders? Were any nearby? If discovered, they could kill her easily. She would not turn herself into prey for those monsters.

After several more futile attempts, Lluava gave up the idea of untying herself. Maybe if she shifted form, her increased weight would pull her to the ground. As Lluava began to metamorphose, the binding cut deep into her growing mass. She stopped immediately.

She growled in frustration. The snapping of a twig was the unsettling reply. Twisting around to get a better angle of vision, she saw Austro step out of the forest. He looked quite bemused.

"Well, isn't this a pretty picture?" he said, more to himself than to her. Was he angry with her? After all, he was one of Apex's companions. Did he blame her for the termination of their contract? Austro studied her a moment longer, then pulled a knife out of his tall, fur-trimmed boot.

Was he going to kill her? Lluava caught her breath and wondered how she could fight him. The Claws had been left with Talos, as she did not need them to hunt deer. Austro walked past Lluava and severed a taut cord. A moment later, the buck came crashing down. The tracker squatted and began to butcher the beast.

"Hey!" Lluava exclaimed. "What about me?"

Without pausing to look over his shoulder, Austro said, "I am sure you are perfectly capable of getting yourself out of this situation."

His words seemed to echo Derrick's. A low growl slipped out, and Lluava once again attempted to rid herself of the bindings. If she could just reach the cord. Her head throbbed madly, and the pain in her leg intensified.

Changing strategy, Lluava humbled herself. "Please, won't you help me?"

Austro stood up and moved to her side. With one clean cut, she tumbled to the ground without warning. Austro turned his attention back to the deer. "You are thankful, now, that you didn't eat me, yes?"

Flipping over on her knees, Lluava took stock of herself. She was going to be all right.

"I was and still am sorry about that. It was a mistake, you know?"

"A mistake you will never make again," Austro's curt voice was terse but not angry.

Was he making fun of her? Lluava didn't care. She was alive and back on solid ground. "Never again," she affirmed.

As she slowly got to her feet, she noticed how efficiently Austro worked. Every slice he made was perfect. He knew exactly what he was doing. His expertise was undeniable.

"Did you make these snares?" Lluava asked as she touched a sticky patch of blood on her forehead.

"No," admitted the small man. "Wod built them. He has many scattered around the Beltline."

Although impressed by that knowledge, the thought of falling victim again was highly unsettling. What other traps were hidden nearby? Derrick's words rang out in her mind again. They needed the expertise of these huntsmen. Without them, they had little chance of succeeding.

"If there was some way to—" Lluava hated herself for what she was about to say. She had to be crazy for broaching this subject. "To, uh, work together again, what would that take, and would it be possible?"

Austro turned to face her. "Work for you again?"

Lluava wished she could read between his words. "I'm not saying that we would, but is it a possibility? In the future? Could it happen?"

"Anything's possible," grunted the man. His large ears seemed to move on their own, ever so slightly.

Closing her eyes, Lluava inquired, "Would Apex agree to that?"

"I am not Apex. I cannot say what he would choose."

Thinking for a moment, Lluava posed another question. "If Varren changed his mind and wanted to talk to you or Apex about working together again, how would we find you?"

Austro cleaned his blade on a scrap of cloth tucked into his pocket. Then he reached into his coat and pulled out a small silver object. He handed it to Lluava. "Use this."

The minute whistle fit perfectly in the palm of her hand. A thin cord was connected to one end. "What if the sound alerts the enemy?"

Austro smiled, exposing his large front teeth much like Chat had once done. "The whistle was made for Theriomorphs. Do not worry about your enemy."

Although Lluava could not help but eye Austro suspiciously, she kept the unexpected gift. Slipping its cord over her neck, she slid the whistle under her tattered shirt. Austro returned to the job at hand, and Lluava left to find her own comrades. She still hoped they would not have to summon the huntsmen and Apex, but she took comfort in knowing that she could contact them if needed.

A raven cried out in the distance. Soon the flapping of dark wings alerted Lluava to the incoming animal. Onyx flew down and perched on the girl's shoulder. Moments later, Varren appeared; it was clear that he had followed the bird's caws.

"There you are," he sighed. His relief was obvious. "I was beginning to worry."

Before the prince could ask, Lluava answered, "I was caught in a snare. Took a little time to get free."

"Only you." Varren smiled, his eyes tenderly looking her over. "Well, if you are all right, are you up to helping me and Derrick bring the carcass back to camp? Then we can get Rosalyn to look at you."

"Of course."

***

The following day, as they rode side by side, Lluava observed Byron's behavior closely. She had an unsettled feeling, thanks to Derrick, and she needed to resolve it.

"Byron," she began.

He looked at her. "Hmmm?"

"How are we doing? And please be honest with me."

Byron's features grew slack; he shook his head slightly. Nothing more needed to be said. The Raiders were getting away. Lluava caught the stern look that settled on Derrick's face. He must have overheard their exchange. She knew what she must do.

Lluava rounded her horse and caught up with Varren. "Byron is unable to track the Raiders. Our plan is failing."

"I know." His voice was serious, his look hard.

"Maybe we should rehire the huntsmen." Once the words were spoken, Lluava's stomach knotted up. She was repelled by the situation, but what choice did she have?

Varren looked aghast. "What? How can you say such a thing? Especially after what Apex did to you?"

Steadying her nerves, Lluava tried to answer logically. "Nothing actually happened. I was able to stop him."

"I will not allow Apex anywhere near you again. A man like that can never be trusted. Anyway, this mission is too important."

Lluava had to stop herself from smiling. Forcing herself to be serious, she said, "I am more than capable of taking care of myself. I am trained in combat; he is not. I am quite strong, you know. I stopped him before, and I can prevent that situation from happening again. Now that I am aware of the sort of person he is, I will be on the alert.

"Varren," she said, speaking calmly to soothe the fierce anger in the prince's eyes, "without him and his comrades, our mission will fail. We will fail. Elysia will fail." Lluava repeated Derrick's words. "We have to push past that incident."

Varren's jaw tightened. "There has to be another way."

"What?"

"I do not know, but there has to be one."

Lluava was not amused. "Do you think I want them back? I hate Apex more than you can imagine," she spat out, "but we cannot let the Raiders escape. We cannot let them win."

Varren remained silent.

"Just think about it, okay?" she said.

For the better part of the day, Varren kept to himself; stress lines appeared on his furrowed brow. Lluava could not blame him. What she asked was something she, too, wished were not the only viable option. Although she had hoped for a better alternative, it was clear that they were floundering in the forest. There was nothing to be gained if they continued without help.

That evening, Lluava took leave of her friends to walk in the woods. Tensions were so high that she could feel them like a physical presence. She needed to step away for a bit. She shifted into her dual form, reveling in the earthy perfumes all around her in the dusk.

Listening to a disturbance in the underbrush, Lluava approached a small rabbit. She made sure this was no Theriomorph. Had she been human, she would have grinned; it was just a rabbit. Her small band of friends would be eating meat from the deer for days. Wouldn't it be nice to have a different flavor to add to the mix?

As she bounded forward, another large shape mirrored her response. The animal collided with her. She snarled and struck at the other beast. A sharp bite on her rear leg caused her to turn and face the challenger. Instantly, Lluava saw that color had drained away; the world around her had taken on a cast of cool hues. The desire to attack, to kill, took over.

"Lluava!"

Varren's voice rang out. She blinked. The world returned to normal, its colors bright and strong. Derrick stood in front of her, looking perturbed— and why wouldn't he? Hadn't she just struck him? What was going on with her?

"What were you doing?" her partner asked heatedly.

Lluava did not respond; instead, she pivoted and returned to camp. She needed time to think. When she fought the giant Raider, she had lost control of herself completely—as though some other force had manipulated her body, pushing her out. This evening, it had almost happened again. And if it had, it would have cost Derrick his life.

Thank the gods for Varren, thought Lluava. If it weren't for him, she might have—

"Lluava, I need to talk with you." Varren waved her over to his tent. "You are right. We cannot continue in this manner. We will not succeed unless we have help."

As far as she could tell, Varren was being honest with her. What had made him change his mind? Did it have anything to do with what she had almost done?

He continued, "I am afraid that I have delayed too long. We are miles away from Tinder's Keep."

"Are you sure you want them back?" Lluava asked as she fingered the lip of her cloak's inner pocket.

"No. But do I have a choice?"

"Okay. Let's get the huntsmen back."

After he had gathered their other friends around him, Varren said, "Byron, I know you have tried to do what I asked of you. It was unfair of me to place that responsibility on your shoulders. For that, I am sorry."

"It's nothing," Byron began.

Varren shook his now lengthy locks. "No. I should not have placed you in a position in which you were clearly uncomfortable. What I am about to propose is something I cannot support wholeheartedly. Since you are my trusted friends, I need to make sure that this decision is backed by the majority."

Rosalyn gave Talos a questioning look and then turned toward Lluava; Yamir's features looked gloomy. Lluava wondered if he suspected what Varren was about to say.

"We have found no sign of the band of Raiders since we left Tinder's

Keep. We have lost valued days, and I fear that, if we have not already failed at our reconnaissance mission, we soon will. Therefore, what say you to the idea of—" Varren stopped, summoning his will to finish the proposal, "—rehiring the huntsmen? If there is a chance to finish what we started, would you support that?"

Derrick was the first to speak. "Putting personal issues aside might be in the best interest of the greater good. If working with the huntsmen protects Elysia in any way, I say we should ask them to rejoin our efforts."

Talos was not pleased. He kept silent for a long while; when he spoke, he chose to be logical. "How would we even find them? We left them at Tinder. Do you think they just stayed there? They are long gone—as should be this idea."

Looking at his partner, Byron added, "I wish I were better at tracking. I will keep trying, but the trail went cold a long time ago."

"We should return," whispered Rosalyn, whose health had begun to deteriorate. "We made this journey based on several large assumptions. What if we were wrong, and we are wasting our strength and time on a fruitless mission?"

Rosalyn had a point. What if all this was for nothing? Had they squandered all their time chasing shadows in the woods while Elysia was doing battle with—and possibly losing to—a cruel and evil enemy? Perhaps they should turn around and go back. At least they would not have to worry about whether or not to work with the huntsmen. Lluava would never have to see Apex again. But what if there was a chance? Could they gain important information? Could they prevent a major attack? How many lives might be saved?

Lluava spoke. "Elysia's future is at stake. We can't afford to lose any chance to save our kingdom. Of all of us, I should be the one most opposed to working with the huntsmen, but I support this decision."

Whether it was the truth of Lluava's last statement or the points made by others, several heads nodded in agreement. Though Yamir and Rosalyn still opposed the idea, the consensus was to resume their contract with the huntsmen.

"How are we to find them?" questioned Yamir. He had been quiet for most of the conversation. "If we can't find them, all this talk means nothing."

Several questioning looks passed among them before Lluava reached inside her shirt and pulled out the cord with the whistle. "I know how to call them."

After she explained how she had come into possession of the whistle, Varren gave her a nod. "Give it a try."

Though still skeptical, Lluava took a big breath and blew into the tiny whistle. As soon as she did, she quickly reached up to her ears to block the piercing trill emitted by the tiny object. Even though she had stopped blowing, the ringing echo continued. Looking around her, the noise seemed to bother many of the friends, although Byron and Varren were unperturbed.

"Well?" asked Byron, who was clearly confused at his comrades' odd reactions.

Next to him, Talos was shaking his head repeatedly, his tawny locks whipping around his features. "Did you not hear that?" he exclaimed, disgruntled.

"What?" Byron looked at Lluava. "You blew it?"

The young woman returned the whistle to her pocket, hoping she would not have to use it again anytime soon. "It wasn't meant for your ears," she said.

"How long will it take?" inquired Varren, who was less concerned about the phantom sound.

"I don't know," Lluava admitted. "I guess we just have to wait and see."

At first, everyone stopped as if stuck to their spots, hoping for any sign of approaching figures. As time crept on, one by one they resumed their normal camp duties.

"Maybe you should blow it again," suggested Byron.

Yamir quickly shook his head. "No, don't do that. I can still hear it."

Looking over at her partner, Lluava apologized. "I tried…"

"I know you did," Varren acknowledged. "However, it seems that we are on our own." He began to turn away, but then stopped. "Is that—?"

Lluava peered in the direction the prince was pointing. Apex stepped out of the gloom with his companions at his heels. Lluava felt her heart skip a beat. Had she made the wrong decision? There was no way she would let that monster see her fear. Standing up straight, Lluava watched as the huntsmen approached their campfire.

For a moment, no one spoke. Then Apex broke the silence. "Well? What have you to say?"

Varren approached the burly man. Lluava followed at her partner's side. From this new angle, Lluava could see the yellow-green remains of the bruise Varren had left around Apex's eye. She was glad to see that Varren had hit him so hard. Some of the bilious color overlapped her own claw marks that slanted across the brute's cheek. He finally looked like the monster he really was, and she was glad he was marked for all to see. Still, Lluava found herself moving closer to Varren's side. She would not let Apex see her tremble.

Stopping several feet away, Lluava could not help but sense the deep penetration of the lead huntsman's stare. Maybe she had made the wrong decision. Maybe they all had. A sudden panic began to rise inside her. She wanted to escape from this man and his unwelcome presence.

Lluava felt Varren's hand on her shoulder. Had he realized her inner discomfort? The simple gesture was comforting. She forced herself to meet the gaze of the tracker before her, although she wanted to turn away.

The prince began, "What happened in Tinder's Keep was inexcusable." Varren glanced at Lluava before continuing. "Yet the cold fact remains, we must track down the band of Raiders before it is too late."

Apex seemed about to respond with a snide remark but thought better of it. He stood silently, which forced Varren to speak once more.

"My comrades and I have a mission to complete and, just as before, we need your aid in order to succeed. I will not let my emotions hinder this task. Will you rejoin our efforts?"

"Oh?" Apex raised an eyebrow and glanced in Lluava's direction. She could feel her insides churn. Every bit of her wanted to bolt. Thank the gods Varren was near; she drew strength from him.

Turning his hard gaze on the prince, Apex responded. "In our original agreement, we were to track and you to fight. That deal was made to protect my fellows from risk of injury. That insurance of protection has been violated."

Now Varren was the one holding back the angry retort. Lluava was unable to look away from Apex's bruised eye. Would he really turn them down?

The huntsman answered Lluava's unspoken question. "Before I will agree to rejoin your efforts, I demand compensation for the risk we are all taking in this endeavor."

"What sort of compensation?" inquired Varren. He clearly disproved of the entire situation.

Apex looked at each of his own companions, then stated, "Double the pay."

Varren looked at his partner. Lluava nodded so he would know she accepted the proposal. But did she have any right to make the choice? It wasn't her money.

"That's ridiculous," Talos blurted out.

"Out of the question," agreed the prince.

Tensions were rising as fast as Lluava's discomfort. She looked at Derrick, imploring him to back her. He stared back but did not respond. He was right, wasn't he? They did need these men, no matter the cost?

Lluava leaned toward her partner and whispered urgently into his ear, "We need them. They are angry with us, just as we are angry with them. Give them something, but not all."

She knew her partner was struggling internally, and she gave his arm a quick squeeze. His body relaxed slightly. Varren's eyes never left Apex's face.

"I will raise you a third of your original price."

"We want the money up front."

Varren bit his tongue but said, "I will pay half now and half upon completion of our mission."

Behind Apex, smiles crept onto the brothers' faces. Even Mila seemed pleased. Yet Apex remained stoical. The trackers' leader took his time to weigh Varren's terms.

"Deal."

Glancing at the other huntsmen, Lluava realized they were all grinning. Yamir's next question indicated he realized it, too. "Do you think they planned this? To con more money out of Varren?"

Listening to Yamir's wild conspiracy theories had always been a fun pastime. Yet somehow, this one rang true. Lluava wondered if he were right. Was this all part of Apex's plan?

***

The next morning brought another drop in temperature. Although it was only mid autumn, the weather was already far colder than any winter Lluava had experienced. She shivered as she tried to keep her cloak closed.

"Still refusing to travel in your dual form?"

The snow leopard strolled at Lluava's horse's feet. After leaving Tinder's Keep, Lluava had chosen to ride on horseback to help distance herself from the very people she had just rehired. There had been no time for her to follow Mila's earlier advice. Maybe her winter coat *would* be better.

"Oh, uh…all right." Passing her mount's reins to Byron, Lluava stripped off her cloak, leaped down, and shifted. "Still cold," she grumbled.

Mila snorted. "Give it time. Walk with me."

"I wish my cloak was made of Endun."

"Luckily for us, the rest of our clothes are," agreed Mila.

"Wait, Endun is only made for Theriomorph soldiers, to allow us to shift in battle."

Mila contorted her face in what could only have been a grin. "It is amazing what people will trade, isn't it?"

Lluava was taken aback. "No Theriomorph soldier would sell his uniform."

"Perhaps," acknowledged Mila. "However, the soldier for whom mine was made doesn't need it any longer."

"Are you suggesting that the living military partner sold it for some meat?"

"I am not suggesting," corrected Mila. "I am stating a fact."

"But no partner would do that."

"Are you implying that you are partners to death and beyond?"

"Yes."

"If that is the case, why doesn't everyone here have a partner?"

Lluava sprang to the defense of her friend. "Yamir's partner was killed."

"I am referring to Rosalyn. She must have had one."

"She does," Lluava snapped back rather defensively. "She's just…" Lluava hesitated as she realized that Rosalyn had indeed abandoned her own partner in order to follow Talos when war was declared. The thought was disquieting. Mila slipped away, and Lluava was left to question her own friend's sense of duty.

***

Over the ensuing days, the two groups remained wary of each other. The distrust between them had clearly intensified, and the two parties made camp separately, just as before. Lluava kept close to Varren. She did not go anywhere near Apex and even turned down Mila's offer to hunt together. What was the point of befriending these people, these mercenaries? They were two separate units, working together only out of necessity, and Lluava was glad of it.

To awaken in the morning to chilly air was expected by now; nonetheless, Lluava grumbled every time. This morning was no worse than the last, yet she cursed aloud, her breath making a translucent cloud that trailed into the air. She poked her head out of her tent flap. The world was still and quiet. Tendrils of smoke snaked their way above the firepit. A few ragged snores could be heard in unsteady rhythms scattered through the camp.

Maybe she could go back to sleep.

On the far side of their camp, Talos pulled back his flap.

Or maybe not.

Pulling on her cloak, Lluava headed toward the campfire. A few coals glowed dimly from under mounds of ash. Buried in the smoky smell, a familiar odor caused Lluava to gasp.

"Varren!" she cried out, and her partner fumbled, wide-eyed, out of his tent.

"What is wrong, Lluava?"

Sniffing the air once more, Lluava hissed, "The thief who tried to steal Issaura's Claws has been here!"

Chapter 25

Through the Smoke of Madness

I smell him. The thief…" Lluava tried to keep the shock out of her voice. Varren seemed too stunned to respond. Several of the others had heard her exclamation and headed toward her, but she was in no mood to answer questions.

Lluava slipped on Issaura's Claws; she wanted her weapons at the ready. Her eyes swept the ground, looking for any other signs of the intruder. How had he stumbled upon them? Or had he been following them the whole time?

"What's going on?"

Apex appeared, along with his comrades. They watched as Varren's group moved about their camp almost haphazardly. Lluava refused to answer him directly; she growled out, "Tell him."

She did not want to waste time talking, especially with Apex. All her senses were focused on finding the thief. He had to have left some sort of sign—a strand of hair or fur, a footprint of some sort, a broken twig. While Varren explained, Lluava felt herself growing desperate. The musk had dissipated.

Suddenly, she saw them: several prints left in the soot next to their fire. What were they? She did not know, and as much as she hated to do so, she turned to the huntsmen.

"Help us, please." She took a breath and forced herself to sound more in control. "There are paw prints here. Can you follow them?"

Although the brothers looked bemused, Apex was quite serious. He nodded, and the brothers moved over to examine the faint shapes.

Squatting down, Wod announced, "It's a badger." He turned to look at Lluava. "Your thief's form is a badger."

A northern animal, thought Lluava. *No wonder I did not recognize its smell.*

"Track him," commanded Apex. The huntsmen dispersed silently. Lluava wished she could help, but tracking animals was not her strong suit; besides, the huntsmen knew what they were doing. She had to content herself with waiting with her friends for any word on their intruder.

One by one the huntsmen returned, all bearing the same news: the badger's trail had gone cold. Finally Austro appeared. He hopped into camp lightning fast in his dual form. Watching him shifting back with his eyes still wide, Lluava knew he had brought word; yet it was not what she had expected to hear.

"I found your Raiders," Austro reported breathlessly.

"What?"

"Where?"

"How many?"

Bombarded by questions, Austro took several steps backward. Once his questioners calmed down, he answered, "I spotted three of the largest men I have ever seen, dressed in the garb you previously described and carrying particularly nasty weapons. I think they are headed to the Pass."

"Only three?" questioned Varren, while Yamir interjected, "We are looking for more."

"They could be headed to the others," suggested Talos.

Derrick seemed to agree. "Our best bet is to follow them."

"That is what we will do," affirmed the prince. Lluava grinned. Varren turned to Derrick and gently ordered, "Get word to your troop about this discovery."

"Of course." After giving one long, lonesome howl, Derrick waited for a response. None came. He howled once more, his eyes darkening.

"Give me leave, Your Majesty, to find my men."

As Varren granted permission, Lluava wondered what might have happened to the wolf pack. Could the Raiders have killed them all? How could those brutes have known? How could they have found Derrick's entire troop? Hoping that it was only distance that had gotten the better of them, she turned her thoughts to the conversation at hand.

Varren was speaking to Apex. "That was our agreement. Stay here if you wish; any help would be appreciated."

"I am sure it would."

Lluava realized what they were talking about. The huntsmen would remain at camp. This did not concern Lluava; she was glad to leave Apex behind. Byron's tracking ability would have to suffice. The other three friends would stay behind as well, Yamir to look after Rosalyn while Talos kept an eye on Apex and his comrades.

Lluava thought this for the best. A small party was all they would need to track the Raiders. Three people would move faster and could hide more easily, essential on a mission like this one—especially if those Raiders were anything like the giant monstrosity she had encountered on the battlefield.

With Byron in the lead, they headed north toward the silhouette of the Borren Mountains occasionally visible through the trees. Choosing to stay on foot, they moved like shadows amid the forest understory. Austro's information was accurate; soon they were following three pairs of large footprints. The Raiders appeared to be moving at a steady pace.

As they quickened their own pace, Lluava's keen hearing was first to discern the marauders forcing their way through the scrubby underbrush. It took the humans a few more minutes before they were close enough to hear the Raiders.

Lluava risked a glance around the barricade of tree trunks to get a look at the enemy. The brutes were much larger than most humans; the smallest was almost seven feet tall. They were covered in furs and wore sinister weaponry strapped to them. Austro's judgment was confirmed. They had found the giant Raiders—at least some of them.

Hoping that these brutes would lead them to the rest of the Raiders' party, they followed stealthily. The enemy kept silent as they walked, offering the friends no hope of overhearing their plan. Lluava was disappointed, but what had she really expected? That their adversaries would give a full account of their purpose and military strategies?

As Lluava trailed the Raiders, she observed their behavior. Aside from their size, they seemed normal. She could not sense aggression. There was no smoky residue, no expression of atypical strength.

After a time, the first Raider pulled over his head a full-length ox horn with cord and passed it behind him. The third man pulled out flint and stone and lit whatever substance was in the horn. Placing his lips to one end of the horn, he inhaled deeply once, and then again before passing the items to his comrades.

As the Raiders continued into the forest, the smoker suddenly stopped. Lluava froze. To her right and left, Varren and Byron did the same. The third Raider turned, his eyes fractured with red lines. His body language had changed; exactly how, Lluava could not determine. But something was terribly wrong.

He knows we are here! Lluava's thoughts raced. Balling her hands into fists, Issaura's Claws sprang erect. They seemed so ready for a fight—but was she?

Footsteps thundered through the forest. The Raider charged directly toward them, pulling his large sword from the sheath strapped to his back. Lluava let out a growl as she somersaulted out of the way. The man stamped past her, tearing through the underbrush.

Lluava quickly turned to face her opponent, but the Raider did not return. What was going on?

Turning to the young men, Lluava saw Varren's face blanch as he shouted, "He is heading to our camp!" Catching Lluava's eye, he ordered, "Go after him, Lluava."

"I won't leave you," she hissed. The large silhouette was disappearing rapidly.

"Go!" the prince commanded. "Neither one of us is capable of catching him. Run to the camps. Warn them! Save them!"

"We will be right behind you," Byron added, already on the run.

Rather reproachfully, Lluava shifted and raced through the forest, a streak of white tipped in gold. The hardening earth sent a chill up her legs every time her pads hit the ground, but her thick fur countered the brief moments of discomfort. She had to focus on the one thing that mattered, the marauder before her.

It took several more strides than she liked to finally catch glimpse of the enemy. The man seemed unaware of the large feline approaching him. Or maybe he did not care.

As fast as she ran, Lluava was unable to catch up with the fiend. The massive man burst into camp, swinging his weapon. She heard Rosalyn scream and saw Yamir flung into the air, his throwing quills scattering everywhere. Nearby, the huntsmen's camp was barren. A trail of smoke hung languidly in the still air, the only certain marker that the trackers had actually slept there mere hours ago. Somehow, the cowardice of their disappearance struck deep inside her.

Turning her building rage toward the enemy, she sprang into reach, clawing at the thick material on the Raider's legs. The man spun round to face her. He looked directly at her, yet did not seem to regard Lluava in her entirety. He showed fear. What was wrong with this man? This...monster!

As she evaded his maneuvers, Lluava sensed Talos approaching to help her. Talos swung his sword, but the weapon missed its intended mark. The unfortunate backlash came quickly. Talos barely had time to leap out of range of the lunging longsword. At the same time, the Raider stamped down hard on Lluava's tail, sending a sharp pain up her spine. She scrambled to pull free, but the Raider forced all his weight onto his foot; she was firmly pinned down.

Rosalyn, looking terrified, held Talos's weapon. She was bent over by the sword's considerable weight. Where was Talos? There was no time to stop and ponder. Lluava had to deflect her attacker's massive blade. With every impact, she wondered how much more her golden claws could withstand.

On the fourth strike, the Raider stumbled forward, freeing the tigress's tail. She sprang out of the way. Whipping around, she spied a tawny stag pawing angrily at the ground. Talos! The animal shook its impressive rack haughtily. She was glad it wasn't her back that had been jabbed with the dozen or more points. Lluava knew all too well the danger antlers posed. For now, her own wound would not hold her back.

The Raider turned his gaze on the cloven-hoofed creature as if he had forgotten the tiger lurking among the tents. His face appeared indifferent, yet he approached the animal with a clear intent to kill.

The stag leaped forth. The Raider swung. Rosalyn screamed. Joining the fray, Lluava flung herself on the man's left leg and forced him to step back. Talos evaded the blade.

Lluava heard a low moan emerge from the bushes. The Raider noticed as well. Yamir must be coming to.

Although the tiger still had the Raider's leg in its grip, the monstrous man switched course, dragging the tiger with him. Lluava could taste blood through the furred boot. She bit down harder, but to no avail. How could this be happening?

In a flash of tan, the stag reared up in front of the marauder, pummeling him with its sharp hooves. The man stretched out his forearm, deflecting the deadly jabs. Was this man unstoppable?

Soon a third figure attempted to thwart him. Rosalyn had taken a burning branch from the fire and now swung it at the man's fur cape. The smell of singed fur caused the first quick-thinking response they had seen from their opponent. He grabbed the hot end of the stick and tore it out of Rosalyn's hands. Terrified, she stepped back just as the longsword came slicing down.

"Talos!" Rosalyn cried.

The stag sprang in front of her, knocking her down. The Raider's blade sliced the tallest point off the right horn.

Lluava knew she had to lure the giant Raider away from the camp and her friends. Releasing her grip on the fur-covered boot, she turned her snarl into a deafening roar. The behemoth must have at last deemed her a worthy opponent, for he broke off his assault on Rosalyn and pursued the white tiger.

Lluava kept her pace in check. She wanted the man far enough behind, yet close enough to maintain his interest. She feigned tripping more than once to make sure he continued to give chase.

Once away from the camp, Lluava spun around to face the monstrous brute. She had to hold his attention and keep him at bay until Byron and Varren arrived. They would be here soon, but would it be soon enough?

As she danced around man and weapon, his pungent, smoky smell prickled her nose again. Suddenly a thought came to mind. The last giant Raider she had encountered had reeked of the same smell as this one. Even at a distance, one could tell the brute's eyes were bloodshot. Could the smoke itself be responsible? Was that what caused them to act the way they did, in total disregard of pain?

Drugged. What had been just an idea crystallized into clear truth: the substance in the ox horn had caused this bestiality, this bloodlust.

Lluava's hind legs pressed up against a thicket, and she knew she had to get into the open quickly. This giant was too strong for her to combat by herself. Varren, please come quickly, she pleaded silently.

She heard Onyx cawing from the trees and fluttering from limb to limb. The bird kept the battling pair in sight with his good eye. He seemed to know there was little else he could do.

The Raider's gaze, inhuman in its lack of every emotion but rage, never left Lluava. His offensive tactics were draining her strength. A sudden pain in her side alerted her that her wound had reopened, only adding to her defensive decline.

Suddenly a quick flurry of feet and fur flashed past. The arctic hare darted around the brute's massive fur-trimmed boots, causing the hulk to stumble yet again.

Austro! Lluava was elated. The little huntsmen had come to her aid. If she could have grinned in her dual form, she would have done so. Lluava took full advantage of her new assistance. With the Raider distracted, she leaped into the clearing, just as the Raider punted the rabbit into the air and sent him flying into a bunch of brambles.

Seething, Lluava confronted her opponent. She was close now and had to use her gilded claws to fend off several more strikes from the longsword. The clang of metal on metal reverberated through the forest. Suddenly, the molting brown-and-white ball of fur hopped onto one of the Raider's shoes and began to gnaw quickly through the thick hide. In moments, Austro had found skin; however, the Raider did not even bother to glance down at this unwelcome parasite.

The rabbit glanced in Lluava's direction, its dark eyes sparkling. She hoped he understood they just needed a little more time.

A flash of silver was followed by a squeal cut short. Before her, the Raider had driven his sword down through the arctic hare. Lifting his weapon, he inspected the twitching creature. Lluava stood horrified as Austro reverted to his human form.

Lluava recalled the image of Grand Master Chief Argon, along with all the horror of that last day of his life. It had happened once again, and once again she could not stop it. She wanted to shout and scream, but the sounds stuck in her throat.

The Raider turned his weapon downward and gave it a shake, allowing the corpse to fall unceremoniously to the ground. Lifting his dripping weapon, he sent flecks of red toward Lluava's white fur. As he tested his swing like an executioner, Lluava's only thoughts were on the past: I'm sorry, Argon. Grand Master Chief, I failed you.

Chapter 26

Fallen

Utterly distracted by the eruption of pent-up grief, Lluava should have tried harder to evade the Raider's sword. The blade sliced toward her with astonishing speed.

A resounding clang echoed off the nearby trees. Sparks flared as Varren's sword slid down the length of the larger weapon. The opposing pressure forced his legs to buckle, and he fell to one knee. The prince had succeeded in blocking that murderous swing, but could he withstand the next?

Snarling, Lluava reared to attack. The Raider lifted his weapon and struck out once more. The blade slammed into two sets of golden claws. Varren jumped to his feet and jabbed at the monstrosity. His steel buried itself nearly to the hilt in the Raider's thigh.

But the Raider barely reacted to the wound. Instead, he leaned forward and knocked Varren away from the pommel of his blade. Despite the sword lodged in his thigh, the brute returned his gaze to the tigress. Lluava's hackles bristled.

There was a shout and another thwack. A large segment of the Raider's bear-hide cloak fell to the ground. Byron limped out of striking range as fast as he could on his wounded leg.

Byron should not be here, thought Lluava; the fight was taking a terrible toll on his leg. And she could only protect one of her comrades.

Varren was to her right and slightly behind her. When her tail flicked, it brushed up against his leg. Varren would be helpless without his sword. Lluava eyed the enemy warily. The Raider was clearly ready to attack.

Byron cried out again and charged forward in a less-than-fluid motion.

190

No! You fool! Lluava wanted to scream but instead tried to draw the behemoth's attention with her own high-pitched cry. Failing, she tore into the fur-trimmed boot of the enemy, pulling clumps of hide and hair away. Even as she sank her teeth into his calf, she knew the crazed Raider would not stop; at best she might hinder his progress toward her helpless friend.

Just as Lluava's ludicrous plan seemed to be working, Byron tossed his weapon to Varren. The brute knocked Lluava off with a forceful kick and, freed from the tiger's weight, charged the unprotected Byron. Lluava scrambled after him. Varren followed, brandishing Byron's sword.

Rearing up, Lluava grappled with the leather-bound body, managing to halt the behemoth's progress and provide Varren an opening.

Varren sped up. Using the tiger's back as a springboard, he jumped onto the Raider's beefy shoulders, and with one solid thrust plunged Byron's sword into the soft neck, driving it deep into the Raider's center.

Lluava felt the man's body tense and then relax before she let it fall limply into a pile of leaves. It was over. He was dead.

Lluava looked about for the second body, which had been partially buried by the disturbed leaf litter. From her angle, she could see Austro's milky eyes staring up amid the burnt orange and dulled yellows of fallen leaves.

Nauseated, she stumbled to the side of a pine, shifted back, and purged. The taste of bile coated her mouth until long after they had carried the dead huntsman back to their camp.

***

Apex was the first to approach, his features like stone. Mila slipped around him and softly gasped. The brothers stepped up and demanded to know what had happened.

As Varren began to explain, Lluava watched Rosalyn methodically wash and wrap Austro's corpse as if it were her duty, the look on her face unreadable. Lluava wondered what thoughts were passing through her friend's mind.

Her attention was claimed by the babble of voices growing increasingly loud. It was obvious that the two groups were once again at odds.

"So, you let the others escape to warn their comrades and bring death to us all?" Monk was furious.

The prince's face was stern as he defended his decision. "That one brute could have killed all of you. I made the choice: live to fight another day."

As he looked at Austro's wrapped form, Varren's face softened. He glanced at each of the trackers in turn. When he spoke again, his voice was filled with sadness.

"Austro gave his life to save all of ours. He was brave and fearless. It was his choice, but I regret the cost." Looking directly at Apex, he said, "You do not have to aid us any longer. If you wish to leave, you may."

Apex turned toward the solemn faces of his comrades. "We have much to discuss."

"Whatever you choose," added Lluava, "one thing is certain: Austro will be avenged." She turned to Varren, who nodded back.

"Talos, Byron, Yamir—get ready to head out," Varren ordered. "We are going after those Raiders."

"You are a fool, Varren," snapped Monk. "You can't undo what has been done."

"When have you made a choice that affected others' lives?" Varren shot back.

The prince's words hit their mark. Monk started to respond, but Wod stopped him.

Varren mounted his horse. There was no longer a need for stealth. As Talos did the same, Rosalyn scolded him.

"Get down from there. You almost had your head sliced off."

"I am fine," countered Talos. He tried to placate the young woman. "It was only an antler. They grow back every year. I just have a bad headache."

Rosalyn spun around and captured Byron in her sights. "And what about you? With your bad leg, how are you going to fight?"

Byron tried not to hobble but realized he was trapped. "She is right. The cold affects my injury." He turned toward his partner and argued, "I can still fight, you know."

"I know," said Talos as he looked at his tired friend, "but save it for another day."

With that said, the four remaining soldiers rode off in search of the Raiders. They had lost precious time. Luckily, their enemy was on foot.

They had traveled for several hours when the marauders finally came into view. One of the Raiders dropped the oxen horn. Smoke still wafted up from its open base.

I forgot to warn them! Lluava realized. She cried out to her comrades as they rushed toward their enemy, "Be careful! Whatever they smoke causes them to go mad."

But there was no time for questions. Varren clenched his jaw and barreled ahead, Talos and Lluava close behind. The two giant figures ran at them with glazed eyes. One beelined toward Varren. Lluava vaulted from her horse and shifted. She could hear her panicked mount galloping away as she hooked her claws into the Raider's back. She would deal with her horse problem later. If there was a later.

The second Raider grabbed hold of her swishing tail and attempted to pull her off his comrade. From the corner of her eye, Lluava saw Talos charge in to attack. Where was Yamir?

Varren had dismounted, but not before sharp pain shot up Lluava's spine as the Raider wrenched her tail again. She relinquished her grip as a third jerk propelled her backward. As she slammed into the second Raider's body, Lluava made sure she sliced at his face. The sound of claws raking the metal helmet screamed over the muffled grunts and scuffling sounds.

The giant Raider lost his grip. Lluava whirled around and charged the first marauder once again. Transforming back, she ran to her partner's side. And so their dance began, both partners acting in concert, moving fluidly around each other. Fighting in this manner was almost effortless for Lluava. She needn't worry about exposing her back or turning too slowly. Her other half was there, protecting her, filling her gaps, completing her, and she did the same for him. They were far stronger fighting together as one entity than as individuals. Yet neither was able to score a fatal blow.

"Yamir!" Talos's voice pierced the air.

Lluava had only a moment to see that Talos had been abandoned by his surrogate partner. Running toward Lluava's Raider, Yamir pelted the brute's back with his porcupine quills. Meanwhile, Talos was forced to retreat. He, too, moved in Lluava's direction; however, his intention was not to attack but to evade.

"Look out!" warned Lluava as she yanked Varren out of the way of a stray quill.

With a loud clang, Talos's sword blocked the Raider's steel from slicing into Lluava's head. With no time for thanks, it was Varren's turn to deflect the weapon.

It was taking the efforts of all three soldiers to defend themselves from the massive man's attacks. These were not good odds. Lluava risked a glance around. Where was Yamir? She spotted him through a break in the trees, just as the second brute's fist slammed into the youth's chest, sending him flying backward into fallen leaves.

Yamir did not get up.

Please be all right, Lluava prayed. She wished he would right himself and move her way. His body was so still. Was that why the brute had lost interest? Had he forgotten what he had been doing just a moment before? The Raider's face remained blank. What was in that smoke?

Lluava ducked as Varren swung his sword over her head, slicing into their Raider's garb. Glancing behind them, she saw that the other marauder was leaving the area, apparently choosing to continue his mission rather than fight.

"He is getting away," warned Lluava.

But their attacker persisted in his onslaught on the prince despite his wound. Varren focused his attention on the barrage of sword thrusts.

"Lluava," he shouted. "Go after him!"

As if the hulking man had read Varren's thoughts, he swung at Lluava. Before she could react, Varren had shoved her out of range of the vicious weapon. Regaining her footing, Lluava made sure Talos was coming to

Varren's aid. There was no time to check on Yamir. The young woman raced into the woods to find the second marauder.

Within minutes, the trail of smoky scent had led her right to the Raider. Lluava released a low growl. The Raider did not acknowledge the sound. Moving closer, she prepared to strike.

But before she could attack, the Raider turned, his war hammer at the ready. She fell backward to evade the heinous weapon, then rolled away, sending leaf litter flying.

Leaping to her feet, Lluava growled out, "Hi!"

Hi? What was she thinking? Did she want to converse with this monster? The man stopped.

"Say something." Now Lluava thought she might actually be going crazy. "Can you speak? Or are you just a dumb animal?"

The man let out a low grunt. At least, it wasn't any word Lluava knew.

"Just as I thought."

The Raider took a step toward her.

For some reason, she badly wanted to see if she could spark a response. "My raven says more than you do," she taunted him. Where is that bird? she wondered. Onyx must have stayed at camp. The animal was either smart or just lazy.

The Raider continued to close the gap between them.

Lluava knew the man was too strong for her, his weapon too dangerous. She had to find a place to hide. Turning about, she spotted just the thing she needed. As she skidded around a rock formation, she momentarily paused. She did not need to see the Raider; his thunderous footsteps were loud enough to give warning.

Suddenly the sounds stopped. Lluava pressed herself flat against the cold stone. The man must be on the far side of the boulder. She could hear his breath, heavy and rather rapid. Was he tiring, or was his ragged breath a result of the contents of the horn? Peering around, Lluava tried to determine her best route of escape.

She could feel her shirt sticking to her side as she switched positions. Looking down, she saw that a thin damp streak ran the length of her black top. Her injury had reopened again. That realization and the associated pain of the wound angered her; she could feel fury building inside her. Lluava knew she must not let that get in the way of her need to flee.

A bone-chilling crack erupted from above, and shards of broken stone filled the air around her. Lluava flung her arms over her head to protect herself. There was no time to lose—the massive hammer would strike again; this time it could very well lay claim to her.

She backed away from the stone divider and quickly considered her options. If she had to distract the Raider until Varren arrived, it might take a while. The brute did not show signs of tiring, and Lluava knew that this moment of peace was only a temporary reprieve. Eyeing the huge hammer in the monster's hand, the teen knew Issaura's Claws would be of little help. There was only one thing left to do.

Lluava shifted into her dual form, allowing her weapons to gild the tigress's claws.

The Raider's nostrils flared like a bull preparing to charge, but Lluava made the first move. She veered to the side, hoping to lure the man off his intended path. And so she did. The Raider blundered after her. Lluava had to watch her footing in the loose underbrush; if she stumbled, all could be lost.

Away, she thought. I must keep him away. He must not reach wherever he was headed.

Like a rabid animal lunging to attack, the Raider continued to follow her, even though he, too, almost lost his footing on the slick leaf litter. Finally Lluava slowed, fearing she would lose Varren and the others. She needed them to find her. She could not take down this giant on her own.

Swinging his war hammer, the Raider approached. This was the chance she needed. Lluava charged forward, then skidded in the leaves and slid right through the gap between the man's legs. Her dual form was so large that she felt the coarse fabric of his pants tug against her fur.

Unfortunately, Lluava could not right herself quickly enough. The marauder slammed his hammer into the earth, creating massive divots as large as her head. Lluava lurched aside.

As her wound continued to bleed, the pain from her underbelly began to cloud her thoughts. Red stains started to color her fur. Come on! I can do this, she thought. I just need to hold out a little longer.

But she felt her speed begin to slacken and her muscles stiffen with soreness. She looked about desperately. Varren, where are you?

Without warning, Lluava lost her footing. The loose leaves had become more than a literal downfall.

The next moment brought the unnaturally tight grip of the Raider's outsized hand on the scruff of her neck. Yowling, Lluava tried to fight as she was lifted onto her rear legs. Her attempt to twist her body around proved useless. Where was the hammer? She could not see it.

The pain from her extended torso felt like a hot ribbon splitting her in two. She knew she was bleeding freely now. The searing pain was too much. She had to escape it—and the oncoming impact from the hammer that would seal her fate.

Lluava released the restraints she had placed upon herself. She felt herself retract into her own consciousness. As a blue-green film tinted the world around her, something deep inside her being erupted in a tremendous roar.

***

She was on the ground, sprawled among leaves. Her body felt heavy and sluggish, but mercifully the pain had subsided. Congealing blood had caused leaf letter to stick to her clothes. She had shifted back to human form while unconscious.

Had the hammer impaled her? Was that what had made everything go black? Feeling her chest, she found no tenderness other than the aggravated wound from that blasted stag. However, her stomach was distended to the point of discomfort. In the quiet confusion, as her nausea thickened, Lluava felt something in her teeth. She spat out a minute piece of flesh.

Pushing up onto her forearms, Lluava caught sight of the still form lying beside her. There was only thing it could be; however, it was all wrong. A quick glance confirmed that the mangled remains of the Raider were scattered about her. Most of him was missing.

With shocking and sudden awareness, Lluava could not hold back and vomited profusely on the ground. Again and again she retched, as pulpy masses came up with dark bile. Even after several minutes, she continued to dry heave. One thought filled her mind.

I ate him.

Chapter 27

Ullr's Fangs

The foul aftertaste of bile was far less vile than the knowledge of what she had done. Lluava quickly crept away from the grisly scene behind her. Beads of sweat clustered on her forehead and dripped down her face.

What have I done?

Her whole body shook. She felt listless, drained, weak. She closed her eyes and prayed to the gods that this was just a nightmare. But when she opened them again, nothing had changed.

I'm a monster, Lluava thought, her tears welling up. *And what if it happens again?*

Somehow, this thought proved worse than the knowledge that she had indeed eaten a human. Had he been alive, or had she simply consumed his corpse? What was happening to her? Why couldn't she remember?

A faint cawing sound came from a nearby branch. Onyx. The others! Lluava could not allow them to see what she had done. Forcing herself to her feet, she began to stagger toward camp. They must not find the Raider's corpse.

"Lluava!"

Too late.

Varren ran toward her through the trees. He froze, stunned, unsure of what he saw. As he tried to make sense of the scene before him, Lluava collapsed and fell to the ground, sobbing. "Varren," she cried, "I don't know what's happening to me!"

In a moment, he was next to her, carefully wiping the crusting blood off her chin. He gently moved the tangled strands of her hair away from her face and tucked them behind her ears. Leaning closer, he whispered, "We have to go, Lluava."

Her partner put his arm around her and helped her up. She flinched when his hand accidentally touched her wound. He had to control both his anger at the Raiders and his concern for her injury.

"You are hurt," he said gently, knowing she was in shock. "We need to get you back to camp." Quickly he moved her forward.

A few minutes later, Talos and a very glum-looking Yamir approached, leading her mount along with their own.

"You found her. Thank the gods," commented Talos. "What happened to the other Raider?"

Lluava's eyes widened in panic. Varren gave her arm a slight squeeze and then calmly answered for her. "Lluava killed him, but we must return to camp. Rosalyn needs to treat Lluava's wound, and then she needs to rest. We march tomorrow."

Talos seemed skeptical. He stared hard at Lluava but kept silent after Varren's warning look. They returned to camp in silence. Even though Lluava was on horseback, the journey back seemed long.

Lluava struggled with her thoughts. Did Varren fully understand what she had done? He must have. He had seen her as well as the Raider's remains. His face had betrayed his emotions: shock, disbelief, and then acceptance. Would he tell the others? What did he think of her? She looked over at her partner. His features were strained. She felt like vomiting again.

Byron greeted them when they arrived at the camp, but Rosalyn hung back. From the look on her friend's face, Lluava knew that Talos was about to endure another epic argument. Lluava found that she did not care. She was so tired and still felt very sick. She wanted only to sleep.

"I'm going to lie down," said Lluava as she slid off her horse. Her legs started to buckle. Varren leaped to the ground to steady her.

"Rosalyn," he said with a nod to the other woman, "get your medical supplies and take care of her." Releasing Lluava, he told her to get some rest and then took her horse's reins.

"What happened out there?" Byron asked as Lluava walked heavily away.

Would Varren tell them? Lluava was terrified that the others would find out about the incident in the woods. She glanced over her shoulder; all her friends seemed to be staring at her. Pinpricks raced down her spine, and she hurried toward her tent. She did not want anyone's help, including Rosalyn's. She needed to be alone, away from everyone. She wanted to sleep away this whole living nightmare.

"I want to speak to you." Apex's terse voice cut through her thoughts like a knife.

"Leave me alone," she hissed, and moved quickly around the campfire.

He was the last person she wanted to see.

Apex followed her. "I said, I want a word with you. *Now*."

Lluava's heart began to thump rapidly. This man made her skin crawl—he would not corner her again. Veering sharply away from her tent, she snarled back, "I said, leave me alone."

He pursued.

Lluava ran.

Hearing his footfalls, she ran faster. What would Apex do to her if he caught up? Had he any clue what had happened in the forest? Did this have something to do with Austro? Did he blame her for the death of his friend, or whatever Austro was to him? The idea of the huntsman's fury was nothing less than terrifying.

Risking a backward glance, she saw Apex in pursuit. The expression on his face was both determined and serious. The desire to shift took hold, but Lluava quickly stifled it. She feared she would lose control again and kill Apex. Even he did not deserve that.

"Go away!" she screamed, and almost fell over a root. Regaining her footing, she headed deeper into the woods. She *had* to lose him. But try as she might, he continued the chase. Eventually, Lluava looked back again. Was he catching up? Apex was still running, but the distance had not changed between them. He appeared neither winded nor tired.

Was he unable to get closer? Or was he simply that confident? The third time she glanced around, Apex's pace remained unaltered. She had the impression that he was not actually trying to catch her. Perhaps she was wrong, but she believed it. Either way, she was far too weary to keep up this pace.

She slowed; so did Apex. Lluava stopped and faced him. Apex stopped too.

"What do you want from me?" she cried out, exasperated.

No response. He looked at her, his face unreadable.

"I ate him," she said.

Lluava didn't know why she had said it, or why to him, of all people. The huntsman already despised her. Knowing what she had done could only make things worse. Then again, could he really hate her more than he already did?

Apex's expression did not change. He stood twenty paces away and observed her.

Maybe it was the desire to confide in someone, or maybe it was the feeling of utter desperation, but suddenly the whole story came tumbling from her lips. When she had finished, Apex remained silent.

"Well?" she asked. She needed to know what he thought.

"Run," he stated, nodding toward the forest.

"What?"

"Just run."

What kind of advice was this? Was he trying to be sincere? Lluava had no idea, but she took off once again. This time, Apex positioned himself by her side.

They ran like this, together, for several hours, at a steady pace set by neither one in particular. After a time, Lluava realized that the exertion was driving out her pent-up anxiety. Here in the woods, there was no one to judge her, no enemy to fight, no restrictions or boundaries.

Finally, Lluava found herself struggling for breath; her limbs ached, and there was a sharp catch in her side. Gradually she slowed and paused to catch her breath. The chill air cooled the heat that radiated from her sweat-soaked body.

Apex panted, too. Yet even in his exhaustion, his look was still untamed.

"Thank you," she said, and meant it.

He looked at her. "It's time to head back. Evening is approaching."

Apex was right. The understory was darkening. Had they actually been gone that long? Varren was probably searching for her. She suddenly felt foolish, charging off into the woods like that.

As they began the long run home, a wafting scent made the hairs on Lluava's neck stand on end. Halting, she briskly barked out, "Badger!" She did not have to say another word. Apex clearly understood that if this was her secret stalker, they had to investigate.

Taking the lead, Apex quickly followed the new course. Lluava trailed him, trying to be as quiet as the large huntsman. This time the scent did not dissipate; rather, it strengthened and mixed with the damp aroma of water. Climbing down into a wide ravine, the pair carefully tracked their prey.

Not too far ahead, they heard a high-pitched chittering. Staying just out of sight, Lluava peered around some underbrush. A small brook trickled through the bottom of the ravine, and a large badger paced around a sorry-looking cherry tree. The carnivore's ears perked up in her direction, and Lluava quickly ducked back down.

Please don't run away, she thought. Nearby, Apex's face was serious, as usual.

Lluava listened to the continuous sounds the badger emitted. Fortunately, it seemed to be content with circling the tree. Soon Lluava took another peek. The animal saw her but did not move. Instead it sat down and seemed to wait.

"He's not afraid," whispered Lluava, and Apex moved forward to see.

Now the badger bobbed its head up and down, as if nodding.

"Is he your thief?" whispered Apex.

Lluava tried to sense whether this was another Theriomorph, but it was somehow hard to tell. "I don't know."

"Well, there is one way to find out." Apex approached the badger. It continued to chitter but stayed seated. After a few steps, Lluava stood up to follow the huntsman. As soon as she did, the badger sprang to its feet and snarled.

Lluava and Apex froze in their tracks. Was the animal about to attack? After a tense moment, Apex waved Lluava back. As a huntsman, he must know best, she decided. She squatted down but kept Issaura's Claws at the ready.

Seeing her move away, the badger relaxed and resumed its chittering. Apex took a step forward and then another. Slowly and cautiously, he made his way to the animal. As he approached, the badger began to grow more excited and began to claw at the earth near the base of the cherry tree.

"I think he wants to show me something," Apex said to Lluava as he knelt by the striped beast. The badger clawed the soil once more, then backed off to observe the huntsman.

Lluava was dubious. If the badger really was the one who had tried to steal the Claws, wouldn't he want to deal with her, not Apex? Hadn't the thief been following her the whole time? He would not have allowed them to see his dual form. None of this made sense.

Apex scooped a handful of the damp soil to one side. The badger's chittering became faster and more intense. Lluava leaned forward for a better view. The animal eyed her warily while Apex continued to dig.

Finally he stopped. Wiping off his hands, he exclaimed, "There is something buried here!"

Lluava wished she could go over and look, but the badger was keeping his guard up. She had to be content with seeing Apex uncover a long, thin, wooden box. Purring, the badger seemed beside himself. What was happening?

"What is it?" questioned Lluava as the badger lay down, apparently content.

"I'm not sure. Come take a look."

Lluava approached the huntsman slowly; her eyes kept drifting to the badger, who seemed too relaxed to worry about her.

Kneeling next to Apex, Lluava could see the three-foot-long box up close. Dark wood was hinged with metal trim. There was no line for an opening, although a small knob that resembled a lock without a hole was centered in what was most likely the front. On the lid was carved the image of a monstrous animal that seemed to sneer up at them. Around the four sides of the box, a carved battle scene depicted the same enormous animal ripping apart fleeing soldiers.

"What is that?" Lluava asked, pointing to the unknown animal.

Apex stared at it in silence. Then he attempted to pry open the box. But even with all his might, he was still unable to remove the top. After several attempts, Lluava joked, "It got the better of you?"

In no mood for jests, Apex pulled out a skinning knife and tried to wedge it between the wood and the metal knob. The knife slipped and cut his hand. Cursing, Apex let go of the box and kicked it. Lluava was not the only one who could abruptly lose her temper.

As Lluava picked up the unexpectedly heavy box, she almost dropped it in surprise. She blinked to make sure what she saw was real. Some of Apex's blood had fallen onto the small lock, and as it dripped down, a thin crack appeared across the knob.

"Apex," called Lluava. "Look."

He strode over and reexamined the box, then carefully lifted the lid. Two sets of eyes now absorbed the secrets that had been buried in the forest. Inside the box lay a pair of twin swords, their shape familiar to Lluava but crafted like none she had ever seen. From handle to tip, they seemed wrought from a single piece of coppery metal. Their blades formed a slight teardrop shape, and a snarling creature's face was carved into each pommel.

"They're Gladius swords," explained Lluava. She pointed to the one on the left. "Two feet long, and look at their curve."

"Are they for us?" Apex asked in a tone that oozed desire.

Lluava found herself shaking her head. "I think they are meant for you."

"What do you mean?"

Looking at the weapon's strange container, Lluava said, "I don't think my blood would have unlocked the chest."

As Apex lifted one of the blades to inspect the flawless workmanship, Lluava noticed an inscription on the inside of the lid. Looking at the runes that she had come to understand, she translated aloud, "Ullr's Fangs."

She quickly looked back at Apex, who was staring at her. Suddenly, Lluava wished she had not followed the badger's musk. Now Apex had weapons like hers. Why would he, of all people, be gifted with replicas of the Gladius swords worn by the god of war?

There were so many questions to be answered. Lluava stood up and looked at the badger, or where it had been.

"Apex!" she cried out. "The badger—he's gone!"

Chapter 28

Falling Sky

We have to go after him!" cried Lluava. Moving in the direction the badger was last seen, Lluava turned. "Apex?"

Still examining his new prizes, the huntsman disagreed. "We should head back to camp. It's almost dark."

Lluava was annoyed. Clearly, Apex did not understand the direness of the situation. He was far too enamored with his new treasure.

"But the badger..." she protested. If only she had developed tracking skills.

Apex repacked Ullr's Fangs in their wooden case and slung the long box over his shoulder. Glumly, Lluava followed him back to their camps.

She could not stop thinking about the badger. Why would he try to steal Issaura's Claws, then turn around and show Apex where Ullr's Fangs were buried? The Fangs had been lost since ancient times. How did the thief know where they were hidden? Did he steal them and hide them himself? How could that be? Is that what he had wanted with the Claws—to take them away from her, only to give them to some nameless creature? For what? And what use would Apex have for weapons like these? He knew nothing of combat on the battlefield. He was not a warrior.

Lluava continued to brood until she saw a figure striding toward them. In the gloom, she recognized the prince only by the familiar way he moved.

Varren was furious. "I told you to stay away from her!" he yelled.

Apex said nothing, but he lowered the box to the ground.

Varren's eyes were ablaze. "You are never to be alone with her again!"

"You've got this all wrong—" Lluava began, but Varren cut her off.

"I'll deal with you later," he said, and returned his fierce gaze to its intended target.

Lluava felt herself grow hot with anger.

He continued to address Apex. "You are never to talk to or even look at Lluava when she is alone. Do you hear me?" Coming to a stop directly in front of the huntsman, Varren waited impatiently for a response.

"That decision is not yours to make," responded Apex briskly.

Lluava saw Varren reach for the hilt of his sword. Apex must have anticipated Varren's next move. The huntsman raised Ullr's Fangs to Varren's throat just as Varren pointed his sword at Apex's jugular. Lluava had not even seen Apex open the box.

"Enough!" roared Lluava. This was getting out of hand. From the corner of her eye, she saw other figures running toward them.

"Varren," she said as she pulled him backward by his shoulder, "you may be my partner and my prince, but that does not give you total authority over my actions. I can associate with whom I please."

"With that excuse for a man?" Varren pointed to Apex, who still held the Fangs before him. "That animal! Even after he tried—" Varren cut himself off. His chest heaved with rage.

"Yes, that man." Calmly Lluava said, "He was only trying to help me."

"I don't understand you." Varren scowled at Lluava and glared at Apex before storming off, back to camp.

Lluava knew she should follow. She needed some distance between herself and Apex. As she left, she heard Wod ask Apex, "Where did you get those swords?"

By evening, Varren had calmed down, at least for the time being. After everyone but Lluava had eaten, she walked over to the huntsmen's camp to pay her respects to Austro.

Still wrapped in the cloth in which Rosalyn had bound him, his body appeared untouched. No pyre had been built, no hole dug. What had the others been doing while she had been away?

"Mila," she said to the woman sitting by a small fire. "Are you going to have a ceremony for Austro?"

Looking at the deceased, Mila asked, "Ceremony? Why? Austro's not here anymore. All that's left is his corpse."

Lluava was taken aback at the callousness of Mila's words. "But aren't you going to bury him?"

Turning to Lluava, Mila spoke kindly, though her words were frigid. "Austro was of the forest. He, like the rest of us, understood that there is nothing to come from mourning. People die. Animals die. The dead are consumed to feed the living. That is the way of the wilderness. We will leave him as is."

Lluava left, feeling hollow. Was that all there was? Was there only emptiness to fill the void where the soul had been?

This day had been too hard. Yearning for sleep, Lluava refused to speak with anybody, especially Varren, and retired to her tent. Unfortunately, someone was waiting for her inside.

As Lluava prepared to defend herself, Rosalyn's voice whispered, "Lluava, it is I."

"What are you doing here?" Lluava asked as she calmed herself. "You startled me."

"I am truly sorry for the intrusion. I wanted to check on your wound." Rosalyn hesitated and then looked down. "Actually, I wanted to talk with you alone. You see, I need a favor."

Sitting down on her blankets, Lluava told her dear friend, "Anything. Name it."

Rosalyn knelt beside her. "I want you to teach me to fight."

This was totally unexpected. Lluava stammered, "You were taught how to fight, Rosalyn."

"No," her friend disagreed candidly. "I was taught how to defend myself. General Kentril never wanted to train women to be warriors."

She had a point. At Thowcelemine, the Theriomorph women's training camp, females were taught to be healers and behind-the-lines advisors, not fighters. Lluava regarded Rosalyn's delicate build. Was her friend serious?

"Why don't you ask Talos? I'm sure he would assist you."

Rosalyn laughed. "Talos wants to keep me safe. He, like many of the others, treats me like some fragile doll that might crack if dropped. I am no doll, Lluava. I can learn to fight." Rosalyn must have seen the frown on her friend's face, for she added, "Talos will not teach me; he will do everything he can to keep me away from battle. But Lluava, those battles will come to us, and I must be ready."

"Are you saying that you are not even going to tell Talos about this?"

Nodding her head yes, Rosalyn's eyes brimmed with tears. "I almost lost Talos earlier today." The words came out in broken sobs. "He nearly died… trying to protect me…. All because I could not defend myself…"

"Rosalyn, he only lost the tip of an antler," Lluava reminder her gently.

A fierceness took hold of Rosalyn's voice, and she wiped the tears from her cheeks. "Next time, it could be his head. I cannot allow that. I cannot be responsible. Lluava, I want you to train me until I am able to prove to Talos that he need not protect me all the time."

"I doubt that even the highest skill in combat would prevent him from trying to protect you."

"True," acknowledged Rosalyn. "But at least I could also help defend *him*."

Lluava chewed her tongue as she thought. Rosalyn waited, looking anxious.

"Fine." Lluava had made her decision. "I will begin training you tomorrow evening after we make camp."

"You won't tell anyone else about this, will you?"

Lluava considered Talos's behavior and Varren's overreaction earlier today. How dare her partner think he could control her?

"I won't," she promised.

"Thank you!" exclaimed Rosalyn. "Thank you, Lluava." She left hurriedly, as though she feared Lluava might change her mind.

As soon as the tent flap closed, Lluava once again drifted off into nightmare-filled sleep.

**

The cold had not dissipated by midday. In fact, it seemed to be growing colder. Clouds of breath puffed about everyone's faces. Ulder, Varren's mount, seemed to loathe the weather just as much as Lluava did. Unlike the other northern steeds, his sleek form and coat were not made for this sort of temperature. The horse shivered often under his blanket.

Something icy pricked Lluava's ear. Looking about, she saw nothing unusual. Soon, however, another frigid pinprick hit the back of her neck. Lluava pulled the hood of her cloak over her head. The material had started showing wear, but it still kept her warm and well.

Something white and almost too small to notice fell onto her horse's mane. In a blink, it was gone. Soon another particle fell, and then another. What in the gods' temples was going on? Lluava looked up at the overcast sky and saw a profusion of white flecks sloughing from the gray clouds.

"Varren?" Lluava's voice cracked. "The sky! It's falling!"

Something dark was in the works, and they needed to find shelter. What if the entire sky fell down, clouds, stars, and all? Why was everyone so calm? Didn't they see the crumbling heavens?

Varren laughed. It was a sound Lluava had seldom heard him make of late, and she liked it, even though he was laughing at her. "Lluava, have you not seen snow before?"

"Snow?" Lluava repeated. She knew what snow was. She had read about it in her studies long ago in Rivendale. She had never encountered it before. It was far too warm in the south for such nonsense as snow to occur.

"Look. See," Varren stretched out his black glove before her. Soon a small frozen crystal landed on his palm. Lluava only had a moment to admire its delicate and intricate beauty before it melted and was gone.

Was he trying to make up with her? Lluava was unsure. After their quarrel, he had been coolly polite. Pulling down her hood, she reached out her own hands and tried to catch the drifting white fluff. Varren did not judge her or make fun of her limited knowledge of this frozen precipitation, and for this she was glad.

He smiled as he watched her. "Try to catch one on your tongue. Like this."

Opening his mouth, he attempted to position himself where a flake might land, zigzagging his horse all about. "Got one!" he exclaimed with a grin.

"I want to try," laughed Lluava, and she, too, moved her horse around. Soon the sharp sting of cold landed on her tongue.

"Very good," acknowledged Varren. "With a bit more practice, you could be a professional snow-catcher like me."

Looking at Varren mischievously, Lluava commented, "I bet I can catch more than you can."

So their secret competition began. Whoever nabbed a flake would shout out the number: four, seven, ten. Only when Apex barked out, "We are stopping to eat!" did Lluava finally admit that Varren was by far the more expert snow-eater.

"But," she reminded him, "it's only because you've had more practice."

While she stretched her legs, Lluava heard Wod calling her. What did he want? She had not talked with the other huntsmen since they had left Austro's body behind that morning. She would have liked to avoid them altogether, but traveling in such a small group made that impossible.

Wod was throwing knives at a knot in a tree and hitting the mark every time. Next to him, Monk was fletching arrows. The older brother ignored Lluava's presence, but Wod gave her a large, toothy grin.

"Yeah?" said Lluava.

Wod, still holding three knives, selected one and prepared to aim. "I saw you and the prince playing with the snowflakes."

"I've never seen snow before," Lluava hastily explained, embarrassed at having been observed.

"Really?" asked Wod, who tossed his blade. With a thunk, it sank into the knot. "Then I look forward to seeing your reaction when it actually begins to stick. I bet you will jump into the frozen mounds like me. I can show you how to make winged figures in the snow."

Lluava raised an eyebrow. Was he making fun of her? At seventeen, Wod was close to her own age and seemed honest enough, but would he actually reach out to her in friendship?

"Maybe," she replied hesitantly. She changed the subject. "Aren't you the one who makes all those snares? Can you show me how to do that?"

Wod threw another knife, this time without aiming. He still hit his mark. "Maybe," he said, all smiles.

"Wod, let's go hunt."

Monk had finished with the feathers and had his bow slung it over his shoulder. He gave Lluava a cold look before motioning his younger brother to follow him.

"Catch ya' later," said Wod with a grin. He headed into the woods, his throwing knives tucked into his belt.

Lluava still had enough break time left to check on Yamir. Rosalyn had told her he was lucky to have only bruised ribs after being tossed around in yesterday's skirmish. During the morning ride, Yamir had seemed to withdraw into himself.

Lluava found him seated at the perimeter of the clearing. Varren sat next to him, his arm about their younger friend's shoulders. Moving closer, Lluava stayed just within the range of her hypersensitive hearing. She didn't want to eavesdrop, but her curiosity got the best of her.

Yamir was speaking. "Don't bother saying that. I know the truth."

"And what is the truth?" Varren asked intently.

Chewing his lower lip, Yamir eventually replied, "I know that none of you trust me. You think I'm crazy or something."

"We do not believe that you are crazy," countered the prince, "but we have been concerned about how you are dealing with Chat's death. You two were very close."

Were those tears in Yamir's eyes? Lluava was too far away to tell. She moved closer.

"It shouldn't have been him." Yamir's voice cracked.

"It should not have been anyone," Varren contended, his own voice deepening. "Chat was a true friend to all of us, but to you, he was a brother. Not by blood, that is true, but brother just the same. I know the feeling of losing a brother…" Varren's voice broke as well.

Yamir studied Varren's face; his own showed understanding. "I forgot about Thad. I'm sorry."

They both remained silent for a long time. Lluava, suddenly embarrassed to be listening to their private conversation, slipped away unnoticed. Watching Varren comfort Yamir had reminded her how compassionate he really was. Yes, he had overreacted with Apex the other day, but she knew he did it out of love for her. Regardless, he still should not have responded as he did.

Lluava got back to camp just as a new commotion was occurring. Half-supported by Monk, Wod was stumbling back to their tents. The teen's left leg had swollen to twice its normal size.

"Hey, you!" Monk shouted out to Rosalyn as Wod's face contorted in pain. "Help him!"

"What happened?" she inquired, ignoring Monk's rudeness.

"A spider bit him. I don't know what kind," Worry lines creased Monk's face.

Wod scanned those around him and spotted Lluava. "It was only a little spider," he added.

"Hand me my bag," directed Rosalyn.

As Lluava was closest, she picked it up—it felt remarkably light—and handed it to her friend. Rosalyn took an unusually long time fumbling through its contents. Odd, thought Lluava; there could not have been that much, based on its weight. Her friend finally selected a small vial and placed a single drop on the wound.

Wod yelped.

"Your leg will feel better within the hour, and the swelling should be gone by tonight. If it persists, let me know, and I will administer another dose."

Monk reached over and touched Rosalyn's arm. "Thank you."

By evening Wod clearly felt as if he had never been bitten. Rosalyn seemed pleased. After supper, Lluava followed her friend into the woods.

Lluava selected a spot far away from the light of the cooking fires so no others would see them. Possibly due to the loss of Austro, Apex and Varren had decided to combine both camps; now, with more people coming and going, it was easier to disappear unnoticed for a bit.

Lluava handed Rosalyn a stick; she herself held its twin. "We will begin with these," she stated. "Once you know the appropriate techniques, we will transition to real knives and swords."

"That sounds perfect," Rosalyn gleefully acknowledged. She sounded almost giddy.

"But before we begin, I have something I need to ask you."

"Anything."

"What happened to your medical supplies? I know your supplies are low. I felt the bag."

Rosalyn's shoulders dropped. "It's the cold. Most of my tonics were not meant to withstand this temperature. At least not for any extended period. I had to dispose of them."

"So, what does that mean?"

"It means, Lluava, that I cannot afford to waste anything on minor injuries. Only the most severe cases can be treated."

Lluava chose not to question Rosalyn further. Instead, she began to instruct her in proper stances for battle.

When they had finished for the evening, Lluava returned to her tent. Her wound was irritating her once again. She had not changed the bandage in several days. Peeling back the wrappings, she looked at the long cut down her side. Even in the dark, she could see that it was pink and warm to the touch. She rinsed it off with drinking water and rewrapped it.

Mulling over what Rosalyn had told her, she decided not to bother her with this. It was only a scratch. It would heal in time.

Chapter 29

Dead but not Forgotten

Snow fell more heavily each day; soon high mounds covered underbrush and obscured animal trails. Lluava's attitude toward the ever-piling white fluff quickly turned from admiration and awe to indifference and finally to loathing. Extra time was needed for the caravan to pick its way through the forest. On more than one occasion, they had to dismount and walk their horses through particularly thick drifts. It seemed to Lluava that she was constantly cold and wet. Sulking, she desired the warmth of fires.

To her dismay, Varren would not allow large fires to be built, for fear of alerting any Raiders possibly lurking in the forest. Apex agreed. Actually, Apex seemed to support every order Varren gave. Lluava wondered if this had anything to do with the huntsman's new swords. Ullr's Fangs were always in hand whenever Apex and the troop stopped. Was this the beginning of some sort of obsession?

"You don't even know how to use them," snapped Lluava to Apex after a particularly hard ride. She was sore, tired, and not feeling like herself.

Apex lifted one of the Fangs in a nonthreatening way and pointed it in her direction. "I know well enough."

Somehow, Apex always found a way to stir up Lluava's temper. If the gods did exist, how could they have made a man like that? And why would they bestow such gifts upon such a worthless person? Then again, did a higher power have any say in the actions of the mysterious badger? Lluava peevishly wondered how gamy a badger would taste.

"Will you hunt with me today?"

Mila had appeared in her dappled-gray dual form. She had asked Lluava the same question for days, and Lluava's response was always the same.

"No."

Knowing that there was something monstrous about herself was horrifying; realizing that she could no longer control herself was almost too much to endure. What if, the next time she shifted, she mauled one of her friends? In that blacked-out state, could she differentiate the Elysians from the Raiders? Lluava secretly vowed never to shift again. That part of her, the tigress, could never be allowed to reemerge, if only to keep people like Varren safe.

As far as she could tell, Varren had not exposed her dark secret to anyone else. Lluava was grateful for that. She was not sure she would be able to bear the looks from her friends or the whispers that would follow. However, she still had to deal with the fact that Varren knew she was capable of such unspeakable deeds.

When they were alone, Varren had asked her many questions. Lluava trusted her partner and wanted to confide in him, but she did not understand what had happened either. The questions remained unanswered. Together they decided that it was best for her not to be put in any situation that could unleash such overwhelming anger and trigger her incredible transformation. Lluava had wondered if Varren's feelings for her would change. And they had; he had become even more protective.

Lluava could deal with that. Besides, there were far more pressing matters. Derrick had returned, bringing with him the news that three of his men had been murdered. Now their communication chain, their link with their Elysian army, was incomplete. Derrick reassured them that they would still be able to pass messages, but each member of his pack would have to travel to get into hearing range of the next member. It could slow down their messages by several days.

That evening, Lluava saw Mila's tail twitch before the woman shifted back into her human form. "Take a walk with me," Lluava said.

Together the pair strode through the thinning forest. Looking ahead at the ever-growing mountains, Lluava said, "Tell me about the Pass. That is where we are heading, is it not?"

Mila considered her taller comrade for a moment. "I don't have much to tell. I have never been there."

"Never?"

"Never. People do not leave the Beltline. Those who do don't come back. Only one has ventured into the Borren mountain range and lived to tell of it." Lluava already guessed to whom Mila was referring. "Apex will show us the way."

Lluava snorted. "Of course."

"He is not as vile as you seem to think," Mila assured her.

"He is no charmer," countered Lluava.

"Many a woman would beg to differ," smiled Mila ruefully as she leaped onto the leaning trunk of a fallen tree.

Lluava wondered if Mila were one of those unfortunate women who had succumbed to Apex's supposed charm. She wanted to ask more; however, the many weeks of etiquette training had taught her that tact was always the better route. There was no tasteful way to broach the subject.

Instead, Lluava asked, "If no one travels into the mountain range, why does he? Let me guess; it has something to do with his obstinate contempt for rules."

If Lluava had hoped for a laugh or even a smile from the other woman, she was greatly mistaken. Instead, Mila replied, "He is from there." There was no guile or deceit in her response.

"I don't understand," Lluava said. "What do you mean, 'from there'? Was he born there? What about his parents?"

Slipping off her perch, Mila said, "One thing you must understand in regard to Apex: ask no questions. That is the secret to getting along with him. Time for dinner. Let's go."

Lluava did not have a moment to mull over this information; it would have to wait.

Back at camp, she observed a distance between Rosalyn and Talos. Though not physical, the estrangement manifested itself in different ways. As they gathered for the meal, Byron tried to make light of the situation and sat down between the two, hoping to spark a conversation. Lluava knew he meant well, but his attempt seemed only to draw the attention of others to the betrothed couple's personal problems.

Taking a seat beside Lluava, Varren placed his hand on the small of her back. He leaned close and whispered, "May we never have a falling out like that."

Although she appreciated the gesture, Lluava could not stop herself from retorting, "Just don't think you can control me again!"

Varren clenched his jaw, dropped his hand, stood, and left to sit somewhere else. Lluava felt bad about offending her partner, yet her point was as valid as his. Prince or not, he did not have full control over her, especially here in the Outlands.

After a quiet supper, Lluava met Rosalyn in the forest. Lluava led the way farther into the woods so as not to alert the camp of their practice. They moved as quickly as possible through the snowdrifts, for they could escape only for short periods of time.

Once she found a place sufficient to meet their needs, Lluava placed Issaura's Claws on the ground. The weapons traveled with her all the time now; she would not risk being caught off guard by a marauding Raider or risk losing them to the Theriomorph thief. Her body ached as she bent over, as it had for the last several days. Lluava attributed the pain to her lack of sleep.

Nightmares disturbed her slumber. Images of burning castles and monstrous beasts were always accompanied by the cries of the dying.

"Ready?" Lluava inquired as she picked up her stick sword.

Rosalyn corrected her stance and replied, "Whenever you are."

"Let's begin by reviewing some of the combinations I showed you yesterday."

Watching Rosalyn practice her moves brought a smile to Lluava's face. She thought of Domar at the castle and remembered the steps he had used to teach her to fight with a sword. It was true that Lluava had already had some rudimentary training with the weapon at Durog, yet Domar's steps were easier to follow, so those were what she used to instruct Rosalyn.

"You're doing well," observed Lluava as she paused to reposition Rosalyn's shoulders at the right angle. "There. Now, I want you to repeat that again, but this time act as if I were actually combating you."

Rosalyn's expression was a mask of seriousness. Taking a deep breath, she began to go through the motions; however, Lluava noted the lack of force behind them. She would have to find ways to help build up her friend's strength.

As the lesson continued, Lluava forgot to hold back and in one stroke disarmed Rosalyn, sending the woman's stick flying into the underbrush.

"Sorry, I'll get it," apologized Lluava as she went to retrieve the stick.

She was poking through the snow-burdened underbrush when Rosalyn called out in a frightened voice, "Lluava? Lluava, get back here!"

Running at full speed, Lluava found Rosalyn, pale as ever, staring back at her. "What's wrong?"

"Behind you!" Rosalyn screamed.

Lluava turned to face a wall of golden-brown fur that seemed to rise into the tree canopy. She stared at the massive black muzzle that adorned the snarling features of a Great Mountain bear.

"Argon?" she questioned aloud, not realizing the ludicrous nature of her plea. Staring at the beast, Lluava recalled another forest and the final moments with Grand Master Chief Argon, the man who had become her friend, who had died saving her life.

"Lluava, watch out!" Rosalyn's cry forced Lluava to refocus on the present and the approaching swing from the animal's lustrous black claws. It was not the blow itself but the resulting impact as she hit the ground that made her gasp. Her shoulder, her weak link, had become dislocated.

Lluava glanced at her friend. Rosalyn was shaking with fear, but she had picked up Issaura's Claws. Was she going to attempt to fight? Lluava knew that would mean certain death for her unskilled companion.

"Rosalyn!" she shouted. "Get help! Leave the Claws and go!"

Lluava had no time to watch her friend flee toward camp. She found the strength to get to her feet and face the bear once more. Tears brimmed and rolled down her face; she wiped them away with her good arm.

The animal dropped down onto all fours. It swayed side to side, clacking its teeth. Sensing what she hoped was fear, Lluava backed away from the animal to show that she was not a threat. Why try to fight this beast, when one could just leave it be?

Slowly she took a step back, and then another. The bear lowered and began to swing its head from side to side. She paused and waited for the swaying motion to decrease. clutching her injured arm closer to her body. Bears don't go after the smell of blood, do they? Lluava hoped not.

Just as the space between them had widened beyond striking range, Lluava tripped and fell. This startled the bear. It lunged slightly, ears folded back. Lluava scrambled to her feet.

Where were the Claws? She spotted their golden glint, but they seemed so far away. She had to reach them. Even with her injured shoulder, she would have a better chance of defending herself with Issaura's Claws.

The bear made another short lunge at her.

Should she shift? At the very least, as a tiger she might scare the bear away. But what if she lost control and her friends showed up? What if she attacked one of them? Or Varren?

The bear stamped its forelegs. Lluava felt the ground tremble. Eyeing the long black claws, the teen knew that if they struck her again, she would end up with much more than a throbbing arm.

Lluava decided to make a run for her weapons. As soon as she bolted, the bear charged, cutting her off. Slipping on the frozen snow, she spun around and ran off in the opposite direction toward a leaning tree. If she could just slide under the fallen pine, maybe she could get away from the bear.

The rising moon was before her, illuminating her destination. Its soft glow somehow gave her hope. Behind her, the heavy thuds of the blundering brute resounded in pursuit.

Almost there, she told herself.

Suddenly, a dark form leaped onto the tree in front of her. The light of the moon shone on the silhouette of a second monstrous animal.

Lluava halted. She was now trapped between two enormous beasts. Behind her, the bear had also paused. Raising her good arm above her eyes, she tried to discern the features of this new creature.

The sudden comprehension hit her hard, making her want to curl up and disappear. Upon the fallen pine tree stood the monster from her nightmares—the creature carved on the mysterious box. Not a leap away stood a living, breathing Yorrick wolverine.

Lluava was caught between two supposedly extinct beasts. The only question was, which one would kill her first?

Chapter 30

Exposed

The two fabled beasts glowered at each other. Lluava was caught squarely between them, and her desire to shift was strong. But due to her injured shoulder, even if she did not lose control in her dual form, she would hardly be able to defend herself.

The monstrous creature on the log raised its hackles, which increased its size by a third. Even without being able to make out the Yorrick wolverine's features, Lluava quickly realized she would rather face the bear.

Behind her, the Great Mountain bear stood on its rear legs to engage in physical intimidation. The bear gave an impressive roar to scare off its new opponent. The Yorrick wolverine met the bear's mighty bellow with its own. Lluava clutched her ears, trying to dampen the horrendous noise.

Although both creatures were focused on each other, Lluava's fear of being pinned between these aggravated beasts was too much. She desperately looked around for an escape route. As she did so, the wolverine leaped from its post. Lluava watched the huge mass soar overhead, its bronze fur a metallic shimmer in the moonlight. When it landed, it faced away from her. To Lluava's relief, she was not worth its attention. At least, not right now.

Immediately, the two giant beasts collided. Fangs and claws tore at each other's hides. The force of the bear falling to all fours knocked the wolverine backward. Lluava had to leap out of the way as the animals hurtled past her.

Scurrying behind a clump of nearby trees, Lluava was oddly captivated by the sight of these animals brawling through the woods. The ground shook; branches broke; clumps of fur were sent adrift in the air.

All at once, the bear turned around and charged Lluava. She should have tried to escape and not waited until she became the bait. As she darted aside, the wolverine grappled with the bear, forcing the animal to slam into the ground.

Where were Issaura's Claws? In all the commotion, snow and leaf litter had been tossed everywhere. Lluava got her bearings and recognized the general area where she had left her weapons. Carefully circumnavigating the combating beasts, Lluava made a dive for the Claws and snatched them up. Weapons in hand, she tried to make a dash toward camp, but the wrestling animals cut her off.

"Lluava!" Varren's shout reached her over the din.

In the gaps between kicking limbs and snapping jaws, Lluava saw that the others had arrived. Looks of horrified awe stained their moonlit features. Varren had his sword in hand, but what could he do? Attack the already engaged beasts?

Lluava tried to dodge around the fighters, yet the animals blocked her every attempt. Finally, she saw an opening and took a chance. Moving as quickly as she could, Lluava skirted the flailing beasts, bounded over a fallen tree, and leaped into Varren's arms. But instead of a welcome embrace, her partner threw her to the ground. She felt the hiss of air as his sword slashed away a rogue paw.

As the wounded bear screamed in pain, the wolverine pulled it backward. Lluava muffled her own cries, for she had landed on her throbbing shoulder. The pain was unbearable, like knives stabbing the joint.

"What's wrong?" Varren asked as he pulled her away from the still-enraged beasts.

"My shoulder," Lluava admitted, tears rolling down her face.

Varren's brow furrowed with comprehension. "I thought it had mended."

Lluava shook her head. She was afraid of sounding weak if she spoke through the pain.

Varren looked displeased. "We will talk more about this later. If you are not in fighting condition—"

"I'm fine," she hissed. She hoped he saw how serious she was.

"I will not lose you," Varren said as he helped the young woman to her feet, then ordered, "Everyone back to camp!"

As they retreated, Lluava looked back to see the wolverine tearing into the back of the fallen bear. In a few more moments, it would be over. Only one mighty beast would survive. From her angle, Lluava could see the pain and fear in the bear's face.

"No!" she screamed. She shrugged Varren off and took a step toward the wolverine. "Leave him alone!"

"What are you doing?" demanded Varren as he grabbed her good wrist.

"I don't want it to die." The new wave of tears was not for herself.

Looking into her eyes, Varren released her. "Empathetic to a fault. Well, what do you want to—"

Lluava picked up a broken branch and threw it directly at the wolverine's face. The animal looked up, its golden eyes scorching.

"Go!" Lluava screamed. "Off with you!"

Looking at Lluava quizzically, the Yorrick wolverine slipped off its victim. In the next moment, the bear was on its feet. It lumbered off, emitting a trail of moans.

"Lluava," Varren said hesitantly, "we should go back—now."

The wolverine approached them, its eyes on Lluava. As it moved, it began to shift. Both Lluava and Varren inhaled sharply. Apex stood before them, eyes still locked on Lluava. He wiped the blood off his bristly chin with his arm and pushed past them.

Back at camp, Lluava hurried to find Apex. Varren followed her. "You're a Yorrick wolverine!" she exclaimed. "Why didn't you tell us? Don't you think that is knowledge we should be privy to?"

Apex stripped off his blood-spattered Endun shirt. His blood or the bear's? Lluava could not tell, nor did she care.

"The need to tell never came up," he growled as he inspected a bite on his biceps.

"You have a god's form!" she angrily accused.

"Why so shocked? You have one as well," said Apex offhandedly.

"But your form! Ullr's form! The Fangs!"

Apex pulled out another unmarked bottle from his stash and poured some of the alcohol on his arm. "Do you believe in fate?" he grumbled.

"No," declared Lluava matter-of-factly.

"Neither do I." Apex turned to Varren, who had been quiet during this exchange. "What say you about this matter?"

"I say," Varren began, "that you deserve thanks from me as well as from Lluava. You did save her life."

This seemed to actually surprise Apex.

"Lluava," Varren continued, "you should thank him."

Should she? This was the man she hated, wasn't it? Did he truly deserve her appreciation?

"Thanks," she mumbled.

Feeling awkward and unsure of her emotions, Lluava turned to leave, but not before Varren had reached over and touched her shoulder. She winced.

"We need to get that taken care of," he said. She could hear the concern in his voice.

As they neared Rosalyn's tent, the usually gentle nurse was waving Talos off. His face was angry; Lluava had an idea why. Spotting Lluava, Talos demanded, "Why were you and Rosalyn alone in the forest?"

Lluava looked at the couple and then back at her own partner. She realized she had to confess, even though Rosalyn would be angry with her. This secret could not be kept anymore.

"I was training Rosalyn to fight."

"You were *what?*" questioned Talos angrily.

Varren seemed to take the news calmly. He only asked, "Why?"

Rosalyn chimed in, "Because I asked her to. I need to know how to defend myself."

"You almost got yourself killed," snapped Talos. Varren gave his friend a sympathetic look.

"Lluava," Varren began, "you should not have wandered off without telling me. We are not only partners; I care for your safety."

"I can take care of myself."

"Are you certain? That is not what I saw."

Lluava bit her tongue just as Rosalyn pointed to Talos. "You almost got killed. Do not forget that either."

Varren's words came as a shock to all of them. "It would be beneficial for Rosalyn to learn how to fight. Actually, it would be beneficial if every one of us had those skills." He looked at the huntsmen, who were talking among themselves.

"But Rosalyn's not like Lluava. She —" Talos was cut off by an abrupt slap in the face.

Rosalyn's voice was icy. "I could be."

"Varren," Talos pleaded.

Varren shook his head. "Rosalyn will learn, as will all the others. We will train them in the evenings."

"As you wish, Your Majesty," Talos replied stiffly. With that, he left Rosalyn to tend to Lluava's dislocated shoulder.

"You should have told me, you know," Varren said as he assisted Rosalyn.

Was he disappointed that she had not confided in him? "I thought you would stop us," replied Lluava as she sat down.

"I was referring to your arm. You said it was better."

Varren held Lluava as Rosalyn directed. His face lost its color, and his eyes widened. Lluava took a breath and closed hers. With a crack, Rosalyn realigned the joint.

"You wouldn't have let me come," Lluava panted out. "Don't lie."

"You are right," her partner acknowledged. "I would not have." He knelt before her and took her hands in his. "I have half a mind to send you back, but I will not. You say you are fit to fight, and I will believe you. However, if anything changes, I want you to promise me that you will return to Elysia if I ask you to."

Lluava fought the impulse to chew her lip. She had told neither Varren nor Rosalyn about the ache in her side. Well enough. This would be the last lie she would tell Varren.

"I promise."

***

The journey north was surprisingly smooth. Training had begun for the huntsmen as well as Rosalyn. As put out as Talos was at the notion of his betrothed attempting to swing a sword, he did as commanded and assisted in the instruction.

Of all of them, Apex displayed the most promise. Lluava was not surprised. He refused to start out with pointed sticks, insisting instead on learning with Ullr's Fangs. He even proved superior in hand-to-hand combat. Apex advanced through the lessons at a rate that made both Lluava and Varren nervous. Yet the huntsman adamantly denied ever having been taught weaponry.

Even Yamir, their spiky-haired companion, seemed much more rational after the talk Varren had had with him. However, Lluava was not convinced. Part of her wished she had heard the rest of their conversation, although she kept telling herself that eavesdropping was not a good thing.

Lluava hoped that Yamir could earn back at least some of their confidence. To deal with the loss of a friend was hard for anyone, yet one could not allow oneself to be consumed with grief. Somewhere inside her, she, too, felt that she had yet to come to terms with the guilt she had buried along with the grand master chief. Surviving the attack by the Great Mountain bear was a first step. Wasn't it?

***

Three days out from the Pass, Lluava awoke covered in a film of sweat. She must have had another nightmare. She had had plenty of those lately. Her body ached, probably from their ride over rough terrain the day before, and she let out a low moan. Sitting up, she began to feel a bit nauseous. She quickly left her tent to vomit just outside of camp.

Nearby, Derrick was seated outside his own tent. He looked at her quizzically. Lluava waved him off. No reason to draw more attention to herself, but she could not shake off the sick feeling.

While eating their cold breakfast, Sköll trotted up to Lluava and sniffed her side. His nose twitched in disgust. Lluava shoved the dog away; he was aggravating her already extremely tender side. The way the wolf-mutt observed her sent a shiver down her spine.

Catching Rosalyn's attention, Lluava asked, "Can you check on my cut?"

Rosalyn raised an eyebrow. "Has it not healed already?"

Lluava shook her head.

Rosalyn quickly rinsed off her bowl. "Come with me to my tent."

Once inside, Lluava removed her shirt. Her uncared-for bandages had seen better days. A thin line of moisture tinted them. Lluava chastised herself

219

for not changing them after she sweated. Riding horses and dodging bears would do that to you.

"Take those off," Rosalyn said in an unusually testy manner.

Lluava began to unpeel the wrappings. A vile odor escaped. What was going on? When the last cloth fell to the floor, Lluava wished she had not seen what it covered. The long cut was badly infected. The swollen skin had turned violet all the way down her side, and a filmy fluid seeped from the crack. Much of the damaged skin was covered in blisters.

"What should I do?" asked Lluava as she turned to see terror on her friend's face.

"Lluava," Rosalyn asked, "How long has this been going on?"

"I don't know. Some days now."

"You should have come to me sooner," hissed the raven-haired woman. Rosalyn's right hand hovered over Lluava's wound as though she were afraid to touch the burning flesh. "This... this..." she stammered. "I have never seen anything this bad, and never in this location. Fingers and toes, but never a torso."

"Well, what do I need to do?" Lluava asked. Rosalyn was making her nervous.

Rosalyn pulled back her trembling hand. "Nothing. There is nothing I can do for you. If...if you had come to me earlier, I might have been able to—" Rosalyn's voice broke, and she could not continue.

Lluava said, "Why don't you give me some of those drops you gave Wod? They worked for him. Maybe they will work for me."

Rosalyn shook her head. "I do not have any medicine that can combat this sort of infection. Maybe, back in Elysia, there is a slim chance that help can be found. There are healers who might be able to do what I cannot."

"I am not going back to Elysia," snapped Lluava. She turned her wound away from her friend's eyes.

"If you do not go back immediately," Rosalyn said with a shaky breath, "you will die."

Chapter 31

Entering the Pass

I don't...I don't understand," stammered Lluava. She must have heard wrong. It was only a scratch.

"Lluava, your infection—it is too severe." Rosalyn was visibly upset. "We need to get you home."

"But it's just a scratch," Lluava complained. Rosalyn must be wrong. The deer had not cut her that deeply. The injury just needed more time to heal. Just a little more time.

Rosalyn dabbed at the discharge oozing down Lluava's side. "It will only get worse. Your time on this mission is over."

"No." Lluava stepped backward and flattened herself against the side of the tent.

"This is not the time to be foolish," hissed Rosalyn.

"We are so close."

"You do not know that."

"I'm staying."

Rosalyn scowled. "Did you not hear me? You will become feverish and begin to vomit until you are incapable of keeping anything down. Diarrhea will dehydrate you. Be it lack of food or water, or the infection itself, the result will be the same. You will die."

Why was this happening to her? Lluava wondered. What had she done to deserve it? She didn't want to die. Though life was rather miserable right now, she still had Varren and her friends. She was fighting for them, for her family, for everyone she had ever met.

"How long?"

Rosalyn's features softened. Did she think Lluava was about to comply?

"In all truth, I do not know. You might have weeks, days, or even hours. This type of infection can intensify rapidly. You need to leave this instant."

"It will take days to return to the border. From what you said, I might not have that long."

"You must take that chance."

Lluava thought for a moment. "Suppose I get there; then what are my chances? You said there might be a chance. Might."

Looking like a bird in a snare, Rosalyn admitted, "There is no certainty that you will survive this. Nevertheless, it is a risk you have to take. You just have to."

"I'm going to stay."

Rosalyn stepped forward, waving the soiled cloth she still clutched. "What is it with all of you and this mission? Why do all of you so adamantly believe that we will find some saving grace in the middle of this godless forest? This cause of yours has been for naught. We have lost time and people and…and…" Her voice broke in a sob. "I will not lose you."

"Do you really believe that?" Lluava asked. Before Roslyn could answer, Lluava raised a hand to silence her. "Do you, deep down, believe that all of this has been for nothing? I don't. Something in me has been telling me that we are on the right path. We are Theriomorphs, Rosalyn. We trust our instincts more than our human companions do. It is part of what makes us *us*. I know we are doing the right thing. Are you telling me you don't feel the same way?"

Rosalyn did not answer for some time.

Lluava took Roslyn's hands in her own. "If my life, my one life, is lost in order to save everyone else's, I think that would be worth the risk."

Her friend struggled to hold back a new freshet of tears. "I cannot change your mind?"

Lluava shook her head.

"What are you going to do about Varren? We both know that he would do anything to save you."

"We won't tell him."

"He will find out," cautioned Rosalyn. "As your symptoms worsen, he will realize that you are ill."

"Let's hope that by that time it will be too late to turn around."

***

Several days later, the small caravan was about to enter the Pass, a valley that cut through the enormous white-capped mountain range. From their vantage point, the walls of rock rose up like the jagged teeth of some deceased giant eternally waiting to bite down on those travelling through.

Lluava shivered. For the last day and a half, she had ridden with the hood of her tattered cloak over her head, for she did not want the others to realize how much she was perspiring. The frigid air chilled her sweat, causing her to feel colder than she already was. Whenever Varren gave her a questioning glance, she forced herself to smile. Her body ached and she looked forward to their short rests.

This stop was different. Apex had commanded everyone to halt and then walked over to Varren. What was Apex up to now? Was he going to ask for more money? She wouldn't put it past him.

"Leave your horse," Apex bluntly commanded, speaking directly to Varren and no one else.

"And why would I do that?" questioned Varren dubiously.

"Because you are fond of the beast." Before Varren could inquire further, Apex continued, "Your animal was not bred for these conditions and will not withstand the harsher terrain ahead. The others," he said, gesturing to the shaggy equines, "are bred for the north. Your thoroughbred was not."

Varren seemed insulted. "Ulder is as good as any."

"Do what you will," acknowledged Apex. "But if you ride him into the Pass, he will not return."

Varren studied Apex for a long while. Nearby, Sköll scratched his large ears and yawned. Finally the prince slid off his horse.

"What are you doing?" inquired Talos.

Yamir added, "We cannot afford to be one horse short."

Turning Ulder to face him, Varren stroked the long black muzzle, outlining the starburst. "I raised Ulder from a colt. Broke him in myself." He moved his hand down the lean musculature of the stallion. "He has been with me through so much."

Lluava noticed that the horse was shivering even more than she was. While it was obvious that Varren loved Ulder, Lluava wondered if she could ever love her ratty bird. She felt sorry for the choice her partner had to make.

"Apex is right this time." Varren moved back to the unkempt mane.

"So, what are you going to ride?" questioned Yamir, looking darkly at Apex. Lluava wondered if he were concocting more conspiracies.

"Apex can walk the path. So can I."

"Take my horse," offered Talos. "I do not deny your ability, but if anything should go awry, you need a good mount. Out of all of us, you must be the one with a horse."

Everyone knew what Talos meant. The sole heir to Elysia's throne must be protected. Varren's jaw tightened; Lluava could tell that the prince hated being constrained by his birthright.

"I, too, must insist that you ride," added Derrick. Of course, he would back up Talos's idea.

Byron gave a sideways glance at Talos. "He could ride one of the pack horses. Then everyone who came with a horse would still have one."

Talos smiled, "I like that idea, too."

"And what of the supplies?" asked Yamir, clearly uncomfortable with the whole situation.

Varren took charge. "We will consolidate our belongings and carry what we can. Extraneous items will be discarded."

After casting off unnecessary supplies and rearranging what remained, the caravan was ready to ride once again. Varren took several moments to say goodbye to his old friend. Then, slapping his hand on the animal's rump, he sent Ulder trotting off into the forest.

As Varren mounted his new horse, Lluava thought she saw tears in his eyes. She gave his shoulder a quick squeeze.

Apex barked out, "We are about to enter the Pass. Once we cross the threshold, whatever *I* say goes." He looked over at Varren. The prince gave Apex a silent nod.

Apex continued, "We will travel single file. No more side-by-side socializing. There will also be no, and I mean *no*, loud noises from anyone. Especially you, Lluava."

"Me?" Lluava was insulted.

"Yes, you. So keep your growls to yourself. Let's go." Apex waved them forward.

As Lluava fell into place behind her partner, she spoke just loudly enough for him to hear. "What does he mean by that?"

"Avalanches, I think," answered Varren.

"What are those?" She knew he would not judge her naiveté.

"When walls of snow come crashing down." Varren would have explained further, but Apex gave them a sign to be quiet. Ignoring the initial warning, Varren lowered his voice, "Are you sure you are all right? Your cheeks are rather flushed."

"Silence," Apex barked out, and their conversation was over.

In truth, Lluava was far from all right. During the next couple of days, her fever did not just persist but worsened. She had to force herself to do everything. Her body yearned for a warm bed. She was thankful that the other symptoms Rosalyn had described had not yet appeared. Perhaps this meant that she had more time. She needed more time.

Whenever she ate, she felt nauseated. She found that consuming multiple small portions minimized the urge to throw up. Something as obvious as that would certainly draw Varren's ever-vigilant attention.

Ahead, everything was covered in white: the ground, the few evergreens that sprouted defiantly forth, and the enormous mountainsides that flanked the caravan. Whenever Onyx flew, the raven stuck out like a sore thumb. Lluava wondered if there were other ravens in the Pass; if not, Onyx might draw unwanted attention.

Maybe it was the extreme brightness of sunlight reflected off snow, or perhaps it was the wear and tear of the journey, but Lluava began to struggle to focus. Onyx, who had perched on her shoulder for most of their travels, took wing.

Dratted bird, she thought. It was true that she was shaking, but was it really that bad?

Lowering her head further, she loosened her grip on the reins. Her horse would follow the others. She should save her energy. She should...

In the next moment, Lluava felt herself slipping sideways. Unable to react quickly enough, she began to fall to the ground. Strong hands suddenly grabbed the back of her cloak and jerked her upright.

Varren was beside her, speaking. Lluava blinked and tried to concentrate on his words. "You are sick," he stated, in a mix of anger and worry.

Unable to maintain her balance, Lluava allowed him to help her off her horse. She was embarrassed but too ill to pretend anymore. The truth would have to come out.

Talos assisted Varren, and together they sat Lluava down with her back resting against the trunk of a spruce.

A cloud drifted in front of the sun, casting a shadow on the silent group. Lluava reached out and took hold of Varren's glove. "I'm dying," she said. Her words sounded hollow.

"What are you talking about?" he cried out as loudly as he dared, his features pale. "Rosalyn! Here, quickly!"

"It's no use," Lluava murmured. Her voice was weak and tired. She yearned to sleep, to be rid of all the pain.

Lluava sensed that Rosalyn had run to them. She was aware that words passed heatedly among the gathering group, but she did not register their meaning. She couldn't stop trembling. The cursed snow began to fall again. There was nothing they could do, so why all the fuss?

Bits of the conversation occasionally made sense. Lluava forced herself to concentrate. Her input was still valuable, was it not? As long as she was alive, she had a say.

"Byron, Wod, Monk, scout the area to make sure it is secure until we can get Lluava ready to ride back," commanded Varren. As the trio slipped away, Lluava realized that Varren intended to send her home.

"No," she croaked, but no one heard.

Then Rosalyn spoke in a firm, clear voice. "It is too late, Varren. She will not survive the journey back."

"Lluava's strong," Varren argued. "She will make it." He knelt down beside the desperately sick girl and touched her burning forehead.

"It's too late, Varren. It was always too late," Lluava tried to explain, but Varren refused to listen.

"You will be all right." He kissed her forehead. Then he turned to Rosalyn and said icily, "If anything happens to her, it is on your head, Rosalyn. You are responsible. She needed to return to Elysia." He glared at the small woman who stood before him with her hands on her hips.

"She did this for you," Rosalyn snapped back angrily. "She did it for all of us. Lluava wanted to continue on in case you found your godforsaken information."

"We have come so far," stated Derrick bleakly. "She would want us to finish what we started."

"I'm not dead yet," mumbled Lluava.

Varren looked at her apologetically, "I know. This is why you must return to Elysia." Lluava began to protest, but Varren quietly shushed her. "The only thing that matters to me right now is getting you back home."

From the defiant sparkle in his eyes, Lluava knew he would not accept that she was dying. He would not let her go so easily. The pain in his features broke through the stoic honor to which Lluava had been holding fast. She nodded her consent.

"We need to make camp. Let her rest," ordered Varren.

"It will not matter," Rosalyn gently insisted.

Varren glared at her darkly. "We ride out at dawn."

While the others busied themselves setting up tents and bedding down horses, Lluava's eyes followed her partner. Varren came over to her and wrapped her in his mount's saddle blanket.

Oh, Varren, she thought. You will survive this. You must.

As the others settled in, Lluava's ears picked up the steady crunch of boots on snow. She smiled. Turning in the direction of the sound, she waited until she spotted three forms through the veil of snow. As the silhouetted shapes approached, they grew in size and stature.

Was Byron that tall? Wod certainly was not. Something was wrong.

Lluava forced herself to be still. Instinctively, she knew she should not draw their attention. Then she recognized the horned helmets of Raiders.

Chapter 32

Nestled Below

In only moments, Lluava would be discovered. The path the Raiders were taking would bring them straight to her. She needed to hide, but where? She gathered her strength and slid her back up the trunk of the tree.

In a blur of motion, Varren grabbed her, pulling her back and down behind a large snowdrift. They huddled so close she could smell his rosemary-tinted breath. Did he know how terrified she was? The thought of fighting in her condition was not a welcome one.

Lluava hoped the others had hidden themselves too. She was afraid to turn and look; the last thing she wanted was to lure those brutes toward herself and Varren. She tried to steady her breath, but every time she exhaled, it sounded like thunder. Did she always breathe that hard?

As the crunching of snow came closer, Varren took her hand in one of his. With the other, he grasped the hilt of his sword. With a sharp squeeze, Lluava warned her partner not to do anything foolish. If it took three people, on average, to kill one of those brutes, this was not the time for heroics.

The footsteps stopped. Lluava held her breath, as did Varren. She glanced aside and saw Varren's brows furrowed in concentration. Was he, too, calculating how far from them the Raiders stood? She guessed they were just the other side of the mound, but there was no telltale smoky odor to help her pinpoint their position. Lluava wanted to flatten herself down more, but even that simple move might alert them.

The icy kisses of snow continued to fall, coating them in white. Everything around them seemed to still and slow down. Lluava blinked as white flakes feathered her eyelashes.

The footsteps began again, this time moving away. One set, two. Where was the third?

An explosion of ice seemed to encapsulate them briefly. A Raider's war hammer must have demolished the entire top of the compacted snowdrift. There was no chance to look, for Lluava was violently tossed backward. In the next second, the resounding clang of metal on metal shattered the serenity of the mountainside.

Varren stumbled back from the Raider's blow. Lluava was not sure he could defend himself against another swing like that. She must stand up, move, and assist her partner. She cursed her weakened state.

Shouts erupted around them as weapons were seized and fighting broke out. Lluava pushed herself up to her knees, but once again she was grasped roughly and yanked—upward this time, then tossed like a carcass over a broad shoulder.

"Apex!" she screamed. "Put me down!"

Beating her hands against his back, she heard him curse. She noticed too late that Issaura's Claws had inflicted damage on his shoulders. Part of her didn't care. What did he think he was doing? She shrieked at him to stop, yet he continued to run.

Suddenly he heaved her onto the ground, with no attempt to soften her fall. "Stay here," he growled, then turned back to the fight.

Glaring at his retreating form, Lluava found herself spitting out dark words. How dare he take her away? How dare he think he could make that decision for her? She was trained; he was not. She stood a better chance in the fray than he did.

Lluava's eyes narrowed as she focused on the furious activity at the campsite. Derrick was in retreat. Was Rosalyn really coming to Talos's aid? He appeared to yell at her to stay away, but the girl proved too stubborn. Varren and Yamir were engaged with the third Raider. Mila was nowhere in sight.

Coward! thought Lluava. That was something she would never be. Her body throbbed, and her ears rang with every beat of her heart. It did not help that Apex had tossed her down so horridly. When she fell, one of the Claws had dislodged itself from her grip and now lay a few feet away.

"Damn you, Apex," she cursed again and crawled over to the golden weapon. Fumbling, she slid the Claw over her hand, noticing as she did so that the little finger on her left hand was swollen. Although this injury was not as significant as the others, once she took note of it, she was conscious of its incessant throbbing.

But there were more immediate problems. Lluava turned her attention back to the fighting. Everyone had switched places; Rosalyn and Derrick fought as one, while Yamir rapidly approached their brute from behind. Talos stood his ground next to Varren as they countered a Raider's enormous sword. Apex engaged the third brute by himself.

Damn him, Lluava thought once more, as she forced herself to stumble toward the chaos. Her legs would not move fast enough. It took almost all her energy to focus on shuffling each foot forward.

Not yet, she thought. *Not yet.* She still had fight in her! She stumbled on.

Lluava gasped as she saw Yamir trip. His Raider reached down to grab him but retracted his hand quickly, pierced by countless quills when Yamir shifted. Hurriedly, the porcupine waddled away. Taking advantage of the distraction, Rosalyn flung her dagger into the brute's eye. He cried out, and as he stumbled Derrick finished him off.

Nearby, Varren and Talos had taken down their marauder. Each sword had found its mark, and each comrade now pulled his respective weapon from the huge corpse. At least, Varren was all right—but no thanks to her, Lluava thought sourly.

Turning to the last Raider, she saw Sköll, that dratted wolf-dog, tearing at the leg of the man, whose swing had missed its mark. Apex's brute fell backward. Stepping closer, Lluava realized the Raider's jugular had been ripped out. He collapsed onto a pile of reddening snow. She wondered whether Apex or Sköll were responsible.

Suddenly it was over, and Lluava had not offered any actual assistance. In fact, she had been deemed useless and a risk, tossed aside to keep her from being underfoot. This did not sit well with her at all. What would the Elysians think if they heard about this fight? Their idol, the one they called Theri, Issaura, was as weak and helpless as a newborn cub. Lluava was furious at Apex for carrying her off. The insult would not be forgotten; she would make sure of that.

Once her friends had evaluated their situation, they moved their camp farther up the side of the mountain.

"The valley is too dangerous," declared Varren, as he looked in Lluava's direction.

"So it is," Apex agreed.

"Well, the horses are gone," muttered Yamir in exasperation.

"So is Mila," Lluava pointed out, an edge to her voice.

"You don't think—" Yamir began, but Apex interrupted with a grunted "Let's gather our supplies."

With Rosalyn's help, Lluava had almost finished packing her tent. She caught Rosalyn's eye. "You were brave out there," she told her friend.

Rosalyn did not smile. "I was terrified. I did what I had to do in order to survive."

"That is all any of us can do," Lluava assured her.

Horses' hooves were heard. Looking up, they saw that Mila had returned, with all the animals in tow.

"They ran off in the commotion," huffed the woman. Her long braid swayed as she halted her horse. "It took me a while to corral them."

Lluava felt instantly guilty. Did she actually believe that Mila would abandon them in their moment of crisis? Is that how she viewed the female huntress?

Apex led them to a more protected location. Once again, as they began to pitch their tents more footsteps were heard. Lluava cast a wary glance in Apex's direction. She would not let him haul her off again.

Through the gray blur of snow, another trio approached. This time, Lluava's comrades were ready. There would be no attempt to hide. As the helmeted figures approached, Sköll made the first move.

Stupid mutt, thought Lluava. Couldn't Apex control his mongrel?

Sköll trotted up to the figures, tail wagging. Belatedly, Lluava recognized the three: Byron, along with Wod and Monk. Thank the gods, she thought. They were back.

"Byron!" Talos sighed in relief and hugged his partner. "You will not believe what has happened."

Wod and Monk nodded to the other huntsmen. Monk stated flatly, "You moved camp."

"What is wrong?" asked Talos. He looked at his partner's bleak expression and then toward the brothers. "Where did those helmets come from?"

"You need to see this," Byron told them. The other two kept silent. Lluava knew instantly that whatever it was would not be good.

Talos, Varren, and Apex grabbed their gear and headed diagonally up the slope. Lluava followed. Apex gave Varren a backward nod, turning Varren's gaze toward her.

"What do you think you are doing?"

"I'm coming along," she answered, a bit shocked at the question. Why wouldn't she?

"I think not," disagreed Varren. "You are too ill."

"I feel fine." Lluava knew the lie was obvious, but she didn't know what else to say.

"I am sorry, Lluava, but—"

Varren's statement was cut short by Wod's tentative voice. "I think she would want to see this, too."

Lluava gave Wod a weak smile. Was he really the only one who believed in her?

Varren's gaze lost focus for a moment. Then he ordered, "Stay by my side, okay?"

Lluava nodded. She was not about to say anything that might change his mind.

The small group worked its way farther up the slope. All too soon, Lluava realized that Varren had been right. The snow was slippery, and she was no longer agile. Her partner helped her whenever he could, and she quietly acknowledged that she needed his assistance.

The pair had fallen behind due to Lluava's weakened state. The others were already crouched in a low line near a ridge. Varren pulled Lluava up, and the pair looked down over the valley. The view was simultaneously breathtaking and horrifying.

"Is that...?" Lluava questioned aloud.

"Yes," Varren's voice was a whisper.

"But that's impossible, that would mean—" Lluava lost her voice. Sheer terror crawled up her spine.

The faces around hers had blanched. Even Apex looked disturbed. No good could come from what lay below.

Nestled in the midst of the valley was a fortress of a magnitude greater than any in Elysia. Great spiked walls contained countless wooden structures, long and lean. Built in even rows, each one could house fifty or more men. Great fires burned throughout, illuminating a multitude of figures. Though they appeared minuscule at that distance, Lluava instantly knew that these men were all abnormally large.

This camp was not new. No, this was an established fortress, one that must have existed undetected for some time. Lluava's thoughts were going wild. This meant that the Raiders had been in Elysia far longer than anyone had thought. Obviously, the force had been massing for years. Now they commanded an army large enough to take over the entire kingdom.

Chapter 33

Avalanche

Could there really be that many of them? Lluava noticed Talos's lips silently moving as if he were trying to count them all. They had learned the Raiders' purpose for journeying into the Yorrick Forest. They had discovered this years-old encampment, the source of the attack to come. She should be happy, Lluava thought, but she was not. Far from it.

They did not stay long. Though each of them wanted to take it all in, Apex motioned them to move back. Those left at camp must be wondering what Byron and the brothers had found.

On their return, everyone gathered to discuss their current predicament. Lluava wrapped herself in the saddle blanket and took a seat among them. But there were no easy answers. There were too many Raiders. Just too many.

Derrick spoke up. "Allow me to send out this information."

Varren nodded. "Right away."

"No," barked Apex, looking warily about. "Not here. You must not make any noise until you have left the Pass. Or do you want to bury us alive in a tomb of snow?"

"Evening is still several hours away," Varren pointed out. "We have time to saddle up and start moving in that direction." Looking at Lluava, he added, "Every moment counts."

"As you command," said Apex. Lluava could not tell whether his words were serious or sarcastic.

Lluava was told to rest while the others packed. She did not argue, for her fever was rising. Instead, she watched her friends and wondered if there was anything else she could do before... She did not want to think of her end. Lluava knew she would not make it. She would die here in the ice and snow. Had she done everything she could?

Since Apex had no mount of his own to saddle, he had pulled a bottle from his pack, choosing to focus his attention on it. What a waste, Lluava thought as she watched him smile at Ullr's Fangs.

Lluava's mind drifted back to the fortress. Judging by the troop movements she had observed, the Raiders were not yet prepared to attack. They were waiting. For what, she could not fathom. At least, Derrick's warning would travel to Vidrick and his men in a matter of days, a week at worst. If only they could have sent the signal out tonight.

"Too much noise," she griped. "Too much…"

Struggling to stand up, she exclaimed, "I've got it!" Then she quickly covered her mouth.

"Are you all right?" asked Rosalyn as she began to check Lluava's temperature.

Lluava shrugged her friend off. "I know how to destroy the Raiders."

"Which Raiders?" asked Byron, as he and the others began to gather around their exuberant friend.

"All of them."

Byron laughed, then quickly quieted down when he realized she was serious. "All of them?"

"Yes." Lluava grinned. "All of them."

"How?" asked Varren.

"We cause an avalanche."

Several of those around her looked at her as if the fever had made her crazy.

"I'm serious," Lluava defended herself. "Their fortress is located at the base of the Pass. If we cause an avalanche, we could bury all of them in the snow. We could destroy this entire threat in one move. Check and mate."

"And how would we do that?" asked Talos, as if he were considering the matter. Lluava knew that if she could get him on board with her plan, the others would follow.

"By a great noise. Apex has been warning us about this the whole time."

Apex was standing not far off, still holding his bottle. His face was bleak. Lluava knew she could not rely on him for support. But what about the others?

Derrick furrowed his brows. "I know better than most that it is almost impossible to control the direction of sound. If we make a large enough one, we can't predict where the avalanche will fall. It could kill us just as easily."

"Wouldn't the angles of the mountains help focus the sound?" Lluava was desperately reaching for any hope. She was losing them.

Derrick thought. "There is a slight possibility. I'd have to get a better look at the area around the Raiders' encampment."

"I'll go with you." Mila's statement surprised the others, but Lluava smiled at her friend.

As Derrick and Mila headed up the slope, Varren stated, "If this is going to work, we need to have one noise that is certain to be loud enough to cause an avalanche. We will only have one chance. Once the noise is made, the Raiders will know we are here."

"You are right," agreed Talos, backing up his prince.

"I'll make it," Lluava said. "It is my idea. My roar is loud. I can do this."

"Out of the question," said Varren.

Rosalyn agreed. "You are too weak as it is. Your roar might not be loud enough."

Lluava knew her friends meant well, but they were wrong. "I know that I am dying. I will not be able to survive the trip back."

"Do not say that. You *must* not say that." Varren's heart was breaking, and so was hers. This was not fair. She deserved to live out her life by her partner's side. She had earned that right, had she not? But then, would their kingdom still exist in the future? By the looks of things, that was highly questionable.

Lluava affirmed her earlier statement. "I know I will not make it back. Please, Varren, as my partner, as my prince, please let my death be worthwhile. Let me do this for Elysia."

"Why did it have to be you?" His words came out in a hoarse whisper. He walked off to consider Lluava's proposal and to hide his face from hers.

As Lluava sat down to preserve her strength, Apex lumbered off with Sköll at his heels. She realized she did not care where he was going. Of their entire small group, Apex was the one Lluava worried about the least.

It was not long before Derrick and Mila returned. "If there is a chance, it would be in the hands of the gods," swore Derrick.

Mila added, "A chance that I would not take."

"What other choice do we have?" Lluava asked.

Varren looked sadly at her before turning to their dark-skinned companion. "Derrick, you will leave immediately and warn your troop about our discovery. You will wait for the rest of us to meet you at the opening of the Pass. Is that clear?"

Derrick nodded, shifted, and was off. Clearly, he had been anticipating this order.

Varren turned to the others; his eyes scanned each individual. "The rest of you will pack up and ride down the slope. Once you hit the Pass, you should travel as far away from this mountain as you can. When it begins to darken, make camp and wait."

"What do you mean, 'The rest of you'?" questioned Yamir. "You sound as if you will not be joining us."

"I will be standing at my partner's side. I will always be there."

"You cannot be serious," grumbled Talos unhappily. "Of all of us, you are the one who must not take that risk."

"Do not tell me what I can and cannot do," Varren replied angrily.

Talos was not about to back down, "Someone has to be the voice of reason. What you are proposing is just foolish."

Lluava listened in shock. This had been neither her intent nor her plan. "Listen to Talos," she implored. If things did go wrong, she did not want anything to happen to Varren. "I can do this on my own."

Mila joined the conversation. "The best angle for your heroic stand is three miles farther up the slope." She paused and looked directly at Lluava. "The walk is a slippery one. Assistance might be needed."

Was Mila trying to sabotage her plan? By the look in Varren's eyes, he was now more determined than ever. "I am the prince of Elysia." He spoke authoritatively. "You will do as I ask."

"Very well," Talos reluctantly consented. "I cannot stop you, but we will wait here for you. If it looks like things will go badly, we will be ready to leave. If all goes well, we will travel back together."

Varren now looked as angry as Talos, yet neither would stand down. "As your future king, I command you to wait at the base of the mountain. There, you will have a better chance of escaping if the plan fails."

Byron stepped up to Talos and placed his hand on his partner's arm. "And that is what we will do."

"Talos," Varren began again, his tone more controlled. "I want you to take this."

He pulled the royal signet ring from his finger and handed it to his friend. "If anything does happen, I want you to take this ring to my grandfather and tell him you have my blessing."

"I...I..." Closing his hand around the ring, Talos said, "Thank you."

Watching this interchange, Lluava realized she had a gift of her own to make. "Rosalyn," she called out. When her raven-haired friend drew close, Lluava continued, "In my tent, there are a sword and sheath. General Domar gave them to me when I lost Issaura's Claws. The sword's name is Vjeran. I have the Claws again and have no need of the blade. I want you to have it."

Rosalyn looked dumbfounded.

"You are ready," Lluava assured her. "May she be the most faithful amongst the faithless."

***

Leaving the others to pack up, Lluava followed Varren as they rode up the slope. Mila had given them directions to the ideal location, a wide ledge that overlooked the fortress. The path hugged the mountainside, and an overhang of rock offered some protection from above. Off and away from camp, Lluava spotted Apex reclining on the ground, still tending to his bottle. She shook her head and continued on.

As they neared their destination, they slipped off their horses and tethered them to the branches of a cedar. Lluava was trembling. Although she wanted to blame it on the cold, she knew it was a combination of nerves and fever.

As she trudged up the steepening incline, Lluava's earlier nausea returned and she stopped to purge what little remained in her stomach. Varren knelt next to her, although she wished he were not there at all. She had wanted him to stay with the others.

Varren helped her to her feet. Lluava needed him to realize that she was still capable of this. She could do it. Yet just as she tried to move ahead, she slipped back on the ice and into his arms.

"Let me help you," he whispered gently in her ear.

Giving in, Lluava allowed herself to be assisted the rest of the way. She needed to conserve strength. She would have only one chance. One. Relying on Varren to lead her safely, she closed her eyes.

A few moments later, Varren murmured, "We are here."

As the prince placed his arm under hers for support, the pair stood and looked at the breathtaking scene before them. Evening was fast approaching, and with a break in the clouds the molten hues of the declining sun cast indescribable colors and shadows throughout the mountain range. Deep in the valley below, the fortress was aglow with lantern light and bonfires.

Lluava slipped her hand into Varren's. He held it tightly.

The winter panorama seemed peaceful, beautiful. Standing next to Varren, feeling the rise and fall of his chest, Lluava wished that this moment could last. She closed her eyes, hoping to capture every detail.

"Are you ready?" Varren asked. By the tremor in his tone, he was not.

"No," she admitted. "But here goes."

Remaining in her human form, Lluava took several breaths, each larger than the one before, expanding her lung capacity to its fullest. She angled herself toward the far mountain and let out the loudest and longest roar she could remember making. Her bellowing cry continued to grow like thunder, reverberating and strengthening with every second. When she finally broke off to catch her breath, the resounding rumble continued. The mountains rang out as the valley echoed and amplified her roar until it seemed that dozens of enraged tigers were bellowing forth from the sky above.

As the echoes died away, Lluava felt herself vibrate with nervous energy. She scanned the snowy slopes and felt a rush of disappointment. But suddenly there was a crack, more a visual movement than an actual noise, and a thin line appeared in the snow bank on the mountain across from them. Then the slab broke off.

It did not seem very large at first and made no more noise than a gust of wind. Nevertheless, as the snow continued to roll down the mountainside, it built and built until a wall of ice charged forth. The rumbling, crackling white mass struck down trees and boulders in its path. Lluava watched, awestruck and horrified, as the entire side of the mountain collapsed upon the unsuspecting fortress below.

When the gray of icy discharge had dissipated, a new layer of snow-packed earth seemed to have wiped the Pass clean of any signs of the Raiders' stronghold. In a matter of mere minutes, it was over. Elysia's greatest enemy was destroyed.

In the next moment, Lluava and Varren were in mid kiss. Lluava was elated, but suddenly her legs gave way, and she would have fallen had not her partner's strong arms supported her. She was grateful when Varren helped her down the slope toward their mounts.

The noise had spooked both horses; the steeds bucked and pulled at their tethered reins. Even Varren, whose skill with horses was well known, calmed them with difficulty. When Lluava collected her reins, her mount reared and pulled free, then galloped off down the mountainside.

Varren helped Lluava onto his saddle and swung up behind her. She swore under her breath, but Varren soothed her. "It will be fine. We will find him."

As Varren began to carefully guide his own finicky mount, Lluava felt something. It was like a shift in the wind, a subtle vibration underfoot. A moment later, a muffled noise came from above. Lluava looked up, horrified. A massive slab of ice had cracked off and begun its descent down their mountain.

"Avalanche!" she shouted as Varren spurred his horse forward.

Lluava did not need to look back. She could vividly imagine the building clouds of icy death mounding up behind them and picking up speed. The low rumble grew to a noisy growl and then into a deafening roar. Like a monstrous beast lunging at them for its supper, the great wall of white was fast approaching.

Holding Lluava tightly, Varren steered the horse around trees and over thick drifts of snow. With every hoofbeat, Lluava hoped they could elude the snow racing toward the base of the Pass. Varren angled them down the mountain. They had to move out of the path of the snow, since heading downward to the valley meant certain death.

They were almost at their old campsite when Lluava spotted Sköll running in circles. Why wasn't that dratted mongrel escaping? Then she saw: Apex had bolted up from his drunken stupor and was stumbling down the mountain. In moments, Lluava and Varren would pass him by. He stood no chance.

"We have to help him," yelled Lluava over the growing noise.

"We have no time," Varren replied as he kicked their mount past the hopeless huntsman. Lluava risked a glance back. The wall of white was approaching quickly. Apex was not at a full run.

"This is wrong," she said.

Varren began, "We have no roo—"

Lluava tugged the reins to the side. The horse stumbled. Varren fell. Lluava could not prevent it. She clung to the horse with all her strength as it slid away from her partner. As soon as the steed righted itself, she saw another horse and rider approaching.

As Varren stood up, Talos pulled him onto his own horse. There was no possible way that Talos could have reached them this fast if he had been waiting where he was supposed to. But he had disobeyed his prince. He had never left their campsite. For that, Lluava was grateful.

"We have to go," Talos shouted to her and turned his horse around.

Lluava could see Apex running toward her. Shift, you fool! she thought. Yet she knew that in his drunken state clear thoughts were a rarity. He was so close that she saw the fear in his eyes.

"Ha!" she cried, as she kicked her horse toward their guide. Behind her, Varren yelled her name.

"We have to go back!" shouted Varren.

Talos's voice cut through the oncoming rumbles. "You are more important."

Lluava chose not to care. She had her own mission in mind. Her horse was resisting her commands, its fear too great.

"Hurry!" Lluava yelled out to Apex. "Come on!"

As soon as Apex jumped onto the horse, Lluava spurred the animal on, following the trail left by Talos's steed. Lluava thought she heard Apex talking to her, but every sound was swallowed by the horror behind them. Bits of snow began to fall in front of them, then huge boulders of ice shot overhead, exploding on trees and partially hidden rocks. A dislodged tree slid past, startling all three. Apex grabbed the reins and turned the horse just in time as another boulder of snow rolled down in their direction.

With Apex in control, Lluava glanced back, then wished she had not. The edge of the avalanche looked like a massive cloud that increased in size with each mass of snow it overtook. Trees and other dark forms rolled about inside the white and gray. Large sections of snow were ejected ahead of them like the projectiles of siege engines she had seen the night the war began.

They were moving too slowly. The wall of snow and ice was upon them. Lluava did not have a chance to turn away. She was flung into the air and then sucked into the hard yet soft wall of white.

Chapter 34

Cavern's Keep

As if caught in a rip tide, Lluava flailed about, trying to stay near the surface. She thought she heard their horse scream and glimpsed buried hooves flashing past. She felt herself being tugged under. No, it was more as though a heavy blanket had been tossed on top of her. The frigid casket of deepening gray tightened around her. She could not move on her own; her body continued to roll, over and over again. She gulped air in frantic spurts. And she was cold, so very cold.

When the upheaval finally ended, Lluava lay immobilized, feverish but calm. She should be afraid, even terrified, entombed like this in a cave of ice. Her hands had protected her face and formed a pocket of air, so she might actually be able to last a while. But did she want to? Was freezing to death or suffocating any worse than the likely outcome of her infection?

Should she try to call for help? She felt so tired.... With nothing to focus on, Lluava closed her eyes and thought of her family. Her mother, her sister, and her baby brother were together in Rivendale. As autumn was ending, they were probably preparing for the harvest festival, a three-day celebration of food, fire-eaters, stilt walkers, and dancers. Lamb would actually be old enough this year to participate in the town's play, and in a few more years little Mouse would, too. If only she could have seen them and her mother's smiling face once more.

Something shifted alongside her. A noise like snowdrifts breaking began, then continued. Lluava wanted to look toward the sound, but she did not have the strength.

A moment later, strong hands broke through her prison, grabbed her, and began to pull her free. Her body moved sideways, then upward, toward an unbearably dazzling light. Was that the sun, or was the moon unusually bright? How long had she been buried in the snow? Lluava kept her eyes shut. Any movement she attempted brought pain and exhaustion. She felt hands at her throat, pressing down hard, and then heard her rescuer stand up and move away.

"Varren," she called, but her voice slipped out in a whisper.

Then there was a new noise, akin to scratching or maybe dragging. Lluava felt herself being picked up. How gently, she could not tell, for every movement made her want to scream, but her voice had disappeared along with the rest of her waning energy. She was laid on her back on top of something hard and uneven. From the sensation at her fingertips, it was needles and bark. Her rescuer must be hauling her back to the others using a makeshift stretcher. She wanted to smile. She really did.

There was a change in the angle at which she lay. Now she was moving upward. Why would she be carried in that direction? Wouldn't the others be waiting closer to the opening of the Pass? Hadn't that been the plan?

She couldn't stay with the thoughts. Her fever was overpowering; she felt herself slipping away, and at last allowed herself to give in to sleep. She stirred briefly when the sound of shuffling footsteps approached. Lluava felt her shirt lifted up and something warm and wet spread on top of her skin. Rosalyn, she thought, but then weariness claimed her once again.

Then next time Lluava registered sound, she was lying down, warm despite her high fever. Something soft and thick was wrapped all about her. She attempted to open her eyes, but her lids felt like lead weights. After several tries, she was able to focus through a narrow crack. Although her vision was extremely blurry, she was able to discern a stone ceiling.

Someone approached. His look was familiar, but Lluava could not make out any details. A hand slipped under her head and tilted it, then a warm liquid was dripped between her parched lips. Lluava had not realized how dry her mouth was until the bland sustenance slipped down her throat. After a moment, her attendant stopped.

"Rest," she heard him say. Closing her eyes, she obeyed.

When she awoke, she was groggy. Carefully, Lluava turned onto her side and found herself gazing out the opening of a cliff-side cavern. Exhausted by even that small physical task, she silently took in the sight. Reflected sunlight on snow seemed unbearably bright. Slowly she began to identify the figure standing at the cliff's edge.

For the first time, Apex looked like he was where he was meant to be, as though he belonged to the harsh, untouched wilderness below. He stared off into the distance; at what, she could not tell. The chill wind played with his dark hair, so similar in hue to Varren's yet as different as the two men themselves. Apex's locks were straight and shaggy and shone bronze in the direct sunlight. Although Apex was not as tall as Varren, he was more powerfully built, especially through his wide chest. Lluava could make out the tips of the Fangs resting on his shoulder. He seemed comfortable with them now. They had become, as the Claws had for Lluava, an extension of himself. His free hand scratched the top of his mongrel's head. The dog peered off in the same direction as his owner. Even in her weakened state, Lluava felt safe with Apex standing guard. Her tired body called to her, and again she slept.

The next time she opened her eyes, she had regained some strength. She still faced the opening of the cave, but starlight had replaced the two figures. From deeper in the cave, a second source of light flickered. Lluava slowly turned over on her other side, fighting the layers of furs spread on top of her.

In the back of the cavern, Apex sat by a small fire. Mounds of animal skins were scattered around him, and over his lap were spread beautiful white furs that would be the envy of many at the capital. For a time, Lluava lay quietly and watched him sewing his wares, until Sköll lifted his head in her direction and alerted his master.

Apex slid the furs off himself, then picked up a steaming bowl and moved toward her. "Drink," he said, after blowing off some of the excess heat.

Lluava did not argue. She was famished. But just as she started to gulp down the broth, he pulled the bowl away.

"Rest, now," Apex ordered, then returned to his former position.

Rather reluctantly, Lluava slept once more. For the first time in days, she dreamed. A great estate stood before her, haloed in the glow of fire. Screams came from within, the voices of people she knew: Talos, Rosalyn, Yamir, Byron. Lluava ran toward the palace. Her side was free of pain, and she moved swiftly. Reaching the doors, she tried to tug them open, but they would not budge. They were locked from within.

There had to be another way inside the enormous structure. Stepping back, she saw a figure staring out a window several stories up. Varren. He was banging on the glass. Did he see her? Lluava was not certain. Behind him, the light from the flames grew.

Before she could scream his name, a movement farther up caught her eye. Something broke free. Something was falling. A woman's body hurtled to the ground and landed next to her. Long black hair spread over the noblewoman's dress. Horrified, Lluava looked back at the window, where Varren stared down at her. The fire had entered his quarters.

"Varren!" Lluava screamed. "Varren!"

Lluava sat up and looked around the cave. "It was a dream," she said to reassure herself. "Just a dream."

Apex was not around. Outside, the sun shone brightly. It must be close to midday, she thought. As she moved under the furs, she felt something hard and stiff on her side. Pushing the coverings down, Lluava pulled up her shirt. Underneath, a cracked, drying poultice encased her wound. The whole thing itched, and she wanted to rip it off. Taking hold of one end, she began to slowly peel it away. Beneath the caked mass, her skin was nothing less than miraculous. The oozing, rotting, infection had vanished, leaving only a raised, pale-pink scar.

"What are you doing?"

Startled, Lluava released the poultice. Apex stood by her side.

"Leave that," he ordered, and moved farther into the cave. A moment later, he returned with more steaming broth.

"Here," he said as he handed her the bowl. "It's hot."

He stood there watching her drink, monitoring the amount she consumed and the speed at which she did so.

When Lluava was done, she asked, "Where is Varren?"

"You need to rest," Apex said as he took the bowl away.

"I'm tired of resting. I want to know what happened to Varren. We should be out looking for them."

"Stay inside and sleep," he growled, and then headed out of the cave.

Sköll was sunning himself on the slab of stone in front of the opening. He rose at the sound of Apex's whistle, and the pair headed down the mountain.

Lluava's restlessness grew. Where had Apex brought her? By the looks of this place, he had used it many times. Why didn't he take her back to the others? Were they hurt? Were they looking for her? Varren would be. But why hadn't he found her? Had something happened to him? Had he been caught in the avalanche?

Unable to remain still any longer, Lluava made a move for the cavern's opening. She felt terribly weak, yet at the same time she was much stronger than she had been in days. But just how many days had that been?

Carefully, Lluava stood up. Her legs felt wobbly, but they held her. She shuffled toward the ledge. The sun was not terribly warm, but it still felt pleasant on her face. She sat down at the edge of the stone that served as sort of a balcony overlooking the mountain range below. Lluava wondered how Apex had managed to carry her all the way up here. They must be near the top of the small mountain.

From this perspective, everything looked different, foreign. Lluava wondered if this was even the same mountain they had been on before the accident. Under a clear sky, everything seemed so peaceful. There was no breeze, no sound of any kind. With her feet dangling over the ledge, Lluava leaned back and relished the sunshine. She never wanted to be without it again.

Footfalls. Apex, returning, a brace of pheasants and rabbits swinging over his back. Sköll carried his own bird in his mouth. When Apex saw her reclining outside, he dropped his catch and violently pulled her to her feet.

"What are you doing?" he snarled. "I told you to stay inside."

Lluava was shocked at this unwarranted reaction.

"I just wanted some sun," she replied. Her voice revealed how weak she really was.

"Do you know what you have done?" he barked, looking wildly about. "You want to go so badly, fine! We leave right away."

He stormed into the cave. Lluava was dumbfounded. What was going on? All she did was enjoy some fresh air. What was he so afraid of? She peered down the side of the mountain. Everything looked serene.

A moment later, Apex came out with a large bundle of furs tucked under one arm. Issaura's Claws were tethered by the rope that bound the hides. With his other hand, he began to half drag Lluava down the steep slope.

She did not deserve this. She had almost died twice. What was wrong with him?

Lluava pulled herself free and fell back into the snow. When Apex reached out to grab her again, she scooted back. "No," she said. "I will not go another step until you tell me what is going on."

"You should have just listened to me," stated Apex.

"I don't give a rat's ass what you think I should or shouldn't do," hissed Lluava. "I want answers. What was that place? How long were we cooped up there? What happened to the others? What is going on?"

Apex put down his bundle and took a breath. "The avalanche caught you. I dug you out and brought you somewhere safe. You needed to heal, or you would have died."

"How long?" Lluava asked again. If Apex had expected a simple thank you, he was clearly mistaken.

"Four days today."

"Four?" Lluava had not expected that. "Why didn't you find the others? They are probably worried sick." Then, looking about once more, Lluava asked, "Where are they?"

Apex shrugged. "I don't know. I haven't seen them since that day."

"Didn't you look for them?"

"No."

"What have you been doing all this time? Trapping for your betterment?"

Apex looked as if he would hit her.

"Go on," she egged him. "You know you want to."

Balling his hands into fists, Apex turned away from her. "I took you away to keep you safe. If I hadn't, those Raiders would have killed you."

"The Raiders are dead," argued Lluava.

"Some survived."

Lluava thought about that. Could any have made it out of the snow? She certainly had. Suddenly, Lluava felt ashamed of her reaction—but Apex should have told her. She had a right to know.

"So, you never went back to look for the others, not even Wod, Monk, or Mila?"

Apex shook his head.

"Well," Lluava declared, standing up again. "We will find them now."

As they began to head down the mountain, Lluava selfishly hoped the others had not been left for dead. She hoped that somewhere not far away, all her friends awaited their return. Yet what was her life compared to the kingdom? If Talos had his way, they would be heading to Elysia. He had made that absolutely clear. She wasn't "valuable." Derrick was no different; always thinking of the greater good, he would adamantly push to rejoin his partner and Vidrick's troop.

Abruptly, Lluava realized that her reasoning had changed, that she no longer wanted Varren to be waiting for her. If any Raiders had survived, he would be at risk, and so would the others. With Apex's help, Lluava would find them eventually. Once she was back in Elysia, it would be easy to discover where the prince was. Of course, that was contingent upon Varren's being alive. What if he had not made it? What if Talos's valiant effort was too late? Firmly, she resolved to think no more about what-ifs.

Apex pulled Lluava down under the low limbs of a cedar tree. She was not sure what was going on, but from his expression she knew not to make any noise. She crawled farther under the widespread branches while Apex turned and wiped away their closest tracks.

As the huntsman lay next to her, he gave her a handful of snow. "Eat it. Quickly."

This time Lluava did not hesitate. The cold numbed her tongue, but she held the snow in her mouth as it melted. She noticed that her breath no longer showed when she exhaled.

Apex held a finger to his lips, then pointed ahead of them. Although Lluava could not see much from under the tree limbs, she made out three sets of fur-trimmed boots. They were moving in their direction.

Chapter 35

Beyond the Bend

Slowly Apex reached for the hunting knife tucked in his belt. Lluava would have tried to untangle the Claws from his bundle, but she knew that in her weakened state they would be little help.

Sinking lower into the snow, Lluava hoped the Raiders had not spotted them. These larger Raiders seemed to travel in threes. Did they always? It was true that on the frontlines at the outpost she had confronted two of them, but if her other observations were correct, a third large Raider would have been nearby. Maybe this was all coincidence, but it was worth considering.

Apex appeared ready to spring out and fight. Did he expect her to turn tail and run? Or did he want her to fight alongside him? He gave her no clue as to his strategy. That is, if he had a strategy.

The Raiders kept moving forward. As they neared the tree, they stopped, and one bent down to look at something in the snow. Was it their footprints? Apex had tried to erase them, but snow could be unforgiving. Even though the Raider's ruddy beard covered most of his features, he was obviously intently examining something—but what?

Suddenly, the marauder looked up. Apex held himself back, waiting. The Raider was staring, not at them but at something beyond their tree. Too afraid to turn her head, Lluava had to rely on what she could see out of the corner of her eye.

Something large and gray sprinted past—Sköll. The wolf-dog snarled at the trio of men and loped away. One of the Raiders took a shot at the animal with his crossbow and missed. Sköll turned around, growled, and limped off, with the Raiders in pursuit. Was the dog hurt?

Apex motioned her to be quiet a little longer. Finally, he slid out from under the tree. Lluava followed suit, and he led her in the opposite direction from Sköll's.

"What about—?" Lluava whispered, but Apex quickly said, "He's fine. Just an old ploy."

They continued quietly for some time before Lluava tried to strike up conversation once more. "Where did you learn that trick with the snow?"

"To survive out here, you learn many things, like how to disguise your breath in order to approach your prey." And before she could ask another question, he snarled, "Quiet." There was no further conversation.

Abruptly, Apex stopped. Even in the evening's waning light, Lluava could see the tension in the huntsman's face. She did not have long to wonder why, for she picked out the sound of approaching footsteps. Another Raider? She did not want to find out.

For cover, they would have to make a dash to the nearest cluster of trees. Unfortunately, the person was approaching from those very trees. There was no other choice. They would have to fight.

"Toss me Issaura's Claws," Lluava murmured. Unexpectedly, she heard the beating of wings in the air above. A raven flew straight at her and landed atop her shoulder.

"Onyx?"

The bird cawed once, ruffled his feathers, and settled down. If this was her bird, then that would mean…

Byron stood by the edge of the tree line, his mouth slightly ajar, his face that of a man seeing ghosts.

"Lluava?" Byron's voice wavered. "Is that really you?"

"Of course it is," she said, grinning.

Before they could rejoice, Byron glanced warily about. "Follow me," he directed. "Quickly."

He led the pair through a patch of woods to a small camp, where others huddled around a small fire. Illuminated faces turned in her direction, but Lluava focused on only one.

"Varren!" she cried out and ran toward him. He, in turn, moved to her with the hesitancy of disbelief. When they met, Varren gently held her face between his shaking hands, as though she might disappear like a mirage in the desert.

"It's me," she whispered. "I'm really here."

Tears began to fill his bloodshot eyes. In a perfect mix of tenderness and passion, Varren leaned down and kissed her. The touch of his lips sent a warmth coursing through her, a warmth she had not felt in a long while. She wrapped her arms around his neck, and they kissed again and again, one kiss after another. His hands moved over her features as if to memorize them; she entangled her fingers in his loose curls. For the moment, nothing else mattered, nothing else existed. Lluava felt him brush tears from her own cheeks; she had not realized she was crying. Eventually, Varren pulled away. He stared deeply into her eyes.

This is where I am meant to be, she thought. Right here beside him.

At the edge of awareness, Lluava's ears began to register other sounds. She remembered that there were others present, but she did not care. Leaning in to kiss Varren again, she heard Apex demand sharply, "What happened to them?"

Varren heard it, too, for he stepped back and looked at the lead huntsman. Hugging Lluava to his chest, he said what the others would not. "They were captured."

"Captured?" Lluava repeated, finally paying attention to the group. Three were missing. The brothers were nowhere to be seen; neither was Talos.

"Oh, gods!" Lluava exclaimed, staring at Rosalyn. Her friend looked as bad as Varren had in the moments before he recognized her. "What happened?"

Derrick was the first to speak. He seemed the one least affected by the recent events. "After several days of waiting, I came in search of all of you. When I found the others, I was told that they thought you had both died." Derrick nodded at Apex and Lluava, and then glanced at Varren. "Well, almost all of us. Prince Varren refused to leave until he found you."

Lluava couldn't help noticing Derrick's lack of shame. He would have left her and Apex to fend for themselves. "Since no one could convince Prince Varren to leave, we stayed and searched for you in shifts."

Or for our bodies, thought Lluava darkly.

"Last night, Talos, Wod, and Monk went out to search for you and did not return," Derrick added bleakly.

Yamir put in, "We retraced their steps and found signs of a struggle. They were dragged back to the Raiders' encampment."

"That encampment was destroyed," said Lluava. "I saw it swallowed whole by the avalanche."

Byron shook his head. He sat down next to Rosalyn, who had barely moved since Lluava's return. "They have another."

"Impossible," asserted Lluava. There was no way that could be true, could it? At the same time, she knew her friends were telling the truth.

"Something has to be done," she said.

"We have been trying to come up with a plan," added Varren. "So far, we have none. However, I am so glad that you are alive. At least now some hope has returned."

Mila stalked up to Lluava and inspected her. "Yes. How is it that you are alive? You were dying."

"It is only thanks to Apex," Lluava admitted. "He saved me."

Without releasing Lluava, Varren looked directly at Apex. "Thank you.

I am eternally grateful. You saved the person who is most precious to me in the world." He kissed Lluava's forehead.

"What about Talos?" Rosalyn cried out. "What are we going to do about him?" She stood up and looked around, her eyes fiery. "They have him. They have my Talos. He is precious to *me*."

Lluava forced herself to move away from Varren and run to Rosalyn. Kneeling before her distraught friend, she vowed, "I will do everything I can to rescue Talos."

"You will?" Apex's question came as a surprise. "How do you intend to infiltrate their fortress? You will face hundreds of those giants. You can barely walk as it is."

If Apex were trying to make her doubt herself, Lluava would have none of it. Still, she hesitated as she tried to think of a plausible plan. Last time, the Raiders had not been these freakish behemoths. Last time, they had held Varren captive in a traveling camp, not behind impenetrable walls. Last time, Lluava had had greater numbers to assist her. This was not like last time.

"Have you seen their fort?" Lluava asked.

"Only from a distance, when we were looking for you," acknowledged Derrick.

Lluava nodded. "Then maybe the first thing we must do is get a better look."

Beyond the mass of newly fallen snow and ice, the Pass arced to the left. The Raiders' secondary settlement was nestled in the curve of this bend. As large as the first fortress, this second one seemed even larger, swollen and pregnant, ready to give birth to a plague of death and destruction.

Lluava and her comrades could detect no weakness in the mighty walls. The vicinity was secured with trios of Raiders keeping watch at multiple positions. Lluava did not know whether they always patrolled in such numbers or had increased them after the loss of the other fort.

Outside the walls, numerous structures and tents housed even more of the vile marauders. Were some of them refugees from the other encampment? Lluava was unsure. More important, with all those Raiders on watch, how could Lluava's group hope to rescue their friends?

Something had to be done, and quickly. There was no telling what these brutes were doing to their captives. If Lluava were religiously inclined, she would have prayed. But to her, prayer was a waste. Who would be listening? What creative power? Any almighty force that would sanction such vile attacks on their kingdom by these villains was no god she cared for.

There was movement on her right. Lluava motioned to Varren and the others. Moments later, a band of twenty or so Raiders appeared, headed toward the fortress. They must have come west through the mountain range. Reinforcements. The Raiders were still increasing their numbers. Was that the purpose of the band of Raiders they had followed from the war front?

Had they been merely reinforcements for this hidden stronghold, in preparation for some heinous attack?

One thing struck Lluava as odd—among this approaching band of massive brutes were women, perhaps half a dozen of them. Lluava remembered hearing women's voices inside the first settlement. Were they wives of the Raiders? Were they as massive and strong as the men?

A darker thought slipped into Lluava's mind. Had she killed innocent women and children when she buried the fort under a mountain of ice? Lluava suddenly had to focus on her breathing, which had turned to quick little gasps as if strangled by those thoughts. What had she done? Nearby, Apex growled to himself as if he, too, were displeased at the sight of those fur-trimmed women.

Lluava's comrades regrouped at their own campsite. For many, the reconnaissance mission had borne no fruit. There was no need to stay and watch the Raider females travel toward the fortress. The idea that these women might be searching for their mates upset Lluava. For the first time, she realized that the brutes had homes with wives and families. Before, they had only been harsh faces to cut down. Now, she would always be aware that other people were tied to them.

Lacking the heat of a fire, the friends clustered together as they wracked their brains for any plausible solution.

Rosalyn had scouted with them; now she spoke up. "Does anyone else think it odd that the Raiders would bring their wives with them? If it were up to Talos," she said, briefly pausing, "he would not have risked my life in this sort of situation."

"Maybe they are that confident," responded Yamir sulkily.

"Humph," grunted Apex. "Those aren't wives. They are whores."

Lluava and several others looked askance at him.

Apex clarified, "The way they moved, touched, acted toward each other—it was all wrong for married women. Some came with them; some are from the Beltline. They follow the brutes from camp to camp." He spat on the ground. "They deserve no kindness or pity from us. They are whores and do not care who or what they service. They are whores, here to serve as relief for the marauders."

"How would you...?" Lluava paused. "Of course."

Apex almost grinned. "You might not approve of my chosen companions, but one thing I do know is how to spot a whore."

Lluava wrinkled her nose; this was the man with whom she had lived alone for four days. Suddenly she felt dirty. Was this how those women felt? She could not imagine making a living by going from man to man throughout that fortress. Or any other fortress.

"I can rescue Talos and the brothers."

Everyone turned toward Lluava. She looked at Rosalyn; the hope that leaped in the pale woman's eyes was inescapable. Please let this work, Lluava thought. Then she announced, "I can infiltrate the settlement by dressing as one of those whores."

Everyone seemed to speak at once.

"That is out of the question."

"Are you crazy?"

"You're not serious."

"Lluava!"

But Lluava would not be deterred. "Hear me out," she demanded. "If I dress in woolens and furs, I can slip into their camp. Why else would a woman be wandering the mountain range? Once inside the walls, I can search for Talos. For Wod and Monk. I can do this."

The disbelief and shock of those around her was palpable. Lluava turned to the one person who might possibly back her idea.

"Apex?"

She could tell that he wanted to belittle this dangerous scheme. Yet he didn't.

"You can use some of my furs," he said as he turned to unload his travel pack.

Varren was at his wits' end. "Lluava, if you do this, I will not be able to go with you, to protect you. I just got you back. You are still weak. How could you think of doing this?"

"I know. I know it all," agreed Lluava. "But I need you to trust me on this."

Looking deeply into her eyes, Varren nodded. His reluctance was evident, yet the fact that he would still back her idea was gratifying.

"I will go with you, too."

Lluava was caught completely off guard by Rosalyn's words. Although Lluava's first inclination was to talk her friend out of it, she knew that nothing she could say would matter. The woman had made up her mind. Rosalyn began to select several of Apex's hides.

Sighing, Mila added, "As will I." She joined Rosalyn, and all three women began the process of transforming themselves to blend in with the camp followers. Lluava's hair had to be tied up and hidden under a swatch of fur. She could not risk drawing attention to herself.

Apex pulled her aside briefly and warned, "Be prepared. To act like a whore means to be treated like one."

Lluava shrugged him off and shivered at the thought. It would not come to that, she told herself. She would not let it.

Once the trio had assembled their makeshift disguises and said quick goodbyes, they headed tentatively in the direction of the Raiders' settlement. Varren and Derrick escorted the women as far as the bend and then, with a quick nod for good luck, settled in to wait for the women's return.

Once en route, Lluava did not look back; she hated to leave her partner behind. Swathed in heavy furs, the three women trudged through packed snow toward the enemy settlement. By now it was well into the night. Fires had been stoked and torches lit.

Their fate would be decided in the first moments after they breached the ring of light. Would the Raiders believe them? Would they be attacked on the spot? Would her plan work?

Lluava saw the courage in her friends' faces. *Here goes everything.*

Several Raiders seated near the outer tents jumped up in surprise at the sight of the women appearing out of the darkness. Rosalyn lowered her fur-trimmed wrap and smiled as she strode confidently past them. Mila followed right behind her, and Lluava came last, her pale hair covered by a turban of fur. Her heart raced as the coarse-looking men stared hungrily at them, but the Raiders allowed them to pass unhindered. The women headed deeper into the encampment.

The doors to the settlement's entrance were closed. Three guards were posted at the gate, one on each side of the great double doors and the third directly in the middle. The way the men eyed Lluava and her friends sent a shiver down her spine. She had no idea how to enter.

How were they ever going to do this? What had she been thinking? She had no idea how to act or what to say. They would instantly recognize she wasn't one of them by her voice, wouldn't they? And Rosalyn—that gentle, soft-spoken, educated young girl! This would never work. Had she doomed them all?

The man in the center looked at them with a menacing gleam in his eye. "'Ow goes there?"

Chapter 36

Follow the Leader

She should have come up with a better plan. The guards knew something was up; they had to, didn't they? Lluava resisted the urge to lower her head. She didn't want to be discovered—not here in the thick of the enemy's encampment.

Mila strode forward confidently. She smiled pleasantly and her eyes sparkled. She began talking to the guard in the middle. Lluava hung back; with the heavy furs wrapped around her ears, she could not hear the huntswoman's exact words, but she could make several good guesses. Mila's movements were sensual and alluring, from the way she tilted her head to the manner in which she appeared to unthinkingly brush her hand down the Raider's chest. As the woman spoke, she turned to look at Rosalyn and Lluava.

The guard's grin displayed smokeweed-stained teeth. Lluava's stomach lurched. What had Mila said to him? What had she promised? The guard whistled to his companions, and the trio motioned them past.

As soon as they were out of the guards' hearing, Lluava closed the distance between herself and the self-assured Mila. "What did you tell him?"

"Something that I hope will not come to pass," replied Mila. Lluava thought she heard Rosalyn whimper.

The women made their way farther into the fortress. Its layout was similar to the one Lluava had destroyed, but much larger in scale. Each building was long and rectangular. The walls were built of sturdy wood, probably from the Yorrick Forest; the roofs were thatched. There were no windows or doors, only a single opening in front. Each building looked like the others, with no particular distinguishing characteristic. Lluava saw neither barns nor stables, yet she occasionally heard the deep lowing of cattle or the nicker of a horse.

Rosalyn asked in a hushed voice, "How are we going to find them in this maze? There are so many buildings. We do not have much time."

"We will figure something out," Lluava soothed. She wished she could believe her own words.

As they explored the camp, Lluava noticed another trio of Raiders standing near a building. The other men had moved around casually; these stood rigidly at attention. They were protecting something in that structure. But what?

One of the men saw Lluava looking at them. "Wanta join us?" he called, leering.

Mila, in a harsh accent matching theirs, called back, "Maybe afta."

"We be waitin'," promised the guard as the three women strolled by.

"They are guarding something," whispered Lluava. "Maybe it's Talos and the others."

"Maybe," Mila said, "or maybe not. We do not have time to waste, so we have to be sure before we do anything."

"You're right. We need to make sure," agreed Lluava, but her gut was telling her to go back.

Mila seemed to read Lluava's thoughts. "How do you propose entering with those men standing guard? They are enormous." Mila meant well, but her doubt, combined with Rosalyn's hopeful gaze, only egged Lluava on.

"Let me deal with that. You two see if there might be another building where they could be keeping our men. Okay?"

Instead of criticizing Lluava's hastily formed scheme, Mila smiled and led Rosalyn deeper into the camp. Lluava doubled back and made her way in a wide arc around to the rear of the structure. Uncut logs had been used as siding, and many boards bore thick knots where branches had been hurriedly chopped off. Climbing them should be easy, Lluava thought. Provided her strength held out.

Reaching up, she found a handhold, tested it, and pulled herself up. She wished she had on Issaura's Claws, but they needed to stay hidden under her long cape of furs. At least she had them with her. Rosalyn and Mila were armed only with hunting knives. Lluava hoped that none of their weapons would need to be used.

The building was a story-and-a-half high. Once Lluava pulled herself onto the thatch, she had to be careful where she stepped. Too much pressure on the wrong spot could mean falling through. She was thankful that, years ago, her father had taught her how to thatch their home's roof. Using those skills, she deftly navigated the arched roof.

Shuffling noises came from below. Cautiously, Lluava prised apart the heavy thatching to allow her to peer into the room beneath. It seemed that the back half of the structure was a stable. Bedded in small compartments, animals chewed on scattered hay. She was unable to see into the front part of the building, so with great care she moved on across the thatch.

Here and there, snow and birds had damaged the roof, creating thin spots through which the rise and fall of voices wafted, along with tendrils of smoke. She needed to get closer. Keeping as low as possible, Lluava crawled toward the other end of the structure. Although it was growing dark, she dared not risk being spotted by enemy eyes. Lluava stopped when she guessed she was over the center of those conversing. Squinting through one of the small gaps, she tried to make sense of the smoky room below.

It appeared to be a meeting area. A number of men were seated on benches along the side walls, warming themselves around a small fire. All were massive.

"'Ow can ya be so certain?" questioned a shaggy blond, who spoke to someone just out of Lluava's sight. "Mind ya, I understand th' reasonin', but th' timing's off."

"That is where you are wrong," the other party disagreed. Lluava shifted her position to get a better view. "The timing could not be more perfect. Strike while they are unsuspecting. Slay them while they slumber."

Lluava found another hole in the thatching. Spotting the speaker, she stifled a gasp. Wrapped in the same wolfskin cloak, with a snarling beast's head on each shoulder, stood Alcove, their leader. His well-groomed dark beard had not changed, nor had the patches of gray over each ear. His accent was as thick as the others', yet compared to these massive men his stature, which was average, seemed almost diminutive. Regardless, he clearly held their respect.

Lluava's memory of Alcove had not faded since the last time she saw him. His image had seared itself into her mind as she watched him sail away. On that day, he had told her that the war had only begun. He had been right.

"We have the Berserker Legion here," continued the leader, gesturing to the men around him. His other arm served as a perch for his falcon. "What more do we need?"

Several men smiled and nodded; others looked skeptical. A man seated across from the leader mumbled, "Almost all…"

"What'd you say?" asked Alcove, and the other man straightened up. "I couldn't hear. Come on. Speak louder."

"Wi' all due respect, Ambassador, shouldn't we wait f' *him* to arrive 'fore makin' any military decisions?"

"As it stands now," noted Alcove coolly, "I am in charge of all facets of decision-making. My judgment is final. In three days, we move out and take the Horns." Alcove stroked the back of his bird. The falcon cocked his head toward the ceiling and let loose a cry.

Lluava froze. Alcove tilted his head before reaching into his pocket and pulling out a hood for his pet. Once conversation resumed, Lluava inched backward until she reached the edge of the thatched roof. She checked to see that the coast was clear and then climbed hastily down. Before she could even wonder where to find her friends, they approached.

Rosalyn waved her close. "We found them!"

"We think," countered Mila. Rosalyn ignored the correction and said, "The Raiders are keeping their prisoners in a building off to the left. There are men at the door, but only three."

"Three that we saw," Mila again countered. "Find out anything useful?"

"Maybe, but I will tell you later," said Lluava. "Let's rescue the others."

The long building that served as a prison was different, not in look but in outer design. This structure boasted two rows of large, snarling lizard sculptures flanking the doorway. The grotesque heads were reminiscent of those carved on the bows of the Raiders' long ships. A small fire under each burnished belly illuminated their features in a terrifying way. Steam emerged from holes in their nostrils like smoky breath.

Following Mila's confident lead, the women walked between the ranks of monsters. Low moans issued from the bellies of the beasts. Lluava was relieved once they had passed these groaning metal statues that breathed white steam.

They paused in the doorway, and three haggard men of unnatural size emerged from the darkness. Compared to them, the statues had seemed friendlier. Inside her furs, Lluava brushed her fingers over Issaura's Claws. If only she could use them! She gauged her strength and was disappointed. She was far from ready for combat. But would she have a choice?

The men before them would certainly not allow three women to waltz into the prison, Lluava thought. But when she saw their lascivious expressions, she changed her mind. It seemed Mila had expected this, for her sensual mannerisms had already taken over.

The man on their left grunted to his companions, "Gifts from th' ambassador."

"'Bout time," snorted the one on the right.

The middle guard looked displeased. He was the eldest, with a full head of gray hair. "Not t'night. We's on watch."

Lluava wasn't sure whether he was addressing them or his comrades. Mila continued to smile confidently while Rosalyn played bashful. At least, Lluava thought she was pretending.

The man on the right leered at the women. "We'd be quick."

"We wouldn't 'ave ta leave our post," argued the other man as he pulled Rosalyn toward him. Lluava's first instinct was to jump to her friend's rescue, but then a silvery flash emerged from Rosalyn's furs. Her harasser released her, swiping at the burgeoning ribbon of red at his throat.

A moment of hesitation and surprise ensued, which Mila and Lluava seized. Mila mirrored their raven-haired friend's actions with the second guard while Lluava slipped on the Claws and drove them deep into the stomach of the middle guard, whose face filled with shock as he stumbled back into the building. Lluava fell with him; as she landed onto his torso, she saw the movement of his short sword toward her side. But his attempt died with him, his face gripped in a snow leopard's maw.

Shakily, Lluava got to her feet and looked around. The front room was small, the bulk of the space in the building given over to stables. Each barred gate was locked. By the silence, no animals were bedded here. Was this why this building served as a prison? She hoped that's what it was. It was certainly secure. Looking more closely, she spied several weapons hung within easy reach of the guards. Fortunately, they had not served their purpose this time.

"Quickly," the leopard said as it shifted back into Mila's lithe form. It took all three of them to drag the bodies into the building, out of the sight of passersby. Lluava looked over at Rosalyn, expecting the same expression of wide-eyed shock her friend had worn the day she made her first kill. Instead, she saw a woman standing resolute over three corpses. Rosalyn bent over the closest one and started searching his clothing.

"What are you doing?" Lluava whispered. Experience had taught her that caution was one's best friend.

"Looking for keys," Rosalyn replied as she poked and prodded for pockets or pouches.

Lluava eyed her friend. The dark-haired woman replied, "I panicked, all right? We had to get inside to find Talos."

Lluava raised her hands to show that she wasn't judging. "You just caught me off guard, that's all."

"Rosalyn?" called a rough voice tentatively from one of the stalls.

"Talos!" Rosalyn almost shouted as she ran to the barred enclosure. Lluava and Mila continued to search the bodies for keys and finally found them on the older guard. Quickly the makeshift cells were unlocked and the three prisoners released. Talos embraced Rosalyn, kissing her forehead and cheeks. Then he stopped.

"You should not be here. It is not safe."

"That's an understatement if I ever heard one," said a grinning Wod, and he winked at Lluava with his one good eye. The other was swollen shut. All three men seemed to have been handled harshly.

"Actually, Talos," Lluava responded, "if it hadn't been for Rosalyn's quick thinking, our situation might have turned out quite differently."

Even with his split lips, Talos cracked a smile. "My hero," he said to Rosalyn in a hushed voice. Suddenly, with dawning awareness, he looked at Lluava.

"You are alive!"

"I'm as surprised as you are," she said with a bigger grin than Wod's.

"Welcome back to the living," Monk said earnestly.

Wod nodded. "I knew they would make it."

Monk shoved his little brother playfully before saying, "Now, how are we getting out of here? Anyone have a plan?"

As they began to strategize, Lluava's sensitive ears picked up another sound.

"Shhhh," she hissed. The others stared at her. She disregarded their looks. "Quiet. We are not alone."

Chapter 37

Alcazar

Everyone grew silent. Those who had weapons readied themselves.

"I thought there were only three," murmured Rosalyn as she warily eyed the shadows.

"So did I," acknowledged Wod, who had grown as serious as his older brother.

Monk was by no means flippant at the thought of being imprisoned again. "Spread out. Check all the cells," he ordered.

Lluava had gone farther into the building than the others. She walked down the row of stalls on her right, peering inside each one. They were bare—no chairs, tables, or beds. Many did not even have a layer of straw on the ground; the frozen earth formed the floor.

Empty. Empty. Empty. They were all empty, as far as Lluava could tell. Was she wrong? She could have sworn she heard a noise from the back. Then she heard it again, a heavy sigh coming from the last cell.

"Over here," Lluava said softly, gesturing. Talos picked a flaming stick out of the firepit in the front room. Using it as a torch, he lifted it to the grate, and they both peered into the blackness. In the back of the stall, encapsulated by shadow, was a man. He was sprawled on his stomach, facing away from them. His long blond hair was matted with mud and blood, and his left foot was twisted at an unnatural angle. Yet Lluava noticed something even more important.

"Look! He is wearing an Elysian training uniform."

Talos stared at the incapacitated recruit. "Mila," Lluava called, "bring the keys. Hurry! He's alive!"

"No."

Talos's voice was harsh. Lluava stared at him, aghast.

"What?" She was shocked at her friend's refusal to help. "He is one of us, Talos."

Shaking his head, Talos explained, "We cannot save him, Lluava. Look closely. His leg is clearly broken. I doubt he has the strength to even stand. How do you expect us to move a man in his state out of this fortress, or even out of this building, without getting caught?"

Lluava had no answer.

Talos looked hard at her. "He would only slow us down."

Even though she knew it had hurt him to say that, Lluava was disgusted with her friend. How could he be so cruel?

"I was like that once, remember? I was left for days to die, alone and forgotten, in *that* cell. I was almost dead when Derrick found me."

"But you did not have an injury like that." Talos pointed to the prisoner's leg. "And the Raiders were no longer there."

Rosalyn defended her betrothed. "We came here to rescue Talos, Wod, and Monk. That is all. We cannot risk our success for a man we do not know. I am truly sorry, Lluava. But this is a fight we cannot win."

The others began to leave. Lluava stared into the cell a moment longer, watching the slow rise and fall of the man's chest.

"May the gods be with you," she said as she followed her companions to the front room. She did not know why she had said that. A quick death would be best. But somehow, if he could hear them, her words might offer him some small comfort.

At the doorway, Monk handed Wod his throwing knives. Talos found his sword hanging on the wall and took it down. While Monk counted the arrows in his quiver, Mila spoke out. "We have to split up. It is the only way any of us has a chance to move though this accursed place unnoticed."

Lluava looked at the other five. "Can we travel in threes? It seems to be what they do here. We might blend in more easily."

"Wod, Monk," Mila ordered, "you are with me."

Lluava did not argue, and neither did her friends, who were more concerned about each other. Actually, she was glad to travel with them. The idea of moving though this death trap alone was terrifying. She wanted to be rid of the place for good.

The three men stripped the dead guards of their outerwear, hoping that dressing as a Raider would hide their identity.

"Good luck," she said as the three huntsmen slipped out the door, quiet as shadows.

"Ready?" Talos asked. He looked as bad as Lluava still felt.

"Let's go," she replied as she led Talos and Rosalyn toward the perimeter of the fortress. As they moved out of the building and through the tunnel of metal monsters, Lluava could not shake the eerie feeling evoked by the metallic moaning. Once they reached the perimeter, the trio cautiously moved from shadow to shadow. It seemed that every few buildings, a new group of Raiders would appear. Their progress was painstakingly slow. The night was beginning to wane.

The sight of the still open gates was glorious. Once they passed that portal, they would be through the worst of it. Somewhere on the other side, Varren and the others waited. They could finally return to Elysia. The thought was like a fading dream.

"We need to get past those guards." Talos spoke softly so only they would hear. Rosalyn ventured a smile. Motioning them close, she explained her idea.

Soon the three friends moved toward the gates. Rosalyn had switched clothing with Talos; the oversized male garb made her look smaller than she was. Her long black hair was tucked behind her ears. She led the way. Lluava followed, still hiding her own platinum-blond hair. Talos was bundled in the outer furs his betrothed had worn, all but his eyes hidden.

Would this work? Lluava was doubtful. Yet Rosalyn, assuming full authority, told the central guard, "We have been ordered to service the men in the outer encampment." She nodded at the overflow of Raiders fending off the cold in their tents or near their fires.

The guard looked over and waved them past. But just as they started to slip by, he grabbed Rosalyn's arm.

"I recognize ya. Ya th' one who made us a lil' promise earlier."

Rosalyn looked aghast. "You mistake me, sir."

"Naw. Ya, ya friend," he said, nodding toward Lluava, "and... she's different." He stared hard at Talos's disguise. Even if he had been able to wear Mila's clothing, the height difference would still have been obvious.

"Aye," noted Lluava, trying to replicate the thick accent of the Raiders. "She be different. We're needed out front."

"Then you better pay us quick," replied the guard. His two companions were approaching.

An alarm sounded within the fortress—a war horn's strident and urgent call. The guard holding Rosalyn's arm jerked her toward him. "Sumpin' ain't right." He began to drag her back inside the gates, which were swinging closed.

Talos threw off his fur cloak and drew his sword; yet his act was worthless, for at the same moment an arrow whistled past, striking the guard in the eye. Two more arrows flew through the air to lodge in the throats of the other two Raiders.

In a flash, Lluava tugged at Rosalyn and they raced through the gates. Behind her, Talos followed with Monk, Wod, and Mila at his heels. Monk nocked his bow as he ran. There was no time for words. The six rushed through the outer encampment, passing Raiders who were still strapping on their own weapons. The war horn continued to blare its warning. They had reached the edge of the enemy camp, but a number of giant Raiders were in pursuit.

"Shift, you fools!" hissed Mila as she morphed into her dual form. Talos's stag bounded ahead, and Rosalyn's graceful swan took wing. Lluava's own urge to change was overwhelming, but she would not allow it. The risk was too great. Anyway, she was not alone; Wod and Monk, being human, had to flee on foot.

The giant Raiders were fast, even without drugs to enhance their physical abilities. Wod alerted the others: "We're losing ground."

Lluava saw Monk's expression turn bleak. "Keep going," he ordered as he turned and fired off arrows, each one claiming a life.

All at once, the sounds of pursuit fell silent. It seemed the Raiders had retreated. A moment later, Lluava wished that had not been the case, as a deluge of arrows rained down on them from above.

"Look out!" she screamed and vaulted out of the way of the initial projectiles. The arrows fell rapidly. It took all her concentration to avoid their trajectories. Wod, who had had no direct experience of war, looked panicked. Lluava hoped for a future where she could apologize for dragging them into this mess. The brothers should be hunting happily in the forest rather than dealing with this bloodbath.

Wod cried out. An arrow had caught his throwing arm, and the sudden pain made him stop. Lluava veered in his direction, grabbed his shoulder, and pulled him forward.

Finally, the sound of arrows landing in snow dissipated. They were out of range but not yet in the clear. They had to reach their mounts, then ride as far and as fast as they could from this accursed place.

Ahead, she could see Varren and Apex on horseback, rushing down the ridge toward them. They were so close.

"Monk!"

Wod pulled free of Lluava's grip and turned. Looking back, Lluava saw the form that had been his brother lying on the ground, bristling with the shafts of arrows.

"It's too late," she acknowledged tonelessly. There was no time to mourn, for a large band of Raiders was fast approaching. Lluava assumed they had smoked the vile contents of their horns. "Monk's dead."

"No!" Wod cried and began to run toward his brother's corpse.

From behind her, Apex rode past and cut off Wod's path. Varren had reached Lluava's side; reaching down, he swung her up onto his horse. Wod's screams continued. Jumping from his horse, Apex delivered a quick blow to Wod's head, then slung the young huntsman, now limp and unconscious, across his steed. He remounted and rode after Varren and Lluava. In moments, Monk's body had disappeared under ranks of charging feet.

Over the ridge, the rest of their band waited for them on horseback. Together, they galloped toward the opening of the Pass and into the Yorrick Forest, where Derrick waited. For the first time in a long while, they continued their frantic pace until their horses were exhausted. Saddle sores returned and worsened, even after they had finally slowed.

Lluava lost track of time. The day had come and gone, and now they were finally stopping to rest. During their ride, Wod had regained consciousness, although Lluava was not exactly sure when. He never said a word, just quietly sat up. If Lluava had not looked over at Apex, she would not have noticed Wod. When she did, her heart broke.

It was true that she had never felt a connection with Monk, yet the grief in his brother's face reminded her too well of all that they had lost over the months. Half a year ago, they were each living separate, happy lives. Now, their anger and misery had pulled them together. She wished things were different, especially for those who had lost someone. None of her friends would come out of this unscarred. Although the wounds might not be physical, they could still cripple.

Yamir led his horse over to them. "How quickly do you think they will be upon us? Certainly, some of them have horses."

Varren slid from his mount and helped Lluava down. "We will maintain a rotating watch tonight in case they discover our trail. Since I do not know their plans, I cannot say how soon they will regroup and march out. To move an army as large as that one will take them several days, at least, organizing and preparing supplies. Our best bet is to return to Elysia and summon help there."

"Actually," Lluava interjected, "I did learn something while I was in their camp."

"What is it?"

"I saw Ambassador Alcove—you know, the leader—in a council meeting. He said something about wanting to move those larger Raiders. He called them...." Lluava struggled to remember the strange name. "The Berserker Legion."

Varren asked warily, "Did you hear where he wanted to move them?"

"Um...something about horns."

Varren was confused. "Do you mean animal horns or Theriomorph horns?"

"I don't know," Lluava admitted. "All he said was to take the horns."

Varren's eyes grew large. "He wants to attack Røthe."

"How do you know that?" Lluava asked quickly.

" 'The Horns' is a reference to two rivers, Slidr and Okeanos, that bracket Røthe, our largest northern city."

"What's so important about Røthe?"

Varren furrowed his brow, thinking; then suddenly said, "Because

Røthe's ports are on Okeanos, and that river leads all the way to Pern, a stone's throw away from Cronus!"

Lluava was aghast. "They could take the capital!"

"They will try," agreed Varren. "Let us inform the others."

Once the explanations were made and the new destination agreed upon, Varren approached Apex with one last request.

"I know our contract is over," he told the huntsman. "You did exactly what we asked of you. I also am aware of the great losses you have sustained."

"What do you know of loss?" Wod asked wearily.

Varren paused and looked at the younger man. "More than you know," he answered sorrowfully. Turning back to Apex, he asked, "Will you help us one last time? We need a guide to take us directly to Røthe."

"Our deal is done." Apex crossed his arms and stood resolute. "Pay us now."

Varren pulled his purse from his pocket, saying, "More people will die if we cannot fend off this attack. We need help to reach Røthe before the Raiders do. If not, others will lose family, friends." He handed over the payment to Apex and then implored him, "Please."

Apex counted the coins. Once satisfied, he stated, "We're done."

"I'll help." Wod seemed to have collected himself. "I have lost my brother. Yet I also have the rest of my family to think about—my sisters and my parents. What will happen to them if the mainland falls? How many other families must lose their loved ones? I'll help you."

Sköll trotted up to Apex, who patted the mutt's head before they both headed away together.

"I guess he's gone, then," noted Yamir. "Can't say I'm going to miss him."

"Yamir!" Rosalyn chastised him, yet Byron, who was standing nearby, grinned.

In the morning, the group was packed and ready to travel just after sunup. Lluava was surprised but pleased that Mila had stayed. Wod pointed out the route they would take.

"You'll lose a day that way," a gruff voice declared. Apex walked up to the group. "Since there is no time to waste, you had better follow me."

Wod looked relieved. Lluava guessed he really wasn't sure about this "leading other people" business. She did give him credit for being willing to try.

For several days, they moved at a steady speed, stopping only when necessary and for as little time as possible. Still, it seemed to take too long. Who knew how fast those giant Raiders, the Berserkers, could march? When drugged, they moved so quickly. And Lluava was anxious to return to civilization. Elysia's borders were almost within reach.

Varren appeared tense as well. One evening, Lluava said to him, "You seem nervous. Is something the matter? Derrick has sent word to Vidrick's men. They will meet us in Røthe as soon as they can."

"No. It is not—" Varren took a breath. "There is something you need to know."

"What?"

"Røthe is governed by—"

But he was interrupted by Apex, who was traveling on foot, and had walked up to them. Ignoring their prior conversation, he told them, "We have entered Elysia. Røthe is only a few hours away. We will reach it by supper."

"I need you to adjust our course. Can you take us to Alcazar Castle?"

Varren's questions did not seem agreeable to their guide. "I thought we were going to Røthe."

"There is someone at the castle we must see. Immediately."

The huntsman glared at Varren for a long moment.

Lluava did not understand what the problem was. The castle was only several miles from the city. It was home of the lord whose family's name was now associated with the castle itself. Lord Alcazar governed Røthe. To Lluava, to see him was a smart decision.

"Apex?" she questioned.

The huntsman turned to her, clenched his jaw, and then said, "Let's go."

"Are you all right with this?" Varren asked. "Staying in the Alcazar Castle, that is?"

"Yes. Why wouldn't I be?" countered Lluava.

"You are spectacular." Varren leaned over and kissed her. The thrill of his touch made her flush. Lluava hoped she never got used to it.

Soon the caravan broke from the forest. From this point, they traveled through fields and farmlands, eventually reaching a real road. Sköll had left them at the edge of the woods. He seemed quite content to remain there until his master returned. At one point, as they veered down the other side of the forked road, Lluava glimpsed the lights of Røthe. Stars had popped into sight before Lluava finally caught sight of the castle.

Castle was probably not the appropriate word. The term *palace* came to mind. Unlike Varren's home, this one was far more inviting. Beautifully ornate, multiple towers shot up from its core like pale white blooms in the starlight. The castle was built on a small mound and seemed to grow up and over the trees around it.

"Alcazar is beautiful," commented Lluava wistfully.

Varren's voice darkened. "Yes, she is."

"How well do you know Lord Alcazar?" she asked him.

"I have not talked to him in several years. I have not visited this place since I was a boy."

Once they arrived, the outer gates swung open and several stewards hastily approached to help them from their mounts. Two equerries led the exhausted animals off to the stables. In front of Varren, two doormen pulled open the grand double doors.

Entering the foyer, Lluava gawked at the polished marble floors, the elegant inner columns, and the gold-trimmed double stairwell that led down from the second-floor gallery. A young woman about their age made her way down the stairs with two handmaidens in her shadow. Her flowing purple dress was cinched tightly at her narrow waist, and her dark hair was woven into an elegant updo, which emphasized her flawless features. She curtsied once, then approached the prince.

"Hello, Varren. It has been a long time."

Varren bowed formally. "Hello, Illia. You look beautiful, as always."

Smiling sweetly in front of her was the one person Lluava had hoped never to meet: Varren's betrothed.

Chapter 38

Past Phantoms

Illia's smile was sickeningly sweet. Lluava wanted to vomit—at least, she envisioned doing so—all down Illia's tailored gown. Varren stepped to Lluava's side and began the formal introductions.

"Lady Illia, I would like you to meet my military partner, Lluava Kargen."

By the look on Illia's exquisite features, she already knew who Lluava was. Who didn't? By now, Lluava's fame was more widespread than that of Varren's Northern-born fiancée

Varren continued, "Lluava, this is my betrothed, Lady Illia Alcazar."

"It is a pleasure to meet you." Illia's words were earnest.

Lluava tried and failed to come up with a graceful reply, so she left it with a nod. As Varren introduced the rest of their party, she scrutinized their young hostess. The woman was of average height, slender, but not as frail looking as Rosalyn. Her age was probably close to Varren's, which would make her about twenty. Her amber eyes were thoughtful; her voice was soft and warm, with an undertone of authority. Lluava struggled to find some flaw, yet at this first meeting she could not.

"Allow me to introduce all of you to my father," Illia said. "He is awaiting us in our private dining hall." Slipping an arm under Lluava's, Illia began to guide them through the castle. Her touch was firm but gentle.

"Lady Lluava," she began, but Lluava cut her off.

"I'm not actually a lady."

Illia regarded her with sparkling eyes. "I think you are deserving of such a title, do you not, Your Majesty?" She included Varren with her glance.

Varren stood on Lluava's other side, away from Illia. Lluava wondered

266

whether Illia had noticed the slight or perhaps merely thought her betrothed too tired to engage in formal court etiquette.

Varren replied, "I believe she deserves that and much more."

Illia did not seem taken aback; instead, her smile broadened. "Lluava, will you honor me, when you have time, by sharing some of your marvelous adventures with me?"

Did this woman think that what they had been experiencing was a game? Lluava answered frostily, "War is not to be taken lightly."

Illia paled. "I did not mean to offend. That was a gravely inconsiderate choice of words. I meant only that I wanted to learn more about you. I have heard rumors, but I dislike relying on them. Please accept my apology."

"Of course." Lluava acknowledged grudgingly, and then wondered why she felt as if it were she who should apologize.

Illia stopped in front of a large set of doors. Two more stewards pulled them open and ushered the party inside. The dark, wood-paneled room was filled with one very long table surrounded by high-backed chairs. Fires blazed in the grand fireplaces at each end of the room. The flames' warm glow cast strange shadows on a variety of mounted animal heads that adorned the walls.

At their entrance, the three figures at the far end of the table halted their conversation. One was a well-dressed man whose girth was comparable to his age and who sported a long but well-groomed beard flecked with gray. Lluava assumed this was Lord Alcazar. He held the hand of a lithe woman with a troubled gaze. The third figure was seated to the right of Lord Alcazar, which indicated that he was a guest of honor.

As this man turned to look at them, Lluava exclaimed, "Councilman Hyrax!"

The councilman looked pleasantly surprised. He smiled at Varren and then at Lluava.

Once more, Varren formally bowed. "Lord Alcazar," Varren said, "permit me to make the introductions."

As he presented his comrades, Lady Alcazar suddenly stood.

"If you will excuse me, Your Majesty. I do not feel well," she said as she swept from the room.

Lord Alcazar looked somewhat saddened. "I must apologize," he explained. "Lady Alcazar's health is far from its best. Everyone, please be seated." He snapped his fingers and two serving men appeared. "Bring my guests something to eat," he instructed.

Next to Lluava, Yamir whispered, "I hope it isn't more venison."

"So do I," Talos responded, with a smile that caused a few snickers.

Lluava felt that she could finally relax, at least for the moment. She knew the Berserkers were on their way and that a blood bath would soon follow, but she was relieved, too, that she could finally stop, enjoy food and drink, bathe and dress in clean clothes, and rest. Unfortunately, this sense of security disappeared as she overheard Varren's conversation.

"It has been a long time," Varren said, agreeing with a comment of Lord Alcazar's.

Their host observed, "You two look so lovely together."

Lluava's stomach turned. He was referring to Illia, who was seated across from Varren. How had she expected to avoid meeting Illia, Lluava wondered. Had she really thought she could live out her life without crossing the woman's path? Illia was high born and would eventually come to court, would she not? And what of the betrothal? With all that was going on, would Varren find the time to discuss that arrangement with Lord Alcazar?

Varren seemed to read her thoughts. He reached for her hand under the table and gave it a squeeze. "There is nothing more wonderful than two people in love," he replied.

Illia gave a wan smile. "Yes, that is true."

Soon trays of steaming roast, cheese wheels, and loaves of bread arrived. Lluava salivated as the food was distributed. It had been so long since she had enjoyed a meal such as this. Yet with the first bite, she realized she had lost her appetite. She could not eat with Illia nearby.

More dishes were paraded through the doors, along with platters of figs and pitchers of sweet wine. Before Apex could refill his goblet, two large men approached, seized him by his shoulders, and dragged him to his feet.

"What is going on?" Varren demanded before Lluava could shout out.

"That man, that monster—" Lord Alcazar's tone was censorious as he directed a withering scowl at the lead huntsman, "is to be taken to the dungeons until proper judgment can be passed. You, Varren, could not have known you were associating with a wanted man."

"Wanted?" Lluava repeated. "For what?"

"Murder," stated Alcazar. "Eight years ago, that man took the life of my son, Eran—my little boy. He has been on the run ever since. He must pay for his crimes."

"Is this true?" Varren asked the huntsman, hoping this was just a mistake.

Apex stood erect, his shoulders square. Looking directly at Lord Alcazar, he answered Varren. "I killed his son." There was no guilt or remorse in either his statement or his bearing.

With a quick nod from their host, the two guards led the huntsman to the door. Apex did not resist.

"He saved us," Lluava protested, rising from her chair. "He saved my life. Does that not matter?" But she could see that Lord Alcazar would not be swayed.

Varren looked downcast and motioned for her to sit down. Was he going to abandon Apex just like that? Lluava looked toward her friends for help. Were none of them willing to stand up for the lead huntsmen? Not even

Wod and Mila came to his defense. Would they not fight for their friend? Lluava was mortified. Maybe it was true, then, that the huntsmen were tied together only by their line of work and nothing more. Lluava resumed her seat, lowered her eyes, and remained silent for the rest of the meal.

Hyrax had changed seats after Varren's arrival and now sat across from Lluava. Once, catching her eye, he raised a knuckle to his beard and pushed his chin upward. Lluava was not amused. Unless he intended to help Apex, she did not care.

The councilman turned to the prince. "Your Majesty, what is your reason for traveling here? Last I heard, you and your companions were voyaging north in search of enemy forces."

"It would take far too long to recount all the details of our journey," Varren answered. "To get straight to the matter at hand, we have come bearing news of the greatest importance." Varren looked to their host, whose thoughts were apparently still focused on Apex and his capture. "Lord Alcazar, we believe that Røthe and the surrounding villages will be attacked by the enemy very soon. The Raiders intend to use your ports to travel down the Okeanos to Pern. From there, we believe they will march on Cronus."

"You are certain?" the lord sounded grave.

"If I were not, would you want to take that risk?"

"Your Majesty," Alcazar began, "you must understand that Røthe is a peaceful city, as are all the neighboring villages. Our people are miners and foresters. My guards are few, my people many. We have no means to defend against an attack."

"Derrick," Varren said, gesturing to the dark-skinned man, "has sent word to Lieutenant Vidrick Bern, who is already leading several troops to your city. They should arrive in the next few days."

"And you believe that is enough?" questioned Alcazar skeptically.

Varren shook his head. "We need to send word to the northern training camps. They are the closest source of military support."

"Relying on half-trained men is far from a comforting strategy," replied Alcazar.

"Do not discount them." Varren looked around at his friends. "They might surprise you. Anyway, they are all we have nearby."

"What of my people? I cannot stand by and watch them be—" Lord Alcazar looked abruptly at Illia. "Excuse us, Daughter. Please check on your mother."

Illia seemed to have anticipated such a command. "As you will, Father." She stood and curtsied quickly to the prince. "Your Majesty."

Once Illia had left the room, Varren continued their conversation. "Evacuate them. Send them to the capital. Cronus will house any refugee until the war is over."

"All of them?" Lord Alcazar seemed dubious.

"All those who do not wish or are not able to stay and fight. In the meantime, I will send word to my grandfather asking him for assistance."

"Not the High Council, Your Majesty?" questioned Hyrax.

"I will communicate with my grandfather first."

Varren's words made Hyrax smile.

"What is it, Talos?" Varren asked as soon as he noticed his friend trying to gain his attention.

"We could construct walls—"

"—at least around the city," put in Byron.

Shaking his head, Lord Alcazar said, "If we have mere days, that is not feasible." He paused as he reached his own decision. Waving a steward over, he ordered, "Have Røthe evacuated. Move the people south. If these Raiders attack Røthe, let it be a ghost town."

A new voice spoke up. "May I say something?"

Wod waited for Varren's nod before he continued. "I am a trapper. It's what I know how to do. For as long as I can remember, I have rigged devices to ensnare and capture prey. These devices, if made on a larger scale, could be used on people. I want to trap for you, my lord. I want to trap the Berserkers."

There was a fire in Wod's eyes, a flame that had ignited when his brother died. Lluava had wondered if, after all of this, Mila and Wod would be happy to return to hunting and trapping animals. Now, at least, Lluava knew that Wod was ready to make a stand.

"I can attest to that, Lord Alcazar," agreed Lluava, recalling the snare that had trapped her.

Lord Alcazar looked to Varren.

"Very well," said the prince. "Let us make our plans."

Over the course of the next several hours, Wod was assigned to create several rows of traps running from the edge of the Yorrick Forest to the banks of the Slidr River. Yamir volunteered his services. Lluava wondered if, between the two, they could find other ways to help each other cope with their losses. Talos, Derrick, and Byron would train those who chose to stay and fight. Rosalyn would assist with preparing medical wards and organize the local healers and physicians. Lluava, along with Hyrax and Mila, would help coordinate the exodus of people. Mila's interest in the endeavor pleased Lluava greatly.

They finally made their way to their new quarters in the early morning hours. Lluava was so exhausted she couldn't think straight. But as soon as she slid into bed, there was a soft knock at her door. Having snatched up the Claws, she cracked open the door and readied herself for anything.

Varren stood there.

She let him in. "What do you want?" she asked irritably.

"Before I go to sleep, I want you to know something," he told her. "I will be talking to Alcazar about saving Apex's life."

"Why didn't you do that tonight, before he was dragged out like an animal?" griped Lluava.

"Lord Alcazar was in no mood to have his authority questioned, especially when it concerned the man who admitted to killing his boy," explained Varren. "The law is clear: a life for a life. Yet Apex saved you, and I owe him as much. I have the power to release Apex, but Lord Alcazar is our host and a man I respect. He finally has the person who killed his son; now, he needs time to come to terms with that."

"How much time can you afford?" questioned Lluava. "How much time does Apex have?"

"Enough for me to make amends," replied Varren. He kissed her forehead and bade her goodnight.

***

Lluava awoke late the next day. She hurried downstairs and managed a hasty breakfast. There was much to do before the enemy arrived. Starting with the small farms near the forest's edge, she would help spread the command to vacate homes and seek refuge in the south.

In midafternoon, Lluava returned, profoundly weary. Her strength was still nowhere near what it needed to be. Varren implored her to stay and rest. At first, she balked, but consented as soon as she lay down on a settee in one of the parlors.

It wasn't long before she became restless. Everyone else was working hard while she was resting inside; this did not sit well with her. She needed to occupy her time while she recuperated.

And something else bothered her. Her thoughts had returned to Apex. He had never been the pleasant sort, but she had not expected him to be a murderer. And his remorseless statement last night—was he truly that cold-hearted? Why had he done it?

Lluava spent the better part of an hour wandering the halls of the castle until she found a scullery maid who could point her in the right direction. In the depths of the castle, she found the dungeon. She had anticipated the guards and already had a plan.

"I am Lluava Kargen, military partner to Prince Varren. I was asked to bring the prisoner his dinner ration."

"This early?" questioned one guard.

"Yes, and if he eats it all too early, the worse for him."

The guards scrutinized Lluava and the small roll she held in her hand. "Very well. This way."

One of the guards led her down a corridor to a cell that bore a striking similarity to the one that had once imprisoned her. The damp, dark stone cells gave off a chill, which made her shiver. The guard stopped and rapped on the door.

"Visitor," he barked through the grate. Turning to Lluava, he grunted, "You have five minutes."

"A visitor? For me?" Apex's voice came out of the darkness. Once he approached the door, his face broke into a sinister smile. "You should have said, a *gift*."

"I came to bring you your dinner," Lluava replied.

"I can give *you* something," said Apex.

"I don't need your gifts," she retorted.

"So, no conjugal visit? That's highly disappointing."

"Apex," Lluava hissed, "be serious." What was up with him? Why was he acting this way?

"I've never been more so. Have you ever thought what it would be like— two animals rolling around in the sack?"

Lluava disregarded his question. "Why did you do it?"

"Why did I do it?" repeated Apex. "I do it when there is no other option. I was doing it now before you came."

Lluava was revolted. "What is wrong with you? This isn't like you."

Apex lurched at the bars, pushing his face right up to the grate. "Sweetheart, this *is* me."

Seeing him up close, Lluava could see heavy perspiration filming his brow. "Are you feeling all right?"

"I'd feel better feeling you," he said with a grin. He suddenly stepped back and vomited on the floor.

Behind her, the guard said, "Time's up."

"This man is sick," Lluava called out as the guard came to lead her away.

The man peered in at the prisoner. "That is not my concern. Let's go."

Upstairs, Lluava ran in search of Rosalyn just as trumpets resounded. It was the signal of an approaching army.

Chapter 39

The Arrivals

Lluava pulled aside the first person she saw rushing past and asked, "What's happening?"

The terrified man looked about, wide-eyed, and shook his head. Lluava released him and searched for someone who would know. As she rushed down one side of the double stairwell to the front foyer, she found Yamir.

"They're here!" he exclaimed exuberantly.

"Who? Who is here?"

"Vidrick and his men," he told her with a grin.

Lluava noticed that Yamir had removed a few of his piercings, reducing his collection to half a dozen or so.

He waved her over. "I'm glad I ran into you. Varren told me to send you to the stables. He's saddling up to ride to Røthe, where Vidrick is setting up camp."

"Where's Derrick?"

"Not sure. I'd guess, heading to find his partner as we speak."

After Lluava retrieved Issaura's Claws from her quarters, she and Varren set out for Røthe. Lord Alcazar followed in his carriage.

Although a grand city, Røthe was far less crowded than the capital; this seemed to allow the whole area to breathe. The residents had already begun to vacate their homes. Many a household and shop had already been boarded up and the occupants departed. A company of soldiers occupied one of the squares, while other soldiers dispersed to strategic positions throughout the city.

Upon spotting Varren and Lluava, Vidrick approached, his red hair gleaming in the late autumn sun.

"Your Majesty," he said with a formal bow.

"Lieutenant Bern," Varren replied. He nodded toward Lord Alcazar, who had stepped out of his carriage and then turned to assist his daughter. "Lord Alcazar and his daughter, Lady Illia."

Lluava was surprised that a refined young woman like Illia would even consider leaving the comfort of her home to watch the soldiers arrive.

Vidrick greeted each with respect and then said, "I have brought with me my own cohort as well as twenty other men." For Lord Alcazar's benefit, he added, "Their Theriomorph partners worked alongside the prince in the Yorrick Forest."

Lluava knew Vidrick referred to Derrick and the rest of his wolf pack. She hoped Derrick had already arrived or was at least on the way. He must be glad that his troop would finally be reunited.

"Your assistance is greatly appreciated," replied Varren. "I am sure Derrick's men have filled you in on the details of our current predicament."

"Yes, and after some rest and a warm meal we will be ready to help in any way possible."

Lord Alcazar spoke up. "Food and rest you will have. Your men may stay in any of our inns or households once the occupants have left for the south."

Illia, whose arm was tucked around her father, took her cue from him. "Lieutenant, it would be a great honor if you would stay under our roof for the duration of your time here."

Vidrick looked at her for a moment, then over at Varren. "If it pleases you, I would prefer to stay with my men."

"Of course," both Varren and Lord Alcazar agreed.

"My father and his men should arrive within the fortnight."

"Can he get here that soon?" Lluava questioned excitedly.

"At my request, he split those fighting on the front lines to assist us."

Varren also looked surprised and relieved. "This is the best news I have heard in a long while. Now, allow me to update you on our plans for the coming battle."

***

As Lluava finally returned to the palace that afternoon, she remembered Apex and went in search of Rosalyn.

"Apex is ill," Lluava explained. "He was sweating profusely and vomiting. The guards won't do anything. Please, Rosalyn, come take a look at him."

Rosalyn was loading a cart with medical supplies. "I'm sorry, Lluava. I have to take these to the doctors stationed in Røthe. We are far from ready, and with the Raiders on the way... I don't have time to check on a murderer."

"He helped us," remonstrated Lluava. "Are we going to let him suffer?"

Rosalyn put down the box she was carrying. She looked as if she had expected this response from her friend. "I can tell you what to do for him, but that is all."

"You know what's wrong with him? You haven't even seen him," argued Lluava as she began to assist Rosalyn in loading the supplies.

"That may be true, but I have a good idea," responded Rosalyn. "Knowing Apex and his excessive faults, I believe he is going through the physical reaction that sets in when a person who is given to strong drink is subjected to the withdrawal of his customary spirits. When was the last time he had a drink? And I do not mean water."

"Close to a day, I would gather. How serious is this?"

"Depends on the man," acknowledged Rosalyn. "If he has a fever, it means he is dealing with more severe symptoms." Rosalyn instructed Lluava what to expect and what to do, but the truth of the matter was that there was little that could be done. Apex would have to fight through the worst of it on his own.

Regardless, Lluava felt the need to help him in any way possible. Hadn't he been there in her time of need? He had saved her from the grip of her infection. She would have died but for his care. Lluava could not ignore his suffering; she had to do something.

She made her way back to the dungeon, taking with her a bowl of cold water and several strips of cloth. If he had a fever, maybe she could help ease it. She was not sure.

The same pair of guards awaited her at the bottom of the stairs. "You again," the older one barked. "What is it this time?"

"Your prisoner, the huntsman, is ill," Lluava said. She showed them what she carried. "I've come to help him."

"Can't let you do that, missy," he said as he blocked her path. Lluava took note of a swollen bruise on the side of his face.

Scowling, Lluava countered, "Do you want your prisoner to die down here before Lord Alcazar is ready to pass judgment? If so, be sure to tell his lordship that you allowed it to happen."

She hoped the guard would not call her bluff. Moreover, she hoped it *was* a bluff. Might Apex actually die from not having drink? She wished she had thought to ask Rosalyn. The guard stared at her intently as if trying to read her thoughts.

His comrade nudged him. "I don't want to be on th' lord's bad side."

"Go on," grunted the first guard. "But I'll be checkin' in regular." Hurrying down the dank corridor, Lluava hoped the guard wouldn't change his mind any time soon.

Apex was hunched over in his cell. From the look and smell of the place, he had purged himself several times over.

"Back again? So soon?" Apex's voice rasped through the grate. "They always come back for more."

The guard swung the keys and gave her a questioning look. He clearly wondered if Apex's behavior would change her mind, but Lluava was more determined than ever.

"I don't have time for your verbal abuse, Apex," she said. As she stepped into the cell, she heard the lock click into place behind her.

Apex leaned his head against the stone wall. "What *do* you have time for?"

Lluava gingerly stepped around the congealed puddles dotting the floor. "I wanted to check and see how you were feeling." As she neared the huntsman, Lluava saw that Apex's eyes were closed.

He retorted weakly, "I'm not feeling anything, or anyone, at the moment. And that is a great travesty."

"You're sweating a lot."

"I know how you could make me sweat more."

Lluava was not getting anywhere, but there were other ways to discern how sick he was. His brow was furrowed, and she wondered if he had a headache. With her keen night vision, she could see the dark circles under his eyes. He had not been sleeping. His perspiration was obvious, and his hands clutched the tops of his knees tightly.

"I'm thirsty," he grunted.

"I have water," she acknowledged.

"I thirst for other things," he retorted despairingly.

"Apex, look at me," Lluava demanded. "You're ill." A shiver ran through his body. She observed the slight tremor of his hands. Lluava moved over to him and felt his forehead. "You're so hot."

"You could make me hotter," he grumbled.

Lluava laid one of the water-soaked rags on his forehead. "Your fever is incredibly high. I need to cool you down. Strip off your shirt."

"I thought you'd never ask." Apex didn't resist when Lluava began pulling his shirt over his head. The damp material clung to his chest and seemed to resist being peeled away. "I did wonder if you were a woman who likes being in control."

Dropping the shirt into the bowl of water, Lluava nudged him back to the wall.

"I kinda like it," he admitted.

As she laid the chilled material over his chest, Apex grunted at the cold. "What *I'd* like," she began as she added a new strip of cloth to Apex's forehead, "is for you to shut up."

"So feisty. I like that, too."

Lluava chose not to respond. For a few blissful minutes, the cell remained silent except for the slosh of water and the dripping of cloths as Lluava struggled to lower Apex's temperature. Every time she removed the strips from his chest, she took note of his rapidly beating heart. Could it continue at that pace without rupturing?

Apex began to murmur. Lluava wasn't sure whether he was awake or asleep. His body seemed to be growing hotter as time slipped by. Soon his incoherent whispers formed words: *escape, run, Prema.*

As Lluava rinsed the rags in the warming water, Apex suddenly yelled, "Don't touch that!"

"What?"

"Leave that!" he ordered, and Lluava put down the rags.

"What's—"

Apex leapt to his feet and shoved Lluava to the floor. "That's mine!" he screamed out as his eyes flashed wildly about. "Give it back!"

"I don't have anything of yours," replied Lluava shakily.

Apex was looking not at her but at the shadows in the back corner of the cell. "I'll kill you," he hissed. "I'll kill you!"

Lluava stood up and placed her hand on his arm. "There's nothing there, Apex."

Without turning, Apex swung his arm and knocked her against the wall. She struggled to slip out of the way of his swinging arms. She realized that he was attacking some invisible opponent. Behind her, she could hear the guards fumbling for keys.

"What's going on?" one guard demanded as the door swung open. Without waiting for an answer, both guards charged in and took Apex down, forcing him to the floor. In the commotion, Lluava could not see what actually happened, but when the guards stepped back, Apex lay unconscious.

"This is why I said he needs help," hissed Lluava.

"He was not the one in trouble," grumbled one of the guards.

Lluava questioned them. "Didn't you notice anything wrong with him earlier?" She scrutinized Apex's body sprawled on the floor. When she didn't hear an answer, she glanced at the guards just in time to see the younger guard give the older one an inquisitive look.

"I think," the older one said in a threatening tone, "your time in here is done."

"Has he hallucinated before?" she inquired angrily. "Is that what happened to your face?"

"You need to leave."

"I am military partner to Prince Varren Mandrun. I have the authority to be here." Lluava's voice held a steely edge. "This prisoner is very ill, and I demand that he get the care he needs."

"I think—" the older guard began, just as the younger one shouted out, "Something's wrong with the prisoner!"

They turned to see Apex convulsing on the floor.

"What did you do to him?" the younger one worriedly asked his companion.

Lluava leaped to Apex's side. "He is having a seizure, a fit. Help me hold him down. I need something to place in his mouth so he doesn't bite his tongue."

The guards grabbed Apex's flailing limbs. Unable to find anything to serve as a bit, Lluava could only hope Apex would not lacerate his tongue. Minutes rolled by slowly; finally, Apex's form went limp. His eyes rolled under his lids and his breathing became regular.

"I think it's over," she said, and sat down, panting too.

The guards allowed her to sit with Apex through the rest of the night. He had one more attack before his fever seemed to break. Thereafter, he slept for several hours.

"It's morning." The younger guard had come to inform her.

Lluava stood up and stretched. She checked Apex one last time and was relieved that he seemed over the worst of it. She needed to find a bed somewhere; she was exhausted.

"Leaving so soon?"

Though Apex's voice came out in a whisper, it startled Lluava.

"You're awake! Thank the gods."

"I suspect you're the one who needs thanks," muttered Apex as he slowly opened his eyes.

Was that his form of an apology? Lluava would take it.

"Rest up," she said as she gathered the overturned bowl and spare rags. "You'll need your strength." She paused and waited for some crude comeback, but there was none. "Apex," she inquired as she reached the door, "what's Prema?"

"How do you know that name?" Apex asked bleakly.

"You said it last night," noted Lluava.

"Prema is an orphanage, one of several where I lived as a child."

Lluava would have asked more questions had he been anyone else, but his honesty unsettled her. She followed the guard out of the cell. Once in the main castle, she wandered about until she found her quarters.

***

Over the next several days, their plans took shape. Enormous snares were erected and placed in strategic positions; defenses were laid, offensive plans decided, and men trained. Apex's hallucinations occasionally returned, and Lluava dropped by often to check on him. On the fourth day following his imprisonment, he appeared to be his normal self.

The small towns and provinces had been successfully vacated and Røthe transformed into a military outpost. Vidrick was fully in control, his men and the new volunteers now organized. Lluava assisted in training and drilling the civilians on basic but essential skills. If they were to fight, this instruction might make all the difference.

By nightfall, Lluava felt drained, although she could tell that her underlying strength was coming back. One night, returning from a full day at the training fields, Lluava found Varren knocking at the door of her quarters as she approached. He opened the door for her, and she flopped down on the settee.

Varren seated himself next to her. "I have news."

"You had Lord Alcazar pardon Apex?" she asked hopefully.

"Not yet," he said with a slight frown. "I have different news." He paused, seeming to wait for her to ask another question. When she was silent, he went on. "I spoke with Illia last night. I told her that I was going to break our betrothal. That it was not right to marry someone I did not love."

Lluava's heart was in a flurry of excitement. "And? How did she take it?"

"Surprisingly well," Varren admitted. "She was very understanding. Illia will actually accompany me when I talk with her father tonight." Leaning in, Varren stroked Lluava's cheek. "Everything will work out in the end."

Though Lluava smiled back, part of her could not help but wonder what Illia was up to. How could the woman not be upset? Did she really want to help Varren, or would she sabotage him in the meeting? Yet hadn't she told Varren before that she was in love with another?

"May I accompany you when you meet with Lord Alcazar?"

"If you wish," agreed Varren. He paused. "You look exhausted. Please get some rest."

Just as she stood up to walk Varren out, Lluava heard a noise. Cocking her head to the side, she shushed her curious partner. There it was again.

"Did you hear that?"

"What?"

The subtle sounds were vaguely familiar, but why? Lluava moved to her window, and the sound seemed slightly louder. Lluava threw open the window, disturbing Onyx, who perched nearby. The raven glared sharply at her. Ignoring the bird, the teen looked out at the impressive view of the Yorrick Forest that stretched into the distance. She and Varren stood together for a moment, listening.

The next time the sound occurred, Varren turned in that direction. Together they scanned the panorama. At the next beat, Lluava recognized the sound: war drums.

The Berserker Legion had arrived.

Chapter 40

Breaching Defenses

As Lluava and Varren approached the battlefield, she strapped on the Claws. She had become an expert on manipulating her forearm braces and was comfortable wearing them, although she had only worn them half the time. She was ready for battle.

The opposing force's preliminary waves would face Wod's creations. The outer tree line had been rigged with pressure-sensitive booby traps. Some of them—such as the large logs rigged to swing down from the canopy and collide with unsuspecting victims—Lluava had experienced in her military training. Wod had taken this tactic a step further by adding large spheres of wooden spikes he called hedgehogs to impale the brutes.

The second-wave force would have to deal with leg snares (which Lluava hoped never to encounter again). These had been constructed with extra-long cords to allow the ensnared victim to crash down onto the hardened earth. Wod had made sure the undersoil was peppered with stones. The third-wave defenses consisted of rows and rows of rigged longbows and crossbows. Positioned strategically throughout the forest canopy, these weapons would remain dormant until activated by physical contact with their tripwires. As an extra precautionary measure, Wod had had each arrowhead dipped in poison, so that even if an enemy were merely grazed by a projectile, he would eventually succumb.

Any unfortunate soul who managed to escape these defenses and arrive at the edge of the forest would have to navigate the final array of traps. Several hundred pits had been dug, filled with sharped wooden pikes, and camouflaged to blend with the rest of the recently burned fields. On the opposite end of the clearing, across the narrow Slidr River, the Elysian army waited.

Lluava stood next to Varren as they waited with Vidrick's men for a sign that the Raiders were approaching the booby traps. It was not long before Lluava and her fellow Theriomorphs discerned the sickening thunks of direct impact. There were no screams, no cries of agony, just the sounds of the triggered riggings colliding with their victims.

"They're coming," warned Derrick as his upper lip curled. Since he and his men would not take the field until evening, he would wait until later to shift.

If she concentrated, Lluava could hear the faint whistle of flying arrows and the cracking of skulls on stone. Still there were no other sounds.

"There—almost at the tree line," Talos pointed out. His eyes flitted about the woods, searching for the enemy.

"There!" Wod pointed, peering at movement in the shadowy understory. For a human, the young huntsman's eyes were remarkably keen.

Suddenly, attackers surged out of the forest and onto the field. Like the crest of a wave that has begun to collapse, the rows of enormous marauders seemed to be swallowed by the earth as they tumbled into the pits. They continued to pour out of the woods. Focused only on pushing forward and attacking, the marauders clambered over pits filled with their dying comrades.

The wind shifted. Lluava and those around her could smell the foul smoke, though it was not thick enough to affect her own senses. Wod's creations had taken out many Raiders; unfortunately, their numbers were vast. The seething enemy charged toward them. The time to fight had come.

"Ready?" Vidrick shouted as he watched the Raiders break through the last of the booby traps. Pulling his sword from its sheath, he ordered, "Steady!"

The Berserkers rapidly moved across the field and began to wade across the river.

"Charge!"

Two waves of mortal men collided like a storm at sea. The Berserkers—larger, stronger, and impervious to pain—clearly had the advantage. They continued to kill even as they bled and died from horrendous wounds. The poor men who had volunteered to defend their land had little chance against unnatural giants such as these. Even those trained in warfare struggled greatly. Vidrick fought as hard as he could to save his men, but they fell like stalks of wheat for the reaping.

"There are so many of them," Lluava panted.

Varren yanked his partner backward as a spear landed near her feet. "I am less concerned about numbers," he averred, "than about their capabilities."

"Regardless," Lluava asked, "how much longer can we continue like this?"

Something ran up to them from behind. Lluava turned sharply to attack, but Varren held her back, and for good reason. The porcupine waddled up to the partners with a warning.

"They have broken through the perimeters around Røthe. The city will be overrun. They ripped through our spiked defenses as if they were paper."

"Yamir," Varren addressed the animal, "does the lieutenant know?"

"We haven't been able to find him. His men are scattered about the field."

"Rosalyn is in there with our wounded men!" Lluava exclaimed.

Varren scanned the battlefield and then commanded Yamir, "Lead the way."

Ahead Lluava saw the growing flames take hold of the outer facilities. Røthe would be destroyed in the conflagration. Lluava hoped its people would not go with it.

There was a sharp caw from above.

"Look out!" Lluava cried as a flying sword flashed by.

"Where did that come from?" questioned Yamir warily. He shifted back and peered about. Clouds of smoke made it hard to see. "I'm going to find Wod. He is still working on plans to protect the castle."

"Go," Varren urged, waving him off. "We will search for Rosalyn."

As they entered the city, Lluava was relieved to see that only a few Berserkers had breached its walls. But those few were enough. They stormed from building to building, pillaging.

"We have to stop them," declared Varren.

"What about Rosalyn?"

"If we kill these Raiders, we will be helping her."

"Fine."

Following Varren, Lluava cautiously approached the closest Berserker, who was shouldering his way through a locked door. He turned his head at their arrival, revealing a shredded face that was missing its left cheek. More frightening still was his unregenerate sneer.

Lluava glanced at her partner, who looked mortified at the man rendered monstrous by a smoked drug. The Raider must have lost his weapon; nonetheless he leered at them a moment more, taunting them.

Neither Varren nor Lluava had to say a word. They moved in silence toward their enemy. This Raider, this giant, was just another adversary in the whole scheme of things, just another opponent they must overcome. Yet even without his weapon, the Berserker was unbelievably dangerous. He could kill them easily if he got hold of them with his bare hands. They had to fight smart.

Teamwork, Lluava realized, was to their advantage. All the Berserkers seemed to wage battle as individual entities, neither aiding nor caring about one another. They had one goal only: to destroy any Elysian who got in their way. Once drugged, they rampaged. They could ignore the most grievous wounds, but they seemed incapable of any strategizing or calculated thought. Could this knowledge lead to the Raiders' downfall, as it might for this particular Berserker?

The brute ripped a broken shard of wood from the damaged gate and thrust it like an enormous dagger toward the oncoming pair. Lluava somersaulted under his swing while Varren's sword hacked at the wood, splintering it down to the base.

Now the brute was weaponless again. Lluava and Varren fought ferociously and fast, working to harry and confuse the enormous man with coordinated forays from different directions. Together, the pair achieved the miraculous; the monster could not fend them off. After Varren had swung the final blow, Lluava almost pitied the corpse before her. Once a man, the Raider had chosen to lose himself by becoming a beast.

She did not want to do the same thing. That realization reaffirmed her determination to never again revert into her dual form.

"Look," Varren said, pointing deeper into Røthe. "It seems that Derrick decided not to wait any longer."

In pack fashion, more than a dozen wolves had attacked the Raiders. Several Berserkers already lay dead, and as the partners watched, the few others who had broken through the city's borders were brought down.

Once Røthe had been secured, Lluava and Varren left to patrol the perimeter defenses and search for weak positions. The newly erected walls, shrouded with thorns and briars, had been torn down in several places. Fortunately the majority of the rows of pikes remained.

"The damage can be fixed if we hurry," Lluava pointed out.

"Not all," Varren's chilled voice replied.

Ahead of them were the bodies of several men who had been working on the wall when the Berserkers broke through. Some still clutched their materials in their stiffening arms. They had no hope, Lluava knew that. She recognized one of them.

Lluava ran to kneel by Wod's battered form. One of his arms had been severely broken, perhaps by the swing of a war hammer. His body had been trampled by giant, booted feet.

Carefully, the pair dragged and carried the dead inside the city before heading back to defend her again.

That evening, Varren and Lluava returned to the Alcazar castle. They found that the men defending it had also faced many losses.

"How much longer can we continue?" asked Lluava wearily.

Varren refused to look beaten. "Derrick and his men are among those taking the field now. Yamir volunteered to continue Wod's work; he has been with the huntsman from the beginning of this. The rest of us will rest and resume in the morning."

"Yes, but how much longer can we hold out? How much longer before we have no more men left?"

"I have heard the same murmurs you have. Those still able to fight are thinking of defecting. Their fear of death is too strong." Varren slowed his step. "Do you want to yield?"

"No."

The idea of surrendering was something Lluava refused to consider. She remembered the first time she had encountered the Raiders. They had ransacked Calitron and slaughtered every living thing. Neither Theriomorph nor human survived. Surrender was not an option—but how many options did they have left?

As they entered another room, Hyrax seemed to be having an agreeable conversation with Lady Alcazar. Upon seeing the prince and Lluava, he politely excused himself and approached them.

"I was wondering when you would return," he acknowledged pleasantly. "I am glad to see that Your Majesty and your partner are still well."

"You must forgive me if I seem impolite," Varren replied. He was just as exhausted as Lluava and not in a mood to talk politics. "We are headed to our respective quarters to rest. It has been a long day."

"I can only imagine," acknowledged the councilman. His perfume tickled Lluava's nose. "I have heard of the grievous losses we have sustained."

Lluava found she did not care for Hyrax's use of the term *we* when he had risked neither hide nor hair to defend the kingdom. He meant well, she knew, but he could never understand.

The councilman straightened the amulet that had flipped around on his chest. "I have a suggestion for changing the course of the current battle."

Now all ears were on Hyrax.

"Allow that huntsman to fight for you," he said. "The one with the god's form. Let him use Ullr's Fangs. They are just useless relics sitting around my room. I have been considering what a pity it is that after being turned over to me they will just be sent to the royal treasury."

"Would Ullr's Fangs do any good?" questioned the prince. He seemed extremely skeptical that one man and a simple pair of weapons could change the outcome of the conflict.

"Well, that depends in part on whether my people believe in the man who wields them," acknowledged Councilman Hyrax.

Lluava cast a wary look at her partner. Varren still looked doubtful. "So, the Theriomorphs would need to believe that Apex embodied your god of war, just as they perceive Lluava to be Theri. This would spur them, and hence their human partners, onward."

"It's a simplified theory, but yes." Hyrax ran his fingers along the chain and down to his talisman.

"We have used that tactic before with Lluava," noted Varren. "It is true that faith is a powerful weapon. But will another such figure make that much difference?"

"As you said," agreed the councilman, "faith can be powerful. The bearer must pull his own weight on the war front. To be viewed as a god of war, he must act like one. How capable a fighter is he?"

"He can kill," answered Lluava. "I'm not sure he has had the chance to fully connect with his weapons. He hasn't shifted with them. I don't know if they would change as the Claws do."

Hyrax pondered this briefly. "If he really does possess Ullr's Fangs, they would shift with him. Why don't we give him a chance to try them out?"

"He is a prisoner under Lord Alcazar's orders," reminded Varren, not wanting to overstep their host's authority. His look told Lluava he was not certain about this idea.

"There will not be much land to be lord over if Alcazar does not use all our resources," countered Hyrax. "Shall we see if we can make a deal?"

With no other viable option, Varren agreed, in the hope of saving his people.

As expected, Lord Alcazar was initially appalled by the notion of releasing his prisoner. His wife's reaction was worse. While those of a more levelheaded nature worked on a compromise, she blustered herself into hysterics and had to be escorted to her quarters.

"He will still have to face his punishment when this is over," stated Lord Alcazar.

Varren nodded. "Of course. This does not redress his previous crime."

"And he will return to his cell at night."

Hyrax spoke up. "Please be reasonable, my lord. We are asking him to fight with full knowledge that he will face certain death in the end by the very people whom he would be serving. The very least we can do is provide him with more comfortable accommodations, since he might be the only means of saving your land."

Lord Alcazar stared into the fire. To fend off the cold, it was kept continually burning.

"He will lodge in one of our tower rooms. High enough that he will not attempt to escape. Guards will be positioned outside his doors."

"Certainly," agreed the councilman, pleased with the deal he had struck.

"It is settled." Lord Alcazar added, "That is, as long as you can get him to agree to fight for us."

Lluava could not see how any of those men would be able to convince Apex to agree to their terms. As it stood, he would die either way. Why lose your life in war?

"Do not worry about that, my lord," noted Hyrax. "Lady Lluava will do the convincing for us."

All conversation around the table stopped. Hyrax continued, nodding first to Varren, then to Alcazar, "You must understand, Your Majesty and my lord, that Apex would never agree to any suggestion brought by either of you. One of you has sentenced him to death, while the other flushed him out of hiding, pardon my hunting pun. Apex, I expect, would not trust either of you. I would ask him myself, but he does not know me; there would be no trust, only suspicion."

"But why me?" asked Lluava, who was still quite befuddled. She was not the only one.

"You, my dear, are different. Not only are you a Theriomorph, you are also someone he knows. Moreover, if I remember your tale correctly, he has helped you personally in the past. He may be willing to do so again."

"Fine. But I can't promise anything."

***

Once again, Lluava found herself in the dungeon. As Apex was no longer flirting with death, she was prevented from entering his cell. Through the grate, he saw her before she spotted him.

"Missed me?"

His coy voice seemed stronger. That was good. He would need his strength.

"I have a favor to ask you."

"You?" inquired Apex. "Or your prince?"

"Both, actually." Lluava paused, waiting for a comeback, but none came. "We need you to fight with us on the war front."

Although his face was in shadow, Lluava imagined that he raised an eyebrow.

"Alcazar wants me killed," he replied. "I guess it doesn't matter to him if it be on the front or by a rope around my neck."

There was no way Lluava could counter his statement; she knew it was true. "I'm sorry I asked you to come here. I didn't know."

"You didn't."

Lluava's discomfort showed, and she fidgeted. "If you fight for us, you will be allowed to stay in a real room. Under guard, but you will be out of this cage."

"Why would Alcazar want me to do this?" Apex probed. "It must not be his plan. What's the real reason for this kind offer?"

"There are many people who believe that those who wield mythic weapons like Issaura's Claws have special, god-given abilities. There is hope that since you were..." Lluava searched for the right word, "given Ullr's Fangs, you have the ability to alter the outcome of these battles."

"All this because of some weapons?" snorted Apex dismissively.

"Issaura's Claws are not just 'some weapons'."

There was a moment of silence.

"So they will return Ullr's Fangs and send me to slay their enemy, then have me return to die by the noose?"

"Yes."

Apex looked taken aback. Lluava was not sure if it was because of her answer or because she had chosen brutal honesty.

"I'll do it."

"You have a natural ability to fight."

"I said I'll do it."

Lluava blinked twice. "Oh. Okay. I'll have the guards release you."

She had not expected Apex to be so agreeable. Was he going to use this freedom to escape? He would have to be watched.

Chapter 41

Red Sky at Morning

The front lines were abuzz with news from the night. The Berserkers had secured the Slidr River. Fortunately, due to the early freezes, the river was low and not a viable avenue of travel. Many men were missing, including Derrick and most of his scouts. With no bodies found, the talk of captives ran amok.

Would the Berserkers keep captives alive? As far as Lluava knew, they had only done so a few times. If so, for what reason? Why deal with the difficulty of keeping prisoners?

Apex had been informed of Wod's death. Varren's news seemed to stir no emotion; the man remained silent, focused. Swinging his swords in giant arcs through the air, he merely turned and nodded to the prince.

Varren paused for a moment and said, "If this were any other morning, I wonder how many would have noticed this beautiful sunrise." The sky was afire with deep crimson and vermilion. Cumulous clouds were building up into floating mountains. It was an astounding sight and one Lluava would have missed. There was so little time to enjoy anything anymore.

All too soon, with the red sunrise illuminating their progress, a new wave of soldiers took the field under Vidrick's command. Lluava and Varren kept Apex in sight the entire time. He may have been fighting on their side, but he was a wild card, one neither partner fully trusted.

With Derrick's loss, Lluava was more concerned than ever over the whereabouts of her friends. She had glimpsed Talos and Byron carrying several injured Røthians toward the medical ward. Other than the wear of war that clung to their features, they seemed well enough. Yamir continued Wod's work at the castle, and moments ago she had glimpsed the silvery fur of a snow leopard gliding past.

After she had slain two Raiders, Lluava watched Apex finish off another. The huntsman's handling of the Fangs was still a bit clumsy. Though much improved, his lack of experience had caused quite a few near mishaps. This would not do. He was no god of war. He was more likely to get himself killed than to inspire the weary army at their backs.

"Apex!" she shouted out. "Change into your dual form!"

"And leave my weapons?" he growled incredulously. Another Berserker was approaching fast.

Lluava suddenly realized that Apex had never seen her shift with Issaura's Claws. He had no clue what weapons like these could do. She explained hastily, "They're special. They will shift with you." She hoped it was true.

Apex seemed about to contest her statement but had to lurch backward to evade an oncoming attack. Lluava switched focus back to her own partner as another giant Raider swung a spiked mace. Several evasive moves later, Lluava looked about for Apex. She spotted him farther off. He was in mid shift.

His large form ripped through the human clothing he had been given in prison. Coppery fur sprang forth, agleam in the sunlight. Snout, claws, and tail realigned in their new positions. Lluava's eyes were solely on Ullr's Fangs. They were changing, but not in the way she had expected. Deliquescing into shining streams, they formed metallic tendrils than seemed to run up the Yorrick wolverine's forelimbs, over his shoulders and neck. Once in place, the former twin swords transformed into a metallic casing for Apex's muzzle and teeth. The already monstrous beast could now easily bite through flesh and bone.

"Behind you!" Varren's voice cried out.

In a flash, Varren protected Lluava by taking a blow to his chest from a war hammer. She screamed as he fell to the ground. If she had been concentrating on her partner, this would not have happened.

Lluava would not allow the Berserker to claim his victim. As the large Raider swung his weapon for a death blow, the teen transformed. She ignored the snapping rigs of her braces and let them fall broken to the ground. Issaura's Claws coated her own in sheaths of gold and secured her fierce confidence within a hard, cold casing. The tigress sprang upon the Berserker, clawing and biting at his face and neck.

The feline's weight caused the Raider to tumble backward. On the ground, his struggles were useless, his jugular clamped tightly in the tiger's jaws. Patiently, she waited until the thump of the brute's heart could no longer be felt. Then she released a mighty roar, which was answered by another in the distance. The sounds of the two beasts made men quake.

With many Berserkers still wreaking havoc, Lluava leaped into the fray.

With each kill, a part of her quieted as something else took hold. Soon her normal emotions were subdued, immersed in the green-blue world around her. The beast inside was released.

Flashes. Images. Moments. Lluava's consciousness and awareness returned in spurts. Blood sprayed red against the cool-hued world. Men, Elysians, scrambled out of her way as she charged forth leaving corpses in her wake. There was no sense of pain or exhaustion; she had risen above such physical restrictions. At one point, she stared directly into the eyes of the Yorrick wolverine with its metallic snout. There was no sense of humanity, just darkness and bloodlust. Screams came muffled to her ears. Sounds were distorted. All recognition of friend and foe wavered and blended. She had lost control, but she no longer cared.

As the tigress swiveled her ears, she homed in on a whispery sound behind her. With whiskers flaring, she snarled and leaped around. The young man standing before her took several steps back. His sword was lowered, his empty hand raised in defense. Yet it was the determined and familiar look in his eyes that caused the boundaries of her mental haze to waver. Her blackout slowed and diminished. The man's voice calmed her rapidly beating heart.

"Lluava, it is time to go," he said. "You must return with me."

Her thoughts flickered back to her prey, but the man did not leave. He lowered his empty hand and grimaced as he placed it over his side. He spoke again.

"We must pull back. All our survivors are retreating behind the castle walls."

Colors began to saturate her world. Lluava recognized the man.

"Varren?" she questioned shakily. Her memory was still wavering. She looked around. How had she made it to the river's edge? The clouded water streamed over her striped paws. "What about Røthe?"

Her partner shook his head. "The city could not be saved. But we can."

Lluava wondered if his ribs were hurt. She recalled him crumpling to the ground.

"Can you make it?" she asked as she gauged the distance to Alcazar Castle from where they stood.

"I have no choice."

"Climb on," she instructed. Varren hesitated only a moment before sheathing his sword. Cautiously, he pulled himself onto his partner's sinewy back.

"Hold on," she huffed and began to run forward. Varren nearly slipped off several times, causing Lluava to slow down. She heard him moan each time he was jarred.

Approaching the refuge of the castle, Lluava could not help but think of their retreat behind the walls of Durog, which seemed so long ago now. They had been forced to hide in the training camp as the Raiders laid siege to its walls. That time, they had survived. Would they be so lucky now?

In the near distance, the city of Røthe was ablaze. Its power and might were being eaten away by the hungry fire, its docks now free to serve new masters.

"The Raiders will be able to sail to the capital!" Lluava gasped.

"There is nothing we can do about that now. Live today. Fight tomorrow." A note of sorrow underscored the prince's words. "Anyway, Vidrick sank our ships as a precaution. Unless the Raiders brought their own, sailing to Cronus will be impossible."

They were almost at the gates when Lluava noticed movement. "Are they closing them?"

"They must," Varren affirmed.

"But there are still people outside!"

But Lluava sensed Varren shifting his position. "Stop. Look to your right," he said abruptly. "Is that—it is Ambassador Alcove!"

The leader was traveling with a new wave of Berserkers, who had forded the Slidr River and were headed toward the castle. Lluava, who had begun to slow down, now picked up speed.

"What are you doing?" Varren asked. "He is right over there."

"What are you thinking?" she countered. "There's no way we can reach him."

"We can stop him," Varren argued.

She could feel him tense in anger. Staring at the closing gates, Lluava surged forward. "This is not that day—or have you forgotten?" she growled.

He might have pressed the matter further, but both knew that would have been useless. Lluava sped into the exterior courtyard and then allowed Varren to dismount before she shifted. Behind them, the double doors clanged shut. All around them, men and women scrambled to secure the castle. Survivors of the battle populated the walkways, the grounds, and the Alcazar home itself.

A fierce roar arose beyond the walls. Lluava knew instantly what it was. "Apex is still out there!"

At the same time, Varren shouted, "Open the gates!"

Lieutenant Vidrick, the commanding officer, approached them. "With all due respect, Your Majesty, we cannot risk the safety of those inside the walls for the few who remain outside."

"Some of your men are still out there." Varren, obviously disturbed, pointed to the doors. "A man I ordered released, a man who has fought valiantly for us, is right outside the gates!"

A sentinel shouted down from the ramparts, "The Raiders are approaching fast!"

Vidrick readjusted a bloodstained glove. "I have men out there, too. We must think of the greater good."

Lluava wondered if he meant saving the rest of his men, the defenseless Røthians, or the prince himself. Somehow, she felt it was the last.

"Lieutenant," she pleaded, "I begged Apex to fight for us. I cannot abandon him for doing what he was asked. Please open the gate and let him slip inside."

"I am thinking of the greater good, Private," reiterated Vidrick forlornly.

Apex roared again, this time beating his fists against the gates. Varren shouted to the gatekeepers, "Open the doors!"

The lieutenant's anger was apparent as he countermanded Varren's order: "Keep them closed!"

From above, another shout rang out. "The Raiders are two hundred yards out!"

"Open them. Now!" There was no questioning Varren's authority. This was a command from the prince.

As the heavy gates creaked open, Varren apologized to the young officer. "I'm sorry, Lieutenant, but the greater good is to protect the capital, and in order to do so we must have the help of every warrior."

Apex was safely inside. The gates were hurriedly shut, and none too soon.

For a third time, the lookout's voice gave warning: "They're here—" A dark arrow struck the man. His lifeless body toppled over the parapet, to be dealt with by the enemy.

Lord Alcazar's men escorted Apex to his secluded quarters after first wrapping him in a saddle blanket. Lluava watched with anguish as they stripped him of his weapons and marched him away like some captive beast. At least he was alive. Maybe he could find some solace in that. Maybe she would, too.

Varren, once a healer had tended to his injured chest, held a brief meeting with Lord Alcazar and Lieutenant Bern. Although Lluava would have been admitted, for the first time she felt needed elsewhere. She had to make sure she could account for her other friends. After questioning and searching, she was relieved to find them all, scattered among the other survivors.

When Talos was reunited with Rosalyn, he shared his thoughts on their current situation. "Without ships, the Berserkers will need to regroup before they consider marching south."

"If that is their plan," noted Byron sullenly. "They could try to force us out of here. After all, the crown prince is within these walls."

"Well, they can't have him," affirmed Lluava in a low growl.

"No," agreed Talos, "but we will need to hold on until Colonel Bern arrives with his army."

"Doesn't this seem familiar to you?" questioned Yamir, who, alone of the group, looked like his normal self, for he had not been fighting on the front lines. His hair was freshly spiked; even the edges of his clothing were purposely frayed.

"What do you mean?" asked Byron.

"We went through this in Durog. No help came."

Yamir's words rang true to Lluava. This had already occurred to her. Now she knew she wasn't the only one.

"Last time, nobody knew we needed aid," Talos pointed out. "But Colonel Bern has already sent word to his son, and he is on the way."

"How is Varren?" asked Rosalyn. She was clearly uncomfortable with this sort of talk.

Lluava knew her friend referred to Varren's medical examination. "He has several bruised ribs and one they suspect is cracked."

"Will he still be able to fight?" asked Talos. Was he calculating alternate outcomes?

"Preferably not for a while," admitted Lluava.

"What about Derrick?" Yamir looked directly at Talos, the only other recently held captive. "What do you think they have done with him?"

Talos lowered his head and rested his forehead on his hand. "Nothing good."

A rail-thin steward entered the room. "Lady Lluava, follow me, please."

As bidden, Lluava followed the steward to a grand, fourth-floor living area. Inviting lounge seating was arranged comfortably, a warm fire crackled in the hearth, and the open curtains provided a magnificent view of the Rothian estates aglow in the distance. The city was burning.

Varren was already there, along with Lord Alcazar, Councilman Hyrax, and Lieutenant Vidrick Bern. Lluava did not recognize the half-dozen other grim-faced men who stood ill at ease. Actually, everyone was standing. Lluava could feel the tension resonating among them.

Varren motioned her to his side. Before she could ask, he said in a hushed voice, "A small band of Raiders has approached our gates and asked to speak to the men in command."

"You're not thinking of going out there," whispered Lluava. She could see several fields and orchards still ablaze through the windows. Like shadows, dark forms were moving about.

"We will not leave these walls, but I feel it is necessary to hear what they have to say." Varren nodded toward the windows. "I will listen from the top of the parapet."

"They could easily shoot you down," Lluava hissed.

"I have already been well informed of that." Varren looked toward Vidrick, who stood alone on the other side of the room.

"I don't like this," asserted Lluava.

"Nor do I, but what choice do I have?"

"To stay inside where it's safe. Alcazar or Hyrax could represent you."

"I suspect the Raiders will not talk unless I am present."

"If you didn't request my presence to talk you out of this, why am I here?"

"Why would I not tell you?" Varren rebutted. "You are my partner, my closest confidant, and…so much more."

"You know I'm coming with you."

Varren's face relaxed for a moment. "That is exactly what I was hoping you would say."

***

Outside, the freshening wind swirled columns of ash over the scorched land. Lluava's long hair whipped about her face, and she struggled to see through her silvery locks. Varren seemed to find this amusing, for he smiled at her before climbing the last rung of the ladder to the parapet's landing, where she and Vidrick waited. Lord Alcazar and Councilman Hyrax had remained in the palace. In the event things went badly, they were authorized to make decisions.

Looking over the wall, Lluava counted one hundred Berserkers standing in an organized square. Behind them stood two rows of the wheeled catapults known as onagers. While Lluava eyed the evil-looking siege weapons, Varren addressed a man who had stepped out in front of the massed ranks.

"Ambassador Alcove, you requested a meeting?"

The leader calmly replied, "I had hoped we could speak face to face, like gentleman; yet it seems the spawn of Landon Mandrun received his cowardly traits."

Lluava hoped the insult to Varren's ancestor would not aggravate the prince. But it was Vidrick who became enraged. "Sir! You are addressing Prince Mandrun."

"His lineage," Alcove responded in his thick accent, "is of no concern. The topic of importance is the survival of the people. As it stands, you are cornered, while we are free to move about. It is a bit of a headache that you destroyed your own docks, but Røthe is not the only city perched on the river."

Alcazar paused, and Lluava's stomach knotted. Of course, the Raiders would march on until they could commandeer the ships they sought.

Alcove went on. "Nevertheless, before we continue, there is one thing I must have. Varren Mandrun, surrender yourself to me, and I will spare all who ask for mercy—not only those boarded up in this household but also any others with whom we have contact."

"Don't even think about it!" Lluava snapped.

"They would use you as leverage," stated Vidrick sullenly.

Varren called down to the leader, "From what I recall, the last time we had the misfortune to meet you viewed Theriomorphs as little more than animals. It seemed like genocide was in order."

"I will acknowledge," Alcove began, "that I now realize this species is indeed more than livestock or pets." Lluava thought she saw the leader glance at her. "I will spare their lives, too. So, young Mandrun, will you surrender and save those precious to you?"

Please don't do this. Please don't do this, Lluava silently implored.

"I will..." Varren began slowly, and then his voice took on an edge of steel, "not allow you to use me to reach your endgame. You will not obtain Elysia."

"You are one selfish boy." Alcove almost spat out the words as he turned to leave. Then he paused and turned back. "Wait," he said. "Before I forget, I brought a gift for you to enjoy in case you made this choice."

One of the onagers fired. Both Lluava and Vidrick dove to protect Varren. Its projectile struck the lieutenant directly in the chest, causing him to stumble backward. Had not Varren reached out and pulled him upright, Vidrick would have fallen back into the compound to an almost certain death.

In his hands, Vidrick held the projectile as he screamed and cried out unintelligible curses and profanities. Lluava gasped and shuddered, knowing she would have done the same, for in Vidrick's hands was the head of his father.

Not an idle threat, then, but a certainty; there would be no reinforcements. Lluava could not focus on Varren's words to the unhinged officer. She could only watch in shock and horror as rows of Berserkers picked up four battering rams that had lain by their feet and moved in unison toward the gates. The leader stood defiantly, a smile on his face. He caught Lluava's eye and, with a flick of his wrist, signaled to his onager operators. The heads of hundreds of Elysian soldiers flew through the air toward the castle.

Chapter 42

Completing Vows

veryone inside!" Varren shouted as he struggled to get the deranged and hysterical Lieutenant Vidrick to move. More and more severed heads were catapulted over the wall, many purposely set on fire. They made sickening thunks as they landed on walkways and walls; several broke through windows. Castle Alcazar had been designed as a splendid country home, not a defensible fortress.

Lluava knew that the grisly projectiles were intended not to damage but rather to forewarn. Lluava hated to be threatened. The Raiders might perceive Theriomorphs as monsters, but the invaders themselves were evil incarnate.

With Vidrick refusing to move, Varren's own retreat was at a standstill. How much longer did they have before the onagers started slinging deadlier projectiles? The battering rams at the gates created a steady rhythm that caused subtle vibrations throughout the wall. Had Lluava been human, she might not have felt them. As it was, the tremors were a constant reminder that as long as they remained in the open, their lives were in peril.

Lluava tried to help Varren force Vidrick toward the ladder. The distraught lieutenant shoved her so hard she almost lost her balance.

There was a loud crack as Varren's right hook knocked Vidrick's face to the side. The lieutenant collapsed instantly. Lluava, surprised at her partner's action, gaped at the unconscious body.

"Lluava, help me get him down." Varren pulled the officer to the ladder, but it took both of them, plus the help of several soldiers below, to lower Vidrick to the ground and carry him to safety.

As they entered the castle, Yamir was leading a group of soldiers to the wall.

"What are you doing?" Lluava called out as he passed by.

"Completing Wod's work." The front door shut behind him.

Part of her felt compelled to help her friend, yet she knew that she could not protect everyone. She had to let her friends fight their own battles; there was other work for her to do. The stewards settled Vidrick, still unconscious, in one of the spare bedrooms, and Lluava went to assist in the massive task of organizing those who had taken shelter inside. She spotted Illia working to establish some sense of order amid a sea of frightened and anguished people. As much as Lluava disliked the young highborn, she could not fault her character.

Lluava volunteered to carry a meal up to Apex's quarters in one of the smaller towers. She took care not to spill the hot soup as she climbed the steep, narrow stairs. When the guard unlocked the room, she found Apex seated at the edge of his bed, sewing white furs.

"They might have stripped me of my weapons," grumbled Apex without looking at her, "but at least they returned my merchandise. For what purpose, I don't know. If I am to die, it will all be theirs in the end."

"Perhaps Lord Alcazar changed his mind."

Apex continued to sew.

Lluava's frustration was apparent. "Varren and I are trying to save you."

"I killed the lord's son with my own hands. By law, I should die."

Had Apex given up? "Don't you want to live?" she asked him.

Sitting up straight, Apex stared at the far wall. "I have found that you and the prince live by a code of ethics. I am not sure why, but you do. How ethical is it to alter a law for one man and not another?"

"You're no murderer. The punishment should fit the crime," contended Lluava.

"A life for a life?"

Not knowing what to say, Lluava lowered the bowl onto a small table. "I brought you soup," she said, and left Apex to his sewing.

Downstairs, men and supplies had attained a degree of order. Lluava continued her work for several more hours. At one point, she took a moment to look out the windows of the fourth story, which faced front. Yamir had arranged a number of fire spouts along the parapet. Every other spout intermittently spewed hot tar or flame upon any Berserker within range. Stationed between these contraptions, yeomen loosed showers of arrows. Below them, others worked to reinforce the gates. Yamir stood at the center of the front wall. He looked confident and in charge. He had found himself again

***

That night, with the thrumming of the battering rams providing a constant background, Lluava met Rosalyn outside the doors of the Alcazar chapel. Rosalyn had asked Lluava to stand up for her during this fear-compelled wedding. How could she refuse? Lluava wished that things could have been different, that this hand had not been rushed. Nothing was ideal about it, neither the situation nor the reasoning; but could she blame Rosalyn?

The doors to the chapel opened while Lluava was still smoothing her friend's dress, which matched the intense blue of the young woman's eyes. Lluava had helped her select the gown from Illia's wardrobe. Once again, Lluava begrudgingly acknowledged Illia's genuine kindness.

Rows and rows of lit candles, many burned down to stubs, illuminated the small, dark space. In the hallowed silence, Lluava slowly led the way to the altar. There, Talos waited with Byron at his side. Varren and Yamir watched from their seats nearby.

As Lluava took her place across from Byron, she recalled her earlier conversation with Rosalyn.

"Are you sure you want to do this?" Lluava had asked incredulously. "A wedding should not be rushed."

"Lluava, had it not been for the war, I would have been married by now. My wedding should have taken place a month ago. I want this with all my heart." Rosalyn had placed a pale hand on Lluava's. "This autumn, I almost lost Talos more than once. I know the war for the kingdom is far from over, and you must admit our current situation is grim. If we die—"

"Don't—"

Rosalyn had squeezed Lluava's hand. "If we die here, I want to die married to the man I love. Will you stand up with me tonight?"

Lluava's heart broke at the thought that this couple or any of her friends had to face the possibility of being killed, but she had agreed. Now, as she observed the looks in the eyes of Talos and Rosalyn, she realized that this marriage was right.

The priest who served the Alcazar family began the solemn rites, for no Theriomorph religious man was available. In the flickering candlelight, Rosalyn had never looked so beautiful nor Talos more handsome. As the couple's hands were bound with a white cloth symbolizing their unity, Lluava looked at Varren. Perhaps he sensed her eyes on him, for he returned her gaze. She hoped that they, too, would have a chance for a future together.

There was no celebration after the wedding—no banquet, no recognition of any kind. Instead, each returned to duty: Yamir to the wall, Talos and Byron to the soldiers' quarters, and Rosalyn to the improvised medical ward.

Lieutenant Vidrick had awakened, and Lluava went to check on the devastated officer. As she approached his door, she observed Illia leaving. The look on the woman's face and the blush in her cheeks signified far more than Lluava would have expected. Both women paused and stared at each other; then Illia slipped quickly past.

Vidrick stood in the doorway, his jaw bruised and swollen from Varren's blow. Although his eyes were still red and puffy from tears, Lluava discerned an odd look, like that of a criminal prepared to pay for his crimes.

"I am so terribly sorry about your father," she told him, "but I know that Illia was here with you. It all makes sense now."

Vidrick stared back at her but did not respond. Was he waiting for her to accuse him of improper behavior? Instead, Lluava smiled. "You're the one Illia meant. She loves you. Don't worry; your secret is safe until Illia's betrothal to Varren is annulled."

"He will do that?" Vidrick questioned in a shocked tone. Obviously, he was unaware of Varren's change of heart.

"If we survive this," Lluava answered. The enthusiasm had left her voice.

"Then let me get to work," responded the lieutenant, and he strode off to find his men.

Lluava began to make her way back to her own quarters; it was nearing midnight, and the teen was in desperate need of rest. As she passed the chapel's open doors, she saw Varren still seated inside.

Lluava had vowed to stay out of human churches after her mother adopted the human faith. She had broken that vow for the first time this evening, yet she believed circumstances had justified her doing so. Now, observing her partner deep in prayer, she broke her vow a second time.

Sliding into a seat next to the prince, Lluava looked about in silence. She would not pray to his single god, nor would she ask favors from the many deities who populated her father's beliefs. The gods were not helping them. Their destiny was in their own hands.

Lluava listened to the interminable drumming on the outer gates. How much longer would the gates hold? She envisioned the doors splintering, shattered under the battering. Suddenly she didn't want to be walled up in this gilded prison any longer. She wished she had remained on the outside; at least she could run if it came down to it. Now, all they could do was wait.

Maybe Varren's letter would reach the capital, and the High Council would send help. Once alerted that Varren was in trouble, the council would send men rapidly. That was their purpose, wasn't it? To protect the Mandrun bloodline? Varren was their last chance to save it. They would send reinforcements, but what would they find when they arrived? A palace reduced to rubble? Cities burned to the ground?

A shiver ran down Lluava's spine.

Varren stood up. "Thank you for praying with me."

Lluava felt like a fraud. She had no faith in higher powers, yet she chose not to correct her partner. Let Varren keep his faith. Faith was a powerful thing. At least, that was what she had been told.

As the two reached the door of her room, Lluava looked into the empty darkness inside. "Stay with me," she said to Varren, "at least until I fall asleep."

She realized she sounded far more frightened than she felt. The night was half over. Couldn't she manage by herself until morning?

Varren followed her inside, then sat on the floor with his back against the side of her bed. He looked away as she quickly changed into a clean uniform. Lluava no longer wore nightclothes He could be called into battle at any moment, so she had to be constantly prepared.

In her dreams, large beasts lurked in forests of shadow: green and gold, blue and purple, magnificent animals, bold and unafraid. They passed each other, aware of one another and yet not, a rainbow of creatures all living together. A sound of upheaval was heard. Volatile and abrupt, two enormous animals attacked each other and rolled into the center of the woods. Numerous eyes flashed as they watched a bronze beast combat a white one.

Lluava awoke with her mind still foggy. She had been pulled out of her dream, but not by a jolt of fear or the light of morning. She looked over the side of her bed. Varren was still there, now slumped in slumber.

As she began to move about, her partner opened his eyes. "I had not meant to stay—" he began apologetically.

"That's perfectly fine," Lluava acknowledged.

Varren asked with a yawn, "What time is it?"

The sun had yet to rise, but Lluava slipped out of bed. "I'm not sure. Something has happened," she said. "I can feel it."

Lluava was glad that Varren did not question her. He got to his feet and tightened his scabbard, which had become loose in the night. Lluava picked up Issaura's Claws.

The hall was dark. The candles in the interior sconces had burned out. In this man-made tunnel, it was almost too dark for even Lluava to see. With one hand brushing the wall, she crept down the hall. Her other hand held Varren's as she led him around corners and down stairs.

As they descended a broad staircase, a sudden boom almost caused Lluava to fall. "What was that?" she asked hastily.

"The front doors," came Varren's sharp reply.

The Berserkers had broken through the outer gates and were now beating down the castle doors. It would not be long before they forced entry.

Chapter 43

Leap of Faith

Cracking resounded through the halls.

"The doors are giving way," whispered Varren. A loud splintering noise confirmed this.

"What are we going to do?" Lluava asked in a sudden panic.

"What we must."

Lluava rushed toward the front of the palace with Varren close behind. If the Berserkers were forcing entry, the palace would need all soldiers present. The pair was about to reach the second-story gallery that overlooked the foyer when they heard the echoing thud of the collapsing doors.

"They're inside!" Lluava gasped as she looked down at the Berserkers battling their way through the rows of men who were standing guard. Even with the bottleneck at the door, the enemy was flooding through the opening.

"Where are the rest of the men?" Varren asked as he hurried around the gallery to the stairs. Lluava hoped they were coming to help, not turning tail.

As they reached the top of the stairs, two Berserkers, blanketed in flames from the fire spouts, exploded through the entry. Although their bodies were failing, they succeeded in setting several tapestries alight. Smoke began to billow, clouding sight.

"The Alcazars must be protected," declared Varren. "I see several of their personal guard over there. The lord and his family need assistance."

Lluava eyed the chaos below and recognized Vidrick, who was ordering his men into formation.

"How do you expect the two of us to protect them?"

She had not meant to sound uncaring. Nonetheless, the fact remained that it was difficult enough to slay even one giant with only two people. If there were more Berserkers, Lluava and Varren would have no chance. Varren's life was ultimately of more importance to the kingdom—and to her.

Swinging a maul, a Berserker bounded up several stairs at a time toward the partners. Suddenly, out of nowhere, a large stag rammed its rack of antlers into the marauder's side. It did not stop the Raider, but it slowed him down long enough for Byron to hobble up the stairs and stab him in the back. The tip of the sword barely protruded from the massive barrel chest of the brute. Talos had already begun to shift back when his partner tossed him his sword.

Just as Lluava moved to help her friends, she was stopped.

"Lluava." Varren cleared his throat. "We need to release Apex. We need every man. Everyone."

How could she have forgotten about the lead huntsman? He could help, but the tower that held his closely guarded quarters was far away, on the other side of the castle. Yet with Apex by their side, they would have a better chance of protecting those incapable of defending themselves.

"How are we to reach him?" Lluava asked. "We have to go through those doors." She pointed to a pair near the base of the stairs. Several Berserkers had already broken through them and were pushing deeper into the palace.

"Come on," Varren shouted as he ran past her. Halfway down the stairs, he leaped over the railing and landed on the marble floor. Lluava followed his lead, vaulting the railing just as another Berserker bore down on her. Fortunately, Talos and Byron blocked his path.

The impact on landing was surprisingly jarring. Had Varren sustained further injuries? Lluava helped him to his feet and pulled him through the open doorway and down the hall. As they turned a corner, she jerked Varren backward; another Berserker was just beyond the turn. His massive shadow with its horned helmet flickered mercilessly on the wall—but where was the light coming from? All the sconces had burned out.

Lluava peered around the corner and spotted Mila waving a torch in front of her. Where had the huntress been? Lluava had not seen her since the retreat. Had she been inside the entire time, or had she entered at the same time as the enemy?

In the vermilion glow, Lluava caught the huntswoman's eye. Mila suddenly tossed the flame at the Berserker's face and shifted. The enraged Raider charged at the snow leopard, which quickly retreated into a side room. Mila had lured the Berserker away from them. She had given them a chance, and Lluava was going to take it.

"Let's go," she whispered. She and Varren ran past a darkened doorway, within which they heard furniture crashing about. The rest of their route was clear.

When they reached the tower, they discovered that the guards had left their positions. Either to help fight or to save their own skins; Lluava was not sure which.

"How are we to open the door without a key?" she asked angrily.

Varren gave her a look.

"Fine," Lluava hissed, transforming. Using her golden claws, the tigress began to tear through the thick mahogany at an unnervingly slow rate. Beside her, Varren hacked at the lock with his sword. Eventually, there was a snap as the door broke free of its frame, and the pair pushed inside. Varren dodged a swinging a stool as Apex defended himself.

"Watch it," snapped the prince. The huntsman dropped his multifunctional weapon.

"We need your help," Lluava said. "The Berserkers have broken in, and the Alcazars need assistance."

Lluava realized the irony of her words: She was asking Apex to save the lives of the people who would have had him killed. "If you have any remorse for what you have done in the past, this is your chance to pay your debt and make things right."

"I'll need Ullr's Fangs."

"They are kept in the armory at the back of the palace," said Varren, "but the Alcazars should be hiding in their quarters on the third floor. We must rescue them first."

"I'm going for my weapons," growled Apex as he stepped through the shattered door. "I will find you afterward." He was gone, but the fierce roar of a Yorrick wolverine echoed through the halls. Lluava hoped he would take down a few more Berserkers as he went in search of the Fangs.

Varren was furious, and Lluava couldn't blame him. They had wasted precious time freeing the huntsman instead of rescuing their host and his family. Lluava hoped they were heavily guarded, but were any of Lord Alcazar's men prepared to face something as volatile as a Berserker?

They passed Lord Alcazar's quarters. The doors were open but untouched. There was no sign of forced entry, or of Lord Alcazar either.

"Lord Alcazar must have gone to be with his wife," Varren noted. "They were supposed to stay apart from each other, in case something happened to one of them."

Changing course, prince and tigress traversed several more halls and another staircase before they reached the hall where Lady Alcazar's quarters were located. Bodies of a half-dozen soldiers were cast about; blood splattered the walls. Twenty more men stood near the end of the hall. What had happened?

Seeing the prince, the soldiers created a path to the door for the partners. Lady Alcazar's room seemed to have been turned on end. Shattered furniture was strewn about the floor, along with the bodies of several Elysian soldiers. In the midst of it all, Lord Alcazar knelt on the floor, cradling the limp form of his wife. Tears rolled down his eyes as he rocked her softly.

When he saw Varren, Lord Alcazar exclaimed, "My daughter! You must save Illia. You must save her."

Varren knelt next to the defeated man. "Where is she?"

"She ran to help protect those taking refuge in the castle. She would not listen to reason. Help her. Save her."

"You must leave the castle," urged the prince. "Get away—far, far away from here. We will find your daughter."

Lord Alcazar nodded, although his eyes remained glazed. Lluava wondered if he would actually leave. She doubted it. Meanwhile, time was being wasted; surely more Berserkers were entering the castle. They had to move. She shifted back to her human form.

"Let's find Illia," Lluava said as they headed into the hall. "Where should we start looking?"

"I wish I knew," replied Varren.

With no clue where to look, finding Illia in this enormous household would be difficult. Lluava once again felt the pressure of time slipping past. Others were fighting and dying while they were searching for one woman who might not even be found. Lluava would have argued her point, but Illia was important to Varren, and Varren was important to her.

From up ahead, Lluava's keen hearing picked up the sound of feet fast approaching on the wooden floorboards. By their heavy tread, she knew they were not friends.

"We need to hide," she warned, and the pair slipped through an unlocked door. Barring it from the inside, they backed farther into what appeared to be spare sleeping quarters. Lluava accidentally bumped into a chair. She caught her breath.

Had the Raiders heard? They were almost at the door. Lluava stared at the doorknob, fully expecting to see it begin to turn. It never did. Instead, shouts were emitted and footfalls faded.

Neither Lluava nor Varren made an effort to move. They stood absolutely still, monitoring their breathing, waiting to make sure the enemy had truly left.

Varren carefully pulled his sword from its sheath and slowly approached the door. As soon as he cracked it open, a billow of smoke poured through. Varren widened the opening, allowing Lluava a clear view of the inferno that blazed up and down the hall. Quickly he closed the door and looked at Lluava, his eyes full of fear.

"We're trapped!" Lluava could not help but state the obvious as she retreated to the window. They were four stories up, overlooking a side yard near the stables. Nothing moved below. It seemed that the entire battle was now being fought inside these walls.

Lluava growled. How were they going to get out of this? Smoke had begun to find its way around the doorframe. If they did not die from the fire itself, they would certainly suffocate.

Seizing the chair, Lluava swung it at the glass, shattering it after several blows. Now, at least they had fresh air.

Muffled sounds came from several stories above them. The idea of being trapped made Lluava's heart race even more than when she was in the midst of combat. Was it the smoke that was causing her to struggle for breath?

She and Varren were trapped in the room. Trapped, just as she had been back in Fort Brinsdale's prison. Trapped and waiting for certain death. Lluava sank down and gasped for air in sheer panic. They were going to die, and there was nothing she could do. She had no control.

"Lluava, Lluava, look at me." Varren was beside her. "In and out. You can do this. Just breathe."

Following Varren's example, Lluava concentrated on her own breath. As she found herself relaxing, Varren said, "I love you. I had to tell you."

"I love you, too," replied Lluava. She touched his hands. They were clammy with fear. "I have for a while."

"I want you to know that I would do anything for you." Varren's voice shook. Smoke was filling the space more rapidly.

Lluava responded, "As I would for you."

Varren gently pulled Lluava back up to her feet. "I want you to do something for me. I need you to do this."

Something in her partner's tone was worrisome. "What?"

Varren looked out the window. "I need you to jump down. You can make that leap. I cannot."

"No. I'm not leaving you." Lluava gripped his hands tightly. "We can find another way."

"This is the only way," countered Varren. "I need you to get out of here."

"Varren..." Lluava blinked back tears. "I will come back for you. I'll bring help."

"I know you will."

The way he said it told Lluava he did not expect her to return in time.

Varren pulled her close, and they kissed through the haze of smoke. His lips trembled as they touched hers. She wondered if she, too, were shaking. This would not be the end. She would have to make it back in time.

She would find help, bring water, blankets, anything to smother the flames. She would find a way to reach Varren. She would save him. She must.

Taking a breath, Lluava climbed up onto the windowsill. How could she do this? She had fallen from afar before, when the bridge collapsed in the camps. She had survived, but with injury. If she injured herself here, she was good as dead. The Berserkers would certainly find her, kill her. Varren would die.

"I can't…I can't do this," she stammered.

"You *can*," Varren responded with unquestionable certainty.

She looked about her. There was a small balcony two windows over and two stories down. The leap would only be possible in her dual form. Could she make it? With smoke filling the room, time was running out. She would have to try.

The windowsill was too small for her dual form, but she needed her feline form in order for her plan to work. Lluava crouched down and kissed Varren once more. This time, the prince could not hide his tears.

"I'm coming back for you."

In mid shift, Lluava kicked off from the ledge, hoping she had done so with enough force to vault her onto the balcony. As she began to fall, she saw the railing of the balcony fast approaching.

Claws outstretched, she hooked the railing and struggled to pull herself up. Her rear paws had nothing to grip, so her forearms had to absorb all the force and weight. With one enormous thrust, she toppled over onto the stone floor.

There was only a moment for Lluava to relish the fact that she had survived. Rolling onto her back, she saw Varren worriedly watching from the broken window. Suddenly Lluava felt pain through her coursing adrenaline.

On her left rear leg was a fair-sized gash. She must have cut it on the broken glass. She flipped back onto her feet and transformed. Using the railing to help her balance, Lluava tested her weight on her leg. The pain was sharp and constant, but nothing was broken. She would deal with the pain.

There was a scream from above and a sickening crunch as a body slammed into the balcony mere feet from where Lluava stood. It was a young woman, her dark hair splayed out wildly, like her broken limbs. Her white dress was rapidly turning red.

Lluava was afraid to approach. She already knew who it was. Why did she feel the need to look? Lluava limped over and peeled back a clump of blood-soaked hair, exposing the beautiful features.

She turned her face toward Varren. Even through the sheets of smoke, he seemed to have blanched.

"Who?" Lluava thought she heard him say.

"Illia."

Chapter 44

Vacating the Premises

Varren's betrothed was dead; there would be no more talk of marriage between them. Yet this was not what Lluava had desired. Illia had been like her—a woman unable to marry the man she loved as long as the archaic tradition of marriage contracts continued. For Illia, that day would never come.

Lluava limped to the balcony doors. At least she still had a chance at happiness if she could move fast enough. Who knew how long Varren could last with the threat of fire at his back? Each step she took made her whimper. But pain was a good thing; pain reminded her she was alive. At least, that was what she told herself.

Navigating through the expansive palace, Lluava had been fortunate not to meet a Raider. Abruptly, her luck ran out. A seven-foot-tall Berserker strode toward her, brandishing a sword far too small for his size. It was an Elysian sword. Lluava did not dwell on what might have happened to its owner.

The Claws stood erect on her knuckles; she gripped them tightly. Taking a calming breath, she waited for the Raider to make the initial move. In her weakened state, she had no chance of charging the man. Her tactics must be to evade, to defend. To live.

A man appeared next to her, sword in hand. Lluava glanced to one side and saw Vidrick readying himself to fight by her side. At least she would not have to fight this battle alone.

The Berserker charged.

Though not trained as partners, Vidrick and Lluava fought well together. Soon, the sound of clanging swords resounded through the halls.

While the lieutenant bore the brunt of the attack, Lluava shifted and went for any body part left unprotected.

The Berserker's size hindered his movements in the hall, but not enough to prevent him from inflicting damage. His weapon sliced into Vidrick's shoulder. Miraculously, the lieutenant managed to hold onto his own sword. Grappling with the brute, Lluava prevented a second swing. Switching from his dominant arm, Vidrick attacked once more. As the combatants fought on, Lluava struggled to sink her canines through the Raider's breastplate.

Dropping back to the ground, she skirted the marauder's huge feet. Then, leaping up once more, she thrust her claws into the fleshy mass under the Raider's upraised arm. She had to be near his heart. Shifting back, the teen drove the second Claw deep into the giant's armpit and jerked downward. The Raider gurgled on his blood and spat red droplets at Vidrick. With a final lunge, the Berserker sank down and coughed out his last breath.

"Thank you," Lluava gasped as she tried to catch her own.

Vidrick had his hands on his knees as he nodded.

"Prince Varren is in trouble," Lluava told him urgently. "He is trapped in a room. The entire hall is on fire."

"What floor?" Vidrick asked as he grabbed his weapon.

"The fourth."

"Then we go to the fifth."

***

Lluava had to guess which room stood above Varren's prison. Following the lieutenant's commands, she stripped the room's bed of its sheets. Quickly they ripped the sheets into strips and tied them together as a makeshift rope.

Vidrick tethered one end to the leg of the bed as Lluava opened the window. Clouds of smoke billowed out of the room below. She tossed down the cloth rope.

"Varren!" she screamed. "Varren, look out the window!"

Only smoke poured from the hole. Vidrick was beside her, staring down. At first, Lluava did not know what he was looking at, but then she realized he was catching glimpses of Illia's body on the balcony below them.

She wanted to say, "I'm sorry, Vidrick." Instead, she said, "I'm going down."

"Look!" Vidrick pointed. Coughing and gasping for air, Varren grabbed hold of the improvised rope.

"Help me pull him up," Lluava ordered as she started tugging at the cloth.

The lieutenant had barely begun to haul the prince up when he asked, "Did you hear that?"

Men were heading down their hallway. Large men.

"It's up to you, Lluava," Vidrick said. He gave a final tug and passed the rope to the teen. "I'll keep them away as long as I can."

There was no time for Lluava to argue the point. Vidrick made a dash for the door. She heard it slam shut and then his running footfalls.

Between her injured leg and her weakened shoulder, Lluava did not have the strength to pull her partner up. He would have to climb on his own. Peering over the window ledge, she saw Varren midway up, between the floors.

Suddenly, he seemed to slip for a second. No—he hadn't; one of the knots was coming loose. The rope would not hold.

"Come on! Hurry!" Lluava cried as Varren hauled himself steadily upward.

Lluava could only watch as the knot slowly came undone. He was not going to make it. He would fall—

She leaned over the ledge as far as possible, stretched her good arm toward Varren, and grabbed. His hand in hers had never felt so good.

With a final heave, the prince tumbled over the windowsill and into the room, Lluava noticed a commotion in the barren yard below. Apex, in his dual form, was trapped within a ring of Berserkers. Though he fought violently, even his great brute strength and ferocity could not combat that many. The enemy had him.

A falcon keened as it flew past her window. The Berserker leader looked up. Had he seen her?

"Lluava!" Varren cried out behind her. Standing in the doorway was a Berserker. Once again, they were cornered, but not by fire this time.

A siren sounded. At least, that was the best way Lluava could describe it. The sharp yet deep wail seemed to emanate from somewhere beyond the Slidr River, deep in the Yorrick Forest. Even from afar, the noise blared out like an enormous, angry war horn. The staggering noise was far more strident, more powerful, and more alarming than the siren at the training camp had been.

Looking over Varren's shoulder, Lluava saw the Berserker freeze in place. Then the giant backed out of the room, turned, and left.

For a moment, Lluava was too shocked to say anything.

"He's gone," she finally breathed out.

While Varren continued to stare doubtfully at the door, Lluava turned to check on Apex. In the yard, each of the Berserkers seemed as mesmerized by the wailing sound as the one that had just left. The ring of Raiders surrounding Apex broke apart.

"They're retreating," Lluava pointed out. "All of them."

"Ambassador Alcove," Varren hissed as he strode over to his partner's side and viewed the disarray.

Below, the leader, looking smaller than ever, shouted commands at the unheeding Berserkers, who were in full retreat. He had lost control of his precious legion. The keening sound, the shrieking call, was summoning every one of the giant Raiders back to the woods.

Something, someone, was emitting that sound. Whoever or whatever it was, was clearly in command. Lluava realized that the Berserkers served another. Their true leader was calling them back. Ambassador Alcove's authority had been revoked.

Unlike the enemy, Apex was not mesmerized. He charged at the demoted commander. Several Berserkers suddenly turned their attention to Apex and blocked his path. It seemed the ambassador was still worth protecting.

"We must get out of here and find the others." Varren's voice jerked Lluava back to the present. Other Berserkers might still be lurking; it would be safer to regroup and assess the situation.

With his arm under hers, Varren helped Lluava out of the room. Her leg had bled freely, and she was beginning to feel lightheaded. In the foyer, they rejoined what remained of the devastated Elysian defenders.

Byron and Talos were alive. Lluava did not know how that was possible, but she did not care. She glimpsed Yamir. So, he had made it off the wall. Over the next few hours, others arrived, including Rosalyn, Mila, Vidrick, even Lord Alcazar and High Councilman Hyrax. Apex, it seemed, had disappeared. His body was nowhere to be found.

The people began to tell stories of the heroic deeds and exemplary bravery they had witnessed. These achievements and the people who accomplished them would be immortalized, celebrated for generations to come. Rosalyn had been with the young highborn, Illia, and she tearfully shared what had happened to Lord Alcazar's daughter.

"Illia had led a small group of injured and defenseless people to protected rooms on the upper floors. I was assisting her. We were on our way back with a second group when we heard the Raiders approaching."

Rosalyn was weeping freely. "I had my sword, but she had nothing. Everyone began to flee, and I lost track of her. People were running into rooms, barricading doors. She must have hidden in the room next to ours. I heard a commotion, cries. I wanted to help, but had I left, I would have given away the hiding place of others, who were defenseless."

"Suddenly there was a crash, and she was gone. She saved more than thirty people but sacrificed herself in doing so. Illia was truly a heroine."

Rosalyn's words might not have provided much consolation for Vidrick or Lord Alcazar, but they shed a new light on the woman they both loved.

Teams of soldiers had been sent to scout the palace grounds and outlying areas. Once it was certain that all the Berserkers truly had retreated, Varren and Lluava tried to make sense of it all. Why had the Raiders left? Who or what had called them back? The unanswered questions left Lluava with a bad feeling about what was to come.

The partners sat together near the hearth. "We will survive this together," Varren promised, and kissed her.

"Where's *my* kiss?"

They both turned quickly to stare at Apex. His face was bleak and drawn.

"Don't look at me like that. I was not speaking to you, princeling."

"Where have you been?" Varren asked, surprised. "We tried to find you."

"I had to make sure Sköll was all right."

"You came back?" Lluava was dumbfounded.

"I still have a debt to pay."

"Whatever it was, I promise you," Varren countered, "it has been fulfilled."

Someone knocked at their door: Talos. He looked askance at Apex, then said, "Varren, news has arrived from the capital. You need to come."

Varren and Lluava accompanied Talos to a small meeting room, where they found Vidrick, Hyrax, Lord Alcazar, and a travel-weary messenger already assembled. Since the tables and chairs had been destroyed during the fighting, they stood, ill at ease, near one of the large hearths.

"Your Majesty," the messenger said as he bowed awkwardly several times, "I'm so very glad to see that you have survived."

"What is your news?" Varren asked kindly.

The messenger reached into his coat pocket and pulled out a small scroll.

"Our great ruler, King Thor Mandrun, has died in his sleep. The flags of the kingdom will be flown at half-mast for the span of six weeks. The coronation of the new king will take place upon the return of the crown prince from his noble fight. Until that time, Head Councilman Finch Themis will serve as regent for Elysia. The kingdom mourns this great loss." The messenger straightened his shoulders and stood at attention. With all the strength he could muster, he loudly proclaimed, "The king is dead!" Turning to Varren, he added, "Long live the king."

Lluava wasn't sure whether the last part was written on the scroll or was the customary response.

"May I see the scroll?" asked the prince. Lluava could tell he was struggling to keep his voice steady.

As he reread the scripted words, Lluava asked him, "What are you going to do now?"

"We will return to Cronus. Elysia is on the threshold of great change." Varren handed the scroll back to the waiting messenger. "Most will take place at Cronus."

"If Your Majesty pleases," Hyrax interjected, "I would be honored to escort you home."

"Very well," Varren replied. "We will return within the week."

After Varren and Lluava had left the meeting room and the two could speak privately, Varren told Lluava, "The sooner we return, the better. Themis has held the seat of power since my grandfather's death. I do not want him to get too comfortable."

The next few days were filled with organizing the remaining troops and officers and preparing for the trip to the capital. During this time, a new regiment of soldiers arrived. Hundreds of new privates, fresh from the northern camps, were overly ready for combat.

Lluava did not need to persuade her friends to join her and Varren on their journey. It seemed they all were more than ready to leave the bloodshed behind—at least for a while. Mila, however, left on the second day following the battle.

"This is not my path," she told Lluava. "I wish you well, but I am not meant for high-born society or crowded cities. I prefer to live a hermit's existence. I'll catch you in another life." Lluava hugged Mila and felt her stiffen. Then, in the form of a snow leopard, Mila bounded off toward the Yorrick Forest.

As for the other surviving huntsman, Lord Alcazar had lost all desire for revenge. He released Apex from his confinement and then retired to mourn the loss of his family. Apex had decided to remain at the castle. Lluava could not fathom his reason; she had expected Apex to take Sköll and, like Mila, disappear into the wilderness that he so loved.

The night before their journey to the capital, Lluava caught a scent she had almost forgotten about. Moving silently through the halls, she kept a wary eye out for the animal that was now her prey.

Opening the door of someone's private quarters, Lluava looked about. Black robes lay tossed on top of a partially packed chest at the foot of the bed. It was near the chest that the musk of badger was most potent.

Lluava fumbled through the items. She did not know who had been assigned this room, but maybe something in the chest would provide a clue. Most of the clothing was standard. Blank lettering paper and a vial of ink were tucked in one corner. At the bottom, Lluava's hand brushed something hard. She lifted the object and pulled out a carved obsidian mask. Its foul grimace stirred her memory.

She had seen this mask before, in her dream. That vision of robed men. It had been a dream, right?

"Ah, you're here already."

The voice behind her startled Lluava, and she dropped the mask.

"I have been looking for you."

Chapter 45

The Incarn

Are you all right, Lluava?"

The girl turned to look at Hyrax. He wore his usual councilman garb, adorned with his low-hanging talisman. In the dull light, its radiating eye looked sinister.

"Is this your room?" Lluava asked. She should have smelled his potent perfume, even over the chest's musky odor. Had he forgotten to put it on?

Hyrax eyed the open chest, then looked back at Lluava. "Yes. This is where I am staying. Are you feeling all right? You look rather pale."

"I'm fine. I'm sorry for intruding."

Hyrax brushed the two white stripes on his short beard. "It is fine, Lluava. Curiosity is one of your best traits. As I was saying, I was looking for you, so finding you here is quite fortuitous."

The strong musk in the room had not begun to deteriorate.

"I can't stay. There is much to be done before we depart. Can we talk later?" The hair on the back of her neck was fully erect. Something was not right; she had to get back to the others.

"Hold this, please." The councilman handed her the talisman, then stepped back to the doorway and shifted. There, swaddled in a blanket of dark robes, was the striped creature that had been tracking Lluava. The badger focused its beady eyes on her and huffed before crawling back into the clothes and returning to his human form.

"We should talk," said Hyrax.

Lluava dropped the talisman on top of the chest and made a move for the door. "I don't know who you really are, but I'm leaving."

Hyrax stood in her way. "You won't be leaving for the capital. Don't worry, the prince will be safe. I can assure you of that."

"I'm going to Cronus with Varren." Trepidation slipped into her voice.

"You are not. There is much more work to be done."

"What's going on in there?" Apex's voice growled from beyond the doorway.

"Ah, good. You are both here," acknowledged the councilman. He moved aside to allow the huntsman entry.

"Councilman Hyrax is the badger," Lluava cautioned Apex. "The thief!"

Apex moved to Lluava's side. Like her, the huntsman was not armed, but he was clearly ready to fight.

"Sit, please." Hyrax motioned to a couch. When no one moved, he stated, "I insist."

Hyrax seated himself opposite the pair. "As I was saying to Lluava, I will be returning to the capital with the prince. However, the two of you have a much more important mission."

"I'm done with missions," snarled Apex. He stood up.

Hyrax raised his hand. "Please, let me explain. You will want to hear this. Or do you want always to wonder where the presence that overtakes you comes from? Clearly, you have felt something else in control when you were in your dual form. Or am I mistaken?"

Apex sank back down on the couch.

"You two are quite special. You are members of the Incarn."

"What's that?" Apex asked.

"Patience, please," implored Hyrax. "Members of the Incarn serve as mortal vessels for the gods. The Incarn allow the immortal pantheon to move about this world and do their work. Each god has one. That feeling you get when you lose control occurs when a holy one is doing his or her work through your body."

"So, you are saying that some god uses my body like a puppet?" Apex asked skeptically.

"Not *some* god," corrected Hyrax. "You are Ullr's Incarn, as Lluava is Theri's."

Lluava remembered her blackouts—the lives she had taken, the horrors she had committed. "I will not be a pawn for the gods, not even Theri. She can find someone else."

"Though the gods would prefer a willing host, they can take over at any time. If you fight it, you will only harm yourself. Blacking out is a sign of your internal struggle."

"If the gods are so powerful," Lluava argued, "they should be able to move around as they please, do what they want. Why would they need to use Apex or me?"

"Our world is far different from their own. The longer they stay here, the more clouded their minds become, the more their judgment wavers. They become emotional, unreliable. But by using the Incarn, they can move about without losing their all-seeing ability."

"Too bad," hissed Lluava. "They can find somebody else."

"I don't think you quite understand," countered Hyrax. Lluava disliked the way he spoke to them, like an adult talking down to little children. The councilman continued, "You were not chosen for this role. You were created for it."

Lluava's jaw dropped. Beside her, Apex's did the same.

"None of the Incarn was ever born. Each was specifically made for this purpose. The whole point of your existence is to serve your particular god."

"I have..." Lluava fumbled for words. "I have a family. A mother, father, siblings."

"No," contradicted Hyrax. "You were entrusted to them."

Hyrax retrieved his talisman from the chest. "I am a Guardian—one of many. The Guardians are a secret society of Theriomorphs that have existed since the time of legends. This eye, with its twelve long and short lines, is a symbol of that sect. We are the watchers of prophecies yet to occur. Our sole purpose is to wait for the day an Incarn is created and then to protect him or her until it is time for the Incarn to complete the creator's will. We have been watching you since you were little. Haliden Kargen, the man you viewed as your father, was one of us. He was chosen to raise you."

"That's not possible." Lluava had so many questions. What the councilman was saying could not be true. He must be tricking them for some unknown reason.

Hyrax continued calmly, "Haliden was selected because he was one of the few younger men in our sect who served in the military. Surely you understand that a soldier father would be helpful in the upbringing of the Incarn of Theri, Goddess of War. When the Guardians were made aware of your presence, Haliden was ready and able to do what was required of him. We arranged for him to marry and to claim you as his own child."

"That's not—" Lluava was cut off.

"He was married to Maessa in Bail and sent to raise you in the south so that none of their family or friends would discover that you were not born from them. You are not their child. You have no parents, nor does Apex."

Apex remained silent.

"If that is the case, why did you leave Apex to grow up in orphanages?"

Hyrax turned to the huntsman. "Apex, you were the first Incarn we found. Once we discovered you, we knew the others would be arriving. Our doctrine did not set forth in detail how we were supposed to watch over you. We were told only to stay hidden and not to interfere unless we had to. You were all to develop in your own time and by your own merit. This did not mean we did not watch over you, at least for a while. You were the only Incarn who periodically disappeared from our sight."

"Lluava." Hyrax turned to the young woman. "You, as the youngest and the key to the prophecy, required extra care; thus we placed you with one of our own."

"So, there are others?" Apex questioned. Lluava wondered if he actually believed this fantasy.

"If one Incarn is created, all others are, too. We have found a few of them, for we have scoured the kingdom for years, but there are many still missing. This is why neither of you can return to your regular lives. You must search for the other Incarn. Without them, Elysia will fall, and the world will crumble into darkness."

"How do you know all this?" asked Apex.

"Because the gods would place you on the earth only if the Theriomorph race were on the brink of destruction. Issaura promised she would come back to protect us. The time has come for her to do so."

Lluava thought back on the leader's original plan to eradicate her race. Whatever or whomever controlled him had the authority to command the genocide of the Theriomorphs. But wait—did she believe the councilman's words? If so, her family was not her own. She was an object, created only to serve another. Did that mean she had no free will?

Hyrax was the badger that had followed her since her stay in Cronus. He had been watching her the whole time. It was he who had shown Apex where Ullr's Fangs were buried. He had probably hidden those weapons himself.

"Why did you try to steal Issaura's Claws from me that night in the capital?"

Hyrax actually laughed. "I had heard about you for a long time and knew you had been given Issaura's Claws. I had to make sure they were genuine and not some false representation. I will admit I was doubtful at first, as were others, but I am only mortal; I make mistakes."

"Why didn't you just tell me?"

"The Guardians are not to interfere, as I have already said."

"Then why are you exposing yourself now? What's changed?"

Hyrax sighed. "You, as well as I, have seen what the enemy is capable of, and I feel we have only glimpsed the beginning. I believe we all know they will return." Hyrax picked up his carved mask and seemed to study the ancient workmanship. "The other Guardians warned me not to interfere, to let your journey be your own. However, they have not seen what I have seen. If you return to the capital tomorrow, the kingdom will fall to these monsters. Elysia does not have forces strong enough to protect her."

Moving to the nightstand, Hyrax picked up his empty perfume bottle. "But if you willingly choose to follow your destiny, to seek out and return with the other Incarn, together you can put a stop to these dark forces."

He tucked the bottle into the chest and closed the lid, snapping the latches in place. "I chose to come forward now because your journey begins here."

"Certainly you don't mean at Røthe; the city was destroyed!" Lluava was skeptical; however, Apex asked, "Where do we search for the Incarn?"

Hyrax pulled back the curtain of his narrow window and looked out over the burned fields and the virgin forest. "You must leave Elysia."

Lluava gasped. Go back into that forest again? The Raiders would be massing their army!

"We have searched throughout the kingdom; if the other Incarn were here, we would have found them already." Hyrax pointed to the wilderness beyond. "You and Apex must travel over the Borren Mountains. There you can begin your quest."

"Nothing lives beyond the mountains," stated Apex matter-of-factly. "The land is too cold, too desolate."

"Are you so sure?" questioned the councilman. "Theriomorphs have always found ways to survive where humans cannot."

"It would take weeks just to cross over that range," argued Lluava, thinking back on the length of their journey. "How much time do we have before the Raiders attack again?"

"This is why time is of the essence."

Lluava studied Hyrax. Should she trust him? Should she believe *any* of what he had just said? From the look on Apex's face, he did. Lluava wondered if the huntsman's decision would be influenced by his need to feel valued and respected. She cared little for the thought.

All Lluava longed for was to live peacefully alongside Varren. They deserved a chance for some semblance of a normal life. Yet if this could save her race, her family, and Varren, she had no choice. She must try.

Lluava trusted her instincts. "Fine," she consented. "I'll go. But our other comrades won't like the change of plan."

Hyrax spoke in a steely tone. "Only you and Apex must make the journey. No others."

"He's right," agreed Apex. "It will be a miraculous feat for us to survive, even with the gods' protection."

Lluava's eyes widened in disbelief. Abandon her partner? Travel alone with Apex?

"One more thing," noted Hyrax as he slipped the talisman back over his head. "You cannot tell anyone about the Guardians. We must remain hidden."

Standing up, Lluava hissed, "Do you know what you are asking? You want me to believe that I'm some god's toy, that I have to obey her will, that I must travel to the unknown wilderness alone and not even tell anyone why. Is this what you are asking?"

Apex looked vaguely insulted.

Hyrax replied, "You are a strong person. Both of you are."

The knowledge that there were other Theriomorphs like her elsewhere in the world was thrilling and terrifying at the same time. Then again, what if she were to discover something she wished she hadn't?

"How will we recognize the other Incarn when we see them?" asked Apex. He looked eager to start this new adventure.

"By their dual forms. Look for a god's form."

Apex muttered the names to himself: "Black jackal, purple peacock, emerald anaconda…"

Moving to leave, Lluava said to Hyrax, "Once I step foot into the Yorrick Forest, consider our friendship over."

"If that is the price to pay, so be it."

***

Lluava found Varren reading in his quarters. "This is a collection of ballads about the battles from the time when our races were enemies," he explained. "I wonder what they will write about us. What facts will remain and what aspects will be stretched out to become legends."

"They will write," Lluava began as she took a seat on her partner's bed, "that the handsome prince and the pagan goddess fought valiantly and how, after a great battle in the north, they went separate ways in the hope of saving their kingdom."

"What are you talking about, Lluava?" Varren marked his page in the book before placing it to one side.

"I can't return to Cronus with you. You can't ask me why, but it is important that you know I am doing this to save Elysia."

"I do not understand."

"I must travel back to the Outlands. I believe that I can find a way to save us if I do."

"What aren't you telling me?"

"No questions. You have to trust me."

"Lluava," Varren began, "whatever you think is out there, whatever you will be searching for, is not…you cannot just…"

The prince's strong voice faltered. "I love you, Lluava. I would never hold you back from what you believe is right. I just do not understand this. Let me come with you. We are partners; we pledged to stand by each other until the end."

"You can't come. You must return to Cronus and prevent Themis from controlling the kingdom. Who knows what he would do if he discovered you had left Elysia's borders."

Varren was clearly trying to understand. Lluava desperately wished she could explain. She did not want secrets between them. Yet if she told him the truth, would he allow her to leave? Would he try to follow?

"Will you go alone, then?" Varren asked.

"No," Lluava admitted. "I need someone who can guide me."

Varren's eyes momentarily lost focus. He took a slow breath, then studied her face with care. "Apex will watch your back. I know he will."

"Varren?"

"Yes."

"Tell me what your coronation will be like."

Snuggling next to Varren, Lluava laid her head on his chest. She listened as he described the church with lights streaming through stained-glass windows, his fur-trimmed green and gold wardrobe, and the gleaming golden crown and jeweled scepter. Closing her eyes, she envisioned Varren standing in front of packed pews, proclaiming his vows before the priest, his people and his god.

When he had finished, Lluava promised, "I'll come back to you."

"I know you will," he replied, and kissed her deeply.

***

In the morning, by the crown prince's command no questions were asked about Lluava and Apex's unusual departure. Her friends gave her strange, questioning stares as they said their goodbyes. Lluava felt a bit more comfortable about leaving when she found that Vidrick would join Varren and her friends. "These new privates have their own officers," Vidrick explained. "I am not needed here, nor do I wish to stay and be reminded of all that I have lost."

Lluava respected the redheaded lieutenant. She knew that he, like Talos, Byron, and Yamir, would let no harm come to Varren. After hugging Rosalyn once more, she turned to see Apex and Varren shaking hands.

Apex reached into a sack he had brought from his room.

"This is for you," he said as he handed Lluava the purest white fur coat she had ever seen.

"You made this…?" Lluava was overwhelmed by the huntsman's thoughtfulness.

Apex shrugged. "It's cold out there."

The huntsman walked ahead and waited for Lluava to follow reluctantly. She ran to Varren and wrapped her arms around him.

"Are you sure about this?" he questioned. Was he hoping she would change her mind and return to Cronus with him?

"Yes," she whispered. "Don't make this harder for both of us."

Disregarding their friends, Varren kissed her passionately. Lluava had to force herself to step away from her prince, her partner, her love. As she turned to follow Apex, it took all her resolve not to look back. She knew that if she did, she would never leave Varren's side. Ahead of her stood the Yorrick Forest and the Borren Mountains. Beyond them—the unknown.

I will return, Lluava vowed to herself as she left Elysia's border behind. Whatever happens, whatever must be done, I will return.

Epilogue

Moonlight slipped through the thick curtains and encroached on the woman's face. She awoke and sat up with a sigh, her dark locks falling down her bare chest and back. A silver pendant dipped between her breasts.

Surveying her quarters, lavishly decorated as befitting her status, her eyes eventually rested on the mound of blankets next to her.

"Ah. You're still here."

Receiving no response, she slid out of bed, wincing as her bare feet touched the frigid stone.

"You cannot stay."

She walked over to the ornately carved hearth.

"You need to go."

Stoking the embers until they resumed their earlier enthusiasm, she stood for a moment basking in the warmth. A slight sigh passed her inviting lips as she turned around.

"What a mess we have made."

The woman slowly moved about the room, gathering items that had been discarded in haste. Returning to the warm glow, she ran her manicured nails down the lavish material to the ruffled cuff. Lifting the sleeve to her nose, she breathed in deeply. Then, one by one, she tossed the items into the fire, feeding the flames.

At last, only a pair of gold rings remained. The insignia ring indicated the rank of lord; the band, the vow that had been broken this very night. The woman clutched them tightly in her small fist before tossing them, too, into the blaze. Her free hand gently fingered the metallic teardrop about her throat as it absorbed the heat.

With renewed vigor, she strode to the window. Pulling back the heavy curtains, she let the light of the moon flood through the high, arched panels. She peered down at the countless orbs of light below.

"The capital is beautiful in winter."

A dark cloud momentarily covered the moon, allowing the shadows of the room to dance before they hid from the azure glow.

"I sensed that my abilities were growing."

Returning to her bed, she sat down on its edge and smiled at the patch of golden hair beside her.

"Thank you."

The woman gently pulled down the sheet to reveal the closed eyes.

"Thank you for allowing me to test them."

Carefully, she bent down and kissed the cool forehead, her pendant brushing the slightly parted lips.

"I now know that the time has come."

She pulled the sheet down lower.

"What is to occur, no one will ever suspect."

She slowly ran her fingers down the side of his cheek. Her hand paused briefly above the thick, dark bruise that wrapped itself around his neck like a winter scarf. She inhaled quickly.

Tossing the sheets back, she observed how the purple band ran down his torso to wrap itself several times over crushed ribs.

Everything grew still. Even the fire seemed to briefly settle.

Her skin shimmered metallic.

Then the woman shifted. Chairs and tables were shoved aside to make room for the massive form. Sliding, unfurling, stretching, and uncurling to get into the perfect position. Only the moon observed the man's legs slipping down the anaconda's throat.

APPENDICES

APPENDIX I

<u>Diagram of the Theriomorph Pantheon</u>

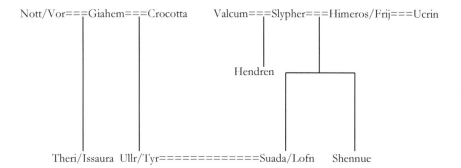

APPENDIX II

The Theriomorph Pantheon

Name	Sex	Divine Realm	Dual Form
Giahem	♂	King/ Husbands/ Fathers/ Heavens/ Males/ Sky	Gold Eagle
Crocotta	♀	Queen/Wives/Mothers/Prophecy/Mating Rights	Silver Hyena
Ullr/Tyr	♂	Young Men/ Inception of War/ Sun/ Courage	Bronze Wolverine
Nott/Vor	♀	Night/ Sleep/ Dreams/ Death/ Underworld	Black Raven
Theri/Issaura	♀	Young Women/ Cessation of War/ Moon/ Wisdom	White Tigress
Ucrin	♂	Ocean/ Water/ Wind	Blue Whale
Valcum	♂	Fire/ Volcanos/ Blacksmiths	Orange Orangutan
Slypher	♀	Earth/ Seasons/ Song/ Dance	Pink Parakeet
Frij/Himeros	♂♀	Love/ Beauty/ Hermaphrodites	Purple Peacock
Hendren	♂	Knowledge/ Virtue/ Health	Scarlet Panda
Suada/Lofn	♀	Lust/ Seduction/ Desire	Emerald Anaconda
Shennue	♂	Mischief/ Mayhem / Illusions	Black Jackal

APPENDIX III

Pronunciation Guide

Acrian	ACK-re-an
Alcazar	AL-ca-czar
Amargo	a-MAR-go
Apex	A-pecks
Austro	AWE-strow
Berserker	bur-ZERK-er
Burok Dûr	ber-AWK DURE
Cherin	CHEER-in
Cronus	CROW-nus
Diaphoranthema	DIE-uh-FOR-an-THEME-a
Dicranum	die-CRA-num
Domar	dough-MAR
Durog	DURE-og
Einherjar	ine-HAIR-har
Endun	EN-dun
Ethril	EE-thrill
Elysia	ee-LAY-szuh
Fárbauti	far-BOUT-ee
Giahem	GUY-a-hem
Giam	GUY-am
Hyrax	HI-racks
Illia	ILL-ya
Incarn	IN-carn
Issaura	i-SAR-a
Kargen	CARG-en
Karmasana	CAR-ma-SAW-naw
Kentril	KEN-trill
Lluava	you-AA-va

Maessa	MAY-es-sa
Maruny	MAR-ou-nee
Mictla	MICKT-la
Mila	ME-la
Nemorosus	NE-mo'ro-sus
Niflhel	NEEF-flell
Ojewa	OH-jay-wa
Okeanos	oak-EE-a-nos
Olingo	o-LING-go
Olio	O-lee-o
Raien	RAIN
Regin	REEG-in
Rosalyn	ROZ-za-lin
Røthe	RAWTH
Selene	sa-LEAN
Shennu	SHEN-new
Sihad	see-HAD
Sihia	sih-HIGH-uh
Skipe	SKY-p
Sköll	SKOHL
Slidr	SLY-der
Slypher	SLY-fer
Sonty	SAWN-tea
Talos	TAL-ows
Themis	THEE-miss
Theri	TH'AIR-ee (rhymes with Carrie)
Theriomorph	TH'AIR-ee-OH-morph
Thowcelemine	TH'OW-cell-e-mean
Vidrick	VEE-drick
Vjeran	VEE'YAIR-en
Yorrick	YOUR-ick

APPENDIX IV

Elysian Military Ranks

Terra Divisions

Private
Corporal
Sergeant
Warrant Officer
Lieutenant
Captain
Major
Colonel
General
Chief General
Master Chief (General)
Grand Master Chief (General)

Aerial Divisions

Private
Airman
Sergeant
Lieutenant
Captain
Major
Colonel
General
Chief General
Master Chief (General)
Grand Master Chief (General)

Marine Divisions

Private
Seaman
Petty Officer
Warrant Officer
Ensign
Lieutenant
Commander
Captain
Admiral
Chief Admiral
Master Chief (Admiral)
Grand Master Chief (Admiral)

Lluava's adventures will continue in Tome Three of The Incarn Saga

Crocotta's Hackles

Tome Three Prologue: Crocotta's Hackles

The translucent beam of moonlight slipped through the perfectly circular opening at the peak of the dome. The sanctuary's sole source of illumination traversed the chamber to its preordained destination. A pair of unblinking eyes, glinting silver, observed the slow procession in silence.

As the light crept up the ancient pedestal, a low hum began to reverberate. Heavy, throaty, almost a purr, the sounds resembled a melody that rose and fell in practiced rhythm.

When the beam breached the lip of the basin, the incantation ended. The vocalist approached and gazed upon the liquid in the hollow. Uttering the scripted words under her breath, she dipped her forefinger into a liquid so dark it seemed to suck all light into its depths. As she lifted her hand high, onyx droplets ran down skin the color of black pearls. As each drop fell, ripples raced across the gently undulating surface of the hollow.

"Crocotta, O magnanimous Queen of the Gods and all that lives, Prophetess, Matriarch of the Blessed. I have come to learn your will."

The moonglow reached the basin's quivering contents.

"Bestow upon me, your servant, keeper of your word, the knowledge you wish to instill."

The small pool calmed and, as the moonbeam hit its heart, an image manifested in the murky darkness of its surface. Two figures trudged in a field of ivory. Torrents of white pelted them from above. Bent low, they clutched at their wind-torn cloaks. A fur-wrapped form blended into the pristine landscape. Tall though not as tall as the other, this one was female.

The vision faded. The light had passed its peak.

In the chamber's deepening gloom, the woman smiled; a pleasant thought crossed her mind.

"They are almost here."

She cast her eyes upward and completed the appropriate rites. Lowering her head, she contemplated the basin for a moment, then briefly closed her eyes.

"It is time to send an invitation."

The woman receded into the shadows until only the silvery reflection of her eyes could be seen.

"It is *time* to bring Ullr and Issaura home."

As she vanished in the blackness, her unhindered laughter bounded upward to meet the observant moonlight.

NOTE FROM THE AUTHOR

As an author, writing the story is just the beginning. Next come revising, editing, formatting, proofreading, and marketing. Surprisingly, marketing requires a huge amount of time. If you enjoy an author's work and want her or him to publish more in a shorter time span, you can help! Spread the word on social media and by word of mouth. Post reviews on Amazon, Goodreads and other websites. Believe me, I would much rather write a new book than spend time promoting the one I have just finished. So go ahead—pin, tweet, post, review, and like.

Thank you!

ABOUT THE AUTHOR

Katharine Wibell's lifelong interest in mythology includes epic poetry like the Odyssey, Ramayana, Beowulf, and the Nibelungenlied. In addition, she is interested in all things animal whether training dogs, apprenticing at a children's zoo, or caring for injured animals as a licensed wildlife rehabilitator. After receiving degrees from Mercer University in both art and psychology with an emphasis in animal behavior, Wibell moved to New Orleans with her dog, Alli, to kick start her career as an artist and a writer. Her first literary works blend her knowledge of the animal world with the world of high fantasy.

LEARN MORE

WWW.KATHARINEWIBELLBOOKS.COM

94817369R00205

Made in the USA
Columbia, SC
07 May 2018